THE ADVENTURES OF
MADAME STOREY

HULBERT FOOTNER

THE ADVENTURES OF MADAME STOREY

VOLUME 1

HULBERT FOOTNER

COACHWHIP PUBLICATIONS

GREENVILLE, OHIO

ISBN 1-61646-236-1
ISBN-13 978-1-61646-236-9

Cover: Madame Storey (Zohair Saleem); Texture (Flypaper Textures);
    Hulbert Footner (George H. Doran Co., 1921)

CoachwhipBooks.com

CONTENTS

"Just one bit of criticism I have to offer. In the current issue four stories had as their heroines, lady sleuths. The stories were good, but I believe even the women prefer the Sherlocks instead of the Shirleys. Mme. Storey is wonderful, though. Give us more of her. . . ." (A reader, to *Mystery: The Illustrated Detective Magazine,* March 1934)

HULBERT FOOTNER,

THE AUTHOR OF THE MADAME STOREY MYSTERIES
GEOFFREY M. FOOTNER

WILLIAM (Bill or Billy, to friends) Hulbert Footner (professionally) enjoyed a life of constant traveling, although he was firmly attached to his rural estate, *Charles Gift,* the beloved residence of the author. He also took great pleasure welcoming an eclectic circle of neighbors, editors and authors to this Calvert County, Maryland, home until World War 2 stopped all travel. Another enjoyable personal habit of Bill Footner was to visit New York to meet his lifelong friend and advisor, Christopher Morley at *Chris Cello Steakhouse* in mid-Manhattan. Mr. Cello's speakeasy flourished through Prohibition, the Great Depression, World War 2, and then long enough after that era ended, for me to visit the restaurant in the 1950s to view the two deceased authors' photograph hanging above a cubby-corner booth in their multi-decade haven.

Christopher Morley was a junior editor at Doubleday, Page & Company in 1911 when he was assigned to handle the publication of Hulbert Footner's first adventure novel based on a canoe trip into the unexplored northwest Canadian territories that had taken place a year earlier. This first novel brought the young author instant fame throughout the English speaking world. As a widely admired Canadian author, who had never made the British colony home, Footner spun off a dozen or so similar adventure books that had a vast international readership. Nevertheless, he experienced a fall in popularity in the years immediately following World War 1.

Christopher Morley, who had in the interim become his close friend, diagnosed the Hulbert Footner problem as over-exposure.

Those earlier novels set in the Canadian territories had featured strong frontier men and their equally strong women. Footner, who was tuned in on the changes around him in post-war America, introduced his readers to two strong and liberated females as memories of the War to End All Wars faded and were replaced by sweeping changes ushered in with the passage of the 18th Amendment to the Constitution, bringing Prohibition to the nation on January 29, 1920, that set into motion a truly unique American decade.

The ban of liquor produced a national lawlessness and the rebellion of young females, called flappers by the nation's press. They led American women's fight for the right to vote, which culminated in the passage of the 19th Amendment that extended voting privileges to the female sex in the national election of November 1920. With this change, after a wait of 126 years, women in a radically altered United States were very much on everybody's minds.

It was into this vibrant decade of change that Hulbert Footner introduces Madame Rosika Storey as a "Woman of Affairs" as she interviews applicants in her office who are responding to an ad for a secretary. These opening scenes of the author's new series allow the successful applicant for secretary, Bella Brickley, to explain her duel role, the first being the alter ego similar to Sherlock Homes' Dr. Watson to this brilliant private investigator who describes herself a "practical psychologist," and whose persona is elaborately drawn by the author so that her idiosyncrasies are constantly on display. Bella's second role in this series of Hulbert Footner mysteries is to be his first-person presenter of the cases that Madame Storey has been engaged to solve, but also to summarize those cases that preceded her employment.

Rosika Storey is everything a woman could be, including being gorgeous and wise, according to Miss Brickley. Bella writes about herself also, explaining that her hair is red and she is plain in appearance. She handles the two jobs the author has given her in an exacting manner, which includes an ever-obvious reverence for her awe-inspiring employer. Bella's precise recital of Madame's high voltage life forms the foundation of her presentation of her cases in a manner that engages readers who are soon submerged with them in this unique era that brought about radical changes in American life.

The detective stories featuring Madame Storey and her assistant Bella Brinkley originally began their successful run in serial form in Munsey's *Argosy-Weekly* in tandem with the political events of 1920. The mystery novelettes, collected and published as books, made a roaring entrance into Manhattan as did the author's two new-wave females, who qualified as liberated, but probably were not "flappers," although their cases moved to the pages of New York's newspapers and magazines and Rosika and Bella into the focus of ever-present cameras.

The Ashcomb Poor Case is the first novelette in the series and is the case that the author uses to introduce Madame Storey, and Bella Brickley as spokeswoman for her boss. The stories that follow the introductory one in this collection are set in New York City, its suburbs or nearby Connecticut. This is Volume 1 of the Coachwhip collection of Madame Storey mysteries. Bella describes the cases that Madame Storey is handling for several very rich and fashionable families of this great metropolitan center of wealth, and for reasons that quickly are made obvious—Footner is fascinated not so much by the rich and very rich victims, but by the fantastic cuisine, great architecture and great old residences, beautiful women and among other fine things, their well-cut clothes of the best materials, and the beautiful art and furniture that Madame Storey's wealthy clients and friends collect, which Bella has the opportunity to describe. Bill Footner, Rosika Storey and Bella Brickley lived during the times when trains and horses were the principal forms of transport and when people walked, talked and read books, magazines and newspapers. They were still adjusting to cars and airplanes, which were the new toys of the very rich.

William Hulbert Footner was Canadian born. His grandfather was a colonist who settled in Canada, and who had arrived there from England in the 19th Century. His mother's family was from South Carolina, proud and boastful about being Loyalists who fled

north to Upper Canada following George Washington and his
French Allies' defeat of a British army at Yorktown. When Billy
was born his father and mother had relocated to New York City
during the period of the 1870s and '80s when a robust portion of
Britain's colony Canada fled to New York in search of jobs that
paid living-wages, which the Footner family (as well as most other
migrants) discovered were scarce in New York City, also.

Young Billy Footner was out on his own while still a teenager.
He was self taught for the most part, educating himself by slipping
into libraries to read the classics and retrieving theatre tickets
dropped by attendees who walked out of Broadway plays at inter-
mission time. His dream was to have a play produced in a Broadway theater, the first of which he wrote when he was age twenty-
one. It was never published, however the very attractive refugee
from starvation joined a traveling theater group that opened in
Baltimore, Maryland, the state where he returned to live perma-
nently in 1916, which was when he purchased the old house that
he rebuilt and named *Charles Gift*—and by the way, which he paid
for with the proceeds of his first successful Broadway production.
It was then, too, he had begun to experiment with various new story
lines, including a male private-eye, who evidently died in print,
since it was soon after his disappearance that Rosika and Bella
appeared on the New York City scene.

This first book of mystery stories are staged in and around New
York. Other volumes will find Rosika and Bella in Paris, London,
Monaco and other places around the western world, that Bill
Footner and his family just happen to be visiting also; the author
with his small Corona typewriter that clicked out new cases in his
hotel room.

THE ASHCOMB POOR CASE

I CANNOT BETTER put that extraordinary woman, my employer, before you than by describing my first meeting with her. It is easier to show her qualities in action than to describe them.

On a certain morning, no different from thousands of other mornings, I was in a subway train on my way to the office when my eye was caught by this striking advertisement:

> Wanted—By a woman of affairs, a woman secretary; common sense is the prime requisite.

Printed words have an extraordinary effect on one sometimes. Something in these terse phrases so strongly appealed to me that though I had a very good position at the time, I interrupted my journey to the office and went directly to the address given.

It was on Gramercy Square. The house proved to be one of the fine old dwellings down there that have been altered into chic more-or-less-studio apartments. Bridal couples of the old Knickerbocker set are fond of setting up in that neighbourhood, I am told. As I approached, other females were converging at the door from three directions. The hall-boy, a typical New York specimen, looked us over with a grin, and without asking our business said:

"Madame Storey ain't down yet. Youse is all to wait in the little front room."

I asked him privately what was Madame Storey's business.

"Search me!" he said cheekily. "She don't hang out no sign."

Her apartment was the first floor front; part of the parlour floor of the old mansion. It was evidently only an office, but such an office! The walls were hung with priceless tapestries, there was an Italian Renaissance table for the secretary, ditto chairs for the clients, and here and there a bit of Chinese porcelain to make a vivid spot of colour. I confess I looked a little dubiously at all this magnificence; somehow it didn't seem quite respectable. All the time I was wondering what Madame Storey's "affairs" consisted of.

There were about twenty women waiting; not nearly enough chairs, so most of us stood. It was funny to see how every Jill of them was busily cultivating an air of common sense. All looked at me as I entered with an expression which said as plainly as words: "You might as well go; you will never do!" It was somewhat disconcerting until I saw that later arrivals received exactly the same look. No doubt I glared at them that way myself. There were far too many of us there already. What did more have to come for, we thought?

We were a motley throng ranging in age from seventeen to seventy. Women who obviously couldn't do a thing in this living world had rushed there to give Madame Storey the benefit of their common sense. One saw that there were as many definitions of common sense as there were women. Some thought it was sensible to paint their faces like a barber-pole; others, and these the larger number, considered that a sensible woman must don a hideous travesty of masculine attire, and wrinkle up her forehead like an ape. As for myself, the moment I saw that exquisite interior realised the incongruity of freckled, red-haired me amidst such surroundings. I had no hope of getting the position, but the whole affair was so funny to watch that I stayed on.

We waited an hour casting haughty glances at one another. But no one got tired and left. At the end of that time the boy from below threw open the door with a flourish and announced impressively:

"Madame Storey, ladies."

There was a dramatic pause while we breathlessly waited with eyes fixed on the open door. Before we saw her we heard her voice—

she was speaking to the boy outside, a slow voice with the arresting quality of the deeper notes of the oboe. Then she entered, and
an audible breath escaped from all us women. I don't know what
we expected, certainly not what we saw.

She was very tall and supremely graceful. It was impossible to
think of legs in connexion with her movements. She floated into
the room like a shape wafted on the breeze. She was darkly beautiful in the insolent style that causes plainer women to prim up their
lips.

She wore an extraordinary gown, a taupe silk brocaded with a
shadowy gold figure, made in long panels that exaggerated her
height and slimness, unrelieved by any trimming whatsoever.
On her head she wore an odd little hat of the same colour with an
exquisite plume curled around the brim. All this was very well, but
what made the women gasp was that snuggled in the hollow of her
arm she carried a black monkey dressed in a coat of Paddy green,
and a foolscap hung with tiny gold bells.

She looked us over with eyebrows registering delicate mockery, and glanced at the ape as if to call his attention to the spectacle. Nevertheless she was not displeased by the sensation her
entrance had created. I suspected that she had lingered outside
especially to create that dramatic pause.

It was funny to see the faces of the waiting women, wherein
strong disapproval struggled with the desire to please. As for myself, having no pretensions to beauty, I don't have to be jealous of
other women. I only knew the moment I laid eyes on Madame
Storey that I wanted that job and wanted it badly. In the first place,
a really beautiful woman is an unfailing delight to my eyes; in the
second, something told me that whoever worked for that woman
would see Life with a capital L. I didn't care much then what her
business might be.

She had kept us waiting a long time, but once there she expe-
dited matters. Without any preamble she turned to the woman
nearest the door—it was one of the near-masculine type that I have
mentioned, and said with a smile:

"There is no need of your waiting any longer."

The woman gasped and turned a bricky colour. "Why—why—" she began.

"I merely wished to save you from wasting more of your time," said Madame Storey kindly.

The woman snorted, glared around at us all, grasped her umbrella firmly around the middle and stumped out.

The next one was a sweet young thing of forty-odd who put her head on one side and wriggled her shoulders when Madame Storey looked at her.

"You needn't wait," said that lady.

The third was a middle-aged woman of determined mien. When Madame Storey turned to her she stiffened up—breathed hard and prepared to stand her ground.

Madame Storey shook her head with a deprecating smile.

"But I am a sensible woman," insisted the other. "Everybody says there is no nonsense about me."

Some of us were impolite enough to laugh.

"I don't doubt it," said Madame Storey, "but you are not what I require."

"I insist on an explanation!"

"Certainly. You do not like me, you see. What would be the use?"

The woman went out with a dazed air.

So it went. In five minutes the room was pretty well cleared. As she approached me my heart sank lower and lower, for I did want that job. But she appeared to overlook me altogether, and I was one of the three left when she completed her circuit. The other two were handsome, assured, well-dressed girls, and I told myself I had as good a chance against them as the traditional snowball down below.

Madame Storey said: "I will see you young ladies one at a time in my own office."

The other two pressed forward, each trying to be the first, but I hung back. I argued that she would not engage anybody until she had talked to all three, and as every lawyer knows, there is a considerable advantage in having the last say.

The first girl, a ladylike blonde in a tailored suit, was not inside more than two minutes. She came out looking red and flustered.

"Well?" we asked her simultaneously.

"Never gave me a chance to say a word!" she said crossly. "Offered me a cigarette. Since she offered it, I knew she must be a smoker, so I took it, not to seem goody-goody. Well, I'm not accustomed to them. I choked over it. She just stood up and said good-morning."

The second girl looked wise, and went on in. But her interview didn't last more than thirty seconds. Reappearing, she burst out without even waiting for me to question her:

"The woman is crazy, if you ask me! Offered me a cigarette, too. Well, I wasn't going to make the same mistake as the other girl. I declined. Said I didn't indulge. She just pointed to the inside of my right forefinger and stood up. It's just a little stained. What does she expect! Smokes like a furnace herself!"

I went into the next room with my heart jumping against the root of my tongue. It was a wonderful room: more like a little gallery in a museum than a woman's office; an up-to-date museum where they realise the value of not showing too much at once. With all its richness there was a fine severity of arrangement, and every object was perfect of its kind. I didn't appreciate all this at the moment. It was only as I came to know it that I realised the taste with which every object had been selected and arranged.

Madame Storey was seated at a great table with her back to the windows. On the edge of the table was perched the little green-jacketed monkey, hands on knees and swinging his feet in an absurdly human way. He was gazing solemnly into his mistress's face and she was talking to him.

"Our last chance, Giannino. If this one fails us, we'll have to go through with the whole silly business again tomorrow."

The ape squeaked sympathetically, and gave me the once over. She waved me to a chair. "What is your name?" she asked.

"Miss Brickley."

"Your first name? It helps one to understand a person."

"Bella."

"Ah!" Giving me a shrewd look, she pushed a great silver box of cigarettes towards me.

I had already made up my mind what to do. "Thanks, I don't smoke," I said.

"Hope you don't object," she said, taking one.

"No, indeed," I answered. "I could acquire the habit as quickly as any one, but it would be an added expense. I have to think of that."

"Ah!" she said, and let the matter drop. Anyhow, the cigarette had not tripped me.

She was regarding me searchingly. It was a kindly look, yet it made me frightfully uncomfortable. I hate people to stare at me, I am so plain. In spite of myself I burst out:

"I suppose you're thinking I wouldn't be much of an ornament to this establishment!"

"Yes," she said quite coolly. "But I was also thinking, that you were not as bad as you thought yourself. Your hair is charming."

My snaky red locks charming! I looked at the woman in astonishment.

"It would make an effective spot of colour against my green tapestries," she went on. "You know you don't have to drag it back from the roots like that."

Her unexpectedness unnerved me a little. Unfortunately when I am nervous I get cross.

"Are you a sensible woman?" she asked with a bland air.

"I don't know," I snapped. "I never gave the matter any thought."

"That's encouraging. Tell me of what you were thinking when you came in just now."

"Well," I replied, "it was clear to me from the experiences of the two who preceded me that they had got themselves turned down by making pretences; the first pretending that she smoked when she didn't, and the second pretending she didn't when she did. So I made up my mind not to bother about what you thought, but to be as nearly honest as I could."

She laughed. "You hear that, my Giannino?"

The ape made a face at me. He and I never took to each other.

"Then you want this job?" Madame Storey asked.

"I do."

"Why?"

"Because I think it's going to be exciting."

She shrugged. "I'll give you a trial," she said casually.

I could scarcely believe my ears. Once I got there I had no doubt but that I could make myself indispensable.

"You have not only the rudiments of sense, but a pretty spirit," she added with that terribly searching kindly gaze.

I was dumb.

"You are surprised that I praise you to your face? It is not my habit. But you, one can see, are suffering from malappreciation. Those two ugly lines between your brows were born of the belief that you were too plain and uninteresting ever to hope to win a niche of your own in the world. And so you are if you think you are. But you don't have to think so. Think that cross look away and your face will show what is rarer than beauty—character, individuality. Old Time himself cannot rob you of that." She turned to the ape. "I believe this is what we were looking for, Giannino."

I felt as if this strange woman had probed my soul.

"Are you employed now?" she asked abruptly.

"Yes."

"What is your salary?"

I named it.

"I shall double it, Miss Brickley. That is only fair, because I shall make great demands on you."

I tried to stammer my thanks.

"Haven't you got some questions to ask me?" she said.

"What is the nature of your business?" I diffidently inquired.

"You will soon see," she said smiling. "I assure you it is quite honest. You may call me a practical psychologist—specialising in the feminine."

2

MOST OF YOU will remember how the murder of Ashcomb Poor set the whole town agog. The victim's wealth and social position and the scandalous details of his private life that began to ooze out, whetted the public appetite for sensation to the highest degree. For years Ashcomb Poor had been one of the most beparagraphed men in town, and now the manner of his taking off seemed like a tremendous climax to a thrilling tale.

The day it first came out in the papers Mme. Storey did not arrive at the office until noon. She was very plainly dressed and wore a thick veil that partly obscured her features. By this time I was accustomed to these metamorphoses of costume. From a little bag that she carried she took several articles and handed them over to me. These were (*a*) a hank of thin green string in a snarl, (*b*) a piece of iridescent chiffon, partly burned, (*c*) an envelope containing seven cigarette butts.

"Some scraps of evidence in the Ashcomb Poor case," she explained. "Put them in a safe place."

I had just been reading the newspaper report.

"What! Have we been engaged in that case already?" I exclaimed. Mme. Storey encouraged me to speak of our business in the first person plural, and of course it flattered me to do so.

"No," she said, smiling, "but we may be. At any rate, I have forearmed myself by taking a look over the ground."

In the rear of her room there was a smaller one that she used as a retiring and dressing-room. She changed there now to a more suitable costume.

Two days later she remarked: "The signs tell me that we shall receive a call from the district attorney's office today."

Sure enough, Assistant District Attorney Barron turned up before the morning was over. Though he was a young man for the job, he was a capable one, and held over through several succeeding administrations. This was the first time I had seen him, though it turned out he was an old friend of Mme. Storey's. A handsome, full-blooded fellow, his weakness was that he thought just a little too well of himself.

I showed him into the private office and returned to my desk. There is a dictagraph installed between Mme. Storey's desk and mine, and when it is turned on I am supposed to listen in and make a transcript of whatever conversation may be taking place. Sometimes, to my chagrin, she turns it off at the most exciting moment, but more often she leaves it on, I am sure, out of pure good nature, because she knows I am so keenly interested. Mme. Storey is good enough to say that she likes me to be in possession of full information, so that she can talk things over with me.

The circuit was open now, and I heard him say: "My God, Rose, you're more beautiful than ever!"

"Thanks, Walter," she dryly retorted. "The dictagraph is on, and my secretary can hear everything you say."

"For Heaven's sake, turn it off!"

"I can't now, or she'd imagine the worst. You'll have to stick to business. I suppose you've come to see me about the Ashcomb Poor case."

"What makes you jump to that conclusion?"

"Oh, you were about due."

"Humph! I suppose that's intended to be humorous. If you weren't quite so sure of yourself you'd be a great woman, Rose. But it's a weakness in you. You think you know everything!"

"Well, what did you come to see me about?"

"As a matter of fact, it was the Ashcomb Poor case. But that was just a lucky shot on your part. I suppose you read that I had been assigned to the case."

"Walter, you're a good prosecutor, but you lack a sense of humour."

"Well, you're all right in your own line, feminine psychology and all that. I gladly hand it to you. But the trouble with you is, you want to tell me how to run my job too."

"No one could do that, Walter."

"What do you mean?"

"Never mind. How does the Poor case stand?"

"I suppose you've read the papers."

"Yes; they're no nearer the truth than usual. Give me an outline of the situation as you see it."

"Well, you know the Ashcomb Poors. Top-notchers; fine old family, money, and all that; leaders in the ultra-smart Prince's Valley set on Long Island. They have what they call a small house at Grimstead, where they make believe to live in quiet style; it's the thing nowadays."

"In other words, the extravagantly simple life."

"Exactly. They have no children. The household consisted of Mr. and Mrs. Poor, Miss Philippa Dean, Mrs. Poor's secretary; Mrs. Batten, the housekeeper; a butler and three maids; there were outside servants, too—chauffeur, gardener, and so on—but they don't come into the case. Ashcomb Poor was a handsome man and a free liver. Things about him have been coming out—well, you know. On the other hand, his wife was above scandal, a great beauty—"

"Vintage of 1910."

"Well, perhaps; but still in the running. These women know how to keep their looks. Very charitable woman and all that. Greatly looked up to. On Monday night Mrs. Poor took part in a big affair at the Pudding Stone Country Club near their home. A pageant of all nations or something. Her husband, who did not care for such functions, stayed at home. So did Miss Dean and Mrs. Batten. Mrs. Poor took the other servants to see the show."

"There were only three left in the house, then?"

"Yes—Mr. Poor, Miss Dean, and Mrs. Batten."

"Go on."

"Mrs. Poor returned from the entertainment about midnight. Mrs. Batten let her in the front door. Standing there, the two women could see into the library, where Poor sat with his back to them. They were struck by something strange in his attitude, and started to investigate, Mrs. Batten in advance.

"She was the first to realise that something had happened, and tried to keep Mrs. Poor from approaching the body. They struggled. Mrs. Poor screamed. The girl, Philippa Dean, suddenly appeared, nobody can tell from where. A moment later the other servants, who had gone around to the back door, ran in.

"Well, there was the situation. He had been shot in the back. The pistol was there. The butler telephoned to friends of the family and to the police. Grimstead, as you know, is within the city limits, so it comes within our jurisdiction. I was notified of the affair within an hour and ordered to take personal charge of the case. Nothing had been disturbed. I ordered the arrest of the Dean girl, and she is still in custody."

"What do you want of me?" Mme. Storey inquired.

"I want you to see the girl. Frankly, she baffles me. Under our questioning she broke down before morning and confessed to killing the man. But the next day she repudiated her confession, and has obstinately stuck to her repudiation in spite of all we could do. I want you to see her and get a regular confession."

"What about the girl's lawyers?"

"She has none as yet. Refused to see one."

"You're sure she did it?"

"Absolutely. It was immediately apparent that the murder had been committed by one of the inmates of the house."

"Why?"

"Because when Mrs. Poor and the servants departed for the entertainment Mrs. Batten, who let them out, turned on the burglar-alarm, and it remained turned on until she let her mistress in again. One of the first things I did on arriving at the house was to make sure that the alarm was working properly. I also examined all the doors and windows. Everything was intact."

"Why couldn't the housekeeper have done it?"

"A simple, timid old soul! Impossible! No motive. Besides, if she had she would hardly have given me the principal piece of evidence against those in the house; I mean her testimony about the burglar-alarm."

"What motive could the girl have had?"

"The servants state that their master had been pestering her—forcing his attentions on her."

"Ah! But this is all presumptive evidence, of course. What else have you?"

"Ashcomb Poor was shot with an automatic pistol belonging to Miss Dean. The butler identified it. At first she denied that it was hers. She could not deny, though, that she had one like it, and when asked to produce it she could not. It was not among her effects."

"Where did you find the gun exactly?"

"In the dead man's hand."

"In his hand?"

"Under his hand, I should say. It had been shoved under in a clumsy attempt to make it appear like a suicide. But the hand was

clenched on top of the weapon. Moreover, the man was shot between the shoulders. He could not possibly have done it himself.
The bullet passed completely through his body, and I found it
lodged in the wall across the room."

"Did the housekeeper hear the shot?"

"She did not. She was in another wing of the house."

"Anything else against the girl?"

"Yes. When she appeared, attracted by Mrs. Poor's cry, though
she was supposed to have retired some time before, she was fully
dressed. Moreover, she knew what had happened before any one
told her."

"Ah! How does she explain these suspicious circumstances?"

"She will explain nothing. Refuses to talk."

"What story did she tell when she confessed?"

"None. Merely cried out: 'I did it! I did it! Don't ask me any
more!'"

There was a silence here, during which Mme. Storey presumably ruminated on what she had been told. Finally she said: "I'll
see the girl, but it must be upon my own conditions."

"What are those?"

"As an independent investigator, I hold no brief for the district
attorney's office."

"Well, there's no harm in that."

"But you must understand what that implies. Neither you nor
any of your men may be present while I am talking to her. And I do
not bind myself to tell you everything she tells me."

"That's out of the question. What would the old man say if he
knew that I turned her over to an outsider?"

"Well, that's up to you, of course." Mme. Storey spoke indifferently. "You came to me, you know."

"Well—all right." This very sullenly. "I suppose if she confesses
you'll let me know."

"Certainly. But I'm not at all sure this is going to turn out the
way you expect."

"After all I've told you?"

"Your case against her is a little too good, Walter."

"Who else could have done it?"

"I don't know—yet. If she did it, why should she have stuck around the house until you arrested her?"

"She supposed it would be considered a suicide."

"But, according to you, a year-old child wouldn't have been deceived into thinking so."

"Well, you never can tell. They always do something foolish. Will you come down to the Tombs? I'll arrange for a room there."

"No, I must see the girl here."

"That's impossible!"

"Sorry; it's my invariable rule, you know."

"But have a heart, Rose. I daren't let her out of my custody."

"You and your men can wait outside the door, then."

"It's most irregular."

"I am an irregular person," was the bland reply. "You should not have come to me."

"Well—I suppose you must have your own way."

"Always do, my dear. With the girl send a transcript of whatever statements have been taken down in the case."

"All right. Rose, turn off that confounded dictagraph, will you? I want to speak to you privately."

"It's off."

It wasn't, though, for I continued to hear every word.

"Good God, Rose, why do you persist in trying to madden me?"

"Mercy, Walter! How?"

"You know! With your cold and scornful airs, your indifference. It's—it's only vanity. Your vanity is ridiculous!"

"Oh, if you're only going to call names, I'll turn on the dictagraph!"

"No, don't, don't! I scarcely know what I'm saying you provoke me so! Why won't you be decent to me, Rose? Why won't you take me? We were made for each other!"

"So *you* say."

"Do you never feel anything, anything behind that scornful smile? Are you a breathing woman or a cold and heartless monster?"

"Bless me, I don't know."

"You need a master!"

"Of course I do. Why don't you master me, Walter?"

"Don't taunt me. A man has his limits! You make me want to seize and hurt you!"

"Don't do that. You'd spoil my pretty frock. Besides, Giannino would bite the back of your neck."

"Don't taunt me. You'd be helpless in my arms. You're always asking for a master."

"I meant a master of my soul, Walter."

"I don't understand you."

"Yes, you do. Look at me! You can't. My soul is stronger than yours, Walter, and in your heart you know it."

"You're talking nonsense!"

"Don't mumble your words. That's my tragedy, if you only knew it. I have yet to meet a man bold enough to face me down. How could I surrender myself to one whose soul was secretly afraid of mine? So here I sit. You know that the Madame I have hitched to my name is just to save my face. No one would believe that a woman as beautiful as I could be still unmarried—and respectable. But I am both, worse luck!"

"It's your own fault that you're alone. You think too well of yourself. You make believe to scorn all men."

"Well, if it's a bluff, why doesn't some man call it?"

"I will right now! I'm tired of this fooling. You've got to marry me."

"Look at me when you say that, Walter."

A silence.

"Ah—you can't you see."

"Ah, Rose, don't torture me this way! Can't you see I'm mad about you? You spoil my rest at night; you come between me and my work by day. I hunger and thirst for you like a man in a desert. Think what a team you and I would make, Rose. There'd be no stopping us short of the White House."

Here, to my chagrin, the dictagraph was abruptly turned off, but when, a minute or two later, Mr. Barron burst out of the inner room purple with rage I guessed that no change had occurred in the situation. He flung across the floor and out of the door without a glance in my direction.

Mme. Storey called to me to bring in my note-book. As I entered she was talking to the monkey.

"Giannino, you are better off than you know. Better be a dumb beast than a half-thinking animal."

The little thing wrinkled up his forehead and chirruped as he always did when she addressed him.

"You disagree with me? I tell you, men would rather go to jail than put themselves to the trouble of thinking clearly."

3

EDDIE, THE HALL BOY, and I had become at least outwardly friendly. In his heart I think Eddie always despised me as "a jane out of the storehouse," one of his own expressions, but as he had the keenest curiosity about all that went on in our shop, he was obliged to be affable in order to tap such sources of information as I possessed. He adored Mme. Storey, of course; all youths did as well as older males. As for me, I couldn't help liking the amusing little wretch, he was so new.

Like most boys of his age his ruling passion was for airplanes and aviators. At this time his particular idol was the famous Lieutenant George Grantland who had broken so many records. Grantland had just started on a three days' point-to-point flight from Camp Tasker, encircling the whole country east of the Mississippi, and Eddie, in order to follow him, was obliged to buy an extra every hour. Bursting with the subject, and having no one else to talk to, he brought these up to my room. This was his style—of course I am only guessing at the figures.

"Here's the latest. Landed at New Orleans four thirty this A.M., two hours ahead of time. Gee! If I could only get out to a bulletin-board! Slept four hours and went on. Four hundred and forty-two miles in under four hours. Wouldn't that expand your lungs? Say, that guy is a king of the air all right. Flies by night as well as day. They have lights to guide him where to land. Hasn't had to come down once for trouble. Here's a picture of his plane. It's the

Bentley-Critchard type. They're just out. Good for a hundred and forty an hour. Six hundred horse. Do you get that? Think of driving six hundred plugs through the clouds. Some team!"

After two days of this I was almost as well acquainted with the exploits of Lieutenant Grantland as his admirer. Every hour or two Eddie would have a new picture of the dashing aviator to show me. Even after being snapshotted in the blazing sun and reproduced in a newspaper half-tone, he remained a handsome young fellow.

Eddie was in the thick of this when they brought Philippa Dean up from the Tombs, but as she was indubitably a "class one jane," his attention was momentarily won from his newspapers. The assistant district attorney did not accompany her. To be obliged to wait outside was, I suppose, too great a trial to his dignity. Miss Dean was under escort of two gigantic plain-clothes men, the slender little thing. I was glad, at any rate, that they had not handcuffed her.

My first impression was a favourable one; her eyes struck you at once. They were full, limpid, blue, very wide open under fine brows, giving her an expression of proud candour in which there was something really affecting—however, I had learned ere this from Mme. Storey that you cannot read a woman's soul in her eyes, so I reserved judgment. Her hair was light-brown. She was dressed with that fine simplicity which is the despair of newly arrived women. At present she looked hard and wary, and her lips were compressed into a scarlet line—but that was small wonder in her situation.

Mme. Storey came out when she heard them. What was her first impression of the girl I cannot say, for she never gave anything away in her face at such moments. She invited the two detectives to make themselves comfortable in the outer office, and we three women passed into the big room. She waved the girl to a seat.

"You may relax," she said, smiling; "nobody is going to put you through the third degree here."

But the girl sat down bolt upright, with her hands clenched in her lap. It was painful to see that tightness. Mme. Storey applied herself to the task of charming it away. She said to the ape:

"Giannino, take off your hat to Miss Dean, and tell her that we wish her well."

The little animal stood up on the table, jerked off his cap and gibbered in his own tongue. It was a performance that never failed to win a smile, but this girl's lips looked as if they had forgotten how.

"The assistant district attorney has asked me to examine you," Mme. Storey began in friendly style. "Being a public prosecutor, he's bent on your conviction, having nobody else to accuse. But I may as well tell you that I don't share his feelings. Indeed, he's so cock-sure that it would give me pleasure to prove him wrong."

I knew that my employer was sincere in saying this, but I suppose the poor girl had learned to her cost that the devil himself can be sympathetic. At any rate, the speech had no effect on her.

"I hope you will believe that I have no object except to discover the truth," Mme. Storey went on.

"That's what they all say," muttered the girl.

"Satisfy yourself in your own way as to whether you can trust me. Come, we have all afternoon."

"Am I obliged to answer your questions?" demanded the girl.

"By no means," was the prompt reply. "Why don't you question me first?"

The girl took her at her word. "Who are you?" she asked. "I have been told nothing."

"Mme. Rosika Storey. They call me a practical psychologist. The district attorney's office sometimes does me the honour to consult me, particularly in the cases of women."

"You'll get no confession out of me!"

"I don't expect to. I don't believe you did it. No sane woman would shoot a man between the shoulder-blades and expect to make out that it was a suicide. At any rate, Ashcomb Poor seems to have richly deserved his fate. Come now, frankly, did you do it?"

The girl's blue eyes flashed. "I did not."

"Good! Then tell me what happened that night."

The girl sullenly shook her head. "What's the use?"

"Why, to clear yourself, naturally."

"They haven't enough evidence to convict me. They *couldn't* convict me, because I didn't do it."

"That's a perilous line to take, my dear. I suspect you haven't had much experience with juries. The gentleman of the jury would consider silence in a woman not only unnatural, but incriminating. Of course, they might let you off, anyway, if you condescended to ogle them, but as I say, it's perilous. Why did you confess in the first place?"

"To get rid of them. They were driving me out of my mind with their questions."

"I can well understand that. Well then, what did happen, really?"

The girl set her lips. "I have made up my mind to say nothing, and I shall stick to it," she replied.

Mme. Storey spread out her hands. "Very well, let's talk about something else. Dean is a good old name here in New York. Are you of the New York family?"

"My people have lived here for four generations."

"I have read of a great beau in the sixties and seventies—Philip Dean. Are you related to him?"

"He was my grandfather."

"I might have guessed it from your first name. How interesting! All the chronicles of those days are full of references to his wit and *savoir faire*. But he must have been a rich man. How does it come that you have to work for your living?"

"The usual story; the first two generations won the family fortune, and the next two lost it. I am of the fifth generation."

"Well, I suppose one cannot have a famous *bon vivant* in the family for nothing."

"Oh, no one could speak ill of my grandfather. He was a gallant gentleman. I knew him as a child. He spent his money in scientific experiments which only benefited others. My poor father was not to blame either. He lost the rest of the money trying to recoup his father's losses in Wall Street."

"And you were thrown on your own resources."

"Oh, I was never a pathetic figure. I could get work. There were always women, not very sure of themselves socially, who were glad to engage Philip Dean's granddaughter."

"That's how you came to go to Mrs. Poor."

"No, that was different. Mrs. Poor didn't need anybody to tell her things. Her family was as good as my own. Her husband was travelling abroad and she was lonely. She engaged me as a sort of companion."

"When did her husband return?"

The girl frowned. "Now you think you're leading me up to it, don't you?"

Mme. Storey laughed. "I suspect you're the kind of young lady that nobody can lead any farther than she is willing to go."

Miss Dean glanced suspiciously at me. "Is she taking down all I say?" she demanded.

"Not until I tell her to," Mme. Storey replied.

"He returned two months ago."

"Do you mind describing their house at Grimstead for me?" asked Mme. Storey. "There's no harm in that, is there?"

The girl shrugged. "No. It's a small house, considering their means, and it looks even smaller because of being built in the style of an English cottage, with low, over-hanging eaves and dormer windows. You enter through a vestibule under the stairs and issue into a square hall. This hall is two storeys and has a gallery running around three sides. On your left is the library; on your right the small reception room; the living-room, a large room, is at the back of the hall, with the dining-room adjoining it. These two rooms look out over the garden and the brook below. Between reception and dining-room there is a passage leading away to the kitchen wing. Besides pantry, kitchen, and laundry, this wing has a housekeeper's room and a servants' dining-room."

"And upstairs?"

"Mr. and Mrs. Poor's own suite is at the back of the house over the living-room and dining-room. My room is over the library. There is a guest room over the reception room. All the servants' rooms are in the kitchen wing. There is no third storey."

Mme. Storey affected to consult the notes on her desk. "Where was this burglar-alarm that there has been so much talk about?"

"Hidden in a cranny between the telephone-booth and the hall fire-place. The telephone-booth was let into the wall just beyond the library door, and the fire-place is adjoining."

"Hidden, you say. Was there anything secret about it?"

"No. Everybody in the house knew of it."

"What kind of switch was it?"

"It was just a little handle that lifted up and pulled down. When it was up it was off; when it was down it was on."

"Describe the servants, will you?"

"How is one to describe servants? The butler, Briggs—well, he was just a butler; smooth, deferential, fairly efficient. The maids were just typical maids. None of them had been there long. Servants don't stick nowadays."

"What about Mrs. Batten?"

In spite of herself the girl's face softened—yet at the same time a guarded tone crept into her voice. "Oh, she's different," she said.

Mme. Storey did not miss the guarded tone. "How different?" she asked.

"I didn't look on Mrs. Batten as a servant, but as a friend."

"Describe her for me."

The girl, looking down, paused before replying. Her softened face was wholly charming. "A simple, kindly, motherly soul," she said with a half-smile. "Rather absurd, because she takes everything so seriously. But while you laugh at her you get more fond of her. She doesn't mind being laughed at."

"You have the knack of hitting off character!" said Mme. Storey. "I see her perfectly!"

I began to appreciate Mme. Storey's wizardry. Cautiously feeling her way with the girl she had discovered that Philippa had a talent for description in which she took pride—perhaps the girl aspired to be a writer. At any rate, when she was asked to describe anything, her eyes became bright and abstracted, and she forgot her situation for the moment.

It seemed to me that we were on the verge of stumbling on something, but to my surprise, Mme. Storey dropped Mrs. Batten. "Describe Mrs. Poor for me," she asked.

"That is more difficult," the girl said unhesitatingly. "She is a complex character. We got along very well together. She was always kind, always most considerate. Indeed, she was an admirable woman, not in the least spoiled by the way people kowtowed to her. But I cannot say that I knew her very well, because she was always reserved—I mean with everybody. One felt sometimes that she would like to unbend, but had never learned how."

"And the master of the house?"

The girl shuddered slightly. But still preoccupied in conveying her impressions, she did not take alarm. "He was a rich man," she answered, "and the son of a rich man. That is to say, from baby-hood he had never been denied anything. Yet he was an attractive man—when he got his own way; full of spirits and good nature. Everybody liked him—that is, nearly everybody."

"Didn't you like him?" asked Mme. Storey.

"Yes, I did in a way—but—" She stopped.

"But what?"

She hung her head. "I'm talking too much," she muttered.

Mme. Storey appeared to drop the whole matter with an air of relief. "Let's have tea," she said to me. "I can see from Giannino's sorrowful eyes that he is famishing."

I hastened into the next room for the things. Mme. Storey, in the way that she has, started to rattle on about cakes as if they were the most important things in the world.

"Every afternoon at this hour Miss Brickley and Giannino and I regale ourselves. We have cakes sent in from the pastry cooks'. Don't you love cakes with thick icing all over them? I'm childish on the subject. When I was a little girl I swore to myself that when I grew up I would stuff myself with iced cakes."

When I returned I saw that in spite of herself the girl had re-laxed even further. Her eyes sparkled at the sight of the great sil-ver plate of cakes. After all, she was a human girl, and I don't sup-pose she'd been able to indulge her sweet tooth in jail. Giannino set up an excited chattering. Upon being given his share he retired to his favourite perch on top of a big picture to make away with it.

While we ate and drank we talked of everything that women talk of: cakes, clothes, tenors and what not. One would never have guessed that the thought of murder was present in each of our minds. The girl relaxed completely. It was charming to watch the play of her expressive eyes.

Mme. Storey, who, notwithstanding her boasted indulgence, was very abstemious, finished her cake and lighted the inevitable cigarette. Giannino stroked her cheek, begging piteously for more cake, but the plate had been put out of his way. Mme. Storey, happening to lay down her cigarette, Giannino, ever on the watch for such a contingency, snatched it up and clambered with chatterings of derision up to the top of his picture. There he sat with half-closed eyes blowing clouds of smoke in the most abandoned manner. Philippa Dean laughed outright; it was strange to hear that sound from her. I was obliged to climb on a chair to recover the cigarette. I spend half my time following up that little wretch. If I don't take the cigarette from him it makes him sick, yet he hasn't sense enough to leave them alone—just like a man!

"Well, shall we go on with our talk?" asked Mme. Storey casually.

The girl spread out her hands. "You have me at a disadvantage," she said. "It is so hard to resist you."

"Don't try," suggested my employer, smiling. "You may take your notes now, Miss Brickley. You needn't be afraid," she added to the girl. "This is entirely between ourselves. No one else shall see them. You were saying that you liked Mr. Poor—with reservations."

"I meant that one could have enjoyed his company very much if he had been content to be natural. But he was one of those men who pride themselves on their—their—what shall I say—"

"Their masculinity?"

"Exactly. And of course with a man of that kind a girl is obliged constantly to be on her guard."

"The servants have stated that he pestered you with his attentions," Mme. Storey remarked.

The girl lowered her eyes. "They misunderstood," she said. "Mr. Poor affected a very flowery, gallant style with all women alike; it didn't mean anything."

Mme. Storey glanced at a paper on her desk. "The butler deposes that one evening he saw Mr. Poor seize you on the stairs and attempt to kiss you, and that you boxed his ears and fled to your room."

Miss Dean blushed painfully and made no reply.

Mme. Storey, without insisting on one, went on: "What were the relations between Mr. and Mrs. Poor?"

"How can any outsider know that?" parried the girl.

"You can give me your opinion. You are a sharp observer. It will help me to understand the general situation."

"Well, they never quarrelled, if that's what you mean. They were always friendly and courteous toward each other. Not like people who are in love, of course. Mrs. Poor must have known what her husband's life was, but she was a religious woman, and any thought of separation or divorce was out of the question for her. My guess was that she had determined to take him as she found him, and make the best of it. Such a cold and self-contained woman naturally would not suffer as much as another."

"Have you knowledge of any incident in Mr. Poor's life that might throw light on his murder?"

"No. Nobody in that house knew anything of the details of his life. He was not with us much."

"Tell me about your movements on the night of the tragedy," Mme. Storey urged coaxingly.

But the girl's face instantly hardened. "It is useless to ask me that," she said. "I do not mean to answer."

"But since you did not commit the crime why not help me to get you off?"

"I do not wish to speak of my private affairs which have nothing to do with this case."

My heart beat faster. Here we were plainly on the road to important disclosures. But to my disappointment Mme. Storey abandoned the line.

"That is your right, of course," she said. "But consider: you are bound to be asked these very questions in court before a gaping crowd. Why not accustom yourself to the questions in advance by letting me ask them? You are not under oath here, you know. You may answer what you please."

This was certainly an unusual way of conducting an examination. Even the girl smiled wanly.

"You are clever," she said with a shrug. "Ask me what you please."

"What were you doing on the night of the tragedy?"

From this point forward the girl was constrained and wary again. She weighed every word of her replies before speaking. It was impossible to resist the suggestion that she was not always telling the truth.

"I was in my room."

"The whole time?"

"Yes, from dinner until Mrs. Poor returned."

"Why didn't you go to the pageant?"

"Those affairs bore me."

"Had you not intended to go?"

"No."

"Where was Mrs. Batten during the evening?"

"I don't know. In her room, I assume."

"In what part of the house was that?"

"Her sitting-room was downstairs in the kitchen wing."

"An old woman. Wasn't she timid about being all alone in that part of the house?"

"I don't know. It did not occur to me."

"You didn't see her at all during the evening?"

"No."

"Where was Mr. Poor?"

"In the library, I understood."

"All the time?"

"I'm sure I couldn't say."

"Did you see him or have speech with him during the evening?"

"No."

"There was nobody in the house but you three?"

"Nobody."

"You're sure of that?"

"Quite sure."

"The servants testified that when the alarm was raised you appeared fully dressed."

"That's nothing. It was only twelve o'clock. I was reading."

"What were you reading?"

"Kipling's *The Light that Failed*."

"What became of the book?"

"I put it down when Mrs. Poor cried out."

"Are you sure? It was not found in your room."

"Of course I'm not sure. I may have carried it downstairs. I may have dropped it anywhere in my excitement."

"Please describe the exact situation of your room."

"It was in the northeast corner of the house. It was over the library."

"Yet you heard no shot?"

"No."

"That's strange."

"The house is very well built; double doors and all that."

"But immediately overhead?"

"I can't help that. I heard nothing."

"You had no hint that anything was wrong until you heard Mrs. Poor's cry?"

"None whatever."

"When she cried out what did you do?"

"I ran around the gallery and downstairs."

"The gallery?"

"In order to reach the head of the stairs I had to encircle the gallery in the hall."

"How long did it take you to reach Mrs. Poor's side?"

"How can I say? I ran."

"How far?"

"Fifty or sixty feet; then the stairs."

"Half a minute?"

"Perhaps."

"What did you see when you got downstairs?"

"The stairs landed me at the library door. Just inside the door I saw Mrs. Batten clinging to Mrs. Poor. She was trying to keep Mrs. Poor from reaching her husband's side."

"Mrs. Poor is a tall, finely formed woman, isn't she?"

"Yes."

"Is Mrs. Batten a big woman?"

"No."

"Strong?"

"No."

"Yet you say she was able to keep her mistress back for half a minute?"

"You said half a minute."

"Well, until you got downstairs."

"So it seems."

"Didn't that strike you as odd?"

"I didn't think about it."

"Did you know what had happened?"

"Not right away. I soon did."

"They told you?"

"No."

"How did you guess, then?"

"From Mr. Poor's attitude, sprawling with his arms across the table, his head down—the pistol in his hand."

"In his hand?"

"Well, under his hand, I believe."

"Did you recognise it as your pistol?"

"I—I don't know."

"Eh?"

"I mean I don't know just when I realised that it was mine. Pistols are so much alike. I hadn't handled mine much."

"Well, how was it that it could be so positively identified as yours?"

"There were two little scratches on the barrel that somebody had put there before I got it. I had shown it to Mrs. Batten, and we had discussed what those two little marks might mean. Mrs. Batten must have spoken of it in the hearing of the servants. At any rate they knew about the marks."

"How do you explain the fact that your pistol was in the dead man's hand?"

"I cannot explain it."

"Where did you keep it?"

"In the bottom drawer of my bureau."

"Was the drawer locked?"

"No."

"When had you last seen it there?"

"Two days before when I—" She stopped here.

"When you what?"

"When I put it away."

"You'd had it out then?"

"Yes."

"What for?"

"To have it fixed."

"What was wrong with it?"

"I couldn't describe it, because I don't understand the mechanism."

"Have you ever fired it?"

"No."

"Then how did you know it was out of order?"

"I—I—" She hesitated. "I won't answer that."

"Surely that's a harmless question."

"I don't care. I won't answer."

"Who fixed it?"

"The man it was bought from."

"Who was that?"

"I don't know."

"You mean you won't tell me?"

"No, it is the truth. I don't know. I never asked."

"Ah, it was a gift then?"

The girl did not answer. She was becoming painfully agitated, twisting and untwisting her handkerchief in her lap. I was growing excited myself. I felt sure we were on the verge of an important disclosure.

Mme. Storey feigned not to notice her perturbation. "How long had you had the pistol?" she asked.

"A few weeks—three or four."

"Was it in good order when you got it?"

"Yes."

"Well, if you had never shot it off how did it get out of order?"

No answer.

"Who had been firing it?"

Silence from Miss Dean.

"What kind of pistol was it?"

"They called it automatic."

"What calibre?"

"I don't know."

The next question came very softly. "Who gave it to you, Miss Dean?"

I couldn't help but pity the poor girl, her agitation was so extreme, and she was fighting so hard to control it.

"I won't answer that question."

"It will surely be asked in court."

"I won't answer it there."

"Your refusal will incriminate you."

"I don't care."

"Tell them you found it," Madame Storey suggested with an enigmatic, kindly look. To my astonishment she arose, saying: "That's all, Miss Dean."

I couldn't understand it. The girl who was deathly pale and breathing with difficulty seemed on the point of breaking down and confessing the truth—yet she let her go. I confess I was annoyed with Mme. Storey. In my mind I accused her of neglecting her duty. The girl was no less astonished than I. Out of her white face she stared at my employer as if she could not credit her ears.

Mme. Storey took a cigarette. "Many thanks for answering my questions," she said. "I see quite clearly that you couldn't have done this thing. I shall tell the assistant district attorney so."

The girl showed no gratitude at this assurance, but continued to stare at Mme. Storey with hard anxiety and suspicion. I stared too. It was perfectly clear to me that Philippa Dean had guilty knowledge of the murder.

"We'll have to hand you back to your watch-dogs now," said Mme. Storey. "Keep up a good heart."

The girl went out like one in a dream. When the plain-clothes men took her, Mme. Storey and I sat down again and looked at each other.

She laughed. "Bella, you look as if you were about to burst. Out with it!"

"I don't understand you!" I cried.

"Didn't you think she was a charming girl?"

"Yes, I did. I was terribly sorry for the poor young thing, but—"

"But what?"

I took my courage in my hands and continued: "You mustn't let your compassion for her, influence you. You have your professional reputation to think of!"

"You are more jealous of my professional reputation than I am," she said teasingly.

"Why did you stop just when you did?"

"Because I had found out what I wanted to know."

"What had you found out that Mr. Barron had not already told you? She was just at the point of—"

"Of repeating her confession?"

"I'm sure of it!"

"That is just what I wanted to forestall, Bella. Another confession would simply have complicated matters."

I simply stared at her.

"Because she didn't do it, you see, Bella."

"Then why should she confess?"

My employer merely shrugged.

"How can you be so sure she didn't do it? Anybody could see she was lying."

"Certainly she was lying."

"Well, then?"

"It was by her lies that I knew she was innocent."

"You are just teasing me," I said.

"Not at all. Read over your notes of her answers. It's all there, plain as a pike-staff."

I read over my notes, but saw no light. "That unmistakably guilty air," I said. "How do you explain that?"

"I wouldn't call it a guilty air."

"Well, anxious, terrified."

"That's more like it."

"Even if she didn't do it she knows who did."

"Possibly."

"Then why didn't you make her tell you?"

"Sometimes young girls have to be saved from themselves, Bella."

And that was all I could get out of her.

4

THE MOMENT PHILIPPA DEAN got back to Headquarters Mr. Barron must have started for our office. He arrived within forty minutes. When I showed him into Mme. Storey's room I followed him, for since the violent interview of the morning, she had instructed me to be present whenever he was there.

He was furious at what he regarded as my intrusion. He said nothing, but glared at me and I breathed a silent prayer that I might not fall into the clutches of the district attorney's office, at least as long as he was there. He sat down crossing and uncrossing his legs, slapping his knee with his gloves, and scowling sidewise at Mme. Storey from under beetling brows. Giannino, who detested him, fled to the top of his picture, where he sat hurling down imprecations in the monkey language at the man's head, and looking vainly around for something more effective to throw.

Mme. Storey was in her most impish mood. "Lovely afternoon, Walter," she remarked mellifluously.

He snorted.

"Will you have some tea? We've had ours."

"No, thank you."

"A cigarette, then?" She pushed the box toward him.

"You know I never use them."

"Well, you needn't be so virtuous about it." She took one herself. The graceful movement with which she stuck it in her mouth never failed to fascinate me—him, too.

He was silent. Mme. Storey blew a cloud of smoke. He scowled at her in a sullen, hungry way. I was sorry for the man. Really, she used him dreadfully.

"Rose, how many of those do you use a day?" he abruptly demanded.

"Oh, not more than fifty," she drawled, with a wicked twinkle in my direction.

She may have spoiled half that many a day, but she never took more than a puff of two of each.

"You're ruining your complexion," he said.

"Mercy!" she cried in mock horror, snatching up the little gold-backed mirror that always lay on her table. She studied herself attentively. "It does show signs of wear. What can one expect? It's six hours old already."

From her little bag she produced rouge-stick, powder-puff, pencils, et cetera, and nonchalantly set about using them. I might remark that Mme. Storey had developed the art of making-up to an extraordinary degree of perfection. In the beginning I had refused to believe that she used any artificial aids until the process took place before my eyes.

Absolutely indifferent to what people thought, she was likely to lug out the materials at any time, but particularly when she desired to be delicately insulting.

Mr. Barron became, if possible, angrier than before. For a moment or two he fumed in silence, then said:

"Please put those things away. I want to talk to you."

"You told me my complexion needed repair, Walter. Go ahead. Making-up is purely a subconscious operation. I'm listening."

They were a strong-willed pair. She would not stop making-up, and he would not speak until she gave him her full attention. There was a long silence. It was rather difficult for me. I sat at my little table, making believe to busy myself with my papers. Mme. Storey put aside the cigarette. That little scamp Giannino came sneaking down, but I got it first, and clapped it in the ash-jar with a cover that he cannot open. He retired, sulking, into a corner, and swore at me in his way.

Mme. Storey finally put down the mirror. "Is that better, Walter?" she asked with a wicked smile.

He puffed out his cheeks.

"I'm waiting to hear you," she said, putting away the make-up.

"It's a confidential matter," he rejoined glancing at me.

"Miss Brickley knows all about the Poor case," she said carelessly. "You needn't mind her."

"Well, what happened?" he asked sullenly.

"Nothing much."

"Did you get a confession from the girl?"

"No; I managed to forestall it."

His jaw dropped. "What do you mean?"

"She was just on the point of making a confession when I sent her back to you."

"Will you be so good as to explain yourself?"

"A confession would simply have puffed you up, Walter, and obstructed the ends of justice. Because she didn't kill Ashcomb Poor."

"I suppose you had your secretary take notes of her examination," he said. "Please let her read them to me."

Mme. Storey shook her head. "The girl talked to me in confidence, Walter."

"But surely I have the right—"

"We agreed beforehand, you know."

The assistant district attorney, very angry indeed, muttered something to the effect that he "would know better next time."

"That, of course, is up to you," she said sweetly. "Anyway, it wouldn't do any good to read you the notes, because I brought out no new facts of importance."

"Then how do you know she's innocent?" he demanded.

"By intuition," she said with her sweetest smile.

He flung up his hands. "Good Heaven! Can I go into court with your intuition?"

"I suppose not. But so much the worse for the court. I haven't much of an opinion of courts, as you know, for the very reason that they throw out intuition. They choose to found justice solely on reason, when, as every sensible person knows, reason is the most fallible of human faculties. You can prove anything by reason."

To this Mr. Barren hotly retorted:

"Yet I never saw a lying woman in court but who, when she was caught, did not fall back on her so-called intuition."

"That may be. But because there are liars is not to say there is no truth. Intuition speaks with a still small voice that is not easy to hear."

"Does your intuition inform you who did kill Ashcomb Poor?" he asked sarcastically.

"I shall have to have more time for that," she parried.

"I thought your intuition was an instantaneous process."

"Since you force me to meet you on your own ground, I must have sufficient time to build up a reasonable case."

"Aha! Then you don't despise reason altogether."

"By no means. But my reasoning is better than yours because it is guided by the voice of intuition."

"Do you expect me to release this girl on the strength of your intuition?"

"By no means. She'd run away. And we may need her later."

"Run away! This paragon of innocence? Impossible!"

"There are a good many things that reasonable men do not understand," drawled Mme. Storey. "Take it from me, though, in the end you will come off better in this affair if you simply hold the girl in the House of Detention as a material witness."

"Thanks," he said; "but I am going before the grand jury to-morrow to ask for an indictment for homicide."

"As you will! Men must be reasonable. According to your theory, she killed him in defending herself from his attentions, didn't she?"

"That's what I intimated."

"Well, as a reasonable man, how do you account for the fact that she was willing to stay in the house with him alone except for the old housekeeper?"

"The point is well taken," he admitted, but with a disagreeable smile that suggested he meant to humble her later.

Mme. Storey continued: "Moreover, she must have put herself in the way of his attentions, for the tragedy occurred in the man's own library."

"I confess that stumped me at first," he said; "likewise the fact that he had apparently been shot unawares. But since this morning some new evidence has come to light."

He waited for her to betray curiosity, but she, who read him like a book, only blew smoke.

"Ashcomb Poor's will was read this morning."

"Yes?"

"He left Philippa Dean ten thousand dollars."

Mme. Storey betrayed not the slightest concern.

"As a testimony to her sterling character, no doubt," she murmured.

"Character nothing!" was the retort. "Well, as far as that goes, Ashcomb Poor's motives do not concern me. The salient fact to me is that the girl knew she was down in his will."

"When was the will dated?"

"Three days before his death."

"Well, she didn't lose any time! How did she know she was named in it?"

"It appears that Ashcomb Poor in his cups talked about the different bequests to his butler, who witnessed the document. The butler told Mrs. Batten, and Mrs. Batten told the girl."

"Was Mrs. Batten mentioned in the will?"

"Yes, for five thousand."

"Perhaps she killed Ashcomb Poor."

"Ridiculous!"

5

MME. STOREY DECIDED that we must interview all the material witnesses in this case.

My desk in the outer office was beside the window. Next morning while I was awaiting the arrival of my employer I saw an elegantly appointed town car draw up below, and a woman of exquisite grace and distinction got out. She was dressed and veiled in the deepest mourning, and I could not see her face, but, guessing who it was, I experience a little thrill of anticipation. The door was presently thrown open by Eddie—it was only visitors of distinction that he condescended to announce. "Mrs. Poor to see Mme. Storey."

I jumped up in a bit of fluster. What would you expect? The famous Mrs. Ashcomb Poor, of whom so much had been written; her beauty, her dresses, her jewels, her charities, and now her tragic bereavement! How I longed to see her face. She made no move to put aside her veil, though.

"Mme. Storey not in?" she said in a disappointed voice.

"I am expecting her directly," I said. "She will be very much disappointed to miss you."

"I do not at all mind waiting," Mrs. Poor replied.

Her voice was as crisp and clear as glass bells. I brought a chair forward for her. I knew I ought to have shown her directly into the adjoining room, but I did want to get a good look at her. Her simple black dress had been draped by a master artist. I cudgelled my brain to think of some expedient to tempt her to put back her veil. I offered her a magazine, but she waved it aside, thanking me. My ingenuity failed me. It was hardly my place to start a conversation.

Mme. Storey was not long in arriving. She was all in black, too, I remember, but it was black with a difference; there was nothing of the mourner about her. And Giannino, who, poor wretch, had to dress to set off his mistress, was wearing a coat and cap of burnt orange.

My employer expressed her contrition at keeping Mrs. Poor waiting, and led that lady directly into the adjoining room. Alas! I was not bidden to follow. I would have given a good deal to be able to watch and listen to the conversation between those two extraordinary women.

I remained at my desk in the deepest disappointment. Suddenly I heard the dictagraph click. With what joy I snatched up the head-piece and pulled note-book and pencil toward me!

At least I was to hear.

Mme. Storey was saying: "It was awfully good of you to consent to come to a strange woman's office. I should not have asked it had I not thought that my coming to you would only have been an embarrassment."

"I was very glad to come," Mrs. Poor replied in her bell-like voice. "You are not by any means unknown to me. On every side one hears of the wonderful powers of Mme. Storey. I was very much pleased to hear that you had interested yourself in my unhappy affairs. One longs to know the truth and have done with it. One can rest then, perhaps."

"And you are willing to answer my questions?"

"Most willing."

"This is really good of you. For of course it's bound to be painful, though I will spare you as far as I am able. If I trespass too far you must rebuke me."

"There is nothing you may not ask me, Mme. Storey."

"Thanks. I'll be as brief as possible. No need for us to go over the whole story. I am already pretty well informed from the police and from my examination of Miss Dean yesterday."

"Ah, you have seen the girl?" put in Mrs. Poor.

"Yes."

"What did she say?"

"Nothing but what has been published."

"Poor, poor creature!"

"You do not feel unkindly toward her?"

"My feelings towards her are very mixed. I could not see her, of course. But I feel no bitterness. How do I know what reason she may have had? And to convict her will not restore my husband to life."

"You have known Miss Dean a long time?"

"Since she was a child. Her family and mine have been acquainted for several generations."

"Has Miss Dean a love affair?"

"No, nothing serious."

"You are sure?"

"Quite sure. I must have known it if she had. Several of the young men who frequented our house paid her attention—a pretty girl, you know—but not seriously."

"I should have thought—"

"I'm afraid young men are worldly minded nowadays," said Mrs. Poor. "She had no money, you see."

"Now I come to a painful subject," said Mme. Storey compassionately. "I am sorry to have to ask you, but I am anxious to establish the exact nature of the relations between your husband and Miss Dean."

"You need not consider me," murmured Mrs. Poor. "I have to face the thing."

"Some of the servants have given evidence tending to show that your husband was infatuated with her."

"I'm afraid it's true."

"What makes you think so?"

"One learns to read the man one lives with—his looks, the tones of his voice, his little unconscious actions."

"You have no positive evidence of his wrongdoing; you never surprised him, or intercepted notes?"

"That would not be my way," said Mrs. Poor proudly.

"Of course not. I beg your pardon."

Mrs. Poor went on bitterly: "If I had wanted evidence against him plenty of it was forced on me—I mean in other cases."

"Nothing that could be applied to this case?"

"No."

"Then we needn't go into that. How did the girl receive his overtures?"

"As an honest girl should. She repulsed him."

"How do you know?"

"I knew in the same way that I knew about him—from her actions day by day; her attitude toward him."

"What was that?"

"On guard."

"That might have been interpreted either way, might it not?"

"Oh, yes. But there was her attitude toward me—open, affectionate, unreserved."

"That might have been good acting," suggested Mme. Storey.

"It might, but I prefer not to think so."

"You have a good heart, Mrs. Poor. How long had this been going on?"

"About a month."

"But if the girl was sincere, how do you account for the fact that she was willing to put up with this intolerable situation?"

"Very simply; she needed the money."

"But if she'd always been well employed why should she be so hard up?"

"She has responsibilities. She supports two old servants of her mother's, who are no longer able to work."

"Ah! But how could you tolerate the situation, Mrs. Poor?"

"You mean why didn't I send her away? How could I turn her off? Ever since I realised what was going on I have been trying to find her a situation with one of my friends, but they thought if I was willing to let her go, there must be something undesirable about her."

"Naturally. Was that the only reason you kept her?"

Mrs. Poor's answer was so low it scarcely carried over the wire. "No; I wish to be perfectly frank with you; I confess, as long as she was there I knew in a way what was going on, but if she had gone away—you see—"

"Then you did have some doubt of her?"

"My husband was a man very attractive to women. He was accustomed to getting his way. I was thinking of her more than of myself. His fancies never lasted long."

"Did you know that he had put her in his will?"

"Not until the will was read yesterday."

"What do you suppose was his motive in doing that?"

"How can one say?"

"May it not have been merely for the purpose of annoying you?"

"Possibly. He was not above it."

"Now, Mrs. Poor, with the situation as it was, how could you bring yourself to leave the girl alone with him except for the house-keeper?"

"That was not my fault. It was sprung on me. I had no time to plan anything."

"What do you mean?"

"It had been understood up to the last moment that Mr. Poor was to accompany me to the entertainment. But at dinner he begged off. What could I do? I had to go myself because I was taking a prominent part."

"Then why didn't you ask her to go with you?"

"I did."

"And she wouldn't?"

"She wouldn't."

"Why?"

"She said she had no dress in order."

"Did you believe that?"

"No."

"You suspected that this staying home might have been prearranged?"

"Oh, I wouldn't go as far as that."

"But if it were not prearranged, why should she have gone to the library?"

"Who can tell what happened? He might have sent for her on the pretext of dictating letters. He had done that before."

"You seek to excuse her. That doesn't explain why she chose to stay at home after she knew he was going to be there."

"Perhaps she was excited—thrilled by his infatuation; girls are like that. Perhaps she was curious to see how he would act—confident in her power to restrain him. And found out too late that she was up against elemental things, and was obliged to defend herself."

"But she must have had some inkling of what was likely to happen, since she took her pistol with her when she went to the library. Did you know that she possessed a pistol?"

"No."

"Now, Mrs. Poor, let us jump to your return home that night. Describe your homecoming as explicitly as possible."

"It was five minutes past midnight. I am sure of the time because I glanced at the clock as I was leaving the club. It was five minutes before the hour then. It took us about ten minutes to cover the three miles, for the road was thronged with returning motors."

"One minute; the entertainment was held in the open air, wasn't it?"

"Yes, and we dressed in the club house. We had the limousine. I rode with my own maid, Katy Birkett, beside me, and the cook and the housemaid opposite. The butler was outside with the chauffeur. When we reached home I got out alone at the front door. I told the others to drive along to the service door, because I thought it might annoy Mr. Poor to have them trooping through the house. The car waited until the door was opened, because they didn't want to leave me standing there alone in the dark.

"Mrs. Batten opened the door. This surprised me, because she was usually in bed long before that hour. I had expected my husband to let me in. I had had the chauffeur sound his horn in the drive to give notice of our coming. I said to Mrs. Batten: 'Why aren't you in bed?' She answered that she thought she'd better wait up— or something like that. I asked her where Mr. Poor was, and she said he had fallen asleep in the library.

"A few steps from the inner door I could see into the library. The door was standing open, as it had been when I left it. I could see my husband sitting at his writing-table in the centre of the room, his back to the door. His head was lying on his arms, and I, too, thought he was asleep. I noticed the fire had gone out."

"Oh, there had been a fire?"

"Yes, Mr. Poor liked to have a wood fire in the library except in the very hottest weather. As Mrs. Batten removed my cloak I called to him: 'Wake up, Ashcomb! You'll get stiff, sleeping like that.'

"He did not move. Mrs. Batten and I were simultaneously struck by the suspicion that something was the matter. We both started toward him. I had not taken two steps before I saw—oh!—a ghastly dark stain on the rug beneath his chair. I saw the pistol. An icy hand seemed to grip my throat. I stopped, unable to move. The room turned black before me."

"You fainted?"

"No. It was only for a second. I started forward again. Mrs. Batten turned and blocked my way. 'Don't go! Don't go!' she cried. Then something seemed to break inside me. I screamed. Then Miss Dean was there. I didn't see her come. I clung to her—"

"One moment. After you screamed how long was it before Miss Dean came?"

"No time at all. She was right there."

"You are sure?"

"Quite sure."

"Perhaps you had cried out before without knowing it."

"Impossible. With that icy grip on my throat."

"Well, go on, please."

"I—I broke down completely then. It was so awful a shock, and—and that dark, wet stain on the rug! The other servants ran in from the back of the house. The maids set up an insensate screaming. Somebody got them out again. The butler examined my—the—the body. He said he was quite dead—cold. I had sufficient presence of mind to order that nothing in the room be touched. I had the man telephone my brother, who lives near, and our doctor—just to be sure. The servants helped me upstairs; people began to come—the police. My recollection is not very clear after that."

"Were you present when the police examined the servants and Miss Dean?"

"No."

"When did you first begin to suspect her?"

"In the morning when I asked for her they told me she had been arrested. That was a fresh shock. I had supposed it was suicide. I only learned the facts little by little, because people didn't want to talk to me about it and I hadn't the strength to insist."

"Did you notice anything peculiar in Miss Dean's manner when she came to you?"

"Not at the time, of course. I was too distracted. But when I thought about it later, she was strangely agitated."

"Well, you all were, of course."

"She was different. Hers was not the impersonal horror and dismay of the servants; hers was a personal feeling. She seemed about to faint with terror; she could hardly speak. She was not surprised."

"What did she say to you?"

"She, too, tried to keep me back. She said: 'Don't go to him. It's all over.' At the moment I thought nothing of it. Afterwards it occurred to me that none of us had been near him then. We didn't know he was dead until the butler came."

"That is very significant," said Mme. Storey.

This ended Mrs. Poor's examination. After the exchange of some further civilities she came out of the inner room. Her veil was pushed aside and I had my wished-for chance to see her face. Her voice over the wire had been so cool and collected that I was not prepared for what I saw. A truly beautiful woman with proud, chiselled features, the events of the last few days had worked havoc there. There were dark circles under her eyes, and deep lines of suffering from her nose to her mouth. I realised how profoundly humiliating the disclosures, following upon the murder, must have been to her proud soul. Seeing my eyes on her face, she quickly let the veil fall and went out without speaking.

As a result of the examination of Mrs. Poor I will not deny that I felt a certain satisfaction. Greatly as I admired my employer, I was not sorry to see her proved wrong for once. It is not the easiest thing in the world to get along with a person who is always right. Mme. Storey's insistence on Philippa Dean's innocence had provoked me just a little. Mme. Storey made no reference to what had taken place between her and Mrs. Poor, and of course I did not gloat over her.

6

AN HOUR AFTER Mrs. Poor had departed I heard a timid tap on my door, and upon opening it beheld a round little body in a stiff black dress and a funny little hat with ostrich tips. She carried her gloved hands folded primly on the most protuberant part of her person, and from one arm hung a black satin reticule. She had cheeks like withered rosy apples, and short-sighted eyes peering through thick glasses. There was a wistful, childlike quality in her glance that immediately appealed to one. At present the little lady was scared and breathless.

"Does Mme. Storey live here?" she gasped.

"This is her office," I said. "Come in."

"I am Mrs. Batten."

I looked at her with strong interest. "Mme. Storey will be glad to see you," I said.

"I told her I'd come," she faltered; "but I'm so upset—so upset, I'm sure if she asks me the simplest questions my wits will fly away completely."

"You needn't be afraid of her," I said soothingly.

I knew whereof I spoke. The instant Mme. Storey laid eyes on the trembling little body, she smiled and softened. She put away her worldly airs and was just simple like folks. I remained in the room. Mme. Storey talked of indifferent matters until Mrs. Batten got her breath somewhat, and brought the matter very gradually around to the Poor case. At the first reference to Philippa Dean the tears started out of the old eyes and rolled down the withered cheeks.

"My poor, poor girl!" she mourned. "My poor girl!"

"You were very fond of her then?" put in Mme. Storey gently.

"Like a daughter she was to me, madam."

"Well, let's put our heads together and see what we can do. You can help me a lot. First of all, where were you all evening while Mrs. Poor was at the entertainment?"

With a great effort Mrs. Batten collected her forces and called in her tears. Her hands gripped the arms of her chair. "I was in my room," she said; "my sitting-room downstairs."

"All alone?"

"Why, of course."

"Please tell me just where your room is."

"Well, the way to it from the front hall is through a door between the reception room and the dining-room and along a passage. Half-way down this passage is my door on the right and the pantry door opposite. At the end of the passage another passage runs crosswise. That we call the back hall. It has a door on the drive—"

"That is the door by which the servants entered when they returned with Mrs. Poor?"

"Yes, madam. And at the other end of the back hall there's a door to the garden. The back stairs are in this hall. The kitchen and the servants' dining-room are beyond."

"I get the hang of it. Wasn't it unusual for you to remain up so late?"

"Yes, it was."

"How did it happen?"

"Well—I got interested in a book."

"What book?"

Mrs. Batten put a distracted hand to her brow. "Let me see— my poor wits! Oh, yes, it was called *The Light That Failed*."

No muscle of Mme. Storey's face changed. "Ah! An admirable story! I know it well! What I particularly admire is the opening chapter, where the young man steps out of the clock case and confronts the thief in the act of rifling the safe."

"I thought that a little overdrawn," said Mrs. Batten.

I gasped inwardly. I could scarcely believe my ears. Our dear, gentle little old lady was lying like a trooper, and Mme. Storey had trapped her. For, of course, as everybody knows, there is no such scene in *The Light That Failed*.

Mme. Storey went right on: "Please tell me exactly what happened when Mrs. Poor returned that night."

Mrs. Batten complied. Up to a certain point her story tallied exactly with that of her mistress, and there is no need for repeating it. Mrs. Batten corroborated Mrs. Poor's statement that Philippa Dean had appeared as soon as Mrs. Poor cried out.

Then Mme. Storey said: "But Miss Dean testified that she had to run all the way around the upstairs gallery and downstairs."

Mrs. Batten gave her a frightened look. "Oh, well, I may be mistaken," she said quickly. "It was all so dreadful. Maybe it was a minute before she got there."

"What did Miss Dean say to Mrs. Poor when she got there?"

"She didn't say anything—that is, not anything regular. She put her arm around her and said: 'Be calm!'—or 'Don't give way,' or something like that."

"Didn't Miss Dean say: 'Don't go to him. It's all over.'"

Mrs. Batten sat bolt upright in her chair, and the near-sighted eyes positively shot sparks. "She did not say that!"

"Can you be sure?"

"I'll swear it!"

"She might have said it without your hearing."

"I was there all the time. I had hold of Mrs. Poor, too."

"But Mrs. Poor has testified that Miss Dean said that."

The old woman obstinately primmed her lips. "I don't care!"

"Wouldn't you believe your mistress?"

"Not if she said that. She was mistaken. She was half wild, anyway. She didn't know what anybody said to her. Why, nobody knew that Mr. Poor was dead then. Not till the butler came."

Mrs. Batten's anxiety on the girl's behalf was so obvious that her testimony in the girl's favour did not carry much weight.

Mme. Storey continued: "Did you notice anything strange about Miss Dean's manner when she came?"

Mrs. Batten sparred for time. "What do you mean?" she asked.

"Was she unduly agitated?"

"Why, of course, we all were."

"I said unduly. Did she behave any differently from the others?"

The little old lady began to tremble.

"What are you trying to get me to say?" she stammered. "She didn't do it! She couldn't have done it! That sweet young girl, so gentle, so fastidious!" The old voice scaled up hysterically. "Nothing could ever make me believe she did it! Like a daughter to me, a daughter! She didn't do it! I will say it to my dying day!"

Mme. Storey smiled kindly. "Your feelings do you credit, Mrs. Batten; still I hope you won't show them so plainly before the jury."

"The jury!" whispered Mrs. Batten, scared and sobered.

"Because if you let them see how fond you are of Miss Dean they won't believe a word you say in her favour!"

"The jury!" Mrs. Batten reiterated, staring before her as if she visualised the dreadful ordeal that awaited her. "I will have to sit up there in the witness chair and take my oath before them all— and everybody looking at me—thousands—and lawyers asking me this and that a purpose to mix me up—" She suddenly cried out: "Oh, I couldn't! I couldn't! I know I couldn't! I'm too nervous! I'd kill myself sooner than face that!"

The little woman's terror was so disproportionate to the thing she feared, that the strange thought went through my mind, perhaps it was she who killed Ashcomb Poor, or maybe she and the girl had done it together. I attended to what followed with a breathless interest.

Meanwhile Mme. Storey was trying to quiet her. "There now! There now! Mrs. Batten: don't distress yourself so. This is just an imaginary terror. It may never be necessary for you to go on the stand. Let's take a breathing spell to allow our nerves to quiet down. Have a cigarette?"

I stared at my employer, for at the moment this seemed like a very poor attempt at a joke. I ought to have known that Mme. Storey never did anything at such a moment without purpose.

Mrs. Batten drew the remains of her dignity around her. "Thank you, I don't indulge," she said stiffly. She was pure mid-Victorian then.

Mme. Storey said teasingly: "Come, now, Mrs. Batten! Not even in the privacy of your room?"

"Never! I'm not saying that I blame them that do, if they like it; but in my day it wasn't considered nice."

"Does Miss Dean smoke?" asked Mme. Storey with an idle air.

"I'm sure she does not!" answered Mrs. Batten earnestly. "I've been with her at all times and seasons, and I never saw her take one between her lips. There was no reason she should hide it from me. Besides, the maids never picked up any cigarette ends in her room. They're keen on such things."

"You have the reputation of being a very tidy person, haven't you, Mrs. Batten?" asked Mme. Storey. "They tell me you are a regular New England house-keeper."

By this time I had guessed from Mme. Storey's elaborately careless air that this apparently meaningless questioning was tending to a well-defined point. The old lady glanced at her in a bewildered way, but she could see nothing behind this harmless remark.

"Why, yes," she said, "I suppose I do like to see things clean—real clean. And everything in its proper place."

"Who does up your room?" went on Mme. Storey in the purring voice that always means danger—for somebody. My heart began to beat.

"I do it myself, always," answered the little woman unsuspectingly. "I don't like the maids messing among my things. I like my room just so. I always sweep and dust and put things in order myself, and I mean to do so until I take to my bed for the last time."

"Every day?" asked Mme. Storey, flicking the ash off her cigarette.

"Every day, most certainly."

Mme. Storey drawled in a voice as sweet as honey: "Well, then, Mrs. Batten, who was it that was smoking cigarettes in your room the night that Ashcomb Poor was killed?"

The little old woman's jaw dropped, the rosy cheeks greyed, her eyes were like a sick woman's. Presently the hanging lip began to tremble piteously. I could not bear to look at her.

"I—I don't know what you're talking about," she stuttered.

"You have not answered my question," Mme. Storey said mildly.

"Nobody—nobody was smoking in my room."

Mme. Storey turned to me. "Miss Brickley, please get me the exhibits in the Poor case that I asked you to put away."

Hastening into the next room, I procured the things from the safe. When I returned neither of the two had changed position. From the envelope that I handed her, Mme. Storey shook the cigarette butts.

"These were found in your room early the next morning," she said to Mrs. Batten. "In the little brass bowl on the window-sill."

"All kinds of people were in the house that morning," stammered the little woman with a desperate air; "police, detectives, goodness knows who! How do I know who passed through my room?"

"It was scarcely one who passed through," said Mme. Storey. "He or she must have lingered some time—long enough, that is, to smoke seven cigarettes. See!" She counted them before the old woman's fascinated eyes.

"I don't know how they came there. I don't know how they came there!" wailed the latter.

Mme. Storey spread the cigarette ends in a row. "They are plain tip cigarettes," she said, "so I assume they are a man's. Women prefer cork tips or straw tips, because lip rouge sticks and comes off on the paper. What gentleman visited you, Mrs. Batten?"

"There was nobody, nobody!" was the faint answer. "Why do you torment me?"

"There's no harm in having a visitor, surely. Your son, perhaps, a nephew, a brother—even a husband. Women do have them, Mrs. Batten."

"Everybody knows I have no family."

"A friend, then. Where's the harm?"

"There was nobody there."

Mme. Storey examined the cigarette ends anew. "One of them is long enough to show the name of the brand," she said. "Army and Navy. One might guess that they were smoked by a man in the service."

The harried little woman gave her a glance of fresh terror.

Delicately picking up one of the butts, Mme. Storey smelled of the unburned end. "The tobacco is of a superior and expensive grade," she remarked. "Evidently an officer's cigarette. But of what branch of the service? That is the question." She fixed the trembling little soul with her compelling gaze and asked abruptly: "Was he an aviator, Mrs. Batten?"

A terrified cry escaped Mrs. Batten.

"I see he was," said Mme. Storey.

Mrs. Batten was gazing at Mme. Storey as if the evil one himself confronted her.

Answering that look of awed terror, my employer said quietly: "No, there is no magic in it, Mrs. Batten. As a matter of fact, later that morning I found in the field across the brook at the foot of the garden marks in the earth showing where an airplane had alighted, and had later arisen again. I was only putting two and two together, you see."

The little woman, seeming incapable of speech, sat there with her hands clasped as if imploring for mercy. It was very affecting.

Mme. Storey went on: "Upon consulting an expert in aviation I learned that such tracks could have been made by none other than one of the new Bentley-Critchard machines, of which there are as yet only half a dozen in service, and those all at Camp Tasker, which is only fifteen miles from Grimstead—a few minutes' flight. All I lack is the name of the aviator who visited you. Who was he, Mrs. Batten?"

The little woman moistened her lips and whispered in a kind of dry cackle: "I don't know. No one came."

"You might as well tell me," Mme. Storey said patiently. "It would not be difficult to find out at Camp Tasker, you know. There cannot be many officers accustomed to driving that new type."

A groan broke from the little old woman. She covered her face with her hands. "You are too much for me," she murmured. "It was Lieutenant George Grantland."

I got out of my chair and sat down again, staring at the woman like a zany. Grantland! Eddie's hero! The popular idol of the day!

Mme. Storey was no less astonished than I. "Quick, Bella! The morning paper!"

I hastened and got it for her. There was his name on the front page, of course, as it had been in every edition during the past two days. Mme. Storey read out the head-lines:

GRANTLAND AT CHICAGO LAST NIGHT
FLEW FROM NEW ORLEANS YESTERDAY
Expected to land at Camp Tasker this A.M. Has circumnavigated the entire country east of the Mississippi in little more than three days. The bold young flier's endurance test a success in every particular. Great ovations tendered him at every landing.

Meanwhile the wretched little old lady was weeping bitterly and wailing over and over: "I promised not to tell! I promised not to tell!"

"Promised whom?" asked Mme. Storey.

"Philippa."

"Well, you needn't distress yourself so, Mrs. Batten. If you love this girl, bringing the man's name into the case isn't going to hurt her chances any."

Mrs. Batten had forgotten all caution now. "But if you convict him," she sobbed, "it will kill Philippa just the same."

"Aha!" murmured Mme. Storey to herself; "so that's the way the wind lies." She looked at the old woman oddly. "So Grantland did it?"

Mrs. Batten flung up her arms. "I don't know!" she burst out, and at least that cry rang true. "I haven't eaten. I haven't slept since it happened. I'm nearly out of my mind with thinking about it!"

Mme. Storey whispered privately to me to call up Camp Tasker. If I could succeed in getting a message to Lieutenant Grantland I was to ask him to come to her office at once on a matter of the greatest importance concerning Miss Philippa Dean.

Through the open door I could hear her asking Mrs. Batten to forgive her for tormenting her.

"But you know you came here determined not to tell me the truth," she said.

In a few minutes I was able to report that I had got a message to Lieutenant Grantland, who had but just landed from his plane, and that he had promised to be in Mme. Storey's office within an hour.

Mrs. Batten was quiet again—quiet and wary. Poor little soul, now that one understood better, one couldn't help but admire her gallantry in lying to save her friends.

"Tell us about Lieutenant Grantland's visit," Mme. Storey said coaxingly.

"There's nothing much to tell," was the cautious answer.

"He came to see Miss Philippa?"

"Yes."

"He had been before?"

"Oh, yes; a number of times."

"Did Miss Philippa know he was coming that night?"

"Yes. He had telephoned just before dinner. It was to say good-bye before starting on the big flight."

"What time did he come?"

"About nine."

"Tell me about it in your own way."

Mrs. Batten shook her head. "You must question me," she said warily. "I don't know what it is you want to know."

Mme. Storey and I smiled, the old soul's equivocation was so transparent.

"Did Lieutenant Grantland always come in his plane?" my employer asked.

"No, that was the first time by plane."

"Didn't the noise of his engine attract attention at the house?"

"No; he shut it off and come down without a sound."

"How could he see to land in the dark?"

"He came just before it got too dark to see."

"But couldn't you see him land from the house?"

"No. He came down at the top of the field which is hidden from the house by the trees along the brook."

"Then how could he get away in the dark?"

"He had the whole length of the field to rise from."

"But in starting his engine didn't it make a great noise?"

"I don't know. We didn't notice it."

"Did you go to meet him?"

"I; no."

"Miss Philippa went?"

"Yes."

"And brought him back to the house?"

"Yes."

"Right away?"

Mrs. Batten bridled. "I don't see what that—"

"Well, what time did they get to the house?"

"About half past nine."

"How did they get in?"

"I turned off the burglar-alarm and let them in the garden door."

"What happened then?"

"Nothing!" said Mrs. Batten with an air which said: You're not going to get anything out of me!

"Well, where did they go in the house?"

"They came into my room. They always sat there."

"You left them there?"

"No, I stayed. Miss Philippa always had me there when he came. So that nobody could have any excuse to talk. That shows you the kind of girl she was!"

"Very commendable. Go on."

"There isn't anything to tell. There we sat as cosy and friendly as could be in my little room. I don't remember anything particular that was said. I wouldn't tell it if I did, for it was just their own matters. At ten o'clock I brought out a little supper I had made ready. The lieutenant was always hungry—like a boy. That's all."

"What time did he leave?"

"At midnight."

"That is, when Mrs. Poor got home?"

"Yes."

"How did you get him out of the house?"

Mrs. Batten bridled again. "There wasn't any getting out about it. He walked out of the same door that he came in. When I went to the front door to answer the bell I left the passage door open. When I switched on the light in the hall, that was to tell them the burglar-alarm was off. Then Miss Philippa let the lieutenant out of the door from the back hall into the garden."

"What was the necessity for all this secrecy, Mrs. Batten? Miss Philippa was treated like a member of the family."

Mrs. Batten was very uncomfortable. "Well, there was no necessity for it, so to speak," she said. "But it seems natural for young lovers to wish to meet in secret, to avoid talk and all that."

"And a moment after the lieutenant had gone you and Mrs. Poor discovered the murder?"

"Yes, but that isn't to say—"

"Of course it isn't! Up to that moment you yourself had no suspicion that there had been a tragedy in the house?"

"No, indeed! No, indeed!"

"After Miss Philippa let him out she presumably returned through the passage. That would explain how she came to be so close at hand when Mrs. Poor cried out."

"I suppose so. But there's no harm in that."

"Certainly not. But why was there so much lying, Mrs. Batten? Why did she tell me she had been in her room all evening? Why did you tell me you were alone in your room?"

"I couldn't give it away that she had been entertaining him."

"Why not, if it was all regular and above board?"

"Well—well, I said I wouldn't tell."

My employer became thoughtful. Mrs. Batten, watching her, began to fidget again.

Suddenly Mme. Storey said: "Mrs. Batten, did Lieutenant Grantland know that Ashcomb Poor had been pestering Miss Philippa?"

"No!" answered Mrs. Batten breathlessly—but the terrified glance that accompanied it told its own tale.

"Now, Mrs. Batten, you're fibbing again! What's the use when your face is a mirror to your soul?"

The little body hung her head. "Yes, he knew," she murmured. "He had heard some gossip or something. He was furious when he came. Wanted to march right into the library and tax Mr. Poor with it—to 'knock his block off,' he said. We had a time quieting him down. The only thing that influenced him was when Miss Philippa said the scandal would injure her."

"But you did quiet him down?"

"Yes. We were all as happy and pleasant as possible together. Then we had our supper."

Mme. Storey fell silent for a while. Her grave and thoughtful glance seemed to inspire the little old woman with a fresh terror. Mrs. Batten struggled to her feet.

"I must go now," she said tremulously. "I've been away too long. They won't know what's become of me."

"Sit down, Mrs. Batten," said Mme. Storey quietly.

The other's voice began to scale up again. "I won't answer any more questions!" she cried. "Not another one! I can't! I'm in no fit state! I don't know what I'm saying! It's not fair to keep at me, and keep at me!"

"Sit down, Mrs. Batten," repeated the grave voice.

The old woman dropped into a chair, weeping bitterly.

"Did Miss Philippa leave the room at any time during your party?"

This was evidently the very question Mrs. Batten dreaded. "Oh, why do you plague me so?" she cried.

"You know the truth has got to come out. Better tell me than a roomful of men."

Mrs. Batten gave up. "Yes, she did," she wailed.

"How long was she gone?"

"I don't know. Just a little while. Not more than ten minutes."

"And did Lieutenant Grantland leave the room at any time?"

"Yes."

"How long was he gone?"

"He left right after her, and got back just before her."

"Ah! What was the occasion of their leaving the room?"

"The bell rang in the pantry. I went to see what it was. The indicator showed a call from the library. It wasn't my place to answer the bell, but I did so because I was afraid if I didn't Mr. Poor might come back. He was at his writing-table. I thought he had been drinking a little."

"Why did you think so?"

"His face was flushed. He had a funny look. He said: 'Will you please ask Miss Dean if she will be good enough to help me out for a little while. I have two or three important letters to get off, and I have such a cramp in my hand I can't write them myself.'"

"Did you believe this, Mrs. Batten?"

"N-no, madam. Not with that look—an ugly look to a woman."

"What did you do?"

"Well, of course I couldn't say anything to him. I just went away as if I was going to do what he wanted. I went back to my room. I was hoping maybe he'd forget. But they saw from my face that something had happened—"

"That open countenance!" murmured Mme. Storey.

"And they gave me no rest until I told them what he wanted. The lieutenant flared up again and said she should not go. Said he'd go instead and write his letters on his face. But she persuaded him not to. She knew how to manage him. She said she must go in order to avoid trouble. She said nothing could, happen to her as long as the lieutenant was there in the house to protect her. So she went."

"Alone?"

"Yes. But when she was gone he could not rest. In spite of all I could do to stop him, he went after her. I stayed there sitting in my room—helpless. Every minute I expected to hear a terrible quarrel—but all was quiet. I could scarcely stand it. I would have gone, too, to see; but my old legs were trembling so they would not carry me."

"You heard no sound while they were gone?"

"None whatever."

"But there were three heavy doors between you and the library."

"The library door stood open all evening."

"But it may have been closed then."

Mrs. Batten wrung her hands. "It can't be! It can't be," she cried. "That young pair—so proud, so beautiful, so loving—"

"Well, murder is not always so detestable a crime," observed Mme. Storey. "Did they come back together?"

The old woman shook her head. "He came back first."

"How did he look?"

"Nothing out of the way. No different from when he left."

"You mean, his face was set and hard?"

"Yes, but he always looked like that when Mr. Poor's name was mentioned."

"What did he say?"

"He said: 'Where's Philippa?' I just shook my head. He turned around to go look for her, but met her coming in the door. They spoke to each other."

"What did they say?"

"It was in whispers. I could not hear."

Mme. Storey fixed the little woman hard with her gaze. "Mrs. Batten!" she said warningly.

But this time the housekeeper was able to meet it. She spread out her hands in a gesture that was not without dignity. "I have told you everything, madam. You know as much as I do now."

"And nothing happened after that?"

"No, madam. We sat down to our supper. Mr. Poor's name was not mentioned again."

"Either one of them could have done it," remarked Mme. Storey thoughtfully.

Mrs. Batten wiped away her fast-falling tears.

7

LIEUTENANT GRANTLAND was prompt to his engagement.

Why is it that aviators, or nearly all aviators, are such superb young men? I suppose the answer is obvious enough; it is the young men with the shining eyes and the springy bodies that are naturally attracted to the air. However that may be, the mere sight of an aviator is enough to take a girl's breath away.

As for George Grantland, he was simply the handsomest young man I ever saw. When he came in how I longed to be comely just for one second, in order to win an interested glance from him. Alas! His eyes merely skated over me. In his close-fitting uniform and marvellously turned leggings he was as graceful as Mercury. At present, whether from fatigue or anxiety—or both—his cheeks were drawn and grey. But his blue eyes were resolute, and he kept his chin up.

You can imagine Eddie's feelings. He had brought the lieutenant upstairs all agog, and now stood just within the door, staring at his idol, and fairly panting with excitement. I was obliged to push the boy out into the hall by main strength and shut the door after him.

I took Lieutenant Grantland directly into Mme. Storey's room. Her glance brightened at the sight of him just as any woman's would. She had mercy on me and nodded to me to remain in the room. Mrs. Batten, I should state, was still with us. Mme. Storey had put her in the back room to rest and compose herself.

"Thank you for coming so promptly," Mme. Storey said, extending her hand.

The young man blushed painfully. "I cannot shake hands," he said bluntly.

Mme. Storey's eyebrows went up. "Why?" she asked, smiling.

"You will not want to shake hands when you know."

Mme. Storey shrugged and smiled at him with an expression I could not fathom—a quizzical expression. "Well, sit down," she said.

He would not unbend. "Thank you, I cannot stay."

"Well, anyway, allow me to congratulate you on your flight."

He bowed.

Mme. Storey went on: "My secretary tells me she got a message to you just as you were landing. I assume that you heard nothing during your flight of what was happening here."

"Not a word!" he said. "But Camp Tasker was buzzing with it. I heard everything there."

"Then we need not go into lengthy explanations," said Mme. Storey. "I need only say that Assistant District Attorney Barron has done me the honour to consult me in regard to this matter. That is where I come in. As for my secretary, she is acquainted with all the details of the case, so you need have no hesitancy in speaking before her. I would like to ask you a few questions, if you please."

"There is no need," he said, standing very stiffly. "It was I who killed Ashcomb Poor."

My heart went down sickeningly—not that I blamed him at all; but at the thought of that splendid young fellow being subjected to the rigour of the law; his career spoiled; that proud head brought low in a prison cell! I don't know what Mme. Storey felt upon hearing his avowal. Her glance betrayed nothing.

"I never dreamed that they would dare arrest her," the young man went on with a break in his voice, "or I should not have gone away. I can never forgive myself that."

"Well, sit down," said Mme. Storey for the second time.

He shook his head. "I am on my way to police headquarters to give myself up."

"Oh, but not so fast!" objected my employer. "There are many things to be considered. Meet Mr. Barron here. You will be at a better advantage."

"I have no desire to make terms," he said indifferently.

"Then let me make them for you. Or lay it to a woman's vanity, if you like. I found you first. Let me hand you over to the district attorney's office."

"Just as you like," he said.

Turning to me Mme. Storey said: "Please call up the district attorney's office and tell Mr. Barron that important new evidence has turned up in the Ashcomb Poor case. Ask him if he will bring Miss Dean up here."

At the words "bring Miss Dean" a spasm of pain passed over the young man's face.

"Do you think he will?" I murmured, thinking of Mr. Barron's former objections.

"What he did once he can do again," Mme. Storey said lightly. "Curiosity is a strong, impelling force." She added in a lower tone: "Mrs. Poor is at the Madagascar Hotel. Ask her to come, too. Then we'll have all the material witnesses."

Then to the aviator: "If you came here the moment you landed you haven't had anything to eat."

"I don't require anything, thanks," he muttered.

"Nonsense! You have a severe ordeal before you. You must prepare for it in any way that you can."

To make a long story short I ordered in a meal. It arrived after I had finished my telephoning, and both Mme. Storey and I saw to it that the young man did justice to the repast. Notwithstanding his situation he developed an excellent appetite. It struck me at the time that we were treating him more like a returned prodigal than a self-confessed murderer; but good looks such as his are like a magic talisman in the possessor's favour. What would any woman have cared what he had done? How delightful it was to see a better colour return to his cheeks. And how grateful he was for cigarettes!

Mr. Barron brought two plain-clothes men and Miss Dean in his own automobile. We received them in the outer office, and Mme. Storey insisted on allowing the girl to enter her room alone. When the door was opened and Philippa saw who was waiting within, a dreadful low cry broke from her that wrung our very hearts. Mme. Storey closed the door behind her, and no one ever knew what took place between those two unhappy young persons.

While we waited Mr. Barron besieged Mme. Storey with questions which she smilingly refused to answer, merely saying:

"Wait and see!"

They were not together long. Lieutenant Grantland opened the door. His face was stony. In a chair behind him the girl was weeping bitterly. It looked as if they had quarrelled.

He said to Mme. Storey: "We must not keep you out of your own room."

Mme. Storey, Mr. Barron and I went in. My employer, much against Mr. Barron's wishes, insisted that the plain-clothes men be required to wait in the outer office.

"I fancy there are enough of us here to frustrate any attempt at an escape," she said dryly.

Mrs. Batten was called in. She was in a great taking at the sight of Philippa and the young officer, but the former kissed her tenderly, and the young man shook hands with her.

When we all seated ourselves the place instantly took on the aspect of a courtroom. I am sure I am quite safe in saying that every one of us—except possibly my inscrutable employer—was shaking with excitement. Our faces were pale and streaked with anxiety. Mme. Storey sat at her table and I was in my usual place at her right. Mr. Barron sat at her left, while Miss Dean, Lieutenant Grantland and Mrs. Batten faced us in that order.

Before anything was said, there was a knock at the door, and upon being bidden to open it Eddie ushered in a heavily shrouded figure that all knew for Mrs. Poor, though her face was invisible. I expect Eddie would have given some years of his youthful life to be allowed to remain, but a glance from Mme. Storey sent him flying. Mr. Barron hastened to place a chair for Mrs. Poor next to Mrs. Batten. The young soldier arose and bowed stiffly. Philippa turned her head away from the newcomer with a painful blush.

Mme. Storey said in a voice devoid of all emotion: "Lieutenant Grantland wishes to make a statement."

Grantland was still on his feet. He came to attention and said in a low, steady voice: "I wish to say that it was I who shot Ashcomb Poor."

The widow started violently. One could imagine the piercing gaze she must have bent on the speaker through her veil. Philippa Dean covered her face with her hands, and Mrs. Batten began to weep audibly. Mr. Barron's face was a study in astonishment and discomfiture; Mme. Storey's a mask.

Mme. Storey said: "Please tell us the circumstances."

"Wait a minute," stammered the assistant district attorney. "It is my duty to inform you that anything you say may be used against you."

"I quite understand that," said Grantland.

"I must have a record of his statement!" went on Mr. Barron excitedly.

"Miss Brickley will take notes of everything that transpires," said Mme. Storey. "Please proceed, lieutenant."

He spoke in a level, quiet voice, with eyes straight ahead, looking at none of us.

"I was calling on Miss Dean to whom I am—to whom I was engaged to be married. We were with Mrs. Batten in her sitting-room. Mr. Poor sent to Miss Dean to ask if she would write some letters for him. I had heard certain things—things that led me to suspect that this was merely a pretext. Anyway it was no part of her duties to look after his correspondence. I didn't want her to go. But she persuaded me that it would be better for her to go. And she went. But when she left the room I became very uneasy. I followed her. Down a passage, and across the main hall of the house. The hall was dark.

"The man was in a room off the hall—library, I suppose. The door stood open, and from the hall I could see all that took place. Mr. Poor, with many apologies, was repeating his request that Miss Dean write some letters for him. He made believe his hand was cramped. But he looked at her in a way—in a way that made my blood hot. I think he had been drinking. I could see that Miss Dean was frightened. I was at the point of interfering then, but I heard her ask him to excuse her while she got a handkerchief, and she came out and ran upstairs. She did not see me in the hall.

"Well, I remained there watching him. The expression on his face as he sat there waiting for her to return drove me wild. I—"

"But he was sitting with his back to the hall," interrupted Mme. Storey. "How could you see his face?"

"There was a mirror over the fire-place hung at such an angle that his face was reflected in it."

"But if you could see him in it could he not see you?"

"No, I was standing too far back in the dark hall."

"Go on."

"The look on his face conveyed an insult no man could bear. I went in and shot him, that's all."

Philippa Dean struggled to her feet. From her lips broke a cry none of us will ever forget.

"It's not true! It was I who did it! He knows it was I. He's trying to shield me!"

She could go no further, but stood, struggling to control the dry sobbing that tore her breast. None of the rest of us stirred.

Grantland did not look at her. One could see that he dared not. "She knows it was I," he said stonily.

With a great effort Philippa regained a measure of control.

"Listen! Listen!" she cried desperately. "I will tell the truth now. Mr. Poor sent for me. He asked me to take some letters. He looked at me in such a way I was afraid—afraid. I asked him to excuse me while I got a handkerchief. I went upstairs. But it was my pistol that I went for. I was so afraid they would meet—and fight. I got my pistol. I came downstairs again. I shot him. Lieutenant Grantland wasn't there at all!"

"I was there!" cried Grantland. "Ask Mrs. Batten. Mrs. Batten, didn't I follow her?"

"Oh! Oh! Oh!" wailed the little body. "Yes, you followed her."

"And if I was not there how could I have known about the handkerchief?" he demanded.

By this time Philippa had nerved herself. She faced him out fearlessly. Never have I seen anything like that look, so hard, so full of pain. "Well, if you were there you didn't wait till I got back. You weren't there when I got back, were you? Answer that."

"No," he admitted, "but—"

She wouldn't let him go on. "Why should I have wanted a handkerchief at such a moment? It was my pistol I went for, and I got it, and I came downstairs and shot him."

"Without warning?" Grantland demanded in his turn.

"No. I sat down and made ready to take his letters. But he had no letters to dictate, of course. He put his hand on my shoulder and I—I shot him."

"How could you shoot him in the back when you were sitting beside him?"

"I reached around behind him and shot him."

"Where did you have the pistol?"

"Hidden in the bosom of my waist."

"The waist you wore that night was closed in front."

"Pooh! What do you know about such things? You never notice what I have on. Mrs. Batten, wasn't the waist I wore that night buttoned in front?"

The little body was completely distracted. "Yes—no—I don't know. I can't remember!" she wailed.

"Now answer *me*," cried Philippa to Grantland. "How could you get into the room when the man was sitting there watching in the mirror for my return?"

"I dropped to my knees out of range of his vision and crept in."

The girl's eyes flashed at him. "Do you mean to tell all these people that you, an officer in the uniform of the United States, crawled in on hands and knees like a thug and shot the man in the back?"

Grantland's head dropped on his breast; a dark flush overspread his face, he gritted his teeth until the muscles stood out in lumps on either side his jaw.

"It is the truth," he muttered. "I looked on him as a kind of wild beast against whom any measures were justifiable."

The girl passionately appealed to the rest of us. "Look at him! Look at him!" she cried. "Any one could see he is lying!"

The spectacle of the two lovers cross-examining each other; facing each other down with hard, inimical glances; each desperately striving to pull down the other's tale, was the strangest and most dreadful scene I ever expect to witness.

The young man stubbornly raised his head, and his glance bore hers down. He had better command of himself than she.

"Your story could not be true," he said firmly. "You were not more than half a minute behind me in returning to Mrs. Batten's room."

"Half a minute was long enough to pull the trigger," she retorted.

A new thought struck Grantland. "You could not have returned that way at all!" he said. "You must have come down the back stairs. I remember now that as you came into the room you appeared from the rear of the house."

"Too bad you didn't think of that before," she rejoined scornfully. "Your tardy recollection will not deceive Mme. Storey or this gentleman. This is all wasting time, anyway. You have not explained the most important thing of all."

"What's that?" he asked sullenly.

"How did you get hold of my pistol?"

She thought she had him there, but he instantly retorted: "You gave it to me yourself a week before to have it fixed. I had had it fixed, and I was bringing it back to you that night."

"Now I have caught you!" cried the girl with wildly shining eyes. "You had returned my pistol to me two days before that night, and Mrs. Batten was present when you handed it to me!" She whirled around. "Mrs. Batten, didn't you see him return my pistol to me two days before that night?"

The little woman, unable to speak, nodded her head.

"Now, who's lying?" cried Philippa.

The young aviator never flinched. "That wasn't your pistol I gave you two days before," he said coolly. "That was a pistol I borrowed from the dealer while yours was being repaired. I got it for you because I believed after what I'd heard, that you ought not to be without the means to defend yourself."

"Why didn't you tell me all this at the time?" she demanded.

"Because I would have had to explain why I got you the pistol, and I didn't want to alarm you unnecessarily."

"Fine tale!" she said with curling lip—but her assurance was failing her. "How about the two little marks on the barrel that identified the pistol as mine?"

"That is the dealer's private mark to protect himself. It appears on all the weapons that he handles."

"Well, if it was really my pistol that you say you shot the man with, why did you leave it there to incriminate me?"

"I thought you had only to produce the one you had in order to clear yourself."

"It's not true! No other was found! There was no other. What did you want to leave the pistol there for anyway, to make trouble?"

"I thought it would be regarded as a suicide."

Philippa had regained her assurance. "Do you expect these people to believe that with your knowledge of weapons you thought you could shoot the man through the back and have anybody think he did it himself?"

Grantland showed some confusion. "Well, I was excited," he said sullenly. "One can't think of everything."

The girl smiled scornfully. "I've no more to say," she said abruptly. "These people will not need any help in deciding who is telling the truth." She sat down.

What the others thought of this confession and counter-confession I cannot say. I believed Philippa was telling the truth.

My employer's face was like a tinted ivory mask.

"Have you anything more to say?" she asked Grantland.

He shook his head.

"Mr. Barron, do you wish to put any questions?"

"I think not," he answered, with a casual air that did not conceal his triumph. "I see no reason to alter my original opinion. Lieutenant Grantland's motives do him credit, but his story simply does not hold water. Leaving aside all other considerations it is preposterous to suppose that after shooting the man in the way he describes, he could fly away and leave the two women to their fate."

Philippa looked gratefully toward him. What a strange, topsyturvy situation that she should actually thank him for expressing his belief in her guilt!

My employer said in the silky tones that always portended danger: "I must differ with you, Mr. Barron. Lieutenant Grantland has explained how he thought he had insured Miss Dean's safety. On the other hand, it is incredible to suppose that a gently reared girl, after having killed a man, could sit down and sup with her two friends as if nothing had happened. A man might, a soldier, but this girl, never! And afterwards allow him, her only protector, to leave her without a word!"

"I had to let him go," sobbed Philippa. "His reputation was staked on that flight!"

I noticed at this point that Mrs. Poor's foot was nervously tapping the floor. In my concern for the two young people, it had not occurred to me what a harrowing business all this must have been for the widow.

"No," said Mme. Storey to Mr. Barron, "you have done me the honour to consult me in this case. I must ask you to put Lieutenant Grantland under arrest. I pledge myself to justify it directly."

Grantland fairly beamed on my employer. I wondered mightily what she was up to. Poor Philippa seemed on the verge of a collapse.

"But how—why—on what grounds?" demanded the puzzled prosecutor.

Mme. Storey's next words fell like icy drops. "At the proper moment—I will produce an eyewitness to the affair—who will swear—that Lieutenant Grantland shot Ashcomb Poor."

"*You lie!*"

This scream—for scream it was—from a new direction, almost completed the demoralisation of our nerves. Every eye turned towards Mrs. Poor. She had leaped to her feet and had thrown her veil back. The pale, proud face was working with intense emotion, her hands were dragging at her bodice, she had lost every vestige of control—a dreadful sight.

"It's a conspiracy!" she cried shrilly. "To railroad him—with his consent! They staged it here together. Can't you all see? That's why we were brought here!"

Mme. Storey turned to the hysterical woman with seeming surprise. "Why, Mrs. Poor, what do you know about it?"

Under that cold glance the woman suddenly collapsed in her chair. Her eyes sickened with terror. The strident voice declined to a whisper. "Of course—of course I don't know," she stuttered. "I am simply overwrought. All this—all this has been too much for me. I am simply overwrought. I beg your pardon. I will retire—if someone will help me to my car."

Mr. Barron made a move to go to her, but Mme. Storey laid hand on his arm and looked at him significantly.

He fell back in his chair muttering: "My God!"

At Mme. Storey's mention of a new witness Philippa had sagged down in her chair. Little Mrs. Batten had flown to her, and now knelt beside her with an arm around the girl. Grantland was staring at Mrs. Poor with a strange, perplexed frown.

"Don't go, Mrs. Poor," said Mme. Storey softly. "Help us to throw a little light on this baffling matter."

Mrs. Poor made an attempt to draw her accustomed garments of pride and aloofness about her, but they would no longer serve. She shivered under our glances like a naked woman.

Mme. Storey proceeded: "How long have you known Lieutenant Grantland?"

"About two years," was the reply.

"Ah, that is longer than Miss Dean has known him, isn't it?"

"Yes."

"Miss Dean met Lieutenant Grantland in your house?"

"Yes."

"Formerly you took a great interest in Lieutenant Grantland?"

"I liked him, if that is what you mean. We were friends."

"Great friends?"

"That is such a vague phrase. I advised him as I could out of my greater experience."

"Like an elder sister?"

"If you like."

"Did you notice any change in him after he met Miss Dean?"

"No."

"But he stopped coming to see you."

"Well, yes. I saw him less often."

"But he was still coming to the house?"

"So it seems."

"Did you know they were engaged?"

"Yes."

"How?"

"Gossip, rumour."

"He did not tell you?"

"No."

Mme. Storey turned unexpectedly to Mrs. Batten. "Mrs. Batten," she said, "why did Lieutenant Grantland come to see Miss Dean secretly? Quick, the truth!"

The little body could not resist that sharp command. She glanced in a scared way at her mistress, and the truth came tumbling out involuntarily. "She—she had taken a fancy to him. They did not wish to anger her."

"That is sufficient," said Mme. Storey.

Mrs. Poor struggled to her feet. "Servants' gossip!" she cried. "This is outrageous! I will not stay to be insulted!"

Mme. Storey rose too, and said in a tone oddly compounded of scorn and pity: "What's the use, Mrs. Poor? You have passed the limit of a woman's endurance. Tell the assistant district attorney who killed your husband."

The other woman with a last effort threw her head back, and tried to face Mme. Storey down—meanwhile her ashy cheeks and trembling lips told their own tale.

"How should I know?" she cried. "How dare you take such a tone to me? Do you presume to accuse me? Oh, this is too funny!" Her laugh had a shocking ring. "You know very well I was performing at the club when it happened. Hundreds saw me there. I returned home with my servants. Ask them!"

"I know all this," said Mme. Storey with a bored air, "but that's only the beginning of the story. Sit down and I'll tell the rest."

Mrs. Poor obeyed—simply because her legs would not support her. As Mme. Storey proceeded, the other woman let her veil fall over her face. Her hands convulsively gripped the arms of her chair.

Mme. Storey sat down and drew from the drawer of her table the several bits of evidence in connection with the case. She had in addition a programme of the pageant given at the Pudding Stone Club. Consulting this, she said:

"You made your first appearance in the second tableau as Starving Russia," she said. "This was at nine-fifteen. Upon leaving the stage your maid dressed you for your second appearance. This consumed about twenty-five minutes. You then went out into the audience to view the performance. Your maid joined the other servants in the part of the grounds reserved for them. You had told her you would not need her again.

"While everybody was looking at a tableau you slipped into the shrubbery surrounding the open-air theatre and made your way to your car. You are an expert chauffeur, as everybody knows. You drove it home. You did not turn in at the main gate but at the lower entrance leading to the service door. You did not drive up to the house, but left the car just inside the gate and walked to the house. The tracks made by the car were found where you had run it just inside the gate, and later backed it out into the road again. It was identified as your car by certain peculiarities in the tires.

"You went to one of the French windows of the library—to be exact, it was the second window from the front door. In order to reach the sill you had to make one step in the soft mould of the flower bed. You turned around on the sill, and stooping over, with your hand you brushed loose earth over the print of your foot. But a slight depression was left there, and by carefully brushing the loose dirt away again I was able to lay bare the deep print made by your slipper.

"I assume that you tapped on the window, and that your husband, seeing you, turned off the burglar-alarm and let you in. This would be about ten o'clock, or just as the other three persons in the house were sitting down to supper in Mrs. Batten's room. Perhaps you glanced through the window of that room as you passed by on the drive. What you said to your husband, of course, I do not know. My guess is that you accounted for your unexpected return by saying that an unforeseen request for a contribution had been made on you. At any rate he sat down at his writing-table and drew out his cheque-book. As he dated the stub you shot him in the back with Miss Dean's pistol which you had previously stolen from her bureau."

A convulsive shudder passed through the frame of the woman in black.

Mme. Storey continued in her sure, quiet voice: "You had wrapped your right arm and the hand holding the pistol in many folds of a chiffon scarf. This was for the double purpose of concealing the weapon and of muffling the report. After the deed you tore off these wrappings, and crumpling the scarf into a ball, threw it on the fire, which the servants have testified was burning in the room. But it must have opened up as it burned. At any rate, a small piece fell outside the embers, and was not consumed. Here it is. The characteristic odour of gunpowder still clings to it faintly.

"My principal difficulty was to establish how you got out of the house. I suspected that you must have contrived some means of setting the burglar-alarm behind you. The string box on Mr. Poor's desk furnished me with my clue. It was empty. When the last piece of string comes out of such a box, a man's instinctive act is to put a fresh ball in at once—if he has one. There were several spare balls in Mr. Poor's desk. Yet the box was empty. I may say that I subsequently found the length of string that you pulled out of that box in a tangled skein beside the road where you threw it on your way back to the club. Here it is.

"When I examined the burglar-alarm all was clear. A tiny staple had been driven into the floor under the switch. It was still there at nine o'clock of the morning after the murder when you had had no opportunity to remove it. You tied the string in a slip-knot to the handle of the switch, passed the other end through the staple in the floor—this gave you the necessary downward pull on the handle. You then ran the string across the floor and passed it through the keyhole of the front door. This door locks with a spring lock, and the original keyhole is not used.

"You went out, closing the door behind you. Your first light pull on the string set the alarm—the handle of the switch moved easily. A second and harder pull slipped the knot, and you drew the string through the keyhole. You returned to the club, arriving there in ample time for your second appearance as Victory at 10.50."

An absolute silence filled the room. We glanced at one another in a dazed way, wondering if we dared credit what our ears had heard. Then suddenly joy flamed up in the face of the two young people—the loveliest thing I have ever seen. But I turned away my head. We all did. We heard them cry each other's names.

"Philippa!"

"George!"

Presently Mme. Storey said: "Mrs. Poor, are the facts not as I have stated?"

The wretched woman sat huddled in her chair like a demented person. I was glad her face was hidden. Suddenly she straightened up and cried out:

"Yes, it's true! It's true! I killed him! I shot him just as you say! Thank God! I've told it! I can sleep now!"

Once the bonds upon speech were broken she could not stop herself. "Yes, I killed him! I killed him!" she repeated over and over. "I couldn't stand it any longer! I'm not sorry for it! Who's going to blame me? What kind of a life did I lead? What kind of a wife was I? An object of scorn to my own servants! No one will ever know what I put up with— Oh, I know what they said; 'The proud, cold Mrs. Poor, she doesn't feel anything!' Proud! Cold! Oh my God! When I was burning up! When I died a thousand deaths daily! What do gabbling women know of what such a woman as I can suffer!"

This was unspeakably painful for us to listen to. Mme. Storey looked significantly at Mr. Barron. He, whose attitude toward Mrs. Poor had undergone a great change during the past few minutes, now stepped forward and touched her arm.

She drew away from him with a sharp, new cry of terror. "No! No! Not that! Not that!" Throwing aside her veil again she turned to Grantland with outstretched arms. "George, don't let them take me away!" she cried. "George, help me! Help me!"

The young man walked to the window. Mrs. Poor was led out, still crying pitifully upon his name.

Mme. Storey turned quickly to Mrs. Batten. "Will you go with her? She needs a woman near."

The good little body hurried after.

Grantland went back to Philippa. Drawing her hand under his arm he brought her up to Mme. Storey's table. After their terrible ordeal they were gravely happy: it seemed not to be necessary for these two to speak to each other; the look in their eyes told all.

The young man said to my employer: "How can we ever thank you?"

Mme. Storey put on a brusque air to hide the fact that she was moved, too. "Nonsense! You owe me nothing! I got my reward in taking the wind out of the assistant district attorney's sails!"

"What a wonderful woman you are!" murmured the girl.

"That's what people always say," said Mme. Storey ruefully. "It makes me feel like a side-show."

Philippa looked at her lieutenant. "What a fool I was to believe he could have done it!"

He looked back. "I was the bigger fool."

"Wonderful liars, both of you!" said Mme. Storey dryly. "You had me guessing more than once. Like all really good liars, you stuck close to the truth. His story was true up to the point where he said he crawled into the library on hands and knees. That was just a little overdone, lieutenant. As a matter of fact, when Philippa didn't come back, you returned to the house-keeper's room to look for her. By the way, that touch about the second revolver was masterly."

Grantland blushed.

Mme. Storey turned to Philippa. "You told the truth up to the point where you said you got your pistol out of the drawer. It wasn't there, of course. After searching frantically for it, you were afraid to return to the library without it, and you stole down the back stairs, knowing you would be safe with your young man anyhow."

They bade her a grateful farewell and went out. They made an uncommonly handsome pair.

Mr. Barron returned to the room. He had a highly self-conscious air that betrayed him.

"Oh, I thought you'd gone," said Mme. Storey.

"No, I sent Mrs. Poor down-town in her own car with my men. I'll follow directly. I want to speak to you."

"Go ahead," said Mme. Storey.

"It's a private matter," he said with a venomous glance in my direction.

Mme. Storey, with a whimsical twinkle in her eye, signified that I might leave. I knew she was going to turn on the dictagraph. She had no mercy on that man.

I heard him say: "Well, Rose, I take off my hat to you! In this case you certainly beat me to it! I confess it. I couldn't say fairer than that, could I?"

"It's not necessary to say anything, Walter."

"But I want you to know the kind of fellow I am. I'm a generous-minded man, Rosie. The trouble is, you provoke me so I fly in a rage when I'm with you, and you don't get the right idea of me. I'm gentle as a lamb if you take me right."

"Well, I'm glad to hear that, Walter."

"Take me for good, Rosie! You and I need each other. Your intuition is all right. With your intuition and my logic we'll make an unbeatable pair. I'll tell you all my cases, Rosie, and let you advise me. Honest, I will. Give me a smile, Rosie. I don't mean that kind of a smile. From the heart! You cut the ground from under my feet with that wicked little smile. Smile kindly on me, Rosie—"

It was indecent to listen to a man making such a fool of himself. I took the headpiece off and laid it down. The next minute Mr. Barron, very red about the gills, banged out of Mme. Storey's room, stamped across my office and downstairs.

Mme. Storey rang for me. She was imperturbably lighting a cigarette.

"I'm ready to take up the Cornwall case," she said. "Bring me the papers from the file."

THE SCRAP OF LACE

ONE MORNING WHEN I was later than usual in arriving at Gramercy Park (Mme. Storey and I had been working the greater part of the night), Eddie, the hall boy, informed me that there was a lady waiting upstairs.

"Upstairs?" I repeated in surprise. I had the key to our offices.

"I placed a chair in the hall for her," he said. "She wouldn't wait down here. She was excited. That's her car outside."

The car (to which I had given an admiring glance on the way in) was a foreign-built limousine perfect in its appointments; the chauffeur one of those exalted creatures with the self-possession of a cabinet minister.

I hastened up the single flight of stairs in no little curiosity. There was the chair where the boy had placed it, but the lady was walking jerkily up and down. It was the more noticeable in that she was of an age and figure not given to unnecessary exertion.

I did not recognize her until I had thrown open the door of my office, letting a shaft of light out into the hall.

It was Miss Teresa de Guion. You could have blown me down with a fan. Not alone the fact that she was there at all at such an hour, but the state she was in. She had left off the famous makeup; her face was streaked and hollowed with distress; and she, often called the best-dressed woman in New York, had evidently thrown on her clothes anyhow. It was the first time I had seen her looking anywhere near her age, which was about sixty, and it shocked me.

But a handsome woman still, with hair black as a raven's wing, and young, dark eyes.

Preceding me into my office, she breathlessly demanded to know where Mme. Storey was. I told her I was expecting her at any moment. Could I not find her on the telephone? I called up my mistress's apartment, and was told, as I expected, that Mme. Storey was on her way down.

Miss de Guion sat on a chair biting her pale lips. I hope I did not show my feelings unduly, nevertheless it made her exquisitely uneasy to have to sit there under my eyes. Presently she asked in a thick voice if she might wait in Mme. Storey's room. I made haste to open the door for her, and she passed in.

Teresa de Guion was one of the notable figures of New York life. She was, I think, the first, and certainly the greatest, of social secretaries. But the word secretary does not do her justice; prime minister would be nearer it. She came of a family of French descent that for several generations had ridden the crest of the wave in New York society. Their wealth originated in South America. Teresa, the last of her line, more than upheld the family traditions, for she was not only beautiful and vivacious, but she had a courage and freedom rarer then than now, and not on that account any the less potent.

It was odd that she had never married. They say she had a swarm of admirers; that it was part of a young man's education to tag after Teresa de Guion for a season or two. But she never distinguished one above his fellows; she was never even reported to be engaged. It may be that with all her beauty and cleverness she lacked something of essential charm. Charm for men, I mean. I suppose it would have taken a deal of charm to gloss over for men, her undoubted masterfulness. She always had devoted women friends.

When she was in her sixth or seventh season, that is to say, still a dazzling young beauty, her father died suddenly—killed himself, I have heard it whispered, leaving her penniless. One of the innumerable revolutions in South America had swept away everything he possessed. The only equipment Teresa had was her social equipment, and she promptly turned that to account. The two or three women who mattered most in New York society were her intimate friends. She undertook to relieve them of the more onerous part of their social duties; arranging their entertainments, keeping their lists, sending out their invitations.

This was one side of her business. The other lay in introducing sufficiently rich people to society. She could do that; she had the prestige and she had never abused it. She made no bones about it, for she was refreshingly frank. Therein lay her strength.

She was a success from the start. Indeed there was never anybody like her; for she had the aplomb of a duchess, and never lowered her colours for a single instant under any circumstances. Her best friend and principal client was the third Mrs. Peter John Cruger, who, as everybody knows, ruled New York society with a despotic hand for almost a generation, and Teresa de Guion was her grand vizir.

The great Mrs. Cruger died about five years ago, and her mantle descended, as a matter of course, to her eldest son's wife, Mrs. Peter John Cruger the fourth. This event, instead of overthrowing Miss de Guion, was actually the means of strengthening her hand, for the fourth Mrs. Cruger, better known as Bessie Cruger, while a beautiful and charming woman, was of a lazy and indifferent temper that found the duties of her exalted station very irksome. She yielded up more and more to Miss de Guion, who was only too ready to assume it; she gave up the entire direction of things social to the family friend. Things have very much loosened up and spread out, these days, but the Cruger set was still *the set*, and the only access to it lay through Teresa de Guion.

She and Mme. Storey knew each other well, of course. It would have been impossible for two such eminences in the little world that centres east of Central Park not to have become acquainted. I had seen Miss de Guion several times before. She was still a very charming woman, more charming than ever, perhaps. She had progressed with the generations; indeed she probably found this free and easy generation more congenial to her than her own had been. No one ever thought of her as an old woman; all her friends were young people; she still moved the gayest among the gay.

Such was the person I was so astonished to find at our office door at half past ten in the morning and in so extreme a state of agitation. I immediately scented a *cause célèbre*.

My mistress was not long in arriving. She had come in with the composed and languorous air that so belies her. She was in a high good humour, I remember.

"Bella, you have a disgustingly virtuous look," she said. "I see you mean to give me a very bad morning."

It is one of her pet fictions that she would never work if I did not drive her to it. I play up to it, of course. "Then your conscience must be troubling you," I replied.

As I have said before, to me Mme. Storey is the most beautiful creature in the world. I would be repaid for all my hard work simply by the privilege of looking at her every day. She is more than physically beautiful; grace hangs about her like a lovely garment. Everything she does, every gesture is therefore bound to be beautifully right.

Upon this day I remember, her tall figure was habited in a slip of warm brown velvet lined with orange silk which was designed to show in the sleeves and the folds of the girdle. On her head was a little straw hat of a peculiar vivid shade of blue that few women but herself could have worn to advantage. This elegant costume with the light-hearted touches suggested that she had planned a serene and ladylike day. I doubted that it would be realised. On her arm perched Giannino, the black ape, in a little orange jacket and cap with gold bells.

I said: "Miss Teresa de Guion is waiting in your room."

She glanced at me with raised eyebrows. But I said no more. I knew she would find out soon enough what was the matter, and she hates unnecessary comment.

She went on into her room, and I ground my teeth a little in chagrin. I did so want to witness the meeting of those two, and to hear what they had to say to each other. I did my best to start to work, but hardly with success, for I guessed there was something afoot far more exciting than the ordinary routine.

In a moment or two, to my joy, the little buzzer under my desk sounded. I sprang to my feet, snatching up my note-book. But at the door I held myself back for a moment, not to appear too eager. My entrance into the great room created a sudden silence. Evidently an important communication had already been made, for Mme. Storey looked grave.

Mme. Storey sat at the wide table with her back to the windows, Miss de Guion at her left, facing her. The latter held a cigarette between her agitated fingers, but she had only half lighted it, and it was already out. Mme. Storey handed over Giannino to me, with instructions to put him in his little house in the middle room. This presaged action. She consulted her calendar of engagements for the day.

When I returned to her desk she started issuing instructions crisply: "Bella, please call up Dr. Pulford in White Plains. Tell him I shall call for him at noon upon a matter of the most urgent importance, and shall ask for about an hour of his time. Then call up Sidney Crider at this number. Tell him to get into touch with Bourne, and to turn over his work on the Rampray case to Bourne. Then tell Crider to take a train for White Plains at twelve o'clock, and that you will be waiting for him in the station there. Before he starts, let him send his brother to this office to take your place, so that there will be somebody here that we can call up. Then call up Governor Rampray, J. G. Cowley, and Coatsworth and tell each one with apologies, that owning to unforeseen circumstances, I shall be unable to keep my appointments with them today, and that I will write or telephone asking for new ones. Young Crider will have to receive anybody else who may come here. Telephone my maid and ask her to come down and get Giannino. He is not to have bananas today. When we go out, leave the key with Eddie, to hand to young Crider when he comes. While you're telephoning I'll change my clothes."

"Must you stop for that?" faltered Miss de Guion.

"My dear! I couldn't undertake a job in the field rigged like this. I have everything here. I'll be ready before Bella's through telephoning."

"Couldn't we leave her to follow us by train?"

"Impossible, my dear! I must have her to take down your statement on the way to Cariswoode."

"My statement!" exclaimed Miss de Guion aghast. "Taken down—"

"Why, of course," said Mme. Storey. "We must be businesslike. Here, you have dwelt too long on this horror. I shall give you a drink before we start."

2

THE EXTRA SEATS in the Cruger limousine were on swivels, so that I was able to turn around and face Mme. Storey and Miss de Guion while they talked. I had a brief-case on my knees, and my notebook on top of it. The car had such wonderful springs I was able to take dictation without too much difficulty.

Mme. Storey was now wearing a trim tweed suit and a sport hat without any trimming. The severity of the costume made her look girlish. It suggested hard work ahead.

"Tell me as detailed a story as you are able," she said to Miss de Guion. "We have plenty of time, and it will save going back over the ground later."

Miss de Guion had got a better grip on herself by now. "I went up to Cariswoode, the Cruger country place near White Plains, on Sunday morning," she began. "I took my secretary, Louise Mayfield, with me, because there was a lot of work to be done in connection with the Elizabethan fête that Mrs. Cruger is giving for charity next month. The letters to those we wanted on the different committees had to be mailed from Cariswoode, because they were supposed to be written by Mrs. Cruger herself."

"What sort of girl was Miss Mayfield?" asked Mme. Storey.

A spasm of pain passed over Miss de Guion's face. "A very handsome girl, if that is what you mean," she said in a low voice. "You will see her."

"No, I mean her nature, disposition," explained my mistress.

Miss de Guion passed a hand over her face. "It's hard for me to describe her to you," she said wearily. "She's been so close to me these last months. She was very capable. She's the only girl I ever had who could come out of herself when it was required, and exert charm, fascination; and when the occasion had passed, immediately become the self-contained secretary again. Oh, she was invaluable to me! Invaluable!"

There was something very affecting in the spectacle of the old lady's dry-eyed despair. She was a hard old lady, and it is much more terrible, of course, to see a hard person cut up than a soft one.

Mme. Storey maintained a businesslike attitude, as the kindest thing under the circumstances. "How long has she been with you?" she asked.

"Eighteen months."

"How did she come to you?"

"She brought me a letter of introduction from a school friend now living in Pittsburgh. My friend described her to me as an orphan of good family obliged to earn her own living. That in itself, so like my own situation, would have warmed my heart to her. And she had other recommendations. She wrote a very characteristic and aristocratic hand. Very like my own, in fact. Almost impossible to find nowadays. Just what I wanted for filling in invitations and addressing envelopes. I engaged her at once for that purpose."

"And gradually discovered her other qualifications?"

"Yes. I found that I could entrust anything to her tact. A natural tact that scarcely required instruction. Oh, I leaned on her so!"

"Well, when you arrived at Cariswoode on Sunday," prompted Mme. Storey.

"There was only a small party. Vera McPeake—"

"The daughter of the lead trust?" put in Mme. Storey dryly.

"Yes; heiress to a hundred millions more or less," said Miss de Guion without perceiving any irony. "Not a bad sort of girl. She will do in time. Willing to learn."

"Who else?" asked Mme. Storey.

"Only Jack Rowcliffe."

"Ah, he and Miss McPeake are engaged, aren't they?"

"Yes."

"Are they in love with each other?"

Miss de Guion looked at her questioner in surprise. "My dear! How should I know? That's their affair. It's a wonderful chance for both of them. She has the prospect of the hundred millions and he has the social position. Each is young and personable, so that it is not a case of either having to swallow a pill."

I suspected that Miss de Guion must have promoted this match. It was right in her line.

Miss de Guion's face began to break up again, and she dabbed her tearless eyes with her handkerchief. "But what has this got to do with my poor—my poor Louise?" she faltered.

"I must consider every circumstance," said Mme. Storey gently. "What can you tell me about Miss Mayfield's friends, associates, lovers?"

"Very little. She had made her own friends, of course, but not very intimate ones, I fancy. My friends and my work consumed most of her time. As regards men, she had a level head, and no little humour. I never heard of, nor suspected, the least entanglement in that direction."

"Well, what did you do upon your arrival at Cariswoode?"

"We lunched."

"Was Miss Mayfield present?"

"No. She was not a guest, you see, though Bessie Cruger was most kind to her. She lunched somewhere; in her room, I suppose; and immediately went to work on the letters. It was a disagreeable day, and none of us left the house. A few people, intimate friends, came in for tea. Louise came down for tea at Bessie's, Mrs. Cruger's, especial request."

"And dinner?" asked Mme. Storey.

"No. Dinner was a formal affair; sixteen covers. Shall I name the guests?"

"No need now."

"After dinner a number of people came in for music. Music on Sunday nights is a regular institution at Cariswoode when the Crugers are there. I have spent a lot of thought on making those occasions unique of their kind. Ischl played, and Doria, the new

Spanish soprano, sang. Louise came down for the music; she was very musical. Afterward we danced."

"Miss Mayfield too?"

"No. She retired early, as she had a busy day before her. Monday, that is yesterday morning, we lay late. I had my breakfast in bed. Afterwards I went to Bessie's boudoir *en négligé*, and we smoked and gossiped for an hour or so. Vera McPeake was there too. During this time Louise was working in the boudoir adjoining my bedroom. Afterwards I wrote a few letters, dressed for lunch, and after lunch Bessie, Miss McPeake and I were driven into White Plains to do a little shopping."

"Where was Rowcliffe?" put in Mme. Storey.

"He went off to the Kenwood Club to play golf."

"Go on."

"We returned to Cariswoode for tea. Immediately afterwards we went to dress, for we were dining at the Heber Bassetts' in Ridgefield before going on to the Van Brocklin dance, also in Ridgefield. We started shortly after six, as dinner was for seven, and we had twenty miles to drive. Louise came downstairs to see us off. She was to dine with some friends in Scarsdale near by, the Hyatts. She did not have to start so early, and she was not dressed yet. She came out on the terrace as we drove away, and that is the last— that is the last—" The old lady was overcome by emotion again.

Mme. Storey patted her hand. "Hurry on. Hurry on," she said.

Miss de Guion pulled herself together. "The dinner? It was just a dinner. There was nobody of any account there. Bessie is much too lax in such matters. The late Mrs. Cruger was always consulted in respect to the people she was asked to meet at dinner, but Bessie will not trouble herself. I would have attended to it, but I was busy in New York. Consequently we were bored. We went on to the dance at the ridiculous hour of nine-thirty. One has to humour the Van Brocklins. Long established people, but hopelessly outdistanced now. Fancy asking people to dance at nine o'clock! Bessie would have dropped them long ago, but Pete Cruger insists on keeping up the connection, simply because old Mr. Van Brocklin was an associate of his father's—"

"By the way, where is Mr. Cruger now?" put in Mme. Storey.

"Fishing, in Canada. He has been telegraphed for."

"Go on."

"There is nothing to say about the dance, either. It was as dull as we expected. A Viennese orchestra, because the Van Brocklins presume to frown upon jazz. Old-fashioned waltzes, fancy! One expected to hear the strains of a schottische or a polka next. We left at the earliest possible moment, about one. It was three when we got home."

"I thought you said it was only twenty miles?"

"We had an accident. We ran out of gasolene on the road. Bessie was most annoyed."

"This car and this chauffeur?" asked Mme. Storey.

"Yes. We had to sit there an hour while he walked back to some place where he could get gas. It was very tiresome."

"Go on."

Miss de Guion's agitation rose afresh.

"It seemed to me," she said, "that I had no more than fallen asleep when I was violently awakened by my maid. The girl was utterly distraught, her hair flying in every direction; she was holding a bed quilt around her. She stuttered out something, I can't tell you what. But the purport was clear. Something had happened to Louise. Louise was dead!" Miss de Guion put a hand over her eyes.

"I sent the girl away to cover herself," she presently went on. "I stopped only for a dressing-gown and slippers, and found my way to the floor above, where I knew Louise was lodged somewhere. I was guided to her room by the sight of a little group of servants at the door—peering in. They parted as I came up. I looked in and I saw—I saw my poor Louise lying on the floor in front of her dressing-table. The chair was close beside her, as if she had slipped from it. She was wearing her prettiest evening dress of yellow malines. I had given it to her. It had not been worn before—

"I could not—I could not bring myself to touch her, but they told me she was already cold and stiff. It was only too evident that she had fallen as she was dressing the night before, and had lain there all those hours!"

"The room?" asked Mme. Storey softly.

"It was in perfect order. No sign of any disturbance. Louise's dress was not disordered; her hair was perfectly arranged. The clothes she had taken off were put away. On the bed lay her evening cloak, side by side with her night gear, ready for her return."

"Doors? Windows?" asked Mme. Storey.

"There was but the door from the hall, and a cupboard door. The door from the hall was locked, they told me, and the key on the inside. The butler had forced it. There was but one large window. It was closed."

"Does that not seem odd in warm weather? Was it locked?"

"I cannot tell you that."

"Go on."

"The doctor had been telephoned for; Dr. Singer. He came. I retired while he made his examination. I—I could not bear it. He reported that it was a case of heart failure. It seemed the obvious explanation, for I remembered having heard Louise laughingly refer to her weak heart."

"What happened then?" asked Mme. Storey.

"Dr. Singer returned to White Plains. He said he would issue the necessary certificate. Shortly afterwards Mrs. Cruger sent her personal secretary in to the—the undertaker to make the arrangements."

"You notified Miss Mayfield's relatives?"

"She had no near relatives. I expected to take the last sad duties upon myself."

"Go on."

"When Mrs. Cruger's secretary—his name is Jamison, got to the mortuary rooms, Singer's car was waiting there. Dr. Singer had brought the certificate. While they were inside the establishment, the two chauffeurs got into talk about the affair, and Dr. Singer's chauffeur told Bracker, our chauffeur—"

"This man again?" asked Mme. Storey with a nod towards the front seat.

"Yes—told Bracker that his master had told him the girl looked as if she might have been asphyxiated, but that it would cost him his practice to bring up anything like that in connection with the Crugers. There is the miserable story that has thrown us into such confusion!" Miss de Guion cried passionately. "Mere backstairs gossip, I dare say. But what were we to do! It is damnable!"

"Let us hope it is only gossip," said Mme. Storey gravely. "At least we will get a dependable verdict from Pulford. He's a good doctor, though not a fashionable one."

"This Bracker is a well-meaning fellow," Miss de Guion went on. "He told Jamison at once, who told Mrs. Cruger when he got back, and Bessie instantly sent for me. I found her in a terrible state. Bessie Cruger is my dearest friend, but I am not blind to her faults. She would almost rather die than exert herself in any direction. She was determined not to take any notice of the matter. I think it is just idle gossip myself, but I pointed out to her that, the story having once been set in circulation, we could not let it go on rolling up credence and support like a wet snowball. It *must* be investigated, I said. She would not hear of calling in the police, but I had the happy inspiration of suggesting your name. Bessie welcomed that, and instantly dispatched me to New York to fetch you."

3

CARISWOODE IS, OR WAS, one of the most famous country-houses in America, and I was full of curiosity concerning it. To reach the house one had to pass through an extensive ornamental park in the English style. The park was a bit too well cared for to my taste. There was something immoral in keeping so much rich land trimmed, prettified, and out of use. The house, when it burst into view, took my breath away by its mere size. With central block and wings it must have had a frontage of close on three hundred feet. I suppose in the three stories there were two hundred windows in view, all brightly polished. All very well for an institution, a hotel, a club, but preposterous for a dwelling. As a matter of fact, it has since become the most fashionable club in Westchester county.

It was magnificent, but it was not beautiful. Built of red brick in the Tudor style, as that was conceived thirty or forty years ago, the errors of taste were now only too apparent. It already looked old-fashioned. But it *was* imposing.

My curiosity respecting the interior was not to be gratified at the moment; for when we arrived it was already time for me to go back to White Plains to meet Crider. I therefore remained in the car. My instructions were simply to bring Crider to the house, explaining the situation to him as well as I was able, on the way, in order to save time later.

Crider turned up, of course. He is absolutely dependable. Of all the men who work for us regularly or on occasion, I set the most store by Sidney Crider; he is so quiet and sure of himself. One of the best things about him is that he can *listen* intelligently. You don't have to wear yourself out in tedious repetition and explanation. He received my strange tale quite as a matter of course.

When we got back, and at last got into the big house, my eyes flew about. It was certainly a *coup d'oeil* as the French say, or, as we would put it, an eye-opener. From the great central hall which rose to the roof with stairways and galleries, a vast corridor led off at either hand, so long you could scarcely see to the end, and with room after room opening off each side. These corridors were lined with paintings in elaborate gilt frames; with statuary, consoles and settees. The decoration was all of the "red" period; i.e., elaborate carved mahogany, thick red carpets, crimson walls and hangings. The richness of it all was simply overpowering, but I could not conceive of anybody being at home in such a museum. Frankly, it intimidated me. I felt like an insect.

Mme. Storey had established herself in a small room immediately to the right of the entrance. One entered it by a door concealed in the panelling. It was evidently an office, perhaps the butler's office; very plain and businesslike amidst all the magnificence.

She was seated in her plain suit at a flat-topped desk with exactly the air of a commanding officer in headquarters. It was soon evident that the vast, unwieldy household now received its chief impetus from *her*. The suffocating opulence had no terrors for Mme. Storey. In the presence of my mistress the great Mrs. Peter

John Cruger herself, as I was presently to see, modified her imperious air. Such is the power of personality.

Mme. Storey banished everybody from the room while she
talked to Crider and me. When we are working with her in the field
she always makes a point of telling us the exact situation before
we start in.

"While Miss de Guion was away fetching me," she began, "Mrs.
Cruger sent again for Dr. Singer. The man swore that he had made
no statement of any sort about the case to his chauffeur. However,
that has no significance now, for Dr. Pulford states positively that
the girl was asphyxiated. She appears to have come to her death as
the result of inhaling a poisonous gas, all trace of which has disappeared. When I got here the body had been lifted to the bed, and
so many people have been in and out of the room, that any evidence there may have been has pretty well been destroyed. However, it seems certain under the circumstances that the girl was
alone when she died.

"The window of the room is twenty-five feet from the ground.
There is no evidence of any ladder having been planted outside.
There is a heavy gutter pipe strongly supported, that runs down
alongside the window. It is possible someone may have climbed
up by it, but it could only have been a daring and nimble climber,
and one inspired by a strong motive. No motive of any sort has as
yet appeared.

"As a matter of precaution I have collected all the objects on
the girl's dressing-table, and I have them here; brush, comb, mirror, powder-box, bottle of toilet water, etc.

"She was supposed to be getting ready to dine with some friends
of hers named Hyatt who live in Scarsdale near her. As it was odd
that the Hyatts did not telephone when she failed to appear, I had
them called up, and learned, through a discreet inquiry, that Miss
Mayfield had not been expected there last night. It was evidently a
ruse. Where she was going is another point that requires to be
cleared up.

"I have one important clew. In a waste paper basket in the girl's
room I found this envelope. An envelope of cheap, soft paper you

see, without any distinguishing marks. Such envelopes are sold by the million. It is addressed to Miss Mayfield in a disguised hand, and was posted in White Plains yesterday. Fortunately for us, the girl slit the end neatly, and dropped it in the basket without crushing it. Now observe!" Mme. Storey dropped the envelope lightly on the desk, and removed her hands from it. "What does that envelope tell you?"

I was dumb. Crider, better trained than I, peered at it closely this way and that without touching it, and said slowly:

"The envelope has been subjected to pressure in the cancelling machine, and the soft paper has therefore taken and held the impress of its contents. It contained something a little thicker than the ordinary sheet of paper, but folded smaller than the envelope itself. It has made a little square bulge in the centre of the envelope. It was of softer texture than writing paper."

Mme. Storey listened with a gratified smile, as a teacher to the recitation of her prize pupil. "But what was it?" she asked.

"A handkerchief," announced Crider suddenly; "a lady's handkerchief."

"Excellent!" said Mme. Storey. "Anything more?"

"If I had a good glass—," murmured Crider.

Mme. Storey produced a reading glass, and handed it over.

"A handkerchief with an elaborate lace border," Crider reported after a further examination. "The cancelling stamp has struck an edge of it, and has shadowed out a confused bit of the design in ink."

Mme. Storey was delighted. "Anything else?" she asked.

But Crider could tell her no more.

Mme. Storey picked up the envelope delicately. "A negative thing," she said, "but important to us. Observe, by looking at it edgewise, you can see the bulge is exactly the same on one side as on the other. That tells us there was no letter slipped either in front or behind the handkerchief. The envelope contained nothing but the handkerchief."

"Where is it?" we both asked.

"That is for us to find out."

4

CRIDER'S JOB was to search the grounds, and later to go into White Plains to establish, if possible, who posted the envelope containing the handkerchief. Meanwhile Mme. Storey examined various persons in the house.

The first she had in was the butler, Glasgow. He was the most perfect butler I ever expect to behold; a man of fifty-odd, slightly bald, with a clear, pleasant skin. He made quite an elegant figure in his morning coat, and I should have taken him for one of the guests until I heard him speak. A slight tinge of deference in his tones placed him.

Glasgow made an admirable witness.

"At eight o'clock this morning I was polishing silver in my pantry," he said, "when Meeker, a housemaid on the second bedroom floor came to me. She came to me because the housekeeper, Mrs. Evremond, was not down yet. Meeker, who was in somewhat of a state, told me that Miss Mayfield had given instructions that she was to be called at seven o'clock this morning, but that after several attempts she—Meeker—was unable to get any answer from her room. I made light of her fears. 'Miss Mayfield has stopped all night with her friends,' I said. However, I got the duplicate key to that door, and gave it to Meeker, telling her to open the door and look. She presently returned to me, saying she could not get the key into the door.

"I then accompanied her upstairs. I found that the key was in the lock on the inside. A prolonged knocking failed to bring any reply. Somewhat alarmed myself, I then got a pair of thin tweezers, and inserting them in the keyhole, contrived to turn the key a little at a time, until I was able to push it through on the other side. I then opened the door with the duplicate key, and found— well, what you already know, madam."

"Will you please illustrate the position of the body as exactly as you can," said Mme. Storey.

The man got down on the floor, and lay on his left side with one arm doubled beneath him, the other flung over in front. His knees were drawn up; his chin pressed into his breast. He had the instinct of an actor. It was horrible. I turned my head away.

"Thank you," said Mme. Storey. "Were her eyes open or closed?"

"Closed, madam," he replied.

"Did you observe a handkerchief in the girl's hand; on the dressing-table; any place in the room?"

"No, madam."

"You might have overlooked it?"

"I hardly think so, madam. The sight gave me such a shock of horror that every detail of the scene seems to be burned into my brain. That fresh young girl with her shining hair, her pretty, light dress—"

The perfect butler was human like the rest of us. It was no moment for emotion, and Mme. Storey interrupted him: "Please show me again the exact posture of the hand you could see."

He held out his right hand loosely closed, the thumb fitted into the crook of the two first fingers. In imagination I could see a dainty handkerchief clipped there.

Mme. Storey made no comment. "Proceed," said she.

He went on to describe how he had sent the trembling maid to arouse Miss de Guion's maid, and Mrs. Cruger's own maid, that their mistresses might be notified. On his own initiative Glasgow had sent a footman to telephone Dr. Singer.

"After the discovery of the body was any person left alone with it at any time?" asked Mme. Storey.

"Only myself, madam," he answered simply. "While I was waiting for the others to come. After that time I think there were always several persons present."

"You have had several hours now to think things over," said Mme. Storey; "has any peculiar circumstance of any sort suggested itself?"

"There was a noticeable smell when I opened the door," Glasgow said slowly.

"What sort of smell?"

"A sweetish, spirituous sort of smell."

"Chloroform?"

"No, madam, not the same as chloroform."

"A strong smell?"

"No, madam, faint. And after a little while it had disappeared."

"You are sure the window was closed?" asked Mme. Storey.

"Yes, madam. Else the smell would have escaped."

"Did it not strike you as strange that the window should be closed on such a warm night?"

"I did not think of it at the moment, madam, being too much overcome. But it does seem strange."

"There is a screen outside the window," said Mme. Storey. "How does it operate?"

"It slides up and down in a groove, like the sash, madam."

Glasgow then went on to describe the arrival of Miss de Guion and Mrs. Cruger on the scene, and later, the doctor, and his examination of the body. This brought out nothing new or significant. After the doctor had delivered his verdict, Glasgow and a footman had lifted the body to the bed, and all had left the room, Glasgow locking the door and taking both keys with him, pending the arrival of the undertaker.

Mme. Storey went back to the night before. "Glasgow, how had Miss Mayfield expected to get to Scarsdale?"

"Mrs. Cruger had offered her a car, madam, but she declined it. I understood she was to telephone for a taxi when she was ready."

"How is it that none of you realised she had never left the house?"

"I can only say, madam, that each one of us thought one of the others had let her out. Many of the servants would be at dinner at that hour."

"Glasgow, how is the mail delivered here?"

"Rural delivery, madam. By Ford car three times a day; eight-thirty, two-thirty and six-thirty."

"Then there was a delivery last evening after Mrs. Cruger and her guests had started for Ridgefield?"

"Yes, madam, I took it in myself."

"Was there anything for Miss Mayfield?"

"Yes, madam. One letter."

"What can you tell me about it?"

"Only that it was contained in a cheap, common envelope, madam. I sent Albert, the second man, upstairs with it."

"Then Albert was the last person who saw Miss Mayfield alive?"

"He did not see her, madam. I presume she was dressing. She told him to slip the letter under the door, and he did so."

"Is this the envelope, Glasgow?"

"Yes, madam."

"Now, is the maid Meeker outside?"

"Yes, madam, waiting your pleasure." Glasgow opened the door, and gave a sign. "Do you wish me to step outside, madam?"

"Not at all," said Mme. Storey. "At the moment I only wish to find out if Meeker's sense of smell is any better than yours."

The maid entered.

"Meeker, did you smell anything when Mr. Glasgow opened the door of Miss Mayfield's room?"

The housemaid was agitated, but she answered readily: "Yes, madam, vi'lets."

"Ah! Are you sure?"

"Ah, yes, ma'am. Vi'let perfumery. It brought the very flowers before my eyes."

"Thank you, that's all."

Meeker retired.

"One last question, Glasgow," said Mme. Storey. "I can see that you are a man of discretion. It has been suggested that a crime has been committed, and for the sake of the good name of this house, we must go absolutely to the bottom of the matter. Can you, as the result of your observation, suggest the slightest reason or motive for such a crime?"

"No, madam," replied Glasgow, but he stumbled over the word, and changed colour. Mme. Storey simply waited with her grave glance fixed upon him. He could not support it. His fresh face suddenly became moist all over. "I'm sure there's nothing in it," he burst out. "I don't want to get anybody into trouble. I don't want to sow suspicion."

"You are an honest man, Glasgow," said Mme. Storey with a reassuring smile. "Never mind: you will not sow suspicion with me. It is my business to sift suspicion."

"Well, madam, I thought maybe Mr. Rowcliffe was too sweet on Miss Mayfield," he said, blushing like a girl.

"He's engaged to Miss McPeake."

"I know. But I caught him looking strangely at the other girl when he thought he was unobserved. It was at tea time Sunday, and again yesterday."

"What do you mean by strangely?"

"Well, passionately, as they say," Glasgow blurted out with crimson face.

"And did Miss Mayfield return these glances?"

"Oh, no, madam! By no means! She never looked at him."

"Thank you very much, Glasgow. I shall respect your confidence."

5

GLASGOW'S FINAL STATEMENT, with the tragical possibilities it suggested, was to me like the first ray of light breaking through the murk that enveloped the situation. I was very much excited by it. Mme. Storey gave no sign. For some moments after the butler left the room, she sat staring at a pad before her, making meaningless dots upon it with a pencil. Finally I could stand it no longer.

"Will you question Rowcliffe?" I asked.

I was sorry as soon as I had spoken, for Mme. Storey merely smiled at me in a tantalising way. "What an ugly little room this is!" she said irrelevantly. "Shall we take a look at the splendour outside?"

I wanted to see the house, but I wanted much more to know what was passing through her mind. However, when she is in this impish mood there is nothing to do but wait for things to happen. I followed her out of the room.

In the great hall there was a nervous and highly self-conscious group consisting of the dignified housekeeper, Mrs. Evremond,

Glasgow, another manservant, and a couple of maids. Notwithstanding the difference in their stations, the common excitement had drawn them close together. They cast looks of respectful awe upon Mme. Storey as we passed. We crossed the hall and continued on down one of the mighty corridors I have spoken of.

Along each side extended an endless suite of rooms. We passed in and out of them, looking at things. I wondered what they were called. The ordinary names of rooms would give out long before you got through. Later I learned that these were the "state" apartments, and wondered what a good American family did with them. The rooms that were customarily used were in the other wing. Every room had several mountainous crystal chandeliers depending from the ceiling, and every room was filled with gorgeous furnishings and pictures; too much; too much; and not in the best modern taste as even I could see. The present Mrs. Cruger had excellent taste, as I was to learn, but was too indolent to overthrow the gilt and red velvet regime of her predecessor.

"Fancy having to dust all this gimcrackery, Bella," murmured Mme. Storey.

"Yes, but why are we looking at it just now?" I asked.

"Just to stimulate curiosity," she drawled.

The rooms facing towards the south had full-length windows giving on a terrace with a brick parapet, below which you could see the marvellous flower gardens of Cariswoode, now in their glory. In one of these rooms we paused before the famous portrait of the third Mrs. Peter John Cruger, by Campoamor y Nuñez, the Spanish master. A truly regal lady was depicted, but one hardly conspicuous for amiability.

"A prudent master, Bella," remarked Mme. Storey drily. "Observe how one of the lady's hands is partly concealed behind her, while the other is hidden under a flounce. Hands are so difficult to paint!"

Out on the terrace I perceived a handsome young man in a miraculously fitting lounge suit. I supposed this to be Rowcliffe. He came to one of the open windows, to look in, and discovering us, hastily turned on his heel. I began to understand Mme. Storey's reference to stimulating curiosity.

There was a stir at the door of the room, and we beheld a tall, blonde lady advancing towards us. I had not seen her before, but there was no need to be told that this was the chatelaine, for she was followed by a deferential trio, to wit: Mrs. Evremond; an immaculate brow-beaten gentleman whom I guessed to be the secretary; and a second younger gentleman, copy of the other, whose position in the household I never did learn. He may have been the secretary's secretary.

Mrs. Cruger and Mme. Storey had talked before. "Is there any way in which I can assist you?" Mrs. Cruger now asked.

"Not at the moment, thank you," Mme. Storey said pleasantly.

Mrs. Cruger looked at the portrait we had been studying as much as to say: "What has that got to do with the case?"

"I was just mulling things over in my head," murmured Mme. Storey.

Mrs. Cruger bit her lip. She was really an exquisite creature. Her oft-published photographs render her a little insipid, but that is because no photograph could convey the air of delicacy and distinction that enveloped her. She looked as rare and precious as a bit of Venetian glass. This ethereal exterior covered very human failings. She turned her head, saying curtly to her followers:

"You needn't wait."

The three vanished silently. I had an impression that they were still hovering about outside the door. What a life, I thought.

"Have you discovered anything?" Mrs. Cruger asked with an extraordinary anxiety.

Mme. Storey shrugged.

"Tell me!" said the other sharply.

"It's all inchoate," answered Mme. Storey. "I cannot report yet."

Mrs. Cruger stared, and her transparent skin showed a bright flush. Evidently this lady was not accustomed to be denied, however courteously. "Surely I have a right to know what is going on in my own house!" she said.

"Assuredly," rejoined Mme. Storey blandly. "What is your theory of the affair?"

"I have none," said Mrs. Cruger. "The girl died of heart failure. That's all there is to it. This storm of gossip has blown up simply because people insist on making a sensation out of anything that happens to us."

"But Dr. Pulford—" suggested Mme. Storey.

"He was called in without my authority!" said Mrs. Cruger angrily.

"It seemed the obvious first step to take," murmured Mme. Storey deprecatingly.

"He's too bolshevik for my taste!" said Mrs. Cruger.

I saw my mistress's eyes twinkle. "I see that," she said drily. "You can depend upon it, I will take everything into account."

"Whom do you suspect?" demanded Mrs. Cruger. "I insist on knowing!"

This was an unfortunate tone to take with Mme. Storey. "As you have reminded me, this is your house," she said softly. "Nevertheless, I must be allowed to conduct my investigation in my own way."

For a moment the two pairs of eyes contended for mastery. It was Mrs. Cruger's that fell.

"I hope you don't suspect me?" she said with rather a silly sounding laugh.

"Why should I?" asked Mme. Storey mildly. "Have a cigarette?"

"Thanks. One needs one," said Mrs. Cruger. They lit up, amicably enough.

"I liked the girl," Mrs. Cruger went on. "Oh, why did it have to happen here? I wish she had never come to the house! What am I to tell my husband when he returns? He never—" She hastily put the cigarette in her mouth.

"Never what?" asked Mme. Storey offhand.

"Never should have gone to Canada," said Mrs. Cruger quickly.

It was obviously not what she had started to say. Mme. Storey affected to take no notice.

"How about Rowcliffe?" asked Mme. Storey, blowing a cloud of smoke.

"Rowcliffe?" echoed the other. Her face cleared, and she became more at ease.

"He's some sort of relation of yours, isn't he?"

"My first cousin," said Mrs. Cruger. "My mother was a Rowcliffe, you know."

"Yes," said Mme. Storey. "What do you think about this match with Miss McPeake?"

"I think the obvious thing," said Mrs. Cruger. "She's so rich she's bound to arrive anyway. Why shouldn't she arrive through him?"

"Why not, indeed?" agreed Mme. Storey. "He's reputed to be rather wild, isn't he?"

"I don't suppose you want me to repeat gossip," said Mrs. Cruger languidly. "I know nothing of my own knowledge."

"Never mind gossip," went on Mme. Storey. "Give me an impression of his character."

Mrs. Cruger entered into this readily. It seemed strange to me that she was so willing to have suspicion cast on her relative. Odd, too, that she should betray no curiosity as to why he should be suspected.

"All I can say is, Jack Rowcliffe's the sort of young man who purrs in every woman's ear," she said. "Even in mine. It's just a bad habit he's got. I suppose there are women who fall for it."

"Have you noticed any particular woman lately?" asked Mme. Storey.

"Oh, no," said Mrs. Cruger. "There wouldn't be any now. This match means too much to him."

This answer still further confused me. Mme. Storey took it as a matter of course. I could see that, as usual, my mistress was not revealing her real objective in her questions.

"What sort of girl is Miss McPeake?" she asked carelessly.

Mrs. Cruger moved a delicate shoulder. "How can one really know a person of that sort? Her life is strange to me. She does not like us, but she strives to make a good impression. I think she has a bad temper," she added as an afterthought.

"Why do you think so?"

"Oh, I don't know. A certain twitch in her eye."

"Where is she now?"

"In her rooms. Wishes to keep out of all this. I cannot blame her for that."

"Of course not," said Mme. Storey. "You can do something to help me, if you will. Go to her, and without revealing your object, try to have her downstairs in half an hour."

Mrs. Cruger, with a curious docility, made as if to obey.

Mme. Storey glanced at her watch. "But not before half an hour, please," she said. "I need that time."

Mrs. Cruger, with a nod of understanding, left us. Mme. Storey glanced at me with smiling eyes. But I was all at sea.

"I can make nothing of her," I said helplessly.

"She's eager to help us," said Mme. Storey, "as long as we don't come anywhere near the truth."

6

MME. STOREY AND I sauntered out on the terrace overlooking the dazzling flower beds—too dazzling, too well ordered, like everything else about Cariswoode. The elegant young gentleman had disappeared, but out of the tail of my eye I caught a glimpse of him watching us from the far end of the terrace. Mme. Storey and I stood at the parapet looking down at the gorgeous chequered design.

"Like a review of flowers," murmured my mistress. "Poor little soldiers on parade!"

Presently at our ears we heard a dulcet male voice: "It reminds one of the grand finale at the Hippodrome, doesn't it?"

Mme. Storey turned with her most delightful seeming smile. "You must be Jack Rowcliffe," she said.

"You have actually heard of me," he murmured. "I am speechless with delight!"

I edged away a little, as I was clearly not expected to take part in this conversation. But there was nothing to prevent me from listening. The other two half sat against the parapet, and continued in the same strain. The foolish young man did not know, of course, that Mme. Storey was most dangerous when she appeared to be willing to philander.

"I had no hope of ever meeting you," he said. "I can't aspire to your circle. Too clever for me."

"It all depends on what you regard as cleverness," said Mme. Storey. "I should say you were quite clever enough for your own purposes."

"Oh, I'm just a humming-bird," he observed with a disarming air.

From time to time he cast a rather hard glance at me, as if to bid me take myself off. Lacking instructions from Mme. Storey, however, I stood my ground. My mistress presently made her wishes plain by introducing me in form. Rowcliffe bowed, and paid no further attention to me.

I studied him covertly. Jack Rowcliffe was at this time the premier young man about town. One could not read a society column without coming upon his name three or four times. It was always written first among the list of bachelors attending a function. One imagined the society reporters rolling it unctuously over their tongues. I had often tried to imagine what sort of young man would be produced by such a life. My instinct told me it was a horribly unnatural one, but if one was young and did not have much fun, one could not help being impressed. I suspect that Jack Rowcliffe figured in the day-dreams of many a girl who had not the remotest chance of ever meeting him in the flesh.

Well, he was uncommonly good looking, with thick, sleek, black hair, and glowing dark eyes a little too big for a man's. He was no tame cat, though; the rest of his features were heavy, and there was a dangerous masculine suggestion about him that, I suppose, constituted his charm for women. His manner was self-possessed to a degree, but I was startled to perceive deep in his eyes, a hint of terror and pain, which he no doubt believed was safely hidden. I felt that in him we were drawing close to the tragedy of Cariswoode.

After a while his sense of the fitness of things impelled him to say: "I suppose we shouldn't be talking like this—under the circumstances."

Mme. Storey shrugged. "Very distressing," she said. "But after all it's not our affair."

I thought I saw a twitch of pain in his face; but he instantly said, with his eyes fixed admiringly on Mme. Storey: "What a big woman you are! Able to be so honest!"

"Well, I feel that I can talk more plainly with you than with the others," Mme. Storey replied. "What is your theory?"

He shrugged, and spread out his palms. "What is yours?" he asked boldly.

Mme. Storey likewise spread her palms.

"Of course, you're not giving anything away," he remarked.

"Perhaps I have nothing to give," she said. "What sort of girl was she?"

This time I was sure I heard the hint of a stammer in his ready voice. "A devilish handsome girl. That's all I can tell you. Only saw her twice when she came in to tea. Then she kept herself very much to herself."

"If she was so handsome," murmured Mme. Storey, "one would suppose you'd try to know her better."

"Oh, I'm on my good behaviour," he answered with a disarming laugh; meanwhile his eyes were perfectly wretched.

Mme. Storey reminded me at this moment of a great surgeon delicately wielding a steel probe. "One thing that hampers me is that everything in the room was changed before I got here," she said. "Did you see it before it was changed?"

"Oh, no!" he cried, off his guard. "I never went near it!" Feeling that he had given too much away, he quickly added: "There's was no reason for me to butt in."

"I suppose not," said Mme. Storey. "Did you know that Miss Mayfield was not expected at the Hyatts' last night? Where do you suppose she was going?"

"Maybe there was a man in the case," he remarked bitterly.

"Why should she conceal it? She had as much right as any girl to her men friends."

"The old party is a jealous old party," he said. "Wouldn't tolerate that Louise should have any interest apart from hers."

"You are observant," murmured Mme. Storey.

He darted a glance of pure terror in her face. Mme. Storey's eyes were cast down.

At this moment we perceived a distinguished-looking trio approaching without haste along the terrace. Mrs. Cruger was in the middle, overtopping both the other women. They made a notable picture in their exquisite light dresses, designed in the perfection of simplicity that only the very rich can attain to; all three moved with the air of those born to command. When they came closer a difference appeared. Miss McPeake lacked the expression of serene repose that the faces of Mrs. Cruger and Miss de Guion wore; an expression that not only hid the trouble of their minds, but denied the very existence of any trouble.

Miss McPeake was more richly dressed than the other two. With all her smartness, she was far from being a pretty girl, and at present her face was drawn and sharp; her eyes frankly tormented. This torment, whatever had given rise to it, revealed a mean nature. There was a hateful jealousy in the way her eyes pounced on Rowcliffe, and then bored rudely into Mme. Storey's averted face. A shocking display there in that highly bred little company. Rowcliffe frowned and rubbed his perfect black moustache.

He made haste to carry off the uncomfortable situation. "Mme. Storey and I have been taking a moment's respite from the horror," he said with his admirably assumed straightforward air. "If we dwell on it exclusively, we'll simply go off our heads."

Like a thunderclap came the girl's cry: "You fool!"

It was significant of the strain we were all under that nobody looked at her after she cried out.

"You fool!" she repeated. "Do you suppose *she's* taking any respite from her work of prying and spying? That's what she's here for! She's been pumping you! I can see it! She's been turning you inside out for her own purposes, and you don't know it, you conceited fool!"

With that she turned and ran away into the house.

It was an ugly exhibition, but there was the deepest pain in the girl's cry, too. One could not but feel sorry for her; for all of them, poor blind creatures! Mrs. Cruger merely shrugged, and Miss de Guion murmured perfunctorily:

"Poor girl! She's quite overwrought!"

It was very clear that neither of these ladies gave a rap for Miss McPeake's feelings in the matter. A curious thing was that Rowcliffe looked absolutely astounded by Vera's outburst. Whatever his own anxieties may have been, one would have sworn he didn't know what his fiancée was up to.

"Better go after her," suggested Miss de Guion.

He hastened into the house.

"You will think we are all lunatics," murmured Miss de Guion, raising her pretty, plump, jewelled hands. The marvellous old lady had recovered her usual sang-froid. "It is the horrible suspense, the uncertainty. Why, even Bessie and I have been quarrelling bitterly all morning."

Mrs. Cruger cast a look of peculiar exasperation on her friend that I could not interpret.

"I believe lunch is ready," said Mrs. Cruger morosely. "But who wants any lunch?"

"My dear, you must eat something," urged Miss de Guion. "The governors of Upwey hospital meet this afternoon. I think you should be present just as if nothing had happened."

"You may think what you please," snapped Mrs. Cruger. "I'm not going!"

"But my dear—"

"That will do!" cried Mrs. Cruger, beside herself with exasperation. "I—" She checked herself with an effort.

The masterful old lady was not to be easily put down. She shrugged elaborately.

Mme. Storey and I left them on the terrace.

7

As we were returning through the silent, thickly carpeted corridor, from one of the rooms on our right came a sound that sharply arrested our thoughts. It was the sound of a poignant whispering; two voices; a reproachful woman's; an angry man's. A whole drama was summed up in it. We could distinguish no word nor see the persons in the room, but we knew the speakers could be none other than Vera McPeake and Rowcliffe.

"Should we not listen?" I whispered.

Mme. Storey drew me on. Her lips shaped the words: "It is not necessary."

The room we were passing had a door towards either end. As we approached the second door, a few words did reach us. We heard the man's angry whisper: "I'm through! I'm through!" and we heard the woman repeat imploringly: "Jack! *Jack!*"

Mme. Storey's gesture signified: "That's all there is to it!"

Events followed fast after that. Upon returning to the little office we found a sealed envelope lying on the desk with Mme. Storey's name scrawled upon it. Upon opening it, my mistress read the letter it contained, and handed it over to me without comment. I read the headlong phrases in astonishment.

> Dear Mme. Storey:
> I cannot keep silent any longer. You're on the wrong track. That girl was not the sweet, pure soul they would have you to suppose. That was just a blind to cover her schemes. I saw through her immediately. She was perfectly *unscrupulous*. She was just a servant, anyway. She was determined to get on, and if she couldn't get on, she meant to make as much trouble for others as she could. That was the kind she was. *Perfectly rotten* under her sweet and dignified airs. It was through men that she worked her schemes. All men were the same to her. She knew how to get them going without appearing to. Whatever happened to her, she *richly deserved it*. A word to the wise is sufficient.
>
> Vera McPeake.

There was a knock on the door. I handed the letter back to Mme. Storey, who slipped it under the pad on the desk. Rowcliffe came in. There was a startling alteration in him. The gallant philandering air had given place to a hangdog look. His eyes were lowered; his chin was on his breast. One instantly liked the man better. This at least was honest.

"I want to speak to you a moment," he mumbled.

"Sit down," said Mme. Storey. "Have a cigarette."

He waved it away. "Can I speak to you alone?" he inquired significantly.

"Miss Brickley is present at all interviews," said Mme. Storey. "It is my rule. You can depend upon it, it would not be so, unless I had absolute confidence in her."

"Makes it harder," he muttered.

There was a silence, for Mme. Storey made no further move to help him out. I was trembling a little with excitement at the prospect of the confession I expected to hear.

"I suppose you suspect me," he began. "It's natural after the way I tried to conceal things from you—foolish, I suppose. But I couldn't help it—oh God! I couldn't bear to expose my heart before everybody! Nobody thinks I can feel anything—I've been through hell today! I can't stand it any longer. At any rate I've just broken it off with Vera. That's something. I've taken a horror of her—"

He fell silent. Mme. Storey presently said: "That is not what you came to tell me."

"No," he answered very low. He was leaning forward in his chair with his arms resting on his knees and his head down "I was lying when I said that Louise was nothing to me. I—I cared for her very much. Oh, I loved her with all my heart! I had seen her before she came up here. Many times. Whenever I went to Miss de Guion's. The first time I saw her she was just another beautiful girl to me. I made up my mind to have her. I thought I had only to make up my mind. But she laughed at me! Perfectly willing to be friends—but nothing doing. Ah! what a laugh she had! I had to laugh with her, though it was at my own expense—I lost my head completely. I adored her. She understood me through and through. I could be honest with her. She was charitable to my faults—but nothing more.

When I told her she was driving me mad, she said she was sorry, but I was simply paying the price for the others. And she was right!

"When she came up here on Sunday it was simply more than I could bear—living under the same roof with her. She kept out of my way. Finally I made up my mind to ask her to marry me. I have no money, but—but we could have made out somehow. I knew she didn't love me, but I thought if it was a case of saving me from damnation, she might—she might— She was so kind! But I never got a chance to ask her. This thing happened. And now it's too late— too late!"

There was a long silence, broken only by his stifled sobbing. To see a man break down like that is too dreadful. I heartily wished myself away from there.

As Mme. Storey made no comment, he finally raised his head. "That is all," he said. "Did you expect something more?"

She shrugged.

"You surely can't think that *I*—" he began, aghast. "Why I—I adored her. It was a *good* feeling, the best I ever had. I would have cut off my hand to serve her! Oh, you're wrong, you're wrong!"

"I am not accusing you of anything," said Mme. Storey mildly.

He presently got up, and made his way heavily towards the door. When he opened it I caught a glimpse of Vera McPeake waiting close outside. Her face was transfigured with hatred and jealousy. She could not have heard what Rowcliffe was telling us, but she must have guessed its purport. The door closed.

Mme. Storey and I exchanged a glance. "Do you believe him?" I asked.

"As far as he went."

"But in that case we are exactly where we were when we started!"

"Oh, I wouldn't say that," she said.

In a few minutes there came another knock on the door, and Rowcliffe entered once more. His face was now as white as paper, his eyes so wildly distraught it was impossible to tell what feeling had given rise to it, whether grief or terror or both. There was simply no sense in his eyes.

"I—I just wanted to ask you—to forget what I said just now," he stammered. "I mean about Vera—Miss McPeake. I must have been out of my senses. We are still engaged, of course. I beg of you—oh, what must you think of me! Well, it doesn't matter, does it?" He turned abruptly and went out.

"I suppose Vera waylaid him outside," suggested Mme. Storey.

"Yes, I saw her," said I.

"Poor wretch!" murmured Mme. Storey. "He is paying!"

8

BRACKER, THE PRINCELY CHAUFFEUR, upon Mme. Storey's invitation, seated himself gracefully. Being a chauffeur, he was entirely at his ease. Perfect men of the world, the chauffeurs of the rich; I wonder it is not dangerous to have them around, they show up to such advantage.

"I won't keep you but a moment," said Mme. Storey deprecatingly.

He took it as a matter of course, which caused me an inward chuckle.

"I understand from Miss de Guion," my mistress went on, "that on your way back from Ridgefield early this morning, you had a stoppage."

"Yes, madam, the tank went dry."

"How did that happen?"

"I'm hanged if I know, madam. We had plenty of gas when we started."

"You think you had."

"I looked."

"Gasolene gauges are so untrustworthy."

"I know they are. So I unscrewed the cap and measured with a stick that I keep for the purpose. There was a good ten gallons."

"And you get?"

"Seven miles to the gallon, madam."

"Then six gallons should have taken you to Ridgefield and back?"

"Easily."

"Perhaps you had a leak."

"No, madam. She was tight, and is still tight."

"How about your speedometer?" asked Mme. Storey.

"I get you," he said with a quick look. "As to the total mileage I can't tell you; you lose track running around. But I set the trip dial every morning in order to keep tab on the gas. When we got home this morning it registered sixty-nine miles. Just what I drove her yesterday."

"But by pulling out a stem anybody can set the trip dial either forward or back?"

"Certainly. But if it's your idea that somebody used the car, I must tell you I have my own way of preventing that."

"Any objection to telling me what it is?"

"Not at all. It's just a hidden switch I installed, back of the main switch under the cowl."

"You left your car, I suppose, while the party was going on?"

"Yes, madam. I locked the body of the car, and went up to Mrs. Van Brocklin's chauffeur's rooms. He was having a sort of party, too. There was a lot of us there."

"Where were the cars parked?"

"Most of them were in a large yard or enclosure at the side of the house, but Mrs. Cruger told me to leave ours out in front, as she would wish to leave early. So I left it in the drive, a few yards short of the front door. It is expected that Mrs. Cruger's car should take the best place."

"Were there other cars in front?"

"Yes, madam. Two or three behind ours."

Mme. Storey tapped reflectively on the desk. "Are you and Mr. Rowcliffe friendly?" she asked suddenly.

"Why, yes, madam," he said, surprised. "Mr. Rowcliffe's keen on cars. An A1 chauffeur and mechanician too. Only last night he rode outside with me so's he could smoke, and we talked."

"Did you happen to mention the chauffeur's party to him?"

"Yes, madam. I mind saying that while he was having his time, we were going to have a time, too. Only there wouldn't be any girls at our party."

"And did you tell him about your patent switch?"

Bracker suddenly clapped his hand to his forehead. "He knew, he knew!" he said excitedly. "Why, we had worked on the car together!"

"And there is just about six gallons of gas to be accounted for?"

"Yes, madam—but surely you don't think—"

Mme. Storey rose. "I don't think anything, Bracker," she said. "I recommend the same course to you."

"Yes, madam. You can depend on me to keep my mouth shut. But—but—"

"That's all just now, thank you."

He made his way towards the door with a dazed air. "Mr. Rowcliffe—oh, my God!" I heard him mutter.

9

IT WAS AN ILL-BALANCED COMPANY that sat down to dinner at Cariswoode that night; five women and one man. I understood that guests had been expected, but the invitations had been quietly recalled. Though that poor girl's body was still lying somewhere upstairs, everybody dressed as a matter of course. During the afternoon Mme. Storey had telephoned to New York for her maid to bring up evening gowns for herself and for me. In her large way she took it for granted that I was to be received on the footing of a guest. It would have been all one to me either way.

Mme. Storey's dress, with a bit of pinning, did me very well. Her maid put up my stubborn red hair in a cunning and effective fashion. I knew it was effective, because it won a glance from even so experienced a connoisseur as Mr. Rowcliffe. I felt monstrously naked as I came downstairs, but I knew I had a pretty neck and arms, and that helped me to endure it.

While we were dressing in our respective rooms, Crider had made a report to Mme. Storey, but that I did not learn until later.

In the dining-room everybody was on parade. The table had been made small enough to bring us close together. It was a point of pride with all not to give the slightest sign of what was passing in every mind. Rather absurd to take such pains to be unnatural; but such was their code, and you could not but admire the gallantry with which they maintained it. Particularly Rowcliffe, who was quite astonishingly witty and engaging, though his eyes still had the dreadful look in their depths.

Only Miss McPeake lacked the requisite gameness to play up to him. Her face was pinched and haggard; she almost never spoke, and made the merest pretence of eating. The one who betrayed most in her face was the least interesting to watch. It was thrilling to speculate as to what was going on behind the smooth and smiling faces. With all the easy talk and laughter you felt that each one was encased in an armour of glass.

Mme. Storey looked positively glorious in a severe velvet gown of a curious shade of cold red, with no ornaments in her dark hair. For reasons of her own she chose to create a simple and stately effect tonight. The peerless Mrs. Cruger, in pale blue, looked like ah exhausted doll beside her. Miss de Guion was all a-shimmer in white and silver. Her complexion glowed, her eyes sparkled, she continually showed her white teeth; she looked ageless. An astonishing woman! It was she, principally, who, with Rowcliffe, kept the conversational shuttle-cock flying back and forth. Mme. Storey put herself forth very little. Her cue was to encourage the others. Rather a cruel pastime, but necessary.

Glasgow directed the serving of the meal from the sideboard, and there were two footmen to wait upon us like marvellous automata. Very handsome young men. The meal passed like a dream for me. I could never remember what we ate; one dish followed another, with a succession of wines which were taken as a matter of course. In that house it was not considered necessary to speak of where they came from.

When the meal at last drew to a close, Mrs. Cruger said: "I suppose you don't want to sit here alone, Jack."

"God forbid!" he answered.

"Then we'll have coffee in the lounge," said Mrs. Cruger. "It's cooler there."

The "lounge" was an immense room which made a great bow at the end of the west wing. The round part had a glass roof which was raised, and there was a whole semi-circle of open windows, so that we were almost outdoors. The open-air effect was heightened by quantities of growing plants and ferns. The furniture was of painted rattan with gay covers. We sank into insidiously comfortable chairs placed roughly in a circle. Presently a softly stepping footman placed coffee on stands convenient to the hand, and his mate followed him trundling a sort of wheeled tray bearing a dozen varieties of liqueurs. Glasgow hovered in the background. A delicious scented breath was wafted through the windows. The place was dimly lighted by shaded lamps along the back wall.

"Rather spooky, don't you think?" remarked Mme. Storey lightly.

"More light, Glasgow," murmured Mrs. Cruger.

He switched on a central dome which flooded the place with brilliancy. My heart beat a little faster, for I guessed what the light was required for.

When the servants had gone, Mme. Storey said quietly: "It is too bad to break the pleasant spell, but I think we ought to go into committee of the whole upon this matter."

One seemed to feel the shudder that all those well controlled people hid from view.

"Close the door, Jack," murmured Mrs. Cruger.

He came back from doing so, and dropped heavily into his chair. A wretched silence fell on us all.

"This is awful!" Rowcliffe cried at last. "Can't you tell us plainly where we stand?"

"I'm sorry," said Mme. Storey deprecatingly, "but you must tell me. I must question you and piece things together."

"Do you mean to say that the explanation is to be had from anybody here?" demanded Mrs. Cruger, sitting up straight.

Mme. Storey spread out her hands.

Again that silence. Rowcliffe was breathing audibly. He furtively dabbed his face with his handkerchief. Mrs. Cruger and Miss de Guion still wore masks of composure, but the strong light was cruel, and revealed that they were masks. Miss McPeake half turned in her chair, hiding her face from the others.

"Have you your note-book, Bella?" asked Mme. Storey.

I had it, and I produced it.

This act electrified them all. The code was broken, and they were outraged.

"I say!" cried Rowcliffe.

"Must we submit to be catechised here, and our answers written down?" Mrs. Cruger demanded toweringly.

"I'm sorry," said Mme. Storey. "I know just how you feel. But consider my position for a moment. I am acting the part of a bad citizen in consenting to keep this matter from the authorities for twenty-four hours. How else could I square myself with my duty but by keeping an exact record of everything that happened, to turn over to them later if necessary?"

Nobody could gainsay this. They relapsed into a sullen silence.

"Mr. Rowcliffe," began Mme. Storey, quite unimpressed by their hostile attitude, "did you leave the dance for a period last night?"

"Certainly not!" he answered indignantly.

Mme. Storey raised her eyebrows. "Why shouldn't you, if you felt like it?" she murmured.

"No reason," he said. "But I didn't, that's all."

"Mrs. Cruger," said Mme. Storey, "can you assure me that Mr. Rowcliffe was present throughout the dance?"

"Mercy!" drawled Mrs. Cruger. "How can I tell? I danced with him a couple of times."

"When, please?"

"Once when we first went in, and again, later."

"Much later?"

"No doubt."

"Miss de Guion," said Mme. Storey, "can you assure me that Mr. Rowcliffe was present throughout?"

The old lady had herself better in hand than her friend. "I can assure you of nothing," she replied calmly. "Everybody was coming and going. In a crowd you do not think of people unless you see them."

Mme. Storey returned to Mrs. Cruger. "Be frank with me," she said. "Is it not a fact that you and Miss de Guion remarked together on Mr. Rowcliffe's absence?"

This question was cunningly calculated. Mrs. Cruger was a proud woman, and could not bear to stoop to compound a lie with another.

She underwent a sudden change of front. "Yes, we did," she said. "You angered me for the moment. I am sorry. Hereafter I will be perfectly frank with you. Let's get this over with as quickly as possible."

"Thank you," said Mme. Storey.

I saw Miss de Guion shrug almost imperceptibly. She seemed to say: If Bessie wants the truth to be told it's all one to me. The experienced old lady could express all that in the cock of an eyebrow.

"Of course the fact that we did not see him is not to say that he was not somewhere about," Mrs. Cruger pointed out.

"Of course not," agreed Mme. Storey.

Miss McPeake suddenly blurted out: "Why don't you ask me if he was present throughout? I can assure you that he was; because I was with him the whole time."

Rowcliffe cast a glance of terror in his fiancée's direction. Clearly he dreaded support from this ill-balanced quarter.

"Ah, thanks," said Mme. Storey to the girl. "Where were you?"

"The dance was tiresome," answered Vera. "We went outside and walked about."

"For two whole hours?"

"I didn't say for how long," cried the girl sharply. "I don't know how long it was. Most of the time we were sitting in the car."

"Mrs. Cruger's car?"

"Of course."

"On the back seat?"

"Naturally. Where else?"

"The body of the car was locked," murmured Mme. Storey.

The girl's jaw dropped. She gazed at Mme. Storey in a sickly consternation that gave everything away.

Rowcliffe tried to save the situation by saying quickly: "That was only a slip of the tongue. We were sitting on the front seat, of course."

"And you went for a drive?" suggested Mme. Storey.

He glanced at her sharply. "Well, yes, we did," he said. "Any harm in that?"

"None whatever. Quite a long drive?"

"Oh, I don't know. I can hardly say."

"Forty miles?" suggested Mme. Storey.

"What makes you set that figure?"

"Six gallons of gas to be accounted for," she said softly.

"It may have been."

"Why did you turn back the trip dial of the speedometer when you returned?"

Rowcliffe bit his lip. "That was just to put one across on Bracker," he muttered. "He's so cranky about anybody else running that car."

"Then you must know to a mile how far you went?"

"Forty-one miles," said Rowcliffe sullenly.

"Too bad you didn't fill up the tank," suggested Mme. Storey.

"Well, I didn't happen to notice a filling station, and I forgot," he said.

"You had other things on your mind," suggested Mme. Storey.

"Yes," he answered thoughtlessly.

"And that was why you went away by yourself to think?"

"Yes," he said—and gasped seeing how he had been trapped.

Vera sneered painfully.

"So Miss McPeake was *not* with you," murmured Mme. Storey.

He shrugged. Exasperation was rapidly rendering him quite reckless.

"Where was she?"

"Ask her."

"Where were you, Miss McPeake?"

"I refuse to answer!" she cried shrilly.

Mme. Storey let that go for the moment. "You drove back to Cariswoode," she said to Rowcliffe.

"Yes, I did!" he cried.

Mrs. Cruger and Miss de Guion stared, pure amazement breaking through their masks. Evidently, though all these people were playing some game, it was not by any means the same game.

"Why?" breathed Mme. Storey.

"I'll tell you!" he cried, now quite beside himself. "Louise had told me she would be back at half past ten. I had asked her to meet me outside the house for five minutes, and I would find some way of stealing home from the dance. At first she refused, but I told her I would do something desperate if she did not come, and at last she promised to meet me at the little fountain in the center of the rose garden at quarter to eleven. That is why I came back!"

Vera McPeake spread her arms on the arm of her chair, and dropping her head upon them, broke into a hard, dry sobbing. One could not feel very sorry for her, because there was at least as much of rage as of grief in the sound.

"Well?" prompted Mme. Storey.

"She didn't come," he said, relapsing into sullenness again. "I waited half an hour, and then I drove back. I was afraid to wait any longer, for fear the car would be wanted."

Vera McPeake suddenly raised her head. "That's true!" she cried. "I was watching him, and I saw. He waited for half an hour, then he drove back."

We all looked at her. It was only too apparent from the terror in her voice that what she asserted was *not* true.

"You were watching him?" said Mme. Storey mildly.

"Yes, I was!" she cried. "I don't care what you think. I was watching him all the time. I had a right to watch him. I followed him out of the Van Brocklin house. I saw him get in the car and drive away. I jumped into the next car. I don't know whose car it was. It wasn't locked. I followed him. When he turned into the main drive at Cariswoode I turned into the service drive, and left the car standing there. I watched him from the shrubbery."

Mme. Storey turned back to Rowcliffe. "So you did not do any-thing desperate," she said.

"Oh, I hadn't meant that," he said.

"As a matter of fact," said Mme. Storey with a deadly quiet-ness, "when she did not come you climbed up to her window."

Rowcliffe jumped up with a cry, flinging his arms up. "If you know it already, why is it necessary to sit there and torture me?"

"I did not know it," said Mme. Storey. "You are telling me."

"All right!" he cried recklessly. "It's true! I *was* desperate. I stood under her window. I saw the rain pipe. I kicked off my pumps and scrambled up it without caring what I did. Make what you like of it!"

"He was only inside a few seconds—a few seconds!" Vera McPeake cried hysterically.

Rowcliffe turned on her furiously. "Ah, be quiet, you fool! You want it both ways, don't you?" He turned back to us. "I didn't know until today that Vera had been watching me. She held me up out-side the office when I came out, and threatened to tell you I had killed Louise if I tried to break the engagement. Well, you know the worst now. Everybody knows. And, thank God, this fool has no further hold over me. I'm done with her!"

"Oh, Jack! Oh, Jack! Oh, Jack!" the girl wailed. It was horrible to be a looker-on at such a scene.

"You climbed up to her window?" Mme. Storey quietly per-sisted.

He seemed to be bewitched now by the necessity of telling everything. "Yes," he said. "I raised the screen and went over the sill. I groped my way across the room. I stumbled over her body. Oh, my God! I put my hand down and felt of her face, her hands. Stone cold! I was terrified out of my senses. I got out—"

"You were satisfied she was dead, merely by touching her?" asked Mme. Storey.

"No," he said, still anxious to be explicit. "I dared not turn on the light, but I struck a match. That gave me light enough to see that she was dead. I didn't know what had happened. I couldn't think. But it was very clear that she was gone—gone! I was half out of my senses. I just got out."

"Did you notice a smell in the room?" asked Mme. Storey.

"Yes, violets," he answered. "I associated it with her."

"Why did you close the window when you went out?"

"I can't tell you. Some notion of guarding her. I didn't know what I was doing."

"You struck a match. You had one long look at her while it burned?"

He covered his face with his hands. "Yes," he whispered.

Mme. Storey rose. "Then give me what you took from her outstretched hand," she said.

Rowcliffe's hands dropped from his face. He stared at Mme. Storey in amazed horror. His eyes seemed to protrude slightly.

"How—how could you know that!" he gasped.

"The handkerchief," said Mme. Storey.

Rowcliffe, dazed, slipped a hand in his inner breast pocket, and drew it out again with a scrap of lace in his fingers. It was extraordinary to see even in his distraught condition how tenderly he fingered it. He took a couple of stiff, jerky steps forward, and let it drop into Mme. Storey's outstretched hand.

"How did you know?" he whispered again, awe-struck.

"There is no magic in it," said Mme. Storey simply. "I could not account for its disappearance in any other way."

"Well, you have it," he said apathetically. "You won't believe me, I suppose, but I took it simply because it had been close to her. I couldn't think; I had such a pain in my breast I couldn't breathe. I snatched it up because it had been near her. I knew I couldn't even grieve for her openly. I wanted some scrap of hers that I could keep in secret. Now, I suppose you'll hang me, eh? Another triumph for the great Rosika Storey. But I swear I've told you everything I know. I loved her. I would gladly have died myself, sooner than have a hair of her head injured."

"I don't expect to hang you," said Mme. Storey quietly. "All I wanted was the handkerchief, which is necessary to my case."

10

JACK ROWCLIFFE dropped back in his chair. Having delivered himself of his passionate confession, he was apathetic to what immediately followed. But the three women sitting up stiffly, were staring at the handkerchief with astonishment and expressions of growing horror. Mme. Storey was holding it up by two corners, revealing it wholly. One would have said that they beheld a dreadful apparition.

"An exquisite specimen," murmured Mme. Storey. "I have
rarely seen anything finer. Almost a museum piece."

No sound escaped from any of the others.

"I must tell you," Mme. Storey said, "that this handkerchief
came through the mail addressed to Miss Mayfield in a disguised
hand. It was handed to her just before she died. The inference is
therefore inescapable that it had something to do with her death,
but there is no proof of that. The chemists must pass upon it."

Still no sound from the spellbound women.

"Tell me," Mme. Storey said to Rowcliffe, "have you put this
handkerchief to your face at any time?"

"Yes," he said bitterly. "It didn't do me any harm."

"According to the report of my agent," Mme. Storey went on,
"the envelope originated here at Cariswoode."

She paused. The women's stony eyes shifted to her face.

"It was collected at the bottom of the slide in the White Plains
post office among a number of letters mailed by you three ladies
yesterday afternoon. Miss de Guion, you told me, you remember,
that you went in together—"

Every word she uttered tightened the screws of suspense. The
pauses were most dreadful.

"Mrs. Cruger, did anybody give you letters to post?"

"No," whispered Mrs. Cruger.

"Miss de Guion?"

"No."

"Miss McPeake?"

"No."

"Then each of you posted your own letters. Mrs. Cruger, have you ever seen this handkerchief before?"

Mrs. Cruger, white to the lips, slowly shook her head.

"Miss de Guion, you?"

"No," said the old lady calmly.

"Miss McPeake?"

"No!" This negative had a defiant ring.

"Mrs. Cruger, may I ring for Glasgow?"

"As you will," murmured that lady.

When the benignant butler entered, Mme. Storey said: "Glasgow, will you please have Mrs. Cruger's own maid, Miss McPeake's maid, and Miss de Guion's maid sent into us one at a time."

No one presumed to object to this high-handed order. Glasgow retired. During the wait no one moved nor spoke. It was shattering to the nerves. Miss McPeake had quieted down. Her quick, small eyes travelled from one to another of us, sparkling with hatred, jealousy, suspicion. Her emotions were as violent and ephemeral as a fire in straw. Clearly a nature with ugly and dangerous potentialities.

The first to be shown in was a fresh-faced girl with a pleasant expression. She wore a neat working dress and plain apron.

"My maid, Agnes," Mrs. Cruger said in a dead voice.

Mme. Storey held up the handkerchief. "Agnes, have you ever seen this handkerchief before?"

After a brief examination the girl answered: "Not that I know of, madam." Her glance was as open as the morning.

"Thank you," said Mme. Storey, and Agnes retired with a wondering air.

The next was an extremely respectable middle-aged woman, who clearly set a high value on herself. Miss de Guion introduced her with a wave of the hand as "Catharine."

Mme. Storey put the same question to her.

She was more careful before committing herself. "No, madam," she said after a close examination. She retired with a perfectly self-possessed air.

The third was a French maid who might have stepped direct from the stage of a musical comedy; coquettish cap, carmined lips, short skirt and lace-edged apron. Upon being asked the usual question, she looked confused, bit her lip, answered "No," at a venture, and glanced at her mistress.

"Speak the truth, Cécile," said Vera McPeake with a sneer.

The girl then said, in excellent English, with a pert air: "I think it is one of a set belonging to Miss McPeake. There are six of them."

"Thank you," said Mme. Storey, and Cécile retired with visible reluctance.

Vera McPeake, shuffling the bracelets on her arm, said at once, defiantly: "It is, or was, one of mine."

"Why did you not say so at once?" asked Mme. Storey mildly.

With a flirt of her head she answered: "Oh, I didn't want to get anybody into trouble."

We stared at what appeared to be her unparalleled impudence.

"It's nothing to me," she went on. "I gave that handkerchief to Mrs. Cruger yesterday morning. She had admired it."

This statement threw the little circle into a fresh consternation. Rowcliffe had come out of his apathy. Vera enjoyed her moment of triumph. Mrs. Cruger got to her feet, struggling for speech. A bright red spot began to burn in either of her thin cheeks.

"How—how dare you?" she stammered.

"Didn't I give it to you—didn't I—didn't I?" the girl stridently demanded.

"You did," said Mrs. Cruger. "But do you dare suggest that I—"

"Pooh! And why not you as well as any of us? Who are you to hold yourself so high? I'm sick of your airs!"

"Be quiet!" said Mrs. Cruger haughtily.

"I shan't! I shan't!" cried the girl, beside herself. "What do I care for any of you now? You all hate me. You only pretended to be decent to me because I was rich. You laughed at me behind my back—"

"What possible reason had I for wishing the girl harm?" demanded Mrs. Cruger.

"How do we know what reasons you had? Perhaps you had a fancy for Jack yourself!"

"Preposterous!" cried Mrs. Cruger and Rowcliffe simultaneously.

"Oh, I don't know," sneered Vera. "There are funny things going on in this house. I thank God I come of common, simple, honest people!"

Mrs. Cruger came down off her high horse. Her face flushed all over; she was just the angry woman like Vera, though in a better style. "I had no reason for harming the girl," she cried. "But *you had!* You hated her. Any fool could see through this attempt to throw dust in our eyes. You have convicted yourself out of your own mouth."

"Certainly I hated her," retorted Vera. "I'm not grieving over her death. But, as it happens, I had no hand in it. That is the handkerchief I gave you."

"You have no proof it is the same one!"

"Then produce the one I gave you."

Mrs. Cruger's manner became faltering.

"Can you produce it?" murmured Mme. Storey.

"It was stolen from me," she said with a helpless gesture.

"Old stuff!" cried Vera with a fleering laugh.

The sound stimulated Mrs. Cruger's anger afresh. "Still she has not proved that is the handkerchief she gave me," she insisted. "She has a number of them."

"I can prove it all right," cried Vera. "I had six. The other five are still in my possession. Send for them!"

"How do I know you only had six? You may have had seven or eight or a whole trunkful!"

"I can prove that, too. They were sold to me by Benitos Brothers. They are unique. Their history is known. It can be easily proved that there are no more than six anywhere."

"Then you gave it to me simply for the purpose of stealing it back again!" cried Mrs. Cruger.

"You know that's not so! When I left the room you had it in your hand. 'Thank you so much,' you said, as I went out of the door. I have not been anywhere near your room since. That can be proved by your maid and mine. When your maid leaves your suite empty, she locks the door after her, doesn't she?"

"Yes," said Mrs. Cruger with a disagreeable smile. "How did you happen to know that?"

"Oh, it's the usual custom," said Vera with a shrug.

Mrs. Cruger's head went down. Her finer nature was at a disadvantage with the termagant, and it was impossible not to feel sorry for her. At the same time there was a suggestion of terror in her attitude that needed to be explained. From the first she had been too anxious to have it all hushed up.

"How about your maid, Bessie?" Miss de Guion asked her with a compassionate air.

"I trust her," Mrs. Cruger said piteously. "You all saw her just now. Such a simple girl. How is it possible she could look like that if she knew anything?"

"Where did you put the handkerchief?" asked Mme. Storey.

"In a drawer of my dressing-table."

"Locked?"

"No."

"When did you discover the loss of it?"

"When we were ready to start last evening and it occurred to me I would like to carry it. It was gone then."

"Had you looked at it during the day?"

"No."

"Have you any reason to suspect anybody?"

"Oh, no, no, no!" Mrs. Cruger, all but wringing her hands, dropped into her chair.

"Well, without suspecting anybody, let us go over the possibilities," suggested Mme. Storey soothingly. "Who may have been in your room?"

"The housemaids, of course, but only when Agnes is there. Agnes is responsible for my things."

"Well, what persons were in your room when you were there yourself?"

Mrs. Cruger did not answer. Her head slowly went down again.

In the silence that followed, it was inevitable that our thoughts should turn to the remaining one of the trio, and our eyes followed our thoughts. Miss de Guion was sitting easily in her chair, with her eyes fixed solicitously on Mrs. Cruger's distressed face. She became aware of our glances with a start.

"Good heavens!" she cried. "You're all looking at me!"

Nobody spoke. Her eyes travelled from face to face, aghast. "You think that *I*—" she stammered.

"Oh, surely it cannot be necessary for me to defend myself against the suspicion of having harmed my own dear girl!" The old lady's bosom began to heave. "The nearest thing to a daughter I ever possessed! Why, she lies there now in the pretty dress I designed for her myself with so much care! Oh, this is too much! After all I've been through today! Is not her loss enough for me to bear without—without—"

She seemed to be at the point of breaking down altogether.

This struck me as a little bit overdone, for, as a matter of fact, Miss de Guion had had herself well in hand since morning. But there! everybody was overwrought and hysterical. The long-drawn-out scene had demoralised us.

"Perhaps you don't believe in my affection for her," Miss de Guion went on. "You think I'm hard and unfeeling. Oh, I know what people say about me—just because I don't wear my heart on my sleeve! Well, leaving all affection aside, I *depended* on her. You must believe that! I am getting to the age when I want to take things easily. And I should trust everything to her. It is impossible for me to replace her. Is it likely that I—that I—"

"Nobody is accusing you," put in Mme. Storey gently.

"Your silences, your eyes accuse me!"

"Let us put aside all thought of accusations," said Mme. Storey soothingly. "The true facts must speak for themselves in the end. You were present when Miss McPeake presented the handkerchief to Mrs. Cruger?"

"Yes," said Miss de Guion with her handkerchief to her eyes.

"You remained on in Mrs. Cruger's room after Miss McPeake had gone?"

"Yes."

"You saw Mrs. Cruger put it away in the drawer?"

"Yes, yes, yes! What does that prove?"

"Nothing. Did anybody else know the handkerchief was in that drawer?"

Mrs. Cruger intervened here. "Agnes knew. She had heard us talking about it, though she had had no opportunity to look at it. She saw me put it away."

"Leaving Agnes out of it for the moment," said Mme. Storey, "what were you and Mrs. Cruger doing after Miss McPeake left?"

"Sitting there, smoking, talking," said Miss de Guion.

"This was in Mrs. Cruger's dressing-room?"

"Yes."

"How is that placed in respect to the other rooms of her suite?"

"The bedroom is on one side of it, the boudoir on the other."

"Was Mrs. Cruger in the room with you all the time?" asked Mme. Storey softly.

"I suppose so," said Miss de Guion. "I can't remember."

"Mrs. Cruger?"

"I can't remember," the blonde lady stammered wretchedly.

"Oh, assume that she and Agnes both passed to and fro between the rooms," put in Miss de Guion impatiently. "Does that prove that I took the handkerchief?"

"Certainly not—if we can show that any one else *could* have taken it," said Mme. Storey.

Miss de Guion sat forward in her chair. "I'll tell you who could have taken it!" she cried with a furious glance at the sneering Vera. "The only one who had any interest in harming my poor girl! That woman!" She pointed with a dramatic forefinger.

Vera laughed in her face.

"But how?" asked Mme. Storey.

"Through her maid, Cécile. You all saw the girl, a shifty, lying jade! She's always running after Agnes. Bessie has spoken to me about it. A most unfortunate influence on the girl. We no sooner come downstairs than Cécile goes running to Agnes in Bessie's rooms. What more likely than that she was there while we were lunching yesterday?"

"That won't hold water!" said Vera contemptuously. "I didn't know where the handkerchief had been put, and certainly Cécile didn't know."

"Agnes may have told her innocently," suggested Miss de Guion.

"We'll ask her," said Mme. Storey.

Glasgow, who had previously been sent up to Miss McPeake's room to obtain the remaining handkerchiefs of the set, now brought them in. He was dispatched for Agnes.

The five neatly folded squares of lace were laid on the little stand at Mme. Storey's elbow. She still had the first handkerchief in her hand.

"With your permission," she said to Vera, "I will keep them all for the present. To guard against any possibility of mistake I will mark the one returned to me by Mr. Rowcliffe. I want you all to watch me do it." She borrowed my pencil from me. "See, two pencil dots in the corner."

Everybody regarded the dainty fabric with awe and horror.

The pleasant-faced girl entered the room, somewhat scared by the second summons.

"Agnes," said Mme. Storey, "I want you to think back and tell me what happened yesterday. When Mrs. Cruger went downstairs to lunch you remained in her room?"

"Yes, madam."

"Did anybody come there?"

"Only Miss McPeake's maid, Cécile," she answered readily.

Miss de Guion glanced triumphantly at Vera.

"Had she come before?"

"Oh, yes, madam. She was always coming in. I couldn't very well refuse her, being Miss McPeake's maid. I told Mrs. Cruger about it."

"Was anything said yesterday about a handkerchief that Miss McPeake had given to Mrs. Cruger?"

"Yes, madam. I mentioned it."

"What did Cécile say?"

"She said: 'Let's have a look at it.'"

"And did you show it to her?"

"Oh, no, madam. It had been put away."

"Did you tell her where it had been put?"

"No, madam. But I may have looked towards the place, unthinking."

"And did you leave the room afterwards?"

"I was in and out, putting away the things. I didn't think I had to watch her, being as she was Miss McPeake's own maid."

"All right," said Mme. Storey. "That's all, thank you."

The instant the door closed behind Agnes, Miss de Guion cried out: "Now you see which way the wind lies!"

Vera laughed. "Nothing in it," she retorted. "That girl is too simple by half! Besides, if I was up to any games I would not take my maid into my confidence!"

They wrangled unpleasantly back and forth.

Mme. Storey rose. "This is getting us nowhere," she said. "The truth is bound to appear tomorrow. I will ask you all to meet me at ten o'clock in the office that Mrs. Cruger has placed at my disposal."

To me this seemed like a reckless move. I could not but feel that the hours of the night would give the real culprit time to destroy true evidence and concoct false. But Mme. Storey knew exactly what she was about, of course.

11

CRIDER WAS WAITING in the office.

"I assume that you have carried out your instructions?" said Mme. Storey.

"Yes, madam. I have three men posted about the house. Should anybody attempt to leave it during the night, he will be detained, while you are communicated with."

"Good! I want you to watch what I am going to do next, so that you can be called upon to testify regarding it. Lock the door, Bella."

I obeyed.

Mme. Storey sat down at the desk. "I have here the marked handkerchief handed me by Rowcliffe," she said. "Observe that I add two additional dots in the corner, making four in all. This handkerchief remains in my possession."

"Be careful!" I said involuntarily.

"In itself it is harmless," she said.

I looked at her, uncomprehending.

"I mean to use four of the remaining handkerchiefs," she went on. "Watch now. I put the two dots in the corner of each one. Next I would like to have them soiled a little bit—not too much."

We looked around the room for some means of accomplishing this. There was a fire-place.

"Scrape a little soot or grime out of the chimney with a bit of pasteboard, and dust each handkerchief lightly," said Mme. Storey. "Make them look exactly alike."

Crider and I did this together. Afterwards Mme. Storey folded and crumpled the handkerchiefs until they exactly resembled the one recovered from Rowcliffe. She put the original handkerchief away in the little velvet bag she carried, and dropped the other four in the drawer of her desk.

Crider was then dismissed. His final instructions were to report to Mme. Storey at nine next morning. It was about eleven o'clock. Glasgow was still hovering in the hall awaiting our pleasure, and Mme. Storey sent me to him to inquire about Rowcliffe. That gentleman, I learned, had not gone upstairs, but was smoking a cigar on the terrace. Glasgow went after him.

Rowcliffe entered the office with the same crushed and stricken air; nevertheless it was clear that confession had in a measure eased his soul; for his eyes no longer had the same tortured look I had marked in the morning.

Mme. Storey drew one of the handkerchiefs from the back of the drawer. "I merely want to return this to you," she said. "After all, you have the best claim to it, and I realise that it will be safe with you. I shall have to borrow it back again tomorrow."

He was so glad to get it, it did not occur to him to question her motives. He took it in his eager hands, and thrust it back in his inner pocket. Stammering his thanks, he bade us good-night.

Mme. Storey's next move was to call up young Crider in New York for the purpose of instructing him how to handle the next day's business at the office. Absorbing as our present task was, there were other things that had to be kept going.

While she was waiting for the connexion she handed me another handkerchief from the drawer, saying: "Hide this in your dress and carry it to Mrs. Cruger's room. Glasgow will direct you. Simply say to Mrs. Cruger that I feel it will be safest in her possession during the night, and ask her to keep it for me until morning.

If either of the other ladies should be with her, do not show it, of course, but ask Mrs. Cruger to step down here."

I found Mrs. Cruger in her dressing-room, a fairy-like pink bower. She was seated at her dressing-table, having her fine, blonde hair brushed, while she stared into the mirror with a face that had a silvery look in its pallor. She was alone but for Agnes. Seeing me, she sent the maid into the next room. I delivered her the handkerchief, together with my message. She nodded, and, dropping the handkerchief in a jewel case, let the top fall.

"It will be quite safe," she murmured.

When I got back to the office Mme. Storey was deep in her conversation with Crider over the 'phone. She had not much more than concluded it when there came a tap on the door, and Miss de Guion entered. The old lady was dressed just as we had last seen her, in the shimmering and artfully draped gown that made her look almost slender. Her back was stiff and her head up; she had the look of one who had conquered human weakness.

"I thought perhaps I could be of some assistance to you after the others were out of the way," she said simply.

"I'm so glad you came!" rejoined Mme. Storey quickly (and quite truthfully). "You *can* help me."

"What is the real situation?" asked Miss de Guion anxiously.

Mme. Storey made a gesture of helplessness. "I wish I knew! I suspect—but have no proof. I can go no further without the assistance of the chemists."

"Whom do you suspect?" asked Miss de Guion.

"Ah, you know!"

The old lady nodded.

"What I want you to do," Mme. Storey went on, "is to keep this dreadful handkerchief until tomorrow. I do not know what efforts may be made to recover it. I have no place to put it. There is a safe here, but Glasgow has the combination, and even Glasgow has his price, of course. Any drawer I might choose to lock it in may have a duplicate key. But the guilty person would never guess I had put it in your keeping."

Mme. Storey produced another handkerchief from the drawer, and offered it.

"I will keep it gladly," said Miss de Guion, tucking it inside her dress.

After some further conversation about the case, which seemed to have great significance, but had none (so I omit it), Miss de Guion went back upstairs.

Having given her time to get out of the way, Mme. Storey said: "Bella, I fancy there must be a telephone in Vera McPeake's boudoir. Ask Glasgow to connect me with her."

It was so, and in a few minutes Vera appeared in the office wearing an all-enveloping white robe of exquisite fleecy Angora, and a remarkable lace cap. Her fine trappings only made the pinched and spiteful face look more common.

She came in with a defiant air. "What have you got to say to me?" she demanded.

"Hardly necessary for me to say anything," replied Mme. Storey blandly. "You and I understand each other. I could not let it appear before the others, of course."

"I thought you were against me, too," muttered the girl.

"By no means!" said Mme. Storey quickly. "And the best proof of that is, that I'm going to ask you to keep the most important bit of evidence I have. No place in this house would be safe for me. I have no assurance that the murderer would not kill me to get it back again. But it would never be supposed that I had given it to you to keep. Will you do that for me?"

Mme. Storey offered her the last handkerchief out of the drawer.

The girl put forth a slow hand for it. She was deeply suspicious. With her sharp black eyes she was endeavouring to bore through Mme. Storey. "Oh, I'll keep it safe," she said with a sneer. "Is that all?"

"That is all," said Mme. Storey pleasantly. "And thank you."

Vera turned and left the room without another word. I began to see Mme. Storey's purpose, and commended it.

"Now to bed, Bella," said my mistress. "We have a day before us!"

12

AT TEN O'CLOCK the next morning Mme. Storey and I were waiting in the little office for the others to gather. That astonishing woman, my mistress, was reading her mail (which had been sent up from town) with perfect coolness, concentrating on each letter in turn, and issuing her instructions concerning it. I remember how I resented her self-command, for my nerves were in strings. I had slept very little. My hand trembled so that I could scarcely make legible notes. These scenes are more than I care for.

An hour earlier Crider had reported that nobody in the house had made any attempt to get away during the night. Crider had received certain other instructions in private, and had driven into White Plains. We were momentarily expecting him back.

Every member of the little house party had breakfasted upstairs, and we had not yet seen anybody. All the usual routine of the great household had proceeded in as quiet and orderly a fashion as if no suggestion of tragedy had ever approached those gorgeous, still rooms. I remember it was a lovely day out of doors. The sunlight was washing the leaves of Cariswoode with liquid gold, and the branches were full of singing birds. How I longed that I might be able to give myself up to it!

The four persons came in practically together. Mrs. Cruger and Miss de Guion side by side, followed by Vera McPeake, and a moment afterwards, Rowcliffe, giving Vera a wide berth. Four of the plain chairs the room contained had already been placed for them in a line facing Mme. Storey at the desk. I was sitting at the end of the desk on her left, resting my note-book upon it. There was a moment's confusion as they seated themselves, owing to Vera's silent refusal to sit next either Rowcliffe or Miss de Guion. They finally arranged themselves with Vera nearest the windows, then Mrs. Cruger, Miss de Guion and Rowcliffe in that order. Nobody had said a single word.

Mme. Storey seemed scarcely to glance at the four. I studied their faces covertly. Nothing conclusive was to be read there. All were agitated according to their several natures; all silenced by agitation; but there was no guilty quality to be perceived any more in one face than in another. It was significant though, that while the three women were breathlessly watching Mme. Storey, Rowcliffe was watching them, just as I was.

"First of all, the handkerchief if you please," said Mme. Storey quietly.

All four made a simultaneous move to produce it, and each, seeing what the others were about, stared in confusion and anger. When all four handkerchiefs were visible: "A trick!" each one murmured in various tones of anger and fright.

"Yes, a trick," said Mme. Storey coolly. "But one that only a guilty person need fear."

Such was their agitation, one would have said at the moment that all four were equally guilty.

Mme. Storey was unconcerned. "Bella, please take the handkerchiefs one at a time," she said. "Mark each in pencil with the initials of the person from whom you receive it."

I obeyed; putting each handkerchief on the desk and writing the initials: V.M., B.C., T.deG. and J.R. All four were placed in a pile under a paper-weight for the time being.

"As you have guessed, none of you had the original handkerchief," Mme. Storey continued. "That has not left my possession; I have it here." She produced it.

"I have taken every precaution that it may be identified," she said. "Before handling the others I added two dots in the corner; Miss Brickley and Mr. Crider looking on while I did so. You can therefore be sure that the handkerchief I hold in my hand is the same one that Mr. Rowcliffe took from the hand of the dead girl upstairs."

Again one seemed to feel the shudder in the air.

"Bella," said Mme. Storey. "See if Crider has returned."

I went to the door. Crider was waiting in the hall. At a sign from me he came in, holding a small object hidden mysteriously under his coat.

"Sit down by the door for a moment," said Mme. Storey. To the others she resumed: "First I want to establish if possible that this handkerchief was really responsible for Miss Mayfield's death; and if so, how. I have not yet had an opportunity to obtain scientific aid; but I have a theory of my own; and I will now undertake a simple experiment to prove whether or not it is the correct one."

Rowcliffe looked at her now. All four white faces remained turned towards her without stirring. Only the eyes seemed alive.

"The person who sent this handkerchief to the girl," Mme. Storey went on, "was perfectly familiar with the doings and the plans of this household. He or she must have known that if it was mailed in White Plains in mid-afternoon it would be delivered here at half past six, or shortly after you had all left for the dinner and dance. I assume that the sender also knew the girl was going out soon after, and that the delivery of the packet would find her dressing in her room. And so it happened.

"From that moment, of course, we can only proceed upon surmise. Miss Mayfield opened the envelope, and was astonished and charmed by the contents. What girl would not have been? She did not know who sent it to her, but I do not suppose she was much put about by that, for every pretty girl receives anonymous gifts. No doubt she had her own idea as to who had sent it.

"After examining it, I think she dropped it on her table while she finished dressing. The handkerchief would furnish just the touch she needed to complete her costume. Being all ready, she would pick it up again, and moisten it with perfume. She was fond of fine scent, but it is a significant circumstance that she used it in the form of a toilet water rather than an extract. The reason is a simple one; the toilet water is much less expensive than the extract. But you have to use more. I have the bottle here that I took from her dressing-table; a violet toilet water of one of the best makers. This bottle was evidently left uncorked all night. Someone who entered the room after the body was discovered, replaced the stopper.

"After she moistened the handkerchief—liberally," Mme. Storey continued gravely, "what would be her next act? The natural, the inevitable thing since she loved the scent, would be to apply it to her nostrils and breathe of it deeply. That, if I am correct, was the last act of her life—Crider, please—"

Crider came to the side of the desk opposite to me. He produced from under his coat—a guinea-pig!

"A guinea-pig," said Mme. Storey, "because the physical reactions of this little animal most closely resemble those of the human organism."

There was a brief-case lying on the desk. A messenger had brought up the letters in it. Mme. Storey threw back the cover, and let it remain so. She then uncorked the bottle of toilet water, and pouring a few drops on the handkerchief, clapped the wet spot over the guinea-pig's nostrils. There was a convulsive movement under Crider's hand. Mme. Storey quickly dropped the handkerchief into the brief-case, and threw the cover shut. Crider removed his hand, the little animal lay dead on the desk.

With the briefest of pauses Mme. Storey went on: "As to these other handkerchiefs: Bella, spread them out on the desk with the initials turned down—now examine them carefully, you and Crider, and tell me if any one of them is changed, since they left our hands last night."

I obeyed her automatically. Crider came around to my side, and we examined the handkerchiefs together. Whereas all four had been exactly alike the night before, one was now unmistakably different from the others. I looked at Crider and he confirmed it with a nod.

"This one has been washed," I said.

"Read the initials," commanded Mme. Storey.

I tried to, but my tongue would not form the sounds. It was Crider who said:

"T.deG."

Miss de Guion pitched forward out of her chair, and crashed to the floor. A scene of indescribable confusion took place. Vera McPeake shrieked; Rowcliffe sprang up, knocking over his chair, and clapping his hands to his head ejaculated hoarsely over and over: "My God! My God! My God!" Mrs. Cruger's head fell backward, and the last vestiges of life seemed to leave her inert frame. As for me, I dropped into my chair like one paralysed.

What happened immediately after this is vague to me. I remember Mme. Storey and Crider hastening to raise Miss de Guion up. Crider must have summoned Glasgow, for I saw the two men carrying the heavy body from the room. What became of Vera and Rowcliffe I do not know. When clear recollection returned, Mrs. Cruger was alone in the room with us. She had covered her face with her hands, and was weakly weeping.

"You suspected this from the first?" said Mme. Storey.

Mrs. Cruger nodded without taking down her hands.

"Explain to me—when you are able."

The other began to speak brokenly: "It was my fault—in a way. But I couldn't foresee this. It began months ago. Teresa irritated me more and more with her masterful ways. And the entertainments she arranged didn't represent *me*. She was growing old— old-fashioned—made a fool of me. And she presumed to dictate whom I might and might not have for friends! Then I saw Louise; so young, so intelligent; she understood. And in a moment of exasperation with Teresa, I wrote to Louise suggesting that she, well, act for me direct. You understand. Louise never got that letter. I found it out from her indirectly. I never told her I had written to her. I knew it had fallen into Teresa's hands—I just drifted—I never dreamed of any outcome like this—"

"Why didn't you tell me this at first?" asked Mme. Storey.

"How could I? It was just a suspicion—it was *too* dreadful. Teresa is so old. I wanted it hushed up!"

That was all. She made her way out of the room unaided. Crider came back.

"Telephone to the police," Mme. Storey said to him, gravely.

POSTSCRIPT

THE SADDEST FEATURE of the case did not take place until the first reports were published in the newspapers. Then, in the frantic young man who rushed to Cariswoode, was discovered the real lover of Louise Mayfield, a splendid young fellow, Ralph Penry. It was with him that Louise had had an engagement to dine in a hotel in White Plains the night she died. They were engaged to be married, but had felt it necessary to conceal the fact, owing to the jealous, imperious nature of Louise's employer. The young man's grief was heart-breaking to witness.

An unexpected outcome was that Penry and Rowcliffe became friends, drawn together by their common loss. Indeed Rowcliffe's regeneration was a bit of good that came of the miserable affair. He went to work, and has made good, I hear. Vera McPeake subsequently found another impecunious young blue blood and married him.

The trial of Teresa de Guion revealed a subtlety, a determination, a patience in that strange woman sufficient to have accomplished wonders if turned to better purpose. Her boldness was evidenced by the fact that it was she who had insisted on the investigation. She was wise enough to realise that it must be gone through with, once the story was started. She was really a mediæval character, completely out of place in the twentieth century.

It was shown that among her thousands of acquaintances was a famous chemist, engaged upon research work in connexion with poison gases. There is no need to bring up his name again. As soon as she resolved upon a poison, Miss de Guion unostentatiously began to cultivate this man, and, little by little by the exercise of her charm and cleverness, drew his secrets from him, without his ever suspecting that he was being used. When he had told her what she wanted to know, she set up a little laboratory in a room she hired secretly for the purpose; and here she conducted experiments at no little risk to herself, until she had produced what she required.

When she went up to Cariswoode she had the poison with her in the form of a powder contained in a bottle. Chance threw the lace handkerchief in her way. She dissolved the powder in water, and impregnated the handkerchief. The poison was inactive in water, and the handkerchief was harmless wet or dry, until a touch of alcohol released its deadly fumes. The chances were a hundred to one that the girl's death would be ascribed to natural causes, but as it happened, the hundredth chance prevailed.

She was found guilty, but in view of her age and broken physical condition (she went all to pieces before the trial) her sentence was commuted to life imprisonment. She died in prison.

THE SMOKE BANDIT

WHEN I ANNOUNCED my intention of writing up the smoke-bandit case, Mme. Storey scoffed at me. "Why, everybody seventeen years old and more," she said, "that is, everybody who was old enough to read the papers six years ago, knows all about it."

"So much the better," said I; "people like to read what they know about. Moreover, there was so much misrepresentation and concealment in the published accounts that I can tell them a few things they don't know. Take your part in the final clearing up of the case; for perfectly unnecessary reasons of delicacy you refused to let that be divulged. I think it ought to be known."

She shrugged, and let me have my way.

1

THE PREMISES of the National Forrest Bank were built during that period of magnificence when the great banks still arrogated the choicest sites in town to their own use, without feeling the necessity of building a sky-scraper overhead to help pay the interest. The little building making a hole in the solid ranks of the sky-scrapers is extremely effective. Here is a case where smallness is impressive. A little building only in a comparative sense, for, inside, the noble dome dwarfs the bank's customers to the proportions of insects. All around under the dome run the celebrated murals of Herbert B. Weatherbee, one of the sights of New York.

On a Friday at eleven o'clock in the morning, when the bank was at its most crowded—for that is the hour when many of the large firms draw their payrolls,—suddenly, without warning, without any sound of an explosion, great clouds of yellow smoke billowed up from the bank's floor, and instantly filled the whole place with an impenetrable acrid fog. In silence, and with a terrifying swiftness, the fumes puffed up, wiping everything out with a single gesture as it were.

The phenomenon was received in an appalled silence. Then the crowd rushed blindly in the direction of the doors. There was a whole row of doors, but the panic-stricken customers jammed there, and frantic cries of fright and pain arose. In a minute or two the smoke had dissipated itself under the spaces of the dome sufficiently for objects to become visible again, but the panic did not subside until every man had fought his way out of the building. Those who had been knocked down crawled out on all fours. By a miracle nobody was seriously injured. The astonished clerks of the bank for the most part never left their places.

The crowd rushing out of the bank met a bigger crowd running from every direction in the streets to see what was the matter. In five minutes so dense a mob had collected that the Broadway traffic was held up, and it took the reserves from two precincts to start it going again. Before any one inside the building could take hold of the situation, a fresh crowd overran the banking-room, and police had to be introduced through the basement to clear it. Utter confusion prevailed. It was not until a quarter of an hour after the affair that a message from the house of H. Tannenbaum and Co., the big clothing manufacturers, informed the bank's officials that the firm's messenger had been robbed of the week's pay-roll as he left the paying teller's window. Then the reason of the affair became clear.

Such was the story that I read in the afternoon papers. No one who was not in New York at the time can comprehend the shock of dismay it caused. We read with equanimity of the robbery of country banks, or even of the branches of city banks in outlying districts; that seems to be part of the natural order of things. But the National Forrest Bank!—whose long history is interwoven with that of the city itself; an institution only a little less sacred than the

United States Treasury; such a thing had never been heard of before! It was evidently a single-handed crime, and that a lone individual had dared to commit such an outrage within the very temple of security almost passed the bounds of credibility. The whole financial world was shaken.

One could not but feel sorry for the police. All the panic-stricken bankers and business men in town put it up to them naturally, and what could they do? The rush of the crowd back into the banking-room had obliterated whatever evidence might have been left there. They had to appear to be doing something, of course, and all sorts of theories were successively inflated and exploded. From edition to edition of the papers the police promised results, but reading between the lines it was only too clear that they were all at sea. The robber had vanished in his own smoke. In the press the story shrank from a full page to two columns, then to one, from sheer lack of new material. But before it got crowded off the front page altogether, one week later at almost precisely the same hour, another smoke bomb was dropped in the Manhattan National on Wall Street, which, as everyone knows, is the largest bank of them all. The first affair being fresh in everybody's mind, an even wilder panic resulted, of which the bandit took full advantage. His procedure was different this time. The smoke was released at a moment when one of the paying tellers' wickets was thrown up to permit the teller to pass out some package of bills to a customer. The customer was not robbed, but, as the teller fell against the back of his cage, an arm reached in through the open wicket, and gathered up bundle after bundle of bills from his desk. The haul was thirty-two thousand dollars. On the first occasion the robber only got seven thousand.

Well, we thought the first robbery had exhausted the possibilities of sensation, but the second far exceeded it. A single robbery might be regarded as an accident, but two were certainly the result of a deeply planned campaign. Everybody felt that, since no method had been devised of meeting this danger, there was no reason why it should not go on indefinitely, whenever the bandit chose to strike. Every moneyed man in town wondered if he'd be next. A sickening feeling of helplessness filled the authorities.

But the police had something to go on now. One of the detectives placed in the bank that morning had marked the very spot where the billowing fumes were released, and was armed with a description of the man who had stood nearest that spot. He had not been seen to throw or drop anything, and it was supposed that he had released the bomb through his pants-leg. A man of medium size, very well built, the detective reported, but with a face hollowed and greyed as from long illness. A thick grey moustache with ragged ends; a fringe of straggling black hair showing under his hat; dressed in worn but neatly brushed clothes. The detective had taken him for the respectable book-keeper of some business house. When the smoke puffed up the detective had sprung forward to seize him, but had only embraced the smoke.

On the floor where the bomb had been dropped, they found some fragments of colored glass as thin as paper. These were evidently parts of a glass ball, such as are used to decorate Christmas trees. The shops were full of them at the time. The neck of the ball was found intact. It had been stopped with sealing-wax. From traces of powder adhering to the glass, the chemists were able to reconstruct the contents of the bomb. The formula was kept secret, for fear somebody else might try on the same scheme.

After the second robbery the big banks adopted the most elaborate arrangements to protect themselves and their customers. The usual method was to rope off the interior of the banking-house so that the customers were obliged to pass through in single file, watched and protected every foot of the way by armed guards. Only one customer at a time was allowed to approach a paying teller's window, everybody else being held back at a safe distance until he got his money. When he got his money he was escorted to the door by a guard. All this entailed a considerable delay in the transaction of business, and was very expensive, to boot. But it was expected that the smoke bandit would be hard put to beat it.

After the second robbery, the regular police not having produced any results, the Banking Association engaged our old acquaintance Walter A. Barron to act independently in running down the thief. He was given absolute *carte blanche* in the matter of operatives and expenses. Barron, you remember, was an ex-assistant district attorney who had set up his own detective bureau when the city administration changed. He was something more than a mere acquaintance of Mme. Storey, as my account of the Ashcomb Poor case revealed. To put it bluntly, he was a suitor to my mistress, with a bull-headed pertinacity that no amount of discouragement had been able to affect. He often came to our office. We did not see him for some days after he had been appointed to the case, and we had no means of following his activities, for at first he refused to talk for publication, thus showing better sense than I had credited him with.

It was realised around town that Friday was an unlucky day to send to the bank for your pay-roll cash, and business firms quickly got in the habit of choosing any day but Friday. Six days after the Manhattan National robbery, that is to say, Thursday, the blow fell again. This time the bandit picked the big Cosmopolitan Trust on lower Broadway, and all the roped lines, armed guards, etc., troubled him not a whit. A sort of groan of rage went up from financial Manhattan. Some extremists demanded that martial law be established, without any clear notion of what good that would do.

The Cosmopolitan owns a forty-storey office building over its banking premises. The banking-office opens on the same corridor that serves the elevators, and during business hours there is always a throng passing in and out. The thief did not enter the banking-room, but must have loitered in the corridor until he saw a pair of messengers come out of the bank with a heavy satchel. Then he dropped his bomb or bombs in the corridor, and, under cover of the impenetrable fumes, snatched the satchel, and made off with it.

This happened only about ten paces from the doors to the street. The despoiled messengers were outside almost as soon as the robber. They saw their satchel making off down Broadway, and set up an immense hue and cry. In five seconds I suppose there were two hundred men in pursuit of the thief. A real old man they said, who ran with a limp. But he showed an astonishing spryness. Nevertheless, he would certainly have been caught, had it not been for his bombs. They saw him draw his hand from his pocket and immediately thereafter the familiar thick billows of smoke rolled up,

filling the canyon between the skyscrapers from wall to wall. A roar
of balked rage went up from the crowd.

The bolder spirits ran right through the smoke, but found nothing on the other side. The thief had evidently darted into one of
the office buildings on the left-hand side of the way. All these buildings had rear entrances on New Street. He made a clean get-away.
His loot was not quite so big this time. Eleven thousand, if I remember aright.

The following week it was the turn of the Textile National, another of the first-line banks. His reward was only a beggarly five
thousand.

These robberies in New York were the sensation of the entire
country, but out-of-town papers reported them with a difference.
They had no call to feel the strain of anxiety, the helpless anger
that every responsible person in the metropolis shared. Indeed,
since, as Voltaire or some other Frenchman has pointed out, there
is something not exactly displeasing to us in the misfortunes of
our friends, there was a good deal of quiet fun poked at the helplessness of the New York authorities. All this was abruptly changed
when, three days after the Textile National affair, a smoke bomb
was dropped in the Quaker National Bank, Philadelphia, and the
bandit got away with sixteen thousand dollars.

A wave of panic swept over the entire country. If Philadelphia,
why not all the great cities, one after another? Moreover, since the
composition of the bombs was said to be very simple, why should
not a score of smoke bandits arise? No way had been found of meeting the menace, though the whole banking business bade fair to be
disrupted by the magnitude of the precautions that were taken.
The smaller banks simply couldn't stand the gaff in armed guards.
But if they did not hire them, they lost what business they had.
The price of armed guards doubled and quadrupled overnight, and
the hard-boiled gentry reaped a harvest.

There was a universal demand for the federal authorities to take
action. I suppose the Department of Justice agents got busy, but,
as they played no part in what followed, I need not refer to them.

2

So FAR, MME. STOREY and I knew no more about the smoke-bandit case than any other newspaper readers. Busy as we were with other matters, we often discussed it. One could not avoid it. It filled the minds of everybody in our part of the world. On one occasion Mme. Storey said frankly:

"A hard nut to crack, my Bella. I'm glad it's not between our white teeth."

One morning while I was taking dictation from her, I heard the buzzer that announced the entrance of somebody into my room outside. It was Barron, a big, red-faced man with an aggressive, cave-man manner. A man of coarse fibre, but with a crude strength of mind, and determined; egregiously vain in the masculine style. Most people cringed a little before him, but he didn't get it in our office. Maybe that was the attraction it had for him. I was no longer impressed by his manner, because I had learned that so far as Mme. Storey was concerned, it concealed a bad inferiority complex.

I was surprised to see him, busy as he must have been; but the reason for his call soon became apparent. As chief of the search for the smoke bandit he had become the man of the hour; his slightest word was good for a box on the front page of all the newspapers. Up to this time he had had the wit to say very little, consequently he had become a man of mystery, as well. It was natural that he should wish to show himself off in this hour of glory before the woman who had always mocked at him.

I followed him into Mme. Storey's room, since it was understood between my mistress and me that I was always to be present when he called. She used me as a buffer against his crude and tempestuous love-making. He scowled at me ferociously when he saw my purpose, but said nothing, since he had long ago discovered that it was useless to object to my presence. Sometimes it had happened that his feelings had carried him away to such an extent he even avowed his passion before me. He did not love me for having been a witness to his discomfiture.

"Well, Walter!" Mme. Storey cried with delicate irony; "we are honoured that the great man could find time to come to see *us*!"

"Oh, my lines are all out," he said carelessly; "at the moment I have nothing to do but await events."

Mme. Storey's little black ape Giannino had conceived a violent aversion to Barron, which he was apt to express in a very disconcerting manner. I was obliged to carry him into the middle room, and put him in his house. There is no love lost between Giannino and me, but we were at one on this subject. "I sympathise with you, you little black devil," I whispered in his ear.

When I came back Mme. Storey was helping herself to a cigarette. She pushed the big silver box in Barron's direction. He refused impatiently. A silence fell between them, a silence that was a sort of duel. Mme. Storey had no intention of helping him out, and he, on his part, was determined to make her betray some curiosity about his work. Foolish man! I felt like saying, you have about as much chance of mastering her as you have of— but I couldn't think of any adequate figure.

He looked about him with a scowl. The long, tall room was as cool and beautiful and simple as an antique Italian villa. Whereas everybody else is going mad over early American furnishings, Mme. Storey, with a sure instinct, clings to the Italian Renaissance. She is herself a figure out of the Renaissance. Barron resented the rare and precious things with which she surrounded herself; he resented everything about her. That was the inferiority complex working. I had always felt sorry for him in a way, but what can a woman do with a man like that? He simply would not take his answer.

At the moment he was better controlled than usual. But he had to speak first. "Well, Rose, a lot has happened since I saw you."

"You appeared to be well pleased with it," she said.

He shrugged massively. "That's your regular line."

"Well, say then, that you are upheld by a secret feeling of confidence."

"Maybe," he said sententiously.

"You have caught your man?"

"I will catch him."

"Within twenty-four hours?" she asked wickedly. This had been the daily promise of the baffled police.

"Oh, I don't have to perform in the newspapers," said Barron, undisturbed. "It may be twenty-four days, but I'll land him in the end."

There was something quite impressive in the man's heavy assurance. Not to Mme. Storey, though. Her charming face was all lighted up with mockery.

"How interesting! You are working on a theory, then?"

"I am. Would you like to hear what it is?"

"Oh, perhaps it wouldn't be right for you to talk about it."

"I wouldn't object to discussing it with you but. . . ." You can imagine the look he gave me.

Mme. Storey appeared to lose interest in the subject. Half turning in her chair, she glanced out of the window at the nurse-maids and the lively children in Gramercy Park. "What a lovely mild day!" she drawled. "It's a sin to be working."

She had him! He had come to talk to her about his case, and talk he had to. He gritted his teeth a little. "My theory is that we have a madman to deal with," he said.

"Never!" said Mme. Storey, glancing at the lighted end of her cigarette.

"Everything he has done proves it by his cunning," Barron said obstinately.

"I've heard of the superior cunning of madmen," said Mme. Storey coolly. "It may be so, but I've never seen it demonstrated myself. In this case I should say that every act of the smoke bandit proclaimed a brain that was working very well indeed."

"Time will tell," said Barron sententiously.

"Surely, time will tell!" said Mme. Storey with a laugh.

The conversation came to a stand again. Mme. Storey glanced suggestively at the pile of letters that was waiting to be answered.

"Come out to lunch with me," Barron blurted out with the sullen air of a child demanding a favour that he knows beforehand will be refused.

Mme. Storey shook her head. "Too busy. I must eat in, today."

"When can I see you?"

"I'm not making any engagements just now."

He drew his breath painfully between his teeth, and there was another silence.

"When I got out of the district attorney's office," he presently began, "you advised me against setting up my detective bureau."

"What of it?" she asked.

"You thought I wasn't smart enough."

"Oh, I wouldn't say that!" she said teasingly.

"I'm in a position to show you now. This is the biggest case I've ever had—the biggest case anybody ever had. It will establish me at the head of the profession."

"If you catch your man," put in Mme. Storey softly.

"Oh, I will catch him," he said confidently. "Make no mistake about that!"

At this moment the buzzer sounded again, and I had to leave the room. Barron followed me out with a triumphant glance. I left the door open, according to instructions.

It proved to be a messenger with a big bundle of documents that were required in a certain case. I had to check them up against a list before receipting for them. While I was engaged in this mechanical operation, I couldn't help but hear what was said in the next room. Mme. Storey took no care to lower her voice, and Barron had no dulcet tones in his.

Barron said: "You'll have to hand it to me, Rose, when I win this case."

"I shall be the first to congratulate you," she said lightly.

"I wasn't referrin' to your congratulations," he said doggedly. "When I've won, I'll come and claim *you*!"

"I don't exactly follow your reasoning," said Mme. Storey mildly.

"Oh, you know what I mean, all right! I'll come for you!"

"But how about my sentiments in the matter?"

"All talk," said Barron roughly. "There's nothing in it. You can put it all over me with your talk. But I'm a man and you're a woman . . ."

"Well, I never questioned that," said Mme. Storey dryly.

". . . And the great truths of nature are not changed by clever talk! A man is the natural master, and in her soul a woman knows it."

"Oh dear!" said Mme. Storey a little wearily. "Where did you pick up that idea, Walter? It's the way prep schoolboys discuss women, isn't it? At the age of sixteen. And schoolgirls adore it. At least they used to. I've an idea that even schoolgirls require to be shown, nowadays . . . What you want is a woman with a schoolgirl mind, Walter. There are millions of them to choose from. Such a woman would look on you as a god. What perversity is it in your nature that forces you to expose your most sacred feelings to a mocking devil like me? I'm a disillusioned woman, Walter, and I have a lot of work to do."

I heard his chair move, and I hoped he was taking the hint. "That's just a clever woman's talk," he said loftily. "I don't pay any attention to it. A man's a man, and a woman's a woman! With all your cleverness you can't change that."

"I don't want to," she murmured.

"I'm never going to grovel before you again," he said. (This suggested that he was near grovelling then, poor wretch!) "It was a mistake. I say no more. When I have established myself I shall come and claim my due."

"You shall have it," she said promptly.

"Have what?" he asked, somewhat taken aback.

"Your due." In my mind's eye I could see the enigmatic smile that accompanied this.

He came out of her room looking very dubious. This quickly changed to a ferocious scowl as he became aware of my glance. The closing of the outer door was not exactly a slam, but he meant it to express his unconquerable will. I sniggered to myself. I haven't the art, but I do love to see another woman put a bumptious male where he belongs. The idea that this coarse-grained creature should presume to aspire to my peerless mistress seemed perfectly preposterous to me.

"Lord, Bella! how helpless men are!" she said to me when I went in to her. "So much emotion and so little sense! It's pathetic when a masterful man is denied his desire."

"The old problem of the irresistible force and the immovable object," I suggested.

"Yes, if there were such a thing. But there is not, remember. Something has to give."

3

THE ACTIVITIES of the smoke bandit continued unchecked. From Philadelphia he jumped to Chicago, where, a week later, he visited the Inland Seas National, one of the premier banks of the West. It was the Inland Seas which, some years ago, built that famous elevated concrete fort in the middle of its banking-room. The walls were pierced with loopholes behind which armed guards were supposed to be stationed during bank hours. I suspect that the fort had been built for its moral effect, or for the purposes of publicity—or both; but if the armed guards were at their loop-holes, they were helpless, of course, against this bandit's novel weapon.

On this occasion he changed his tactics again. Avoiding the paying teller's window, he went to the receiving teller, where, just as messengers from the Union Station were about to hand in a great satchel of cash, he dropped his bomb, and annexed the satchel. He made a clean get-away; no one had so much as a glimpse of him. Being Monday, the satchel contained two days' receipts, or nearly fifty thousand dollars. This was the largest haul he had yet made. The affair stimulated the police and the banks of Chicago to unheard-of measures of protection. But as a matter of fact, the bandit took the first train out of town, and never returned there. He was like a butterfly which sipped honey where it listed.

The worst features of the situation was the frightful waste it entailed. Throughout the country the banks, I suppose, spent in futile measures of self-protection a hundred times the amount of what the bandit took from them.

Five days later he turned up in Milwaukee, where he relieved a customer of the Grain Exchange Trust of some eleven thousand dollars. This bank had installed an anti-smoke device, the invention of a local chemist. The idea was to neutralise the formula of the smoke bombs. Push-buttons in the tellers' cages were to release, in various parts of the banking premises, jets of this chemical substance, whatever it was, that would instantly clear the air. At least, that was the theory. They never had a chance to try it out, for the bandit did not pull off his stunt in the banking-house. Either he knew of the device (he had an uncanny foreknowledge of the measures that were prepared against him) or else he was simply intimidated by the array of guards outside and inside the bank. He followed the messengers of the Creagan Packing Company back to their own offices in the outskirts, and as they ascended a narrow stairway he tossed a bomb before them, and as they reeled back he got their money-bag. Plunging after him down the stairs, the messengers sprawled over a stick that he had placed for the purpose. The momentary delay was all that he required for his getaway.

This was January 22. On the twenty-sixth his return to New York was revealed by an extraordinary accident. At ten-forty in the morning the crowded platforms of the Brooklyn Bridge subway station were suddenly enveloped in dense clouds of smoke. An ugly panic resulted. Many were pushed off the platforms, and a hideous loss of life was averted only by the quickness of a towerman in stopping all trains. When the confusion subsided it was found that no one had been mortally injured—no one had been robbed either. The inference was that somebody had accidentally knocked against the smoke bandit, setting off one or more bombs in his pockets. The fumes, as I said before, while extremely unpleasant, were not poisonous.

Odd as it may seem, no additional description of the bandit was obtained on this occasion. Even those who were closest to the source of the smoke were unable to state from exactly whose pocket it had issued. But I have noticed myself that people in a subway crowd never look at each other.

The hour was significant: ten-forty. It was pointed out that all the robberies in New York had taken place almost precisely at eleven. Everybody speculated as to which bank he had been about to visit when his ammunition was set off. This dramatic signal of his return to New York set all the bank clerks trembling afresh. These poor fellows were sadly demoralised; the mere striking of a match in a bank was enough to cause the weaker brethren to swoon. In particular, half the paying tellers in town were on the verge of nervous prostration.

The leading banks purchased many columns of space in the newspapers to announce that they had taken advantage of the three weeks' immunity so to perfect their measures that it was impossible for the smoke bandit ever again to operate in New York City. In effect they dared him to try. But public confidence was far from being restored by the advertisements. Practically every firm in town was paying its employees by cheque. Employees in turn insisted on paying their little bills by cheque, and an acute shortage of currency resulted. The clearing house was snowed under, and a flood of bad cheques appeared. The small storekeepers were the principal sufferers. The situation was really serious.

The Industrial Trust Company, always one of the most enterprising banks in town, had notified its customers privately that it was prepared to deliver whatever currency they required at its own risk. On the strength of it they had obtained hundreds of new accounts. Their plan (which came out later) had the merit of simplicity. They hired the back premises of one of their customers, a sporting-goods dealer on Nassau Street, and installed several trusted clerks there. Currency was delivered at the sporting-goods store in wooden boxes marked ammunition. The customers fetched or mailed their cheques to the bank, which telephoned the amounts required to the sporting-goods store. The money was tied up in plain manila packages tied with string, and carried around in one of the sporting-goods dealer's delivery cars. Three men accompanied it: one to drive, one to carry in the packages, one always concealed within the body of the car.

The plan worked so well, the Industrial Trust was preparing to establish other *sub rosa* branches about town, when the smoke bandit suddenly called their bluff. This was on February 4, another Friday! The bank messenger, disguised in a faded uniform as a delivery man, was passing through the corridor of the Manhattan Surety Building with two of the manila packages that were to be delivered there. A bomb was dropped, and the usual weird scene followed. This messenger was a plucky youngster who hung on to his packages, and let out a roar for assistance before the smoke choked him. A blow on the head from some blunt instrument stretched him, and the bandit made off with the packages. Their contents totalled about twenty thousand.

A very painful impression was created by this affair. The secret had been so well guarded it was felt that one of the clerks of the Industrial Trust must be in league with the bandit. It was even suggested that he had his agents in every big bank in town. A fresh panic swept over the community, and business was still further disorganised. It was whispered about that the big cash stores were in serious difficulties as a result of the shortage of currency. Heavens! what would happen if the department stores closed their doors, everybody asked. The thousands of buyers from out of town put off their usual visits; the attendance at the theatres fell away; nobody had any money in his pockets. The worst thing of all was averted only because the people were afraid to go to the banks to draw their money. There were no runs.

4

THREE DAYS AFTER the Industrial Trust affair, Mme. Storey received a mysterious call on the telephone. A gentleman with an agreeable voice, who declined to give his name, asked my mistress if she would do him the honour of lunching with him at the Arts Club that day in order to discuss a professional matter. As evidence of his good faith he suggested she bring her attorney or any other person in whom she had confidence. Now the Arts Club is next door but one to our office. Mme. Storey is a member, and she frequently lunches there. In her large style she told the unknown caller that she was lunching at the Arts Club anyway; that she would bring her secretary; that he might address her; and that, if she liked his looks she would accept his invitation.

"Not that I feel in need of protection in the Arts Club," she added to me with a delightful grin, "but if there is any free lunch going, you may as well be in on it, Bella."

In the main hall of the club an extremely elegant young fellow accosted us. Mme. Storey responded somewhat dryly, for his was not the voice which had spoken over the telephone; moreover he was clearly not an important person, but merely ornamental.

He explained that he was private secretary to Mr. Silas B. Fulton, President of the Manhattan National Bank; also President of the New York Banking Association. Mr. Fulton had with him Mr. Henry Balstock, one of the vice-presidents of the Industrial Trust and secretary of the Association. They wished to talk with Mme. Storey upon a matter the nature of which she could no doubt guess. They regarded secrecy as highly essential. Both gentlemen were so well known, Madame Storey also, that for them to be seen publicly lunching together would certainly start a story. They had therefore ventured to engage a private room for lunch; and if Madame Storey would so far oblige them, etc., etc.

My mistress smiled a little at the elaborate explanation, and the suggestion that she might be afraid to venture into a private room—at the ultra-respectable Arts Club! She graciously signified her acceptance, and the young man led us upstairs.

We found two middle-aged gentlemen waiting for us in a small room. Mr. Fulton was a stout, rosy, benevolent gentleman—that is to say, he would have looked benevolent twenty years ago, when such was the fashion for prosperous bankers; now he was trying to hide it. Mr. Balstock was a tiny man, immaculately turned out. He had a powerful glance that made up for his lack of inches, and a crisp style of utterance. Although not nearly so well known in the world of affairs, he was clearly the leading spirit and he did most of the talking.

Unlike other prominent bankers of whom I have heard, these two seemed not to be accustomed to entertaining a pretty woman at lunch. Or it may be that it was the presence of the other that made each one uneasy. At any rate both cleared their throats a good deal and stalled. It was up to Mme. Storey and the secretary to keep the conversational ball rolling. The five of us sat down to a delicious and expensive luncheon. That helped a good deal.

Mr. Balstock finally said: "Madame Storey, there is no need to enter into the details of the dangerous situation in which we find ourselves. You read the newspapers. We wish to obtain your help in running down this fiend who is ruining us all."

"It is hardly my line," objected Mme. Storey. "I am a psychologist. This is no problem of that sort to be solved. This thief reveals his psychology in his operations. It is simply a case of find your man. Work for a detective."

"Well, aren't you . . . ?" Mr. Fulton began.

The astute Mr. Balstock silenced him with a glance. "I don't see the force of your argument," he went on smoothly. "We already have the best detective talent obtainable. We wish to bring skilled psychology to their aid."

"I assume that you refer to Mr. Barron," said Mme. Storey rather bluntly. "I should not care to supplant him."

"Oh, there's no question of that, no question of that," said Mr. Balstock hurriedly. "Our confidence in Mr. Barron remains unshaken. He is doing all that mortal man can do. But the responsibility is ours. We must leave no stone unturned. It has occurred to us that a woman's point of view might start something new. There's probably a woman concerned in it somewhere. We'd like you to undertake a parallel and independent investigation according to your own ideas."

Mme. Storey still shook her head.

"I need hardly say," Mr. Balstock insinuated, "that in a matter of such importance you could name your own figure."

Mme. Storey wagged her hand humorously. "It doesn't appeal to me," she said, sipping her ice with evident enjoyment.

"But should we not put aside our personal preferences in a situation of such urgency?" Mr. Balstock persisted. "A matter of national urgency, I may say. Perhaps you do not fully comprehend the seriousness of the situation. I will make it clear to you. This country lives by business. The banks are the foundation of all business. When confidence in the banks is disturbed, the whole vast structure of credit trembles. A little more of this, and it may well come tumbling down about our ears. In other words, a financial panic. Picture to yourself what that means, my dear madam: a falling market, tight money, passed dividends, and all the evils that follow in their train. I tell you this fiend is aiming a blow at the very heart of your country. I am offering you an opportunity to be its savior!"

Mme. Storey smiled slightly at the little man's board-room eloquence. She said, in her drawling way: "Somehow it's difficult to get one's feelings harrowed up over a threatened assault on the money-bags."

Mr. Balstock stared at her in a shocked way.

"But the poor, madam," put in the handsome young secretary; "think of what hard times mean to them."

"I am afraid you are not giving us the real reasons for your reluctance," said Mr. Balstock a little severely.

"Perhaps not," said Mme. Storey carelessly. "Mr. Barron is an old friend and I do not wish to put myself in a position where I would seem to be competing with him."

"Oh, if *that's* it," cried Mr. Balstock, much relieved, "let me hasten to put your mind at ease. Mr. Barron would have no objection whatever to your coming into the case. He told me so himself."

"Indeed!" said Mme. Storey, not a little surprised. "And might I tell him if I was engaged?"

"By all means, my dear lady! And give him any help that you are able. Or accept his help."

"And would I be supposed to put myself under his direction?" asked Mme. Storey dryly.

"Not at all! I said an independent investigation. My idea was that there would be a greater chance of results from two entirely separate lines of approach."

Mme. Storey deliberated with herself, turning a cigarette between her fingers. The three men hung anxiously on her decision. Finally she said: "Very well, I accept."

"Good!" cried Mr. Balstock. All three gentlemen were jubilant. The elder two insisted on shaking her by the hand; the young one gazed at her adoringly with his fine eyes.

"What a pity we can't have champagne here!" said Mr. Fulton.

The conversation became general, and quite merry.

"By the way," Mr. Balstock said later, "would it best serve your plans to announce that you have entered the case, or to keep the fact secret?"

"For the present, let it be kept a secret," said Mme. Storey.

"I thoroughly agree," said Mr. Balstock. "Now, how can we be of assistance to you?"

"I must get my thoughts in order first," said Mme. Storey. "At the moment only one question occurs to me. In the case of the stolen notes of high denominations, I assume that the numbers of these notes have been advertised through the usual channels."

"Assuredly, madam."

"And have none of them ever turned up in circulation?"

"Not one, madam."

When we got up to go, the young man arrogated to himself the privilege of holding Mme. Storey's coat for her. His eyes were still speaking volumes. There was a moment when the two other men were consulting about the cheque. Mme. Storey smiled encouragingly at the youth and murmured:

"Do come to see me some time."

"When may I?" he whispered eagerly.

"Let me see . . . I shall be dropping in to tea at the Plaza tomorrow at five. You might join me."

"How good of you!"

5

Upon getting back to the office, Mme. Storey's first move was to telephone Barron to drop in when he could. He came on wings. I was present at their interview. He had himself under firm control, but he was not cured of his passion, as one could see from his intent and sombre glances upon my mistress's face. He literally could not drag his eyes away from her. He expressed neither surprise nor anxiety upon learning that she was in the case, but it was impossible to tell really how he was taking it.

"I stipulated that I was to tell you," said Mme. Storey.

"That was square of you," he said.

"We must come to some sort of an understanding," she said. "Are you willing to have me work with you?"

"By all means," he said quickly.

"How far?" she asked, a little dryly.

His face was perfectly unsmiling. "I'll lay before you what general information I have turned up," he said. "No need your wasting the time to go after it all over again. Beyond that, it's only fair to tell you that I have my own theory and certain evidence that tends to support it. That I'll keep to myself."

"Certainly!" said Mme. Storey good-naturedly. "Go ahead with what you can."

"To begin with, we have been furnished with four alleged descriptions of the bandit," Barron began, consulting a note-book. "First, Dave Anderson, a detective employed by the Manhattan National, calls him a man of medium size, well-built, but with his face hollowed and greyed . . ."

"That's been published," Mme. Storey interrupted. "Proceed."

"John Wood, messenger for Kilmer and Brook, bankers,—this was the man who was robbed in the corridor of the Cosmopolitan Trust building; Wood describes him as a real old man; clean-shaven; white-haired; walked with a limp."

"What size man?"

"Average size. Real old."

"Still, when he was chased he got away with remarkable spryness."

"That's right . . . There are a dozen or more of those who chased him down Broadway who corroborate Wood."

"What's the third description?" asked Mme. Storey.

"W. J. Banks of the Creagan Packing Co., Milwaukee, says the thief was a young man of twenty-five or thereabouts; athletic figure and fresh-coloured complexion; very smartly dressed. Pulled a black handkerchief over the lower part of his face as he sprang up the stairs. . . . You see the different accounts jibe."

"Oh, I don't know," said Mme. Storey. "It may be assumed that the bandit is a master of disguise. One gets something from the composite of all three: a man of average size, extremely well-built, muscular and active.”

Barron shrugged. “As for me, I’ve discarded all three descriptions,” he said. “My experience is that when men are excited they imagine anything.”

“Quite true,” remarked Mme. Storey.

“Now the fourth is a *bona-fide* description,” said Barron, “and I go by that.”

“How can you be sure this one is *bona fide*?”

“Because I saw the man myself.”

“Ha!” exclaimed Mme. Storey. “Here is something new! Go on.”

“It is not generally known,” said Barron, “but I was in the Textile National the morning of the robbery there. I kept it to myself because I thought it would injure my prestige if the public knew how close I had been to the smoke bandit without getting my hands on him.

“How I happened to be in that particular bank instead of another,” he went on, “I can’t tell you. A sort of hunch, I suppose. Unluckily I didn’t profit by it. . . . Well, I was in the bank, looking over the customers, when my attention was attracted by a man waiting in line who had a sort of queer look. A man about thirty-three years old . . .”

“Take this down, Bella,” put in Mme. Storey.

“. . . With a sallow face and a shock of dead-black hair that needed cutting. Hung over the edge of his collar. He had a thin face: long nose, hollow cheeks; and he was thin in the body too; real thin. His overcoat was hanging open, and his pants-legs flopped when he walked, as if there wasn’t anything inside them. Wouldn’t weigh more than 115. Wore an old soft hat of black velure, and a dingy grey overcoat. Other times he may have disguised himself, but that was the natural man. It was his eyes that struck me hardest. Brown eyes with pupils that expanded and contracted while you looked at him. When he caught me looking at him, they turned crafty and secret.”

“How was it you didn’t get him?” Mme. Storey asked.

"Just a bit of ill-luck. I only had a general suspicion of him, you understand, and I was watching him close. But a messenger came to me from Hoadley of the Manufacturers Trust saying that he'd had a message his bank was going to get it that day. I hurried over there, and three minutes after I left the Textile National a bomb was dropped there, and the bandit got away with five thousand."

"Was the message you got, genuine?" asked Mme. Storey.

"From Hoadley, yes. But there was nothing in it, of course. If I'd listened to my hunch I'd have stayed where I was."

"But how do you know the bomb was actually dropped by the black-haired man?"

"Oh, I have confirmation of that. From the fellow who stood next to him in the line. Name, Joseph Keating; address, 33 Pineapple Street, Brooklyn. Keating marked the man in front of him because he kept turning his head over his shoulders; without any prompting from me he described him just as I gave it to you. A black velure hat is a little uncommon. Keating swears that the smoke first issued from a spot at this man's feet. Keating says he grabbed at him, but he slipped through his fingers like grease."

Mme. Storey nodded. "Anything more?" she asked.

"Little bits pieced together. The satchel snatched from H. Tannenbaum and Co. was afterwards found on a bench in Crotona Park, as you may remember. That's in the Bronx."

"I remember."

"Whereas the satchel belonging to Kilmer and Brook was found in East River Park."

"Strange he should have left them lying about so openly," remarked Mme. Storey.

"Well, I don't know. A satchel is dangerously incriminating. I suppose he had to drop it where he could. Wouldn't dare carry it home with him. It was the satchel that gave him away to Kilmer and Brook's messenger on Broadway. After that, you notice, he always dropped the satchel at the scene of the robbery, and made away with the contents. How did he carry it? Either in special pockets or in a paper bag. Certainly, the day I saw him in the Textile

National he had nothing in his hands. He couldn't have, you see, because he needed both hands to snatch with."

"But what's the significance of the two Parks?" asked Mme. Storey.

"I'm coming to that. That time he was jostled in the subway, remember; it was the East side subway, Brooklyn Bridge station."

"What does that prove?"

"It doesn't prove anything. But it suggested to me that the East side subway was his beat. Each of the places I have mentioned is adjacent to that line. Working on that, I finally found the girl who sold him the glass balls he made his bombs out of. She works in the five and ten cent store on East 125th. Name, Bessie Rogers. She described him to the life; even the black velure hat. She had marked him particularly because, though he looked out of luck, he bought a whole gross of the glass balls. She couldn't remember the exact date. A few days before the biggest holiday rush began. The first robbery took place December 17."

"Anything more?"

"One other link. The same man has been seen to take trains at the 125th Street station. All the through trains to the West stop there, as you may know."

"Well," said Mme. Storey, "the evidence so far suggests that the man is mad . . ."

"Well, cracked, anyway," said Barron; "a crank."

". . . And since there are five and ten cent stores all over the town, and since he would naturally drop into the one nearest him, the inference is he lives somewhere in the vicinity of East 125th Street."

Barron nodded.

"The probability is, that he lives alone, eh? In a furnished room or cheap hotel. Because if he had a family, they, knowing he was queer, would keep a close watch on him. And he couldn't have any confederates, because no sane man would dare use a crazy man as a tool. It would be too dangerous."

"That was what I figured," said Barron.

Mme. Storey rose. "Well, we start square," she said. "And may the best man win!"

6

DURING THE DAYS that followed I sometimes blamed Mme. Storey in my mind for the apparent lukewarmness of her interest in the smoke-bandit case. To be sure she sent out several operatives to follow up the lines Barron had laid out (I may say here that none of them turned up anything of first-rate importance) but she herself did nothing so far as I could see. She had other cases on hand at the time, but it seemed to me that this one was of such supreme importance everything else ought to have given way to it.

Well, she was not as inactive as she appeared to be. It was simply that she did not choose to confide in me as yet. I have often noticed that she keeps her speculations absolutely to herself until they begin to resolve themselves into facts. So far she was only groping. Three visits that she paid one afternoon had an important bearing on the outcome of the case. The first was to the Public Library; the second to Police Headquarters; and the third to the head office of the telephone company.

One day, nobody else being available at the moment, I was sent up to East 125th Street to investigate a report that a man answering to the description of the one we wanted, was a regular frequenter of the Harlem Y.M.C.A. It took me half a day to run him down, and then it was only to find that he was a perfectly respectable clerk in the Harlem River freight yards. Moreover, he differed in several particulars from the description furnished by Barron.

Thus I had my trouble for my pains. However, in the course of my peregrinations about Harlem, I made the somewhat thrilling discovery that I myself was being followed and watched. My tracker was a blond young man in a belted overcoat buttoned close under his chin, who would have been perfectly inconspicuous had it not been for his steady, watchful gaze. I considered that my discovery was important. It suggested that instead of having a more or less insane individual to deal with as we supposed, we were up against a complete organization. I so reported to Mme. Storey.

She only smiled. "Crider reported that when he was on this case he was trailed," she said. "Sanders and Canby the same."

I said: "Doesn't that prove what I say?"

She blew a cloud of smoke. "I supposed they were just Barron's men. He has a free hand from the Banking Association, remember. He can hire a thousand operatives if he wants."

"But why should he follow us?"

"To make sure that we don't steal a march on him, my Bella!"

I felt somewhat flattened.

"The obvious retort," Mme. Storey went on, musing over her cigarette, "would be to trail Barron . . . But whom could we put on it? If we do it at all, we must do it better than he. And of course he'll be looking for it."

"Crider?" I suggested, naming our best man.

"Barron is too well acquainted with him."

I was unable to think of any one else.

"I have it!" said Mme. Storey. "We'll take a chance on Sampson, that young Englishman who applied for a job the other day. He's a keen and experienced man, and he has cultivated an innocent, wondering air that would deceive the great Lecoq!"

Sampson was duly assigned to the task.

Subsequently I read his reports. They were rather amusing. From them it appeared that Barron, notwithstanding the unpredictable nature of his business, was a model of regularity in his habits. He was a physical culture enthusiast, and he lived at the Amsterdam Athletic Club on Central Park, where he could indulge his tastes to the full. Every day he swam; he boxed; he performed in the gymnasium; he played handball—all presumably in the interests of keeping his growing weight within bounds.

After a variety of exercises he arrived at his office at ten every morning, where he presumably gave interviews and received the reports of his operatives (Sampson could not follow him into his office, of course). Promptly at twelve-thirty every day he went to the Shoe and Leather Club to lunch, always alone. Sampson could not watch him inside the club either, but he never remained there more than forty-five minutes; no more than time to get a meal. Thereafter he always walked up to Canal Street and back, presumably for his precious health's sake, returning to his office at two. At four he returned up-town. But short as his office hours were, he found time twice a day to receive the newspaper reporters in a body. It seemed that he held a regular levee like a Secretary of State.

Back at the Amsterdam Athletic Club, he played handball on the roof, and had a swim before dressing for dinner. He was a sociable soul, and fancied himself as an after-dinner speaker. Being so largely in the public eye he was in great demand at banquets and club affairs. These affairs frequently lasted until all hours. If he got out early, he would go to a cabaret with friends of the evening. He was keen about dancing.

During the whole time that Sampson watched him the routine scarcely ever varied.

"The man is a mere idler!" I said to Mme. Storey. "He's laying back on his case. He's enjoying the notoriety it has brought him, and he means to string it out as long as possible."

Mme. Storey laughed. She said: "It's his leisureliness that impresses me, Bella. The bustling men are negligible. It requires real strength of character to achieve leisure nowaday. Leisure is only the outward seeming. Inside his head I dare say he's as busy as a weaving spider."

"Handball; swimming; punching the bag!" I said. "He thinks about nothing but his gross body!"

"He wants to keep young," said Mme. Storey. "I rather like him for that."

To go back a little in my story; notwithstanding Mme. Storey's wish to keep her part in the case a secret, somebody blabbed, and the newspapers had soon got hold of it. They played it up for all it was worth. The bandit having been quiescent for some days, they needed something to inject fresh interest into the story, and they found it in Mme. Storey's name. It was represented that Mme. Storey and Barron, "the two foremost criminologists of the day," were engaged in a desperate struggle for supremacy. The idea of suggesting that Barron was in the same class with my mistress! The gullible public, of course, bit, and got itself all worked up over the outcome of the "race." For the moment the bandit himself became a quite secondary figure, the grand question being whether Mme. Storey or Barron would win out.

Now Mme. Storey never will consent to "perform in the newspapers" as Barron had put it. When she has nothing to give out she refuses to string the reporters along. Consequently day after day they were turned away from our door, whereas they were sure of a welcome at Barron's. The inevitable result was that Barron loomed larger and larger in the day's news, while we were nowhere. He had now cast aside his former unwillingness to talk. His after-dinner experience had trained him in the art of talking without saying anything. He always had an interesting-sounding story to give out, though it might not possess the slightest significance. He revealed an abounding confidence. He promised "results" very soon now. There came a day when he gave out the description of the man we were all looking for. So exact a description of a being so peculiar, with the various details of his habits, etc., created an immense sensation. Now that everybody knew him, it was felt that he could not much longer keep out of the hands of the authorities. A dozen individuals came forward to testify that they had seen the man in such and such a bank at such a time. Barron's stock went up a hundred per cent. Mme. Storey's name was scarcely ever mentioned in the papers, and the newspaper boys seldom troubled to come to our office.

Mme. Storey smiled at all this, and continued on her serene way. But it made me rage. After all, we lived by publicity and our reputation, and Barron was stealing the one and destroying the other. Furthermore, one could see that what he gave out in the papers was not mere hot air. Every word was deliberately calculated. His confidence was real. He had something up his sleeve. I believed that it was Barron who had given it out that Mme. Storey was in the case, so that he could publicly triumph over her. This showed how sure he was of his hand.

Finally I could stand it no longer, and one morning I exploded in Mme. Storey's presence. "It seems to me you have never realised how important this case is to you!" I cried. "If Barron wins it, it will be a fatal blow to your prestige!"

"Prestige! Prestige! What follies are committed in thy name!" she murmured teasingly.

"Don't laugh!" I implored her. "It makes me positively ill to see the way he puts it over you in the newspapers."

"*Promises* to put it over me," she amended.

"But there's something in it," I insisted. "You can read that between the lines. He's preparing to spring something. He's acting out of revenge, because you have always laughed at him. He thinks he sees a chance to ruin you. Yet you appear scarcely interested. The days pass. Why don't you do something?"

"What would you suggest?" she asked.

Ah! there she had me. I was silenced. Because for me the case was enveloped in a complete fog.

She leaned over and gave me a pat. "Cheer up, my Bella! I am not so idle as you think. Let Barron have his day in print. In the end I hope not to disappoint you."

"Do you mean to say there is actually a chance of our catching the bandit?" I asked eagerly.

"I think there is an excellent chance," said Mme. Storey coolly.

7

MME. STOREY'S CONFIDENCE infected me. I had never known her to assume more confidence than she really felt. As you have seen from the other cases that I have written up, whenever she was at a stand she frankly owned it. I therefore now had reason to believe that *she* had a trick up her sleeve, whereas I only guessed that Barron had. After all, I told myself, it was ridiculous to think that Barron could put anything over on a woman like Mme. Storey.

It was about this time that the smoke bandit made his boldest and what proved to be his last coup. I have described some of the precautions taken by the banks; there were others, of course; each bank had its own plan for meeting the danger. The only place where vigilance might be said to have at all relaxed, was in the banks where robberies had already taken place. There was a psychological reaction in this. With so many banks to choose from, it was felt that the bandit (like lightning) would never strike in the same place twice. In that his extraordinary cunning was not sufficiently taken into account.

The Manhattan National, the richest bank of them all, was the victim of a second outrage on its premises. It occupies, as everybody knows, a magnificent building on lower Wall Street. The customer who suffered this time was the great firm of G. Showalter and Co., manufacturers of printing presses, who have an immense plant on Grand Street with a weekly payroll of sixteen thousand dollars.

For many years Showalter's had sent to the Manhattan National every Friday morning for their payroll, and the old, proud firm disdained to change its habits for the sake of any mere bandit. During all the excitement they had come for their money just the same. They had collected six of the hardest boiled specimens obtainable: a couple of ex-noncoms from the regular army, a pugilist, an ex-bartender and so on. This formidable squad was sent in an automobile openly through the streets to the bank every Friday morning, displaying a perfect arsenal of weapons. They presented their satchel at the paying teller's window; had it filled; and marched out, surrounding it. Showalter's got any amount of fine publicity out of it. It constituted a challenge to the smoke bandit that no one ever believed for a moment he would accept.

But he did.

On the Friday three weeks after the sensational Industrial Trust affair, the formidable six presented their satchel as usual and had it filled. The vast banking-room was never crowded now. Most firms paid by check, and those who had to have cash obtained it through one devious means or another. There were ten or twelve men waiting to draw money, and these were roped off in single file, and held back by the bank's guards, the nearest in line some thirty feet from the paying teller's window. Only one of the line of windows was being used.

As Showalter's men received their satchel, the smoke billowed up in the usual startling fashion. It started at a point some distance from the men with the money, but spread so fast it overtook them before they could reach the door. There was no fault to be found with the actions of the six; they did their utmost. They had often rehearsed what they were to do in such a contingency. They stopped short where they were, and dropping the satchel on the floor, formed a circle around it, each man with his gun in his right hand, and his left hand on the shoulder of the man next him. Thus they waited.

On this occasion there was no panic. Not enough of a crowd in the place to start one. One or two of the clerks fainted in their cages, out of sheer excitement, but there was no noise, no running about. The doors to the banking-room were all blocked by guards, and it was felt that the bandit was certainly trapped at last. Those who were in the place afterwards described the ghastly silence that filled it, while all waited for the smoke to clear.

It was longer than usual in clearing. Some swear that a fresh supply of smoke was released, which was likely true; the bandit had a hard nut to crack. When it finally lifted, the discomfited six, linked together in the middle of the floor with their guns out, beheld their satchel some twenty feet outside the circle, lying on its side, open and empty. And, notwithstanding the guards at the doors, the bird had flown.

I need not dwell on the sensation that was caused by this affair. All that had gone before was as nothing to it. Three weeks had elapsed since the previous robbery, and people had been telling themselves that the depredations were over. It was felt that, since the man's description had been published, and so many details about him, that he would never dare show himself again. But he had dared further than ever before. There now seemed to be an element of magic in it that scared the boldest. How in the world had the bandit succeeded in winning that satchel from out of a linked ring of armed men?

"How did he do it? How did he do it?" I asked.

"Well, my guess," said Mme. Storey, "and it's as good as anybody's, is, that since the smoke rises faster than it spreads sideways, it leaves a clear space of a foot or so close to the floor. If I am right, the bandit works in that, on his belly. How simple to hook the satchel out between the men, and empty it while their heads were lost in the smoke!"

"But how did he get out of the place?"

"In much the same way. It is natural for a man blocking a doorway to stand with his legs spread. I believe that the bandit dived out between one of those pairs of legs at the doors."

"But the guards would have known it," I objected.

"One of them would," said Mme. Storey dryly, "but he wouldn't give himself away."

In the same paper that carried news of the robbery Barron gave out an interview in which he maintained his equanimity and his confidence. He still promised the public quick results. This no longer disturbed me. I told myself that, if Barron knew any more than the rest of us, he should have prevented this last outrage.

As I thought over the matter it had occurred to me that there was something fishy about the thin-faced man in the black velure hat, of whom there had been so much talk. It did not seem reasonable that such a poor specimen, sallow and emaciated, should be supposed capable of the smoke bandit's really brilliant feats of daring. I began to wonder if he might not after all be just an invention of Barron's, put forward to persuade the public that the detective was doing something.

The thought clung to me. The testimony of those who had come forward *after* his description had been published, with accounts of how they had seen him here or there, might be disregarded, I felt. For there are always weak-minded people ready to say anything in order to break into print. There remained the evidence of the salesgirl, Bessie Rogers, and the man, Joseph Keating—but come to think of it, we only had Barron's word for the existence of those two. Nobody else had interviewed them.

When I mentioned my suspicions to Mme. Storey, she smiled at me in her affectionate and teasing way, and said: "'Pon my word, Bella, you are becoming positively acute! Why don't you go over and look up this Keating yourself?"

I did so. I am a little behind my story now, for this was the morning of the Showalter robbery. Pineapple street is on the edge of the fashionable Columbia Heights section. It is a sober street of plain brick-fronted dwellings, old-fashioned and very American. Number thirty-three was a superior boarding-house. When I asked the pleasant-faced landlady if she knew a Mr. Joseph Keating, she nodded, and I thought I had had my journey for nothing. He was not a myth. But when I asked to see him, she said he no longer lived with her.

"He was only here a few weeks," she added. "He's a construction engineer, and he's gone to the Coast on a big job. No, I haven't got his address."

I came away satisfied that "Keating" was merely a plant of Barron's, though I did not suppose that the landlady was a party to it. I so told Mme. Storey.

"I was sure of it," she said coolly. "If you want to, you can go up to the five and ten cent store to ask for Bessie Rogers. But you'll only be told that she was temporarily engaged for the Christmas rush, or something of that sort."

"Then there's no such a person as the thin-faced man in the black velure hat!" I cried.

"Ah, now you're going too fast!" she warned me.

It was then that we read of the Showalter robbery.

That same afternoon Barron dropped in at our office on his way up-town. I don't know what his object was. His talk did not reveal it. Perhaps just a hunger to see my mistress's face. He was as guarded as upon his previous visit, but he couldn't quite conceal the conflict of passions that tormented him. He was mad about Mme. Storey; he was jealous of her, he was determined to injure her if he could, and he clearly anticipated some sort of hateful triumph. All this was suggested in the slow, painful turning of his eyes, and it made me uneasy all over, again.

They discussed the Showalter case in general terms; under the circumstances they could hardly be frank with each other. Later I remember Mme. Storey saying teasingly:

"I have turned up a new clue to the whereabouts of the thin-faced man with the black velure hat. Hope to lay my hands on him in a day or two."

"I wish you luck," said Barron with a slight smile, by which he wished to convey that he knew she was bluffing, and was not in the least disturbed by it.

"You know where he is?" Mme. Storey asked mockingly.

"I have a good idea," said Barron confidently.

"Why don't you produce him, then?"

"I will in good time. My lines are closing about him. He cannot escape me eventually."

"My dear fellow!" said Mme. Storey. "This is merely the jargon of our trade when we're all at sea."

"It may be," he said undisturbed; "but in this case it's the literal truth."

The man's confidence was real, and my breast was heavy with anxiety. Mme. Storey's brow was clear, but you never can tell about her.

To my astonishment she proceeded to treat Barron better on this occasion than I had ever seen her do. Ignoring his surly look, she was entirely friendly and encouraging. So much so that he dropped his guarded air, and almost lost his head. Only my presence restrained him. He cast poisonous looks in my direction, but I sat tight. In the end, however, Mme. Storey carried him on uptown in her car. I could make nothing of it.

At noon on the following day, Mme. Storey issued out of her room, cloaked and hatted for the street. "I'm going to drop in on Barron accidentally," she remarked with a casualness that was simply to tease me. "If he asks me to go out to lunch I'll accept."

I simply stared.

"They say the food is awfully good at the Shoe and Leather Club."

"Do women go there?"

"Yes; I have made inquiries."

She went on. This move was inexplicable to me. I blamed her for her changed attitude toward Barron. Surely she couldn't be going to fall for the man! That was unthinkable. No, it was some long game that she was playing; the corners of her lips betrayed it. But if it was true that Barron had the upper hand of her in this confounded case, it seemed to me that she was compromising her dignity in making up to him. And whichever way the case went, this would certainly be the cause of trouble with him later on.

8

ALL SHE SAID when she got back was: "The food *is* good there; the service wonderful."

She presently asked about Crider's movements. I told her he was due in, to report at four.

I was present when Crider made his report, which had to do with some other case. When I had taken it down, Mme. Storey disposed of that matter with a wave of the hand.

"Tomorrow is Sunday, unfortunately," she said "and we can do nothing. On Monday morning we three must set to work in earnest on the smoke-bandit case."

Crider and I pricked up our ears.

"You have a chauffeur's livery, haven't you?" Mme. Storey asked him.

"Yes, madam."

"I want you to hire me a good-looking car for the day; say a Mackinaw limousine or a Bruce-Vulcan. It must look like a first-class private turn-out. We'll start a few minutes before eleven. We're going to Jersey; near a village called Cranford."

"I know it," said Crider; "near Plainfield."

Mme. Storey went on: "I want you to be prepared to break down in front of a house which I'll point out to you, so that Bella and I will have to wait there a bit while you are fetching assistance."

"The simplest thing would be to run out of gas there," said Crider.

"No. They might have a supply on hand at this house," said Mme. Storey. "That would defeat my whole purpose. I want an hour there, or at least half an hour. What else can you suggest?"

"Well, I could make out my engine went dead, in front of the house," said Crider. "Then when I got out and threw up the hood to investigate, I could break the distributor arm, or some other small part of the ignition. I'd have to telephone to a large town such as Elizabeth or Newark for another."

"Very good," said Mme. Storey. "Let us do that."

To me she went on: "Bella, you wear your prettiest afternoon dress and your new coat. Pull a cloche over your head—people remember red hair so. . . . We must be prepared to answer questions easily and offhand. I'll be Mrs. Wilkinson. I have an apartment on Park Avenue. You are my friend Miss Chassard of Cleveland visiting me for the season." (Mme. Storey entered into these details of make-believe with all the zest of a child.) "We're motoring to Trenton, where my friend Mrs. Esterbrook is entertaining us at luncheon to be followed by bridge But is Cranford on the road to Trenton, Crider?"

"Not quite, madam."

"How could we account for the fact that we were passing that way?"

"A prettier road, madam, and no heavy traffic."

"Splendid! We'll go over all this again on the way there."

Monday morning was clear after rain and bitter cold. There was a whole gale from the Northwest, and even in the well-built car, with a rug over us, we could feel it stealing around our ankles.

"So much the better," remarked Mme. Storey. "Out of common humanity they'll have to ask us in to get warm."

"What are we to do when we get in?" I asked.

"Just keep our eyes and ears open, Bella. I don't know what we will find. Nothing perhaps."

We crossed on the Weehawken ferry, and made our way *via* the Hudson Boulevard to the Plank Road, thence through Newark and on to Elizabeth; not a very interesting route. Beyond Elizabeth we passed through a village or two; then Cranford. A sign on the railway station identified it. According to pre-arrangement we paused opposite the station for a final consultation.

"The house I am looking for is on the road along the river towards Rahway," said Mme. Storey.

"I know the road," said Crider.

"It is described to me as being on the right-hand side of the road about half a mile beyond the Lehigh Valley Railway; a farmhouse about fifty years old, painted white, and having a fancy porch. The name of the people is Colter, but we mustn't ask the way, of course. Do not stop directly in front of the gate; run a little way beyond. But keep the car within range of the windows if you can."

Turning to the right, we proceeded. This cross-country road led us into a silvan neighbourhood lying between the lines of populous suburbs that follow the railways. The views of the fields and the winding river were charming, though everything was bare. We presently crossed another railway, and kept a sharp lookout ahead. All the houses seemed to be about fifty years old and all were painted white. However we were saved from any uncertainty by a neat sign alongside the road, which read:

ABRAM COLTER
Poultry Farm
Chickens and Eggs for Sale

Crider played his part admirably. As we passed the house we felt the power fail, and the car rolled to a slow stop. A surprised look on the face of our chauffeur, and much working of the throttle and spark levers. Mme. Storey leaned forward to ask what was the matter. Shake of the head from Crider. Out of the tail of my eye I perceived a woman at one of the windows of the house, watching us with interest.

Crider jumped out and threw up the hood of his engine. After fussing about inside, he returned to the door of the car.

"The distributor is broke, ma'am. We can't move until I can get a new part for it."

Business of indignation from Mme. Storey. "Whatever shall we do! We'll be late for our appointment. Why can't you see to these things before we start out, Thomas. That's your business!" And so on. And so on. Nothing of this could be heard in the house, of course, but the woman was watching the by-play which accompanied it. "Go into that house, and ask if you can telephone for what you want."

Crider disappeared from our range of vision, and we plumped back in our seats like a pair of excessively annoyed ladies.

"Don't betray any curiosity about the place," warned Mme. Storey; "just appear to be soothing me down."

"Suppose there isn't any telephone?" I suggested.

"Oh, but there is! That's the whole point!"

"I saw a woman at one of the windows," I remarked.

"Yes, and she has sharp eyes! I expect she won't be very hospitable, but we'll demand to be taken in as a matter of right."

Crider was gone a good while. He came back to the car door to report.

"I telephoned to Newark for the necessary part. Ordered them to spare no expense, and so on. They promised to have it here within forty minutes."

"Who let you in?" asked Mme. Storey.

"The woman who was at the window. A decent-looking body, but has a cagey eye. She stuck around while I was telephoning."

"Anybody else in the house?"

"Not that I could see."

"Did she ask us in to wait?"

"No, madam."

"Well, we'll wait five minutes, then make her. You be working over your engine."

At the end of five minutes, with business of shivering, Mme. Storey and I alighted from the car, and retraced our steps to the neat gate in the palings. The whole place was much better kept up than any of its neighbours. Everything spic and span with new paint; the lawn free from litter; glimpses of trim poultry houses and runs in the rear. A short distance behind the house ran the little river.

As we went up the short gravel path, Mme. Storey murmured: "Don't look. Both windows of the upper room on the left are shuttered. Why should a bedroom be closed up, at this season? We must have a look into that room, my Bella."

The woman who opened the door to us was in outward appearance a typical farm wife of the better sort. She wore a neat print dress and spotless apron; a woman in her forties, healthy and comely. But the quiet, wary glance of her blue eyes was significant. You immediately felt that she was much more experienced in the world than the usual farm woman. She was not at all put about by Mme. Storey's elegance, but very much mistress of herself.

"May we come in out of the cold?" asked Mme. Storey, with an assumption of the fashionable woman's condescension towards one whom she regards as an inferior.

The woman was polite, but not at all cordial. "Certainly," she said, opening the door wide.

We were admitted into one of those crude, prosperous interiors which are somehow uglier than the direst poverty. All the furnishings were brand-new and in the worst possible taste. There was a narrow central hall and stairway, and in the wall on either side had been cut an archway flanked with hideous varnished pillars. The living-room was on the left; dining-room on the right. The archways were for the purpose of permitting free circulation of the heat which puffed up in great waves from a pipeless furnace in the cellar. The place was suffocating. Both the visible rooms had a set and unused look, and one guessed that the real business of the house was carried on in the kitchen.

Mme. Storey and I sat down in two of the "over-stuffed" chairs of the living-room suite, while Mrs. Colter hovered in the archway as if of two minds whether to go back about her work or stop and keep an eye on us. The shuttered room was over our heads. Mme. Storey glanced about her superciliously. She was the empty-headed rich woman, to the life. It clearly irritated the woman of the house, but it was well calculated to keep her from conceiving any suspicions of our real purpose.

"Comfortable place you have here," drawled Mme. Storey.

"We like it," said Mrs. Colter.

The conversation did not flourish. Mme. Storey settled her skirts, looked at her finger-nails, moved her shoulders pettishly, toyed with her wrist-watch: in short, the perfect fool. Mrs. Colter watched her somewhat grimly.

Finally Mme. Storey burst out affectedly: "Isn't it too annoying! We'll be late for our luncheon engagement in Trenton. Poor Mrs. Esterbrook! With bridge to follow, you know! And that man has nothing in the world to do but look after the car, and prevent such accidents from happening. Aren't chauffeurs maddening?"

"I don't know," said Mrs. Colter. "I never had one."

Mme. Storey made out not to notice the bluntness. "You drive yourself?" she asked with a stare.

"It's only a Ford," said Mrs. Colter.

Following the direction of her involuntary glance, I saw the car, a new sedan standing in a shed at the side of the house. I made a mental note of the licence number in case it should be required later.

"Fancy! You're braver than I am," said Mme. Storey.

"Oh, it's nothing in the country," said Mrs. Colter.

"How ever can you endure the country in the winter?"

"It suits me very well. I have too much to do to mope."

"Well, I suppose you have neighbours."

"They don't trouble me much; nor I them," said Mrs. Colter contemptuously. "We're from the city."

"Fancy!" said Mme. Storey. "Don't you pine for it?"

"No," said Mrs. Colter. "We were fed up with four-room flats."

"Fancy, only four rooms! And now you keep chickens. I believe it's very profitable."

Mrs. Colter gave her a wary glance through her lashes. "That's what city people think," she said. "We thought so when we came here. And went broke within a year. It's only since Mr. Colter left the hens to me, and took a job in town that we've been able to make out."

This story was not exactly borne out by the aggressive prosperity of the establishment. It appeared to me that Mrs. Colter dwelt a little too much on the humbleness of their circumstances.

"That your husband?" asked Mme. Storey, indicating an ornately framed crayon portrait hanging over the fire-place.

"As a young man," said Mrs. Colter. "But he's changed very little."

Mrs. Colter observed that the portrait hung a little askew, and went to straighten it. Evidently a notable housewife. When her back was turned to us, Mme. Storey gave me a glance, by which I understood that she wished me to pay particular attention to that face.

When I really looked at it I was startled. You know what crayon portraits are. Smug. But with the best will in the world to achieve smugness, the artist had not been able to hide the terrible distinction of this face. No common man, this. Handsome in a certain way; the thick neck and muscular shoulders suggested a fine physical specimen; but he had the *hardest* face I have ever beheld. One could conceive of such a man looking on at the death of his brother unmoved. When Mrs. Colter turned around, I glanced at her with a queer, new interest. Good heavens! what was it like to be *married* to a man without a soul. But she seemed to bear up under it pretty well. She was a hard one herself.

There was another lull in the conversation.

Ever since we had entered the room, something had been making me curiously uneasy. I couldn't tell what it was. Some mysterious intimation to the senses that all was not well in that house. At last, in the silence, it came to me; my hearing is very acute. The merest suggestion of a footfall overhead; the delicate, cat-like fall of a padded foot; wavering, here and there, silent; then back and forth again. It was the aimless effect which was so disturbing. My heart beat painfully.

Mme. Storey, feeling perhaps that my exclusion from the talk was becoming a little marked, addressed her next words to me: "Will you ever be able to forgive me for this, Estelle? You will think that we manage things very badly in the East."

"Not at all, my dear Maud," I answered as carelessly as I was able. "Anybody's car is liable to break down, East or West."

"Miss Chassard is from Cleveland," Mme. Storey said to Mrs. Colter with the mechanical smile that such a woman affects.

"Is that so?" said Mrs. Colter politely, but her cold look at me said plainly that she didn't give a hang for me or my native town either.

Mme. Storey yawned elegantly behind her hand, said: "Oh dear! There's nothing in the world so tiresome as just waiting around! . . . If you have anything particular to do, Mrs. Colter, don't let us keep you from it."

"Nothing particular at the moment," said Mrs. Colter. She sat down.

The move to get her out of the room, if such it was, had failed.

Every time there was a silence I heard the stealthy tread over-head. What was it? I was hopelessly confused. I had got the notion into my head, from Mme. Storey's peculiar glance, that the hard-faced individual over the fire-place was our man; in other words the smoke bandit. And I could well believe it. But what was he doing creeping about the room overhead like a distracted person? Not that man, surely, so hard, so imperturbable, so contemptuous. And why were the shutters closed? Colter must be a familiar character in the neighbourhood. I couldn't get it at all. One thing I was very sure of: I did not want to look in that room overhead. I clasped my hands in my lap to conceal their trembling.

Mme. Storey, continuing her pantomime of boredom, finally said: "Do you care if I smoke?"

Mrs. Colter, with a snap of her blue eyes that said she *did* care, said: "Not at all, if you've a mind to."

Mme. Storey, ignoring the look, produced a cigarette case from her little bag. "Have one?" she said, snapping it open.

Mrs. Colter's only reply was a sort of snort.

"Miss Chassard doesn't indulge either," said Mme. Storey blandly. She took a cigarette, and searched further through her bag. "I declare I have come away without any matches," she said.

I knew this was a lie, because she had smoked in the car on the way out.

"Could I trouble you, Mrs. Colter?" she asked with the offen-sive sweetness affected by the kind of woman she was portraying.

Mrs. Colter bounced up. We understood her to say the matches were in the kitchen.

The instant she was out of sight, Mme. Storey sprang into ac-tion, holding out a peremptory hand to me. There was nothing for it but to obey. In the hall alongside the stairs, a curtain hung down as it to conceal coats and hats.

"Look behind that!" Mme. Storey whispered. "Be quick!"

She herself ran half-way up the stairs, making no more noise than a skipping feather; looked, and ran back. In ten seconds we were back in the living-room and in our chairs. I had looked too.

Mme. Storey's face was all alight. "We're in luck, Bella," she whispered. "The key is in the door."

I could make nothing of that.

"Did you see anything?" she asked.

I nodded, feeling half sick with excitement. "Old black velure hat; dingy grey overcoat," I whispered huskily.

"Ha! that was what I wanted!" she said.

When Mrs. Colter came back with the matches, Mme. Storey was sitting there with her legs crossed, and her cigarette held impatiently in the air. What a woman! Lighting up, she deeply inhaled the smoke and let it float out of her nostrils. Mrs. Colter's face was a study.

Fortunately I was not required to do anything. I was demoralised inside. You see I had made up my mind that the thin-faced man with the black velure hat was nothing but a figment of Barron's imagination; and here was the hat! To be sure, there is more than one old velure hat in the world, but I knew from Mme. Storey's exclamation that this must be *the* hat. Well if he was the bandit, where did Colter come in? It was supposed to be a single-handed job. All I could do was to watch my mistress and wait for the next act in the drama. Suddenly the fog of my confusion was pierced by a little ray of triumph. Anyway, we had stolen a march on Barron!

The fitful conversation had been resumed. Amidst the empty chatter of a conceited woman, my mistress insinuated some shrewd questions, but Mrs. Colter as shrewdly evaded them. The insolent manner of her visitor kept the woman of the house in a simmer of exasperation, but it was clear that she never suspected us to be other than we seemed. How clever my mistress was! An ordinary person would have set out to conciliate the hard and wary Mrs. Colter, and would thereby certainly have aroused her suspicions.

Finally I saw a service car roll up and come to a stop behind our car. Now for the dénouement, I thought. With a great effort of the will I sought to quiet my shaking nerves.

"At last!" cried Mme. Storey jumping up. "Now you will soon be relieved of us, Mrs. Colter."

The woman murmured something polite, in which her hard eyes had no part.

"How can I *ever* thank you for your kindness!" cried Mme. Storey with palpable insincerity. "I wish I could repay you in some way. . . . Can I buy some eggs?"

"Certainly, if you want," said Mrs. Colter coldly. "Eggs are high now."

"No matter," said Mme. Storey. "I'm sure the lady we're going to see would adore to have some fresh eggs—that is, if they are fresh."

"We don't keep eggs at this season," said Mrs. Colter with a bored air; "they're worth too much. I'll have to fetch them from the nests. The others have been shipped."

"Oh, goody!" cried Mme. Storey. "Think of having eggs out of the nest, Estelle!"

Mrs. Colter went out through the dining-room. Presently we heard the kitchen door close. Mme. Storey seized my hand, and pulled me towards the stairs. I dragged back in a panic of terror. The man would put up a frantic struggle, I thought, and only us two women! It seemed to me that Mme. Storey had taken leave of her senses.

"Wait . . . wait for the men!" I stammered.

Mme. Storey laughed a single note—astonishing sound in my overwrought ears! "Oh, we're not going to take him into custody," she said. "Come on!"

I followed her up the stairs blindly. A short turn around the landing, and we were at the door of the room over the living-room. Mme. Storey turned the key and softly opened the door. She kept her hand on the knob. On account of the closed shutters we could not see anything at first. But we heard the gasping breath of the creature inside. Then we saw him, arrested midway in his prowl to and fro. He crouched there, staring at us; his black hair hanging down over his shadowy, distended eyes.

There could be no doubt but that it was the same man who had so often been described; I saw the attenuated frame; the gaunt, sallow face with its long nose; the lank, black hair. He was wearing felt slippers. There was a bedstead in the room, with a mattress upon it, but no bedclothes. There was not a thing else in the room.

One long look, and Mme. Storey closed the door again, and softly turned the key. I was hopelessly confused in my mind.

"But why . . . but why?" I whispered.

"I want you to be able to testify that you saw him here," she said.

We returned downstairs. A moment or two later the woman came back with the eggs. I was in a daze. I found myself outside the house without any clear notion of how I got there.

As we went down the path I asked incredulously: "Are you going to leave him there?"

"For the present," Mme. Storey answered inattentively.

"But having seen us, he's warned now. They'll spirit him away!"

She merely smiled at me abstractedly. Her mind was far away; busy with some knotty problem.

We met Crider coming to tell us the car was ready. We started. At the first turn to the left we circled back towards New York. All the way back to town Mme. Storey was in a deep study, smoking one cigarette after another, and I dared not question her.

On reaching the office I was relieved to hear her give orders to Crider to have the house near Cranford watched throughout the night.

9

BUT IT SEEMED as if the precaution was taken too late; for that very night the blow fell. It is my habit to sleep with a window raised, and towards one o'clock I was awakened by a noise in the street. When I collected my senses sufficiently, I heard a raucous voice bellowing:

"Wuxtra-a-a! Wuxtra-a-a!" An indistinguishable murmur followed, then louder: "Wuxtra-a-a!! . . . Wuxtra-a-!!"

My heart leaped into my throat. The effect of such a bellowing in that quiet street of sleepers was nerve-shattering. Then I became hotly indignant. To think that such a thing should be permitted in a civilised city! I had not the least doubt that it was a hoax. But I began to reflect that this particular nuisance had been pretty well abated during the last few years. Formerly such false alarms were a regular feature of New York life. There must be something in it this time, I told myself, or the first policeman on his beat would have stopped the racket.

The noise came closer. "Wuxtra-a-a! Wuxtra-a-a! . . ." Then I distinctly heard the words: "Smoke Bandit!" I sprang out of bed, and, shoving my feet into slippers, threw a robe around me, and started down for the front door.

On the stairs I met several of the other boarders similarly attired, and I allowed one of the men, Mr. Steele, to show himself out on the stoop. He came back waving the paper over his head.

"The smoke bandit's caught!" he cried.

A little cheer went up from the knot of half-dressed people in the hall. I did not join in it, for I suspected the worst.

"Who caught him?" somebody asked.

"Barron!" cried Steele.

Knowing that I had a special interest in the case, Mr. Steele thrust the paper into my hands. I read in letters four inches high across the top:

SMOKE BANDIT CAUGHT

The rest of the paper was merely a reprint of one of the evening editions, with a square cut out of the middle of the page to allow for an insert in black-face type. Only twenty lines.

At 11:15 tonight the smoke bandit was nabbed by Walter A. Barron in the abandoned cemetery of St. Aloysius', South Brooklyn. Over two weeks ago Barron discovered the bandit's loot hidden in the disused receiving-vault of the old cemetery. The secret was kept, and ever since Barron and his men have been watching the spot night and day in expectation of the bandit's return. He came last night to stow away the proceeds of the Showalter robbery. Barron himself was on watch. The famous detective locked the iron gate of the vault on his man, and by pre-arranged signal fired his pistol in the air to summon his men who were waiting near by. When the young bandit realised that it was all up with him, he put a pistol to his temple and pulled the trigger. He was dead when they dragged him out of the vault. Barron gave out that his name was Ralph M. Vallon of Brick Church, N. J. Vallon escaped from a mental sanatorium in West Orange on the night of December 11. He answers to the published description of the wanted man. As a result of one of the cleverest bits of work in criminal history, practically every dollar of the loot has been recovered. Further particulars will be found in the morning edition.

Sick at heart, I went back to my bed, leaving them all in their bath-robes and kimonos, excitedly threshing the matter out. Their pitying glances in my direction made me grind my teeth in bitter chagrin. Mme. Storey was a hundred times cleverer than the bull-headed Barron, and it drove me wild to think that Barron was able to make her look small in the public mind.

There was no further sleep for me. Shortly after daylight I was up again, and down at the corner, buying the morning papers. Divested of the usual repetitions and redundancies, the clearest account ran as follows:

Walter A. Barron is the greatest man in America this morning. He has destroyed the menace under which the whole financial world has been cowering during the past two months. Like a modern St. George, Barron has slain the dragon that threatened us all. The smoke bandit, cornered, lies dead by his own hand. Practically every dollar that he stole has been recovered.

Throughout all the excitement of the past weeks, Barron, a steady, dogged man, has been calmly pursuing his own course. From the first he has consistently been promising the public results, and now

he has made his words good. Those who have intimated that he was talking in the air owe him handsome apologies. The events of last night further reveal that none of the other persons who have been
busy investigating the affair has ever been within
hailing distance of the truth. There is no one on the
map today but Barron.

Nearly one hundred years ago a small cemetery
was laid out on the banks of Callopus creek, a beautiful winding stream amidst silvan surroundings
south of the rapidly growing city of Brooklyn. It was
christened St. Aloysius'. The quaint coloured prints
of that old time depict a beautiful spot with weeping
willow trees hanging over the silvery stream, and a
pretty wooden Gothic chapel by the entrance gates.

All that is changed now. The city spread with
unlooked-for rapidity, and the cemetery filled up.
The pleasant stream became an evil-smelling canal,
the fields disappeared under close-ranked factories
and tenements. No permits for additional burials in
St. Aloysius' have been issued for many years. The
chapel burned down, and it was not worth while
rebuilding it. Only the dead trunks of the willows
remain, and the verdant grass was long ago choked
by weeds. The spot bears an evil reputation in the
vicinity. The superstitious believe it to be haunted by
evil spirits. Such was the scene last night of the final
act in the celebrated drama of the smoke bandit.

It now appears that the astute Walter A. Barron
has been working all along on the theory that he
would discover evidence of the bandit in a cemetery;
an old and neglected cemetery, by preference. In and
about New York there are many such places. In his
patient search from one to another, Barron came at
last to St. Aloysius'. There was an old receiving-vault
there, dug into the side of the old creek-bank, lined

and fronted with brick; closed by a gate of thick iron bars. Barron's falcon eyes informed him that the lock on the door had been tampered with. He had it opened.

J. G. Brannan, one of his operatives, was with him when he entered the place,—this was two weeks ago, but the secret has been carefully kept. A single glance inside revealed to them that they had reached their goal. A number of the glass bombs were strewn about, and the simple apparatus for making them. And this was not all. The musty receiving-vault was another Aladdin's cave. In a far corner was a pile of three suit-cases, each one bursting with greenbacks and yellowbacks of large and small denominations: $149,000 in all; or within a few hundreds of the total amount of the bandit's takings, previous to the Showalter robbery.

The money was removed, and the suit-cases left as found. It was at this juncture that Barron permitted himself to promise the public that the robber would be taken. From that moment there was never an hour that the vault was not under surveillance. It so happened that there was only suitable cover for one man; this was a niche between the cemetery wall and the trunk of a dead willow opposite the vault. The watcher was there, while his mates waited in a flat that had been hired on Fremont Street, a hundred yards distant. There were three men in all, and they stood watch, turn and turn about. On cold nights they relieved each other every hour. Barron himself stood his trick with the others. Two revolver shots was the agreed-upon signal in case the bandit returned to his lair.

Last night it was Mr. Barron's watch from 10:30 to 11:30. At the former hour he took up his station behind the willow trunk. At his back was the six-foot brick wall, and over the wall the sluggish waters of the canal. Between him and the vault ran the old driveway into the cemetery, now much broken and washed. Fremont Street was a hundred yards away at his left. It passes in front of the cemetery, and crosses the canal. All the gates into the cemetery were locked, but as the old wall has crumbled down in several places, it is a simple matter to get in and out. Out in Fremont Street, there were lights and people passing, an occasional trolley car; where Barron watched, it was as dark and silent as the grave itself.

After the boisterous wind of yesterday it had fallen still and cold. Barron had just heard a church clock strike the quarter hour when he saw his man. Distant lights drew a faint reflection on the high ground of the cemetery, but down behind the wall it was as black as your hat. The bandit did not come along the road from the direction of the gates, but crept cautiously down the bank from behind the vault, keeping the structure itself between him and the lighted street.

His movements were perfectly assured, as if he had been there many times before. He carried something white dangling from his hand. He let himself into the vault, and pulled the door to after him, but had no means of locking it from the inside. He dropped a sort of curtain that he had inside. Barron couldn't see this, but guessed it from the sounds that reached his ears. He had seen the curtain hooked up out of sight in the vault.

Barron stole across the road; unhooked the open padlock; and, throwing the staple over the hasp, snapped the padlock on. The man inside uttered no sound, but flung his body wildly against the gate. But Barron had him fast. Instantly there was the sound of a shot from within the vault; whether aimed at him or not, Barron could not tell. He had stepped quickly out of range. He fired his own pistol twice in the air. Not another sound came from within.

Within three minutes Brannan and Ling, Barron's two lieutenants, had joined him. A number of passers-by in Fremont Street heard the shots, but none of them cared to venture into that spook-infested place. The three men yanked the curtain down by putting their hands between the bars, and threw their flashlights into the vault. The fellow was stretched out on the stone floor with a gun in his hand, and the blood running from a hole in his temple.

Barron was provided with a duplicate key to the padlock. When they got the door open they discovered that the man was dead. It was the same gaunt, sallow fellow who has been so often described in the press. But he proves to be much younger than had been supposed. Barron, stern man that he is, was much affected. Only he knew the tragic story that lay behind it all. That story has now been revealed, and no one can feel aught but pity. The man was quite mad.

The white object he carried in with him was a stout paper bag with cord handles. On the side of it was pasted a chromo of two lovers in old-fashioned dress, taking leave of each other. It is the sort of bag that women carry home the day's shopping in. In contained sixteen thousand dollars in bills.

An ambulance was called, to make sure that life was extinct. People swarmed into the cemetery on the heels of the surgeon. Barron locked up the vault, and, leaving a guard there, had the body carried to Griffith's mortuary.

Barron afterwards told the fascinating story of the process of reasoning which finally eventuated in the successful capture. "It was nothing but logic and plain horse sense," he insisted in his bluff style. "I am not one of these story-book detectives who can solve a crime for you from a pinch of ashes or a single hair out of the dead man's head. In the beginning, as you may remember, I was furnished with several conflicting descriptions of the bandit, and I have no hesitation in saying that I made no real progress until I saw him that day in the Textile National, as I have already told.

"It was clear to me from the beginning that the man was, if not completely mad, at least unhinged. No sane thief after making a rich haul ever repeats so quick. That was a sort of insane bravado. He didn't even spend what he stole; we knew that all along, because none of the stolen notes ever appeared in circulation. Every bank in the country was on the lookout for those notes, you may be sure.

"Well, if he *was* mad, it stood to reason that he was working alone. An insane man never has any accomplices, because two insane men couldn't turn a trick together. And no sane man would trust an insane man out of his sight. It was further clear that he must live alone, since anybody he lived with would certainly get on to the smoke bombs, etc., not to speak of the quantities of loot he had to dispose of. He had a house, a flat, an unfurnished room, I told myself; some sort of place that nobody else had any right to go into.

"Nothing came of that. All the landlords in town were circularized without avail. I was driven back on the hotels. It is easy enough to trace anybody through the first-class hotels, because they keep a pretty close watch on their guests. Nothing doing there. I was forced to believe that my man was a habitué of cheap lodging-houses. There you're up against it, for men drift in and out of such places, and nobody pays any attention to them, so they have their two bits or half a dollar or whatever it may be for a bed. I still think that Vallon slept in cheap lodging-houses from the night of December 11 until last night, but I cannot tell you which ones.

"I had to proceed without that. Now the frequenters of such places never have any baggage to speak of; I knew it would be impossible for the bandit to conceal his smoke bombs and his big bunches of money in a flop house. So I proceeded on the assumption that he had some kind of cache or storehouse away from the place where he slept. Where would a homeless man be able to find a place to hide anything in the city? That was the grand problem which confronted me.

"I had other lines out, of course. One of them was to investigate the escapes during the past year from all the mental institutions, public and private. There are a lot of these in and around New York, and progress was slow. Over in West Orange I finally turned up rich ore. I learned that Ralph M. Vallon had escaped from the Patching Sanatorium on December 11. From the description furnished me, I knew this was my man. It was a long step forward.

"I say 'escaped' from the sanatorium, but in reality he just walked out, as he had every right to do. A very tragic story came to light. Vallon, who was only twenty-four, though he looked so much older, was, until two years ago one of the most promising young men in Brick Church. He was the only child of George Vallon, a railway official of some prominence. He had been to the best schools and to Columbia University, where he was taking a post-graduate course when his father died. Newspaper readers may remember the first Vallon tragedy. Two years ago last November, George Vallon, in a fit of temporary insanity, shot his wife dead and committed suicide.

"This terrible occurrence unhinged the boy's mind—though not all at once. He had been left well provided for, but he had not a relative in the world. He gradually lost his grip. The doctors told me that in the beginning there was nothing the matter with his mind, but only the ever present fear that he might have inherited his father's madness. He brooded on that until he was indeed no longer responsible. Melancholia.

"Finally, of his own free will, he went to the sanatorium and asked to be taken care of. Whenever he fell into that moody state the impulse of self-destruction came upon him, and he begged to be saved from that. A good part of the time, the doctors told me, he was as sane as you or I. But then these fits would come upon him, and he lost hold entirely. Never violent, you understand; at no time was he considered dangerous to anybody but himself. They watched him carefully to see that no weapon came his way. When he was normal, he was allowed a good deal of liberty, but was always accompanied by an attendant when he left the institution. The worst of these cases, they tell me, is that they are progressive. The patient is always losing ground.

"Finally, as I have said, on the night of December 11, he disappeared. The local police were notified, but no determined steps were taken to apprehend him, because he had never been regularly committed, you see. In the eyes of the law he was still sane. The doctors believed he would return.

"When I learned all this, my first task was to undertake a study of Vallon's boyhood and early youth. I turned up three highly significant facts: firstly, as a boy, his favourite game had always been robbers or highwaymen; he was a leader in that sport. Secondly, as a high school youth, chemistry had been his hobby, and he spent many spare hours in the laboratory. Thirdly, after the catastrophe which wrecked his life, his mind seemed to dwell exclusively with the thoughts of death and burial. His favourite haunt was the old cemetery attached to St. Christopher's church in Newark. At all hours he was seen mooning about there, and it was that which first gave rise to the suspicion that his mind was affected. Even after he had committed himself to the sanatorium, he would ask to be taken there, and they sometimes humoured him.

"After his escape, he was no longer seen around St. Christopher's, but it suggested itself to me that I would do well to look for him in similar places. Not the great modern cemeteries, which are more like parks, and have almost a cheerful air; but the disused burial-grounds, often neglected and overgrown. There are more of such places in and around New York than most people are aware of.

"I had a list made and visited them one after another. St. Aloysius', which looks nowadays like a bit of the war zone in France, struck me as a likely place, the moment I laid eyes on it. And the old receiving-vault; what a hiding-place! It had a rusty old padlock on the barred gate, but it struck me it was not quite rusty enough. Still, the original padlock might have rusted off entirely, and another been put on. I examined the hinges particularly, and discovered that they had been oiled. It had been cunningly done; the surplus oil carefully wiped off, and the hinges rubbed with powdered rust. But you know what oil is; there was a thin, dark line along the cracks of the hinges.

"If it was his *cache*, I didn't want to warn him that it had been visited, so I got a locksmith to open the padlock, and to furnish me with a key to it. I have

already described how I entered it with my operative, J. G. Brannan. It is not a large place; say about
8x15; the walls and the arched roof were of brick,
and it was floored with flagstones. There was a cold
damp chill in the place that struck to the marrow,
and an ancient mouldering smell.

"On either side there were niches in the brick
wall for coffins to rest on; six on a side in three tiers.
These were empty, of course, and the bandit had uti-
lized them for shelves. At the back of the vault on
one side we found a number of the finished bombs
and materials for making others. In the niche on the
other side were the suitcases full of bank-notes. Of
all the thousands he had stolen, he had spent but a
few hundreds. Certainly he was mad.

"There were several boxes of the glass balls which
had not been touched yet. Also a supply of chemi-
cals, etc. I am not going to give out the formula, but
I may say that it was a simple one. Two well-known
ingredients that could be purchased almost anywhere, and a supply of fuller's earth. The fuller's
earth was used to make a sort of cushion between
the two active ingredients in the glass ball. The whole
contents were tamped down with a bit of absorbent
cotton, and the neck of the ball closed with sealing-wax.
When the ball was smashed, the two active elements
were bound to mingle. Simple and ingenious, you see.

"Removing the money, we left everything else
just as we had found it. Thereafter, the place was
watched as I have described. More than two weeks
passed. During this time there was no robbery. Then
came the Showalter affair, and I took a hand in the
watching, personally, because I was sure, then, that
the bandit would visit his *cache* to put away his latest
takings. I figured he would come in the late evening
after the city had quieted clown a bit, but before the

streets were empty enough to make him an object of
suspicion to the police. As it proved, I was right."

Such was Barron's story. To read it, did not lessen my bitterness any. The mock-modest tone of it! How could my clever mistress have allowed herself to be overreached by this braggart? I
asked myself.

At eight o'clock I ventured to call her up. She was accustomed
to wake then, and have her early coffee. The telephone was at her
bedside.

"Have you read the papers?" I asked.

"No," she said. Her tone conveyed nothing.

"Didn't you get the extra last night?"

"Didn't know there was one."

"Barron has caught the bandit!" I cried, full of my bitterness.

"Really!" she said, in the tone she uses when she is thinking of
something else.

It was too exasperating. "In an old cemetery in South Brooklyn. Apparently the same young fellow we saw yesterday afternoon.
When he found himself trapped, he killed himself."

"I will be at the office in an hour," she said coldly. "We will get
busy at once."

When Mme. Storey uses that tone I know she is strongly moved.
By the first law of her nature she is obliged to hide her deeper feelings. I knew it, but, loving her as I did, I never could help resent-
ing it. It makes her seem so inhuman.

Get busy! I said to myself, as I hung up. It seems to me that
everything is over, but the shouting.

I did not learn, until I saw Crider, that Mme. Storey had in fact
received a report of the whole affair from him before twelve o'clock
the night before.

10

THINGS WERE BUSY at the office that morning. Nobody had time to
explain the situation to me, but I quickly gathered that the smoke
bandit case was not closed, and my spirits began to rise.

Mme. Storey went down to Police Headquarters to interview the Commissioner. I understood that her purpose was to obtain the arrest of the man known as Abram Colter at his work in town. At the same time Crider was dispatched to New Jersey, armed with the authority to order the arrest of Mrs. Colter, and to have her house sealed. I heard Mme. Storey say:

"I do not want the woman particularly, but I must make sure that the evidence in that house is not tampered with."

Crider returned shortly before noon, having accomplished his purpose. Mrs. Colter was greatly astonished, he said, but accompanied the officers quietly. That was a woman nothing could put out of countenance.

Mme. Storey then instructed me to call up Mr. Fulton of the Manhattan National, and ask him if she could see him at once "for the purpose of laying before him some additional evidence in the smoke-bandit case."

Mr. Fulton said, in a rather excited voice: "We're all here at my office now. We're waiting for Mr. Barron. Let her come right down if she wants."

His casual tone towards my mistress angered me. People—even bank presidents, are not accustomed to treat her so cavalierly. However, Mme. Storey appeared not to mind it. She said Crider and I must accompany her, and the three of us set off in a taxi-cab. She carried a book.

To our astonishment we found Wall Street below William choked with an immense crowd. It was with the greatest difficulty that the police were keeping a lane open through the middle. The windows up and down the street were lined with hundreds of additional heads. We had fairly to fight our way under the imposing portico of the Manhattan National. The broad-shouldered Crider opened a way for us. Once, when we were brought to a stand, I asked a boy beside me:

"What's it all about?"

He looked at me pityingly. "Ah-h! Walter A. Barron's going to be here at twelve o'clock."

"Such is fame!" murmured Mme. Storey, with a curious smile.

The board-room of the Manhattan National is on the second floor, overlooking Wall Street. The destinies of a hemisphere are directed here. It is a magnificent chamber; big as the throne-room of a palace. There is a long row of tall windows down one side. There were about fifteen men present; the executive committee of the Banking Association, I understood, including some of the most prominent men in town. A festive air prevailed; all pretence of business had been given up; they were crowding to the windows, commenting on the crowd below.

The large, rosy-gilled Mr. Fulton came to meet us. In repose he was quite impressive, but excitement gave him rather a fatuous air. He tittered. "Did you ever see anything like it? We're expecting Barron at any moment. What a reception he'll get! Well, he's earned it . . . he's earned it!"

"I have important evidence to lay before you," said Mme. Storey firmly.

Mr. Fulton spread out his hands and hoisted his shoulders. "He's caught; he's dead," he said. "What could be important now? . . . Can't it wait? we're hardly in the mood for business."

"It cannot wait," said Mme. Storey.

"Well, Barron is the proper one to pass on it," said Mr. Fulton, with his head over his shoulder. "He'll be here directly."

"I'll wait for him," said Mme. Storey composedly.

Mr. Fulton was already trotting back towards the window. The three of us sat down in chairs near the door. Beyond a curious glance or two, very little attention was paid to Mme. Storey. They were cutting up like schoolboys; cracking jokes, and clapping each other on the back. Ridiculous in fat bankers. I sat there simmering with indignation.

Presently we heard, a good way off at first, a great roar sweeping along. "He's coming! He's coming!" they cried at the windows.

The roll of cheering voices swelled up in an overpowering crescendo. It culminated immediately below the windows in earth-shaking roars; wave upon wave of sound, breaking only to re-form again. It was thrilling, as any great natural phenomenon is thrill-ing. What a tribute to any man not of the blood royal. Whether it were deserved or not—that was another matter.

Two minutes later Barron, flushed and grinning widely, entered the room. He had the grace to look a little bit flustered by the mag-nitude of his reception. I felt a little better disposed towards him for it. He was followed by two plain-clothes men who were fight-ing back the crowd that had forced its way into the corridors. They got the door closed, and held it.

The portly bankers rushed for Barron *en masse*, with out-stretched hands. What a scene of handshaking and back-thump-ing ensued. All were slightly hysterical. I hope they did not mean all they said. The gist of it was, that Barron might have anything in the world he expressed a wish for.

In the midst of it Barron caught sight of Mme. Storey, and his face changed. He came to her, quickly.

"What, Rose, you here?" he said in a tone of hypocritical solici-tude. "I'm sorry."

"Why sorry?" she asked composedly.

"Well . . . this can't be very pleasant for you."

She smiled the same smile that I had seen in the street below. "I have a communication to make to these gentlemen," she said, "I wish you'd get them to listen to me."

"Tell me," he said, condescending and confidential.

"I said, 'to these gentlemen,'" said Mme. Storey. She took a step beyond Barron; all the bankers were staring at us. "Gentlemen," she said, "it was not poor Vallon who robbed your banks, and your customers."

They stared at her with fallen chops—then a babble arose: de-risive laughter, scorn, some anger. "Ho! Ho! . . . Did you hear that! . . . Ridiculous! She's only trying to get into the spotlight!"

"What, gentlemen!" she cried in a voice strong with scorn. "That poor wretch to keep you all in terror! A hypochondriac, wasted by disease! Consider!"

The babble increased. A voice was heard to cry:

"Well, who did it then?"

"That's what I'm here to tell you," said Mme. Storey. "It's a long story. You'd better sit down."

"Sit down, gentlemen, sit down," said Mr. Fulton nervously. "We have retained Mme. Storey. We must at least hear what she has to say."

They dropped into chairs around the long directors' table. Crider and I remained in the background. Mme. Storey stood at Mr. Fulton's right. Unlike most men in a similar situation, she required the support of neither table or chair, but stood alone, a gallant figure. Unwilling admiration glinted sideways out of the eyes of the bankers. Barron also stood, on the other side of the table; his face a hard mask, his eyes fixed on my mistress's face like a preying animal's. He had the whole company with him, and he was not as yet seriously disturbed.

Mme. Storey said: "The man who robbed you, gentlemen, passes under the name of Abram Colter; his real name is Charles or 'Finger' Gahagan. Does that suggest anything to you?"

Heads were shaken about the table. She had at least won their attention.

"Well, it is true, his operations were directed against your *confrères* in the West," said Mme. Storey. "Ten years ago he was famous west of Lake Erie. A bank robber, who was a sufficiently good chemist to manufacture his own explosives. Mark that. I secured his history from the archives of the New York police department, which also furnished me with these photographs." She passed two cards down the table. "He is now forty-seven years old, and looks ten years younger. A man of fine physique, you see. I may add that he is of a tireless activity, and daring to a degree. The first three descriptions of the smoke bandit corresponded roughly to such a man under different disguises. I have secured those disguises, gentlemen. That is your man."

"But the money," said an incredulous voice; "Barron found the money in Brooklyn, and returned it to us; almost every dollar."

"I'm coming to that," said Mme. Storey. "Let me establish Colter or Gahagan first. In the old days he always got away with the loot, and he always evaded the police. For fifteen years he kept them guessing. Then at last, seven years ago, they ran him down, and he was brought to trial for the robbery of the Manufacturers' Trust in Waukesha. They did not lack evidence against him; nevertheless, through the efforts of a clever Chicago lawyer, he escaped through technicalities. He has never been in prison."

Barron had kept his composure; his face was red as ever, but his lips were ashy. "Where is this man?" he demanded.

Mme. Storey glanced at her wrist watch. "In the Tombs," she said dryly. "Since quarter to twelve."

"When Gahagan was acquitted," Mme. Storey went on, "he disappeared from the ken of the police. As a matter of fact he came East; established himself on a poultry farm in New Jersey, where he lived very comfortably on his ill-gotten gains; and, so far as I know, kept within the law."

"Where does Vallon come in?" a voice asked.

"Patience, for a moment," said Mme. Storey. "Three months ago Finger Gahagan was tempted by a friend to engage in a new sort of crime; a dangerous crime that appealed to his daring; a crime that was not a crime, because the loot was afterwards to be returned. Whether it was Gahagan or the friend who suggested the smoke bombs, I can't say. Probably Gahagan; he was the chemist. Neither can I tell you which man picked up the unfortunate Vallon. I know that the plot was already under way when Vallon escaped from the Sanatorium, because it was November 25 when Finger's friend obtained a job for Finger in New York. The job afforded them a means of communication nobody would ever suspect."

When Mme. Storey got to this point the blood began to pound in my ears. I simply could not credit the staggering dénouement that I saw looming ahead.

"Fortunately for me," she went on, "they had sometimes to communicate by telephone also. It was through tracing the telephone calls that I was led to Finger's poultry farm."

Mme. Storey's hearers were frankly confused. "Where does Vallon come in?" the same voice idiotically repeated.

"Where does Vallon come in?" said Mme. Storey, indignation got a little the better of her; "That unhappy youth was kept a prisoner in Finger Gahagan's house up to last night."

"How do you know that?"

"Because I saw him there yesterday at noon. Locked in an up-stairs room. My secretary saw him also."

"This must be looked into," said Barron.

"Who was Gahagan's friend?" cried several voices at once.

"The lawyer who got him off when he was tried," said Mme. Storey.

"Who was that? . . . Do you know his name?"

"Walter Barron."

Absolute silence fell on the room. The discomfited bankers stared at my mistress like puzzled sheep. The only thing to be heard was the murmur of the crowd in the streets. Hundreds had remained there, waiting to see Barron come out again. It lent a ghastly touch of irony to the situation. What a summit for a man to be dashed down from! He had brought it on himself, of course. I stole a look at him. The blow seemed to have robbed him of all sense. His mouth was open, his eyes staring vacantly before him.

He finally got out in a smothered voice: "It's a lie!"

Mme. Storey went on relentlessly: "The job you got for Finger Gahagan was that of waiter at the Shoe and Leather Club where you lunched every day alone—at Finger's table."

"I don't know him," murmured Barron.

Crider had the book Mme. Storey had brought. She held out her hand for it. Exhibiting it to the bankers, she said:

"This handsomely-bound volume is entitled: 'The New York City Government, 19—.' You know the sort of thing, gentlemen; a monument to vanity! Here is a handsome photo-engraving of each city official that year, with his biography facing it. Barron was an assistant district attorney. Here he is. I need not read you the entire biography, but only three lines:

"'Practised law in Chicago, 1907-1912; first attained prominence through his defence of the celebrated Charles or "Finger" Gahagan, accused of bank robbery. Gahagan was acquitted.'"

"But why should Barron put up a job like *this*?" somebody gasped.

Mme. Storey waved her hand in the direction of the murmuring crowd below. "For that," she said.

It was a sufficient answer.

"But I don't understand," wailed Mr. Fulton. "What about the cemetery vault, and the wretched young fellow who was caught there, who killed himself?"

Mme. Storey was betrayed into a gesture of pain. "Until yesterday," she said in a moved voice, "I thought this was just going to be a sort of gigantic practical joke: you were to get your money back, Barron was to get his publicity, Gahagan had his excitement and was to get whatever reward was going; no great harm to anybody. I thought they meant to produce the poor mad youth as the criminal; that he would be returned to the sanatorium, and the matter done with. I never suspected that his death was contemplated, or I should have acted very differently. . . . Please listen to one of my operatives." She beckoned to Crider.

Mme. Storey sat down. Crider spoke from behind her. Barron was a ghastly sight; the mere shell of his former self.

"According to Madame Storey's instructions," Crider began, "I was to watch the house of Abram Colter on the outskirts of Cranford, New Jersey, throughout the night. I proceeded there in a car with another operative, timing myself to arrive about six, or shortly after it became dark. I stopped the car a quarter of a mile down the road in front of a house as if it belonged there. I left my partner inside, and proceeded on foot. The arrangement was, if I didn't return in three hours he was to come and relieve me.

"I concealed myself alongside a shed to the north of the house. From this point I commanded both the front and the back doors. Shortly before eight o'clock Colter came out of the back door, carrying a body in his arms, a slender man, no weight at all for Colter. At first I thought it was a stiff. Colter carried him down through the back-yard to the water's edge; it's the Rahway river there, a small stream.

"Colter had a canoe lying on the bank; one of these paddling canoes. He laid the man on the ground, while he put the canoe in the water. I had a chance to creep up and look close in the man's face. He was gagged; also handcuffed. It was Ralph Vallon. Colter laid him in the bottom of the canoe and pulled a canvas over him. He set off down-stream. There was a good bit of water on account of last week's thaw; swift current.

"I didn't have any boat, and it was out of the question to follow along the river shore. The nearest place I could get a boat was the town of Rahway, three miles or so south. Colter was headed that way. I figured if he was only going some short distance, I could pick him up again later, but if he was going to Rahway or beyond, I'd better be waiting there in a boat.

"I ran back to my car, and we beat it for Rahway. I knew I'd have about half an hour's start of him there, the river winds so. Tide-water begins at Rahway. All the boats lie in a sort of pool below the bridge. My partner and I hired a motor-boat with an engineer, and lay in it quiet. Pretty soon the canoe came under the bridge, and passing us, tied up to another motor-boat, further down-stream. There was a man waiting in that boat. They set off down the river, towing the canoe. We unhooked from our moorings, and drifted after, giving them a long start in the river.

"To make a long story short, we followed them out of the mouth of the Rahway river, through the Kill von Kull, around Staten Island. They showed lights, and we took a chance and ran without any. They cut across the upper bay, and turned into the Callopus canal basin. Here they loafed a little while without doing anything. I suppose they were too soon for their appointment.

"We couldn't follow them into the narrow canal without their spotting us, so I got out on a wharf, and followed the other boat as best I could on foot. On the right-hand side of the canal, the buildings came right to the water's edge, but on the left side there was a narrow road, the tow-path, I suppose. Coal-yards, lumber-yards, junk piles alongside. As dark and solitary a spot at night as you could find in all the five boroughs.

"The engine of the motor-boat was no more than just turning over. I could follow her by reason of her being painted white. A third of a mile or so from the basin there was a cemetery on the right-hand side—the side opposite to me. I know now that it is St.

Aloysius'. The lights of the city cast a sort of faint glow on the high ground, but where I was it was pitchy. The motor-boat was just a grey streak on the oily canal.

"They came to a stop near the corner of the cemetery, beside a place where the wall had fallen. I was real anxious, because I couldn't see proper, or follow if they left the boat. The Fremont Street bridge was about three hundred yards up-stream, but I was afraid if I ran around that way I'd miss everything. So I just slipped into the water, and swam across—"

"In February!" somebody exclaimed.

"It isn't above seventy feet wide," Crider explained apologetically. "And I knew it was essential to Mme. Storey's plans, for me to get full information. I tied my overcoat at the back of my head to keep it dry as well as I could. I landed below the motor-boat, and making a little detour, skinned over the brick wall, and crept back inside it. A third man had joined the other two while I was swimming. They hadn't much to say to each other. It seemed as if everything was all arranged.

"One said: 'Is he conscious?' Another answered: 'Sure!' Then the first voice said: 'Don't start your engine right away, but scull down quietly until you're well away from here.'

"I was just inside the wall, you understand. A little bit of light was reflected through the break in the wall, enough for me to see a man come through, carefully picking his way over the fallen bricks; a heavy man wearing a Chesterfield overcoat and a soft hat turned down all around. He was carrying Vallon. Inside the wall there was a sort of road. He walked along that and I followed. Quite a ways; two hundred yards, maybe.

"He came to the vault. He went in a little way, but I could still see his back, I couldn't go up close, because of the light reflected from Fremont Street, which was pretty near to the vault. He was there a minute or so. I supposed that he took off the gag, because I heard a sort of groan from Vallon. I can't tell you exactly what happened, because I couldn't see. Barron backed out of the vault and I heard a shot inside. I saw him fire his pistol twice in the air. In no time at all two men came running from the direction of Fremont Street."

"You say it was Barron," asked a voice from the table. "Can you swear to that?"

"Yes, sir," said Crider. "When the two came, all three had their flashlights out, throwing them this way and that. And I saw the face of the big man in the Chesterfield overcoat. It was Barron. He's wearing the same coat now."

Again the silence of stupefaction fell upon us all.

"I want to say, gentlemen," added Crider, "that nothing that was said indicated that the two operatives were privy to his schemes. From the moment of the firing of the shots everything happened just as he said it did."

At the end of Crider's matter-of-fact story, Barron, who had held himself so stiffly throughout, suddenly collapsed. It was a shocking sight. He dropped into a chair, and his head fell forward on the table. A scene of great confusion followed. Mme. Storey and I and Crider got away as quickly as possible, leaving the bankers to deal with Barron. As a matter of fact, he, who had been cheered into the front door by a thousand throats, was taken out of a rear door handcuffed, and rushed to the Tombs.

That's the story. Nobody will ever know for sure if Barron fired the shot that killed young Vallon. Crider's testimony indicated that he did not. Why should he, when he knew that a pistol had only to be shoved into the unfortunate young man's hand for him to kill himself. But, though it was impossible to bring him to trial for murder, I don't think anybody ever felt that Barron was insufficiently punished. What a fall! He got fifteen years. He will never be heard of again, of course.

Finger Gahagan turned state's evidence, and got off with ten years. His story on the stand filled up the gaps in Mme. Storey's hypothesis. The original proposal for a series of fake robberies came from Barron. Finger invented the smoke bombs, and planned the details. Barron kept him supplied with full information respecting the measures taken by the banks. Finger picked up young Vallon by accident, wandering at night in a demented state over the New Jersey roads. He was just what they required. It was as if the devil had put him in the way of that precious pair.

Finger's price was to be whatever was offered as a reward, with a guarantee of twenty-five thousand. As a matter of fact the reward finally amounted to fifty thousand. Barron could well afford to let him have the whole of it, since he expected to be established for life at the head of his profession. All the details were cunningly thought out as you have seen. "Joseph Keating" and "Bessie Rogers" were two operatives of Barron's.

Mme. Storey never cared to talk much about the case, but once she said: "I knew Barron better than he suspected, but even I had not gauged the depths of his insane vanity. A simple man, you could generally tell in advance what he was going to do. As soon as he was engaged on the smoke-bandit case, he began to behave so differently in all ways from his usual self, that it made me thoughtful. Do you remember that I had tea one afternoon with Mr. Fulton's handsome secretary? I learned from him that it was really Barron who had instigated the bankers to employ me on the case, and it was then that the first little suspicion popped into my head; might not the whole thing be a plot of Barron's to establish himself at my expense?

"At first I laughed at my own thought; it seemed so perfectly preposterous. But one little thing after another strengthened my suspicions: Barron's pretended anxiety to help me, the obvious falsity of the evidence he turned over. Finally I went to work definitely on that theory, and it proved to be the correct one."

THE MURDER AT FERNHURST

IN ORDER TO REST and to escape from the strain of the tremendous publicity that followed upon her success in the famous case of the Smoke Bandit, Madame Storey retired for a few days to the house of her friends, the Andrew Lipscombs, who lived in the Connecticut hills remote from any neighbor. I accompanied my employer, since she insisted that I needed a holiday as well as herself. We simply locked up our offices and went away, leaving the telephone to ring, the mail to accumulate, and the hordes of curiosity-seekers to mill around the door as they would.

We supposed that we had kept the place of our retreat a secret from all, but that fond hope was soon dissipated. Late on the night of our arrival as we were playing bridge with our friends in the blessed quiet of their house, Madame Storey was called to the telephone. She returned to the card table with the grave, remote look that I knew so well, her *working* look, and my heart sank.

"Well, Bella, we have another case," she said.

I laid down my cards. It was useless to protest, of course.

"There's been a terrible affair down at Frémont-on-the-Sound," she went on; "a gentleman has been found in his study, shot dead, and a young girl has been arrested. The man who called me up, evidently the girl's lover, begged me to come and try to get her off. His voice, coming through the receiver, had an extraordinary quality; young and manly; shaken with grief and agitation; yet proud and confident in his girl; it won me completely. I said I would drive right down."

"Murder?" said Mr. Lipscomb, startled; "and so close to us? Who's been murdered?"

"Cornelius Suydam."

"No!" cried our host, springing up. "Why, he's the great man of the neighborhood. His house, Fernhurst, is one of the showplaces! . . . Who is said to have killed him?"

"The girl's name is Laila Darnall."

Both Mr. and Mrs. Lipscomb stared at my employer in stupefied amazement. The former was the first to find his voice. "Merciful Heaven!" he gasped. "She's his ward! Said to be richer than he is. An exquisite young creature; a sort of golden princess; we see her being whisked about in automobiles from one great country house to another. Oh, this will create a terrible sensation! . . . Who called you up?"

"He called himself Alvan Wayger."

"I never heard of him."

"A sort of princess!" Mrs. Lipscomb echoed, aghast; "with everything in the world a girl could wish for! Why on earth should she want to kill her guardian?"

"I don't know," said Madame Storey. "We must go and find out . . . I suppose you will lend me a car and a chauffeur, Andrew."

"Certainly. I'll go with you for a bit of extra protection. I suppose you'll be out the rest of the night. It's near midnight now."

The distance was about twenty miles, and we made it in better than thirty minutes. Fernhurst proved to be an immense country house built of stone in the elaborate style of twenty-five years ago, and standing in its own private park. The house was all lighted up, but we found it perfectly deserted except for a solitary constable on guard, and the young man who had telephoned to Madame Storey. He was a striking-looking fellow with a shock of shining black hair and fiery dark eyes. Somewhat rough in dress and abrupt in manner, but with a glance full of resolution and capacity. It was that kind of terribly direct glance which is disconcerting to ordinary persons, but it is always a sure passport to Madame Storey's favor.

In spite of his grinding anxiety his whole face softened at the sight of my employer's beauty. It was a fine tribute. "I never thought you would be like this," he murmured.

They wasted no time in exchanging amenities. The young man explained that everybody in the house had just gone down to the magistrate's in the village, where a sort of preliminary hearing was about to be held.

"We mustn't miss anything that takes place at that hearing," Madame Storey said crisply. "Drive on down, Bella, and take notes of the proceedings. I will follow as soon as I have looked over the ground here."

I was directed to a large old-fashioned double house standing at the head of one of the village streets. This was the residence of "Judge" Waynham, the magistrate. Already there were half a dozen cars standing in the road, and a knot of people whispering at the gate. A strange sight at midnight in the quiet village! Mr. Lipscomb, who did not wish to intrude himself in any way, waited in the car. Inside, there were people all over the house. No one questioned my presence. The magistrate had not yet come downstairs and everybody was standing about with frozen, horrified faces. A maid-servant was threading her way back and forth between them like a distracted person.

The judge's office was in the back parlor on the left-hand side, and everybody tried to push in there. A quaint room which suggested the era of 1885. I saw the accused girl sitting on a little sofa with her face hidden on the shoulder of a youngish woman in black. Picture a slender, silken girl wearing a flowerlike evening dress of printed chiffon and a white fur cloak which had slipped back. I could not see her face, but the short fair curls that showed against her slender neck were somehow most piteous. She was making no sound, but her delicate, girlish shoulders were shaken with sobs. It was too dreadful to think of anything so fresh and young and fair in connection with murder.

As more and more people crowded in, they opened the folding doors into the front parlor. The distracted maidservant was bringing in chairs. I maneuvered myself alongside a comfortable village matron who looked promising as a source of information. She whispered to me that the lady in black was Mr. Suydam's housekeeper, Miss Beckington. A good-looking woman of thirty-five, I should have said, who appeared younger; very modish, very efficient, one guessed, though at present the tears were rolling down her pale cheeks as she held the girl close. Miss Beckington was something more than a mere housekeeper, my informant said, since she was a person of good family herself, and perfectly capable of acting as hostess to Mr. Suydam's guests. She was wearing a plain black morning dress, a close-fitting hat, and a raccoon coat.

Near these two sat a portly, nervous-looking elderly gentleman, fingering his watch chain. This I learned was "Judge" Gray, the girl's lawyer.

The magistrate entered the room. He had forgotten to brush his hair and it stood straight up all over his head in a very odd fashion. A rosy, kindly old gentleman, he was so nervous and distressed he scarcely knew what he was saying. "Who are all these people?" he demanded. "After all, this is my private house!"

Nobody answered him, and he was obliged to accept the crowd. He had the constable shepherd everybody but the principals into the front room. I got myself a chair in the second row where I could use my notebook without being conspicuous. Judge Waynham sat at his desk facing the rest of us, and a scared village stenographer took a place beside him with *her* notebook.

"Lavell," said the magistrate sharply, "you made the arrest, I assume. It is your place to lay a charge."

This was the chief constable, a tall lanky man with a good-humored, heavily seamed face. Like everybody else connected with the case he seemed completely overcome. He stood beside the magistrate's desk, hanging his head as if he were the guilty one, and mumbled in a scarcely audible voice:

"I charge Miss Laila Darnall with the murder of her guardian, Cornelius Suydam."

One could feel a shiver go through the room.

Suddenly the girl sprang to her feet, showing us all a white and agonizing face, the face of a terrified and uncomprehending child.

Her slender frame was racked with sobs, but her eyes were dry. I shall never forget that desperate face. Though the other woman and the lawyer tried to silence her, she cried out: "How could I . . . how could I have done such a thing? Don't you believe me? Have I not a friend here? Why has everybody turned against me? I am the same girl!" Perceiving three handsomely dressed ladies sitting in the front room (these I learned were her cousins) she ran to them crying: "Helen! Isabel! You believe me, don't you? You know I could not have done such a thing. Tell them all that you believe me!"

"Hush, Laila, hush!" said one of them in cold, correct tones. "Of course we believe you. But let the proceedings go on."

Laila turned from her in despair. "Haven't I a friend here?" she cried.

Miss Beckington held out her arms. "Come, dear," she said tenderly, while the tears rolled down her cheeks. "I am your friend. I know you could not have done it!"

The girl flung herself into her arms. "Oh, thank you! thank you!" she murmured, weeping freely at last. "Forgive me because I have not always been friendly towards you. Once I thought you were cold and unfeeling."

They sank down on the sofa together. It was very affecting, the more so because one could see that Miss Beckington was ordinarily a somewhat hard and self-controlled young woman.

"Do you wish to answer to this charge, my child?" asked Judge Waynham.

"I didn't do it! I didn't do it!" she cried without raising her face from Miss Beckington's shoulder.

"The prisoner pleads not guilty," murmured the magistrate to his stenographer. "Who is your complaining witness?" he asked the constable.

"Mr. Lumley, your honor, Mr. Suydam's butler."

This man stepped forward to testify. A large, soft-looking man with a dead-white skin, he was obviously educated and intelligent, and made a very good impression. He kept glancing at his young mistress commiseratingly. His obvious unwillingness to testify against her gave his evidence all the more deadly effect.

While he was speaking, Madame Storey and Alvan Wayger entered the front parlor from the hall and took seats in the darkest corner. I had a great curiosity concerning this interesting-looking young man who was said to be the heiress's lover. The village matron was still beside me. Calling her attention to him, I asked who he was.

"Oh, that's Alvan Wayger," she said indifferently. "He's nobody in particular. New people here. Haven't made friends much. They say he's a clever inventor, but I never heard of his inventions. Lives with his mother in a little house across the railway tracks. That's his mother against the wall across the room."

I saw a plain, middle-aged woman glancing at her son and his unknown companion with that peculiar jealousy that one sometimes sees in the faces of mothers with an only son. It is a sad thing to see.

Madame Storey had draped a light veil around the brim of her hat so that she could see all without being recognized.

Lumley the butler testified as follows:

"My name is Alfred Lumley. I have been employed by Mr. Cornelius Suydam as butler for the past four years. At the present time the household consists of Mr. Suydam, his ward Miss Darnall, his housekeeper Miss Beckington, myself butler, Mrs. Finucane cook, and five maids. There is also Dugan the engineer, who has a room in the basement; Leavitt the gardener, who lives with his family in the cottage at the park gates; and Pressley and Gordon, chauffeurs, unmarried men who board with the gardener's wife.

"I retired tonight shortly before eleven. There were no guests in the house, and I believed at the time that everybody was in bed except my master, whom I left reading in his study, as was his custom. The study occupies a separate wing of the house, somewhat cut off from the other rooms. I was in bed, but had not fallen asleep when I heard the sound of a muffled shot. Had I been asleep I should probably not have heard it. But I thought it came from inside the house. I sprang out of bed and flung on my clothes. I heard the clock of St. Agnes' strike eleven. My room is on the third floor of the house. I didn't attempt to waken any of the womenfolks. I ran down the two flights of stairs. I knocked on the library door. No answer. I tried the door. It was locked."

"One moment," interrupted Judge Waynham, "was it your master's custom to lock the door when he was in his library?"

"No, sir. No indeed, sir."

"Well, go on."

"I called loudly. There was no answer. My first thought was of robbers. The safe was in the library. I could not tell how many there might be, and I was afraid to venture outside the house alone. So I ran down to the basement and wakened Dugan. He was provided with a gun and electric torches. He threw on his clothes and came with me. We went out the front door and around the house to the library windows. There is a big bay with French windows opening directly on the terrace. The windows were open . . ."

"Cool as it was?" interrupted the magistrate.

"It was my master's custom, sir . . . The room was brightly lighted. We saw . . ." Lumley hesitated, and a shudder went through his stout frame.

"Go on," prompted Judge Waynham.

"My master was seated at his desk in the center of the room. His head had fallen forward on the desk blotter. There was a bullet hole just back of the left temple. His blood had spread over the desk and was already dripping to the floor. He was dead. The door of the safe stood wide open. Beside it lying open and face down on the rug was a little memorandum book. I recognized it as a book my master always carried on his person. On the open page was written down the combination of the safe. The safe was full of papers, none of which appeared to have been disturbed, but there was a little drawer which had been pulled out and emptied. An empty jewel box lay beside it."

"Do you mean to say," interrupted Judge Waynham, "that Mr. Suydam sat in that brightly lighted room late at night with the windows open and unshuttered?"

"Such was his custom, sir," said Lumley, deprecatively. "I had ventured to remonstrate with him about it, but he only laughed at the idea of personal danger. The windows were protected by copper screens, of course. The murderer had fired through the screen, and had then raised it to enter."

"Well, go on."

"Dugan and I searched outside with the electric torches. Bordering the terrace is a flowerbed, and in the loose earth of the bed we immediately found the tracks of the murderer where he had come and where he had left again. Only one set of tracks. They appeared to be those of a large man wearing rubbers, but there was a peculiarity in the tracks . . ."

"Please explain yourself."

"Well, in the middle of the print of each foot there was a roughness which suggested to both of us that the rubbers had been tied to the wearer's feet by strips of rag or something of that sort."

The man's story was almost too painful to follow. A deathly silence filled the room which suggested that his hearers were actually holding their breaths.

"We followed the tracks to the edge of the flowerbed," he went on. "In the grass we lost them, but knowing that a person leaving a place in a hurry usually runs in a straight line, I kept on in the same direction. This took us across a rosebed in the center of the lawn, and here I found the tracks again. By taking a line with the library window and the rosebed we were enabled to find the tracks again where the murderer had struck into the woods. A little way in the woods we came to a place where the earth had lately been disturbed . . ."

"How do you mean?"

"Well, a hole had been dug, and hastily filled in again. We dug there and found firstly a pair of old overshoes gray with dust and dried mud; secondly a thirty-two-caliber automatic pistol; thirdly several pieces of diamond jewelry, tied up in a woman's handkerchief. Dugan immediately recognized the overshoes as an old pair that he used in the winter when he shoveled snow. He had last seen them lying beside the furnace pit where they had been dropped and forgotten." Lumley hesitated, with a piteous glance in the direction of his young mistress.

"Go on! Go on!" said Judge Waynham impatiently.

"The tracks that led away from that place had been made by a woman," said Lumley very reluctantly. "She was wearing what is called, I think, a commonsense shoe, that is a shoe with a moderately broad toe and a low heel. The tracks led us towards the main driveway, but we lost them in the grass before we got there, and of course the hard driveway revealed nothing. So we turned back towards the house meaning to call up the police." His voice sank. "As we approached the house we saw a figure standing in the driveway, its back towards us. The figure of a woman. We stepped into the grass to avoid giving warning of our approach. A moment later I recognized . . . Miss Darnall . . ."

A low murmur of horror escaped from the listeners.

"When I touched her she screamed," Lumley went on. "I thought she was about to faint . . ."

The girl suddenly cried out, "Was that strange? Was that strange? A man coming up on you in the dark without warning . . ."

Judge Gray and Miss Beckington quieted her.

"I led her into the house," Lumley went on unhappily. "As soon as we got in the light I saw—though she was dressed just as you see her now—that she was wearing shoes with broad toes and low heels. Moreover, the gun was quickly identified as one which had been given her by Mr. Suydam some months ago. It was his opinion that everybody ought to be furnished with the means of personal defense. One shot had been fired from it. The handkerchief was also Miss Darnall's. It has her initials embroidered in it."

There was a silence. The girl's shuddering sobs could be heard. Miss Beckington patted her shoulder.

Judge Waynham wiped his agitated face on his handkerchief. "Well, is that all you have to say?" he asked.

"Not quite all, sir," said Lumley in an almost inaudible voice, while we in the front room leaned forward to hear. "I had Miss Beckington roused up, and I delivered Miss Darnall into her care. I forced Miss Darnall to take off one of her shoes—I thought it my duty to do so—and Dugan and I returned to the woods with it. I had read somewhere that the proper procedure was not to attempt to fit the shoe into the suspected tracks, but to make a new impression alongside. This I did. I am sorry to say that the impressions correspond exactly . . . That is all I have to say, sir. When I got back to the house I telephoned for the police."

Lavell the constable laid the sport shoe on the desk.

"One question," said Judge Waynham. "How could Miss Darnall ever have got hold of those overshoes? I assume she was not in the habit of visiting the cellar."

"I asked that question of Dugan, sir," said Lumley. "He told me that a week ago when he was confined to his bed by an attack of tonsillitis, Miss Laila came down to his room to visit him. To reach his room she had to pass the furnace. She must have seen the overshoes then."

The girl tore herself out of the protecting arm of Miss Beckington. Her soft young face worked piteously. "It's a lie!" she cried. "I never saw the overshoes until tonight! It's all lies! I . . . I . . ."

Judge Gray put an arm around her shoulders. "My child," he said soothingly, "be silent! This is neither the time nor the place. You must be guided by me . . ."

She sprang to her feet. "Let me be!" she cried hysterically. "I *will* speak! I won't have these people thinking I did this awful thing! I can explain everything. I have nothing to conceal . . . I had been out of the house ever since nine o'clock," she went on wildly and incoherently. "As for my shoes, I always put on sport shoes when I went out in the park at night. Would they have me wear slippers? . . . Since nine o'clock! I heard no shot. I didn't know anything was the matter. But when I got back to the house I found that the hall was lighted up and the front door standing open. So I was afraid to go in. That's why I was standing there looking at the house . . . My handkerchief . . . my handkerchief, I still have it with me. One wouldn't carry two. In the pocket of my cape . . ." Turning, she searched with frantic trembling hands in the folds of the cape. "It's here . . . I'll show you . . ." Then a despairing cry: "Oh, it's gone! . . . I swear I had it a while ago!" She dropped on the sofa shaken with fresh sobs. It was an unspeakably painful exhibition.

"What did you go out of the house for?" Judge Waynham asked gently. ". . . You don't need to answer unless you wish."

"Yes, yes, I will answer," she cried, striving hard for self-control. "I went out to meet my . . . to meet the man I am engaged to marry. He wasn't allowed to come to the house, I was forbidden to see him. That's why I had to meet him by stealth. I'm not ashamed of it. It's Alvan Wayger . . . ."

A soft, long-drawn Oh! of astonishment escaped from the listeners. In a village where everybody prided themselves on knowing everything this was a startling disclosure. The heiress and the poor young inventor! Everybody looked at the handsome, dark young man who sat there with a perfectly blank mask upon his face. So far as I had observed the two had not once looked at each other during the proceedings.

Judge Waynham energetically polished his glasses. When he recovered from his surprise he looked relieved. I think we all had the same thought. Perhaps after all, here was a perfectly natural explanation of the girl's movements. "Will you answer a few questions, Mr. Wayger?" asked the judge.

"Certainly, sir," said the young man, marching up to his desk.

"Miss Darnall met you in the park at Fernhurst tonight?"

"Yes, sir. We had an appointment to meet at nine o'clock at a certain stone bench under an elm tree near the entrance gates."

"How long did she remain with you?"

"About two hours, sir."

"Can't you tell me exactly what time you left her?"

"No, sir, I didn't look."

"Did you then go straight home?"

"Yes, sir."

"How long does it take you to walk home?"

"Fifteen minutes, sir."

"At what time did you reach home?"

"I cannot tell you exactly, sir. I took no notice."

Here there was an interruption from the front room. "If you please, Judge, I can tell you," said a bitter voice. Mrs. Wayger, the young man's mother, had risen. She cast a look of dislike on the girl. "I was lying awake when my son came home," she said. "After he was in his room I heard the clock in St. Agnes' steeple strike eleven." She sat down again.

Young Wayger received this without a sign of emotion beyond lowering his head slightly. His face was not hard, but simply inscrutable. For my part I could not help but sympathize with his determination not to betray his private feelings before that gaping crowd.

Judge Waynham's face fell. "So," he said heavily, "then it appears you must have left her at quarter to eleven or earlier."

Wayger made no answer.

"Miss Laila," said Judge Waynham, turning to the girl, "if Mr. Wayger left you at quarter to eleven, and Lumley found you at quarter past eleven, what had you been doing during that half-hour! You need not answer unless you wish."

We all held our breaths waiting for what she would say.

"I will answer . . . I will answer," she stammered. "I hadn't been doing anything . . . Just walking up and down the driveway. I was greatly troubled in my mind. I was trying to think . . . to think of some way out!"

It was a deplorably lame answer. In spite of his iron self-control I saw a spasm of pain pass across the young man's face. I think we all gave the girl up for lost then. Judge Waynham's kindly old face was heavy with distress. He tapped his glasses on his desk blotter while he considered. Suddenly a gleam of hope lighted up his eyes.

"The circumstances are unfortunate, most unfortunate," he said, "but no motive for such a terrible deed has been shown, or even suggested . . . Mr. Wayger, I would like to ask you a few more questions."

The young man signified his readiness to answer.

"What were the relations between Miss Darnall and her guardian?"

"I object!" said Judge Gray instantly.

Judge Waynham wagged a soothing hand in his direction. "This is only a magistrate's hearing," he said. "You will have your day before a jury later." He repeated his question of Wayger.

That young man's face hardened. "I don't know that I care to answer that," he said firmly. "It's not up to me to repeat what I learned from Miss Darnall in confidence."

At this juncture Madame Storey raised her clear, distinct voice from the back of the room. If you had heard that voice in the dark you would have known that it belonged to a notability. "Mr. Wayger, I advise you to answer," she said. "The whole truth must come out. By your apparent reluctance you are only prejudicing Miss Darnall's interest."

All the people goggled at the veiled woman, then looked at each other. "Who is this?" you could see them saying.

The young man instantly changed his attitude. "Very well," he said, "the relations between Miss Darnall and her guardian were bad. He was a very oppressive guardian. He had peculiar notions. It is well known that Miss Darnall's income runs into hundreds of thousands of dollars annually, but he would not allow her a cent of spending money."

"What?" exclaimed Judge Waynham.

"It is quite true, sir. Of course, she was provided with everything a fashionable young lady might be supposed to require. She was encouraged to buy whatever she wanted in the shops and have the bills sent in. But she had no money to spend. She was not allowed to drive her own car. In fact she was never allowed out unless accompanied by a chauffeur or a chaperon. All this was very galling on a girl of spirit.

"We wished to get married," he went on in his quiet and self-respecting manner, "but that was quite out of the question, of course. I have all I can do to make ends meet as it is, and Mr. Suydam had absolute control over Miss Darnall's money for two years longer, and partial control for four years after that. He had no use for me at all. He made no bones of calling me an impostor and a fortune hunter. That didn't bother me at all—I have my work to do—but it distressed Miss Darnall very much."

"But this has been going on for some time," suggested Judge Waynham; "this would not account for Miss Darnall's special trouble of mind tonight. Can you tell me what caused that?"

"Certainly, sir. It was what we had been talking about all evening. I have completed an invention. I need not go into detail about it. Properly applied, my invention would revolutionize a certain important industry. Well, I have received an offer from the corporation which controls that industry. Miss Darnall was strongly opposed to my accepting the offer. It was not a good offer, and what's more, there is reason to suppose that they mean to suppress my invention, as is sometimes done. Miss Darnall wanted to finance it, so that we could start manufacturing on our own account in competition with the trust. It was not the money she was thinking of so much as the publicity. She believed it would make me famous. But Mr. Suydam had positively refused to let her have the money."

"And the matter was at a critical stage?" asked Judge Waynham.

"Yes, sir. I am forced to accept this offer. Inventors must live."

"Hm!" said the judge unhappily. "What were the conditions of the late Mr. Darnall's will?"

"I see Mr. George Greenfield in the next room," Wayger said. "He is Mr. Suydam's attorney, and he can answer that question better than I can."

Mr. Greenfield was called upon. He was a handsome, middle-aged man with a youthful air and a good-tempered expression, the sort of man that children instinctively take to. As he came forward, he cast a deeply compassionate look on the unfortunate young girl. In answer to Judge Waynham's question, he carefully explained the provisions of her father's will. I need not repeat them beyond stating that Mr. Suydam was given absolute control of her affairs. In case of Mr. Suydam's death the will provided that Mr. Greenfield himself was to succeed him as Laila's guardian and trustee.

"Do you corroborate what this young man has told us respecting Mr. Suydam's attitude as guardian?" Judge Waynham asked him.

"I'm sorry that I must," he said regretfully, "for Mr. Suydam was one of my best friends. It was not mere harshness that made him behave in this manner. He was actuated by the best of motives. He looked about him and he saw how the young people of today were running wild, as he put it. It was to save Laila from that that he kept her under such strict control. I have often attempted to show him that he was mistaken in his method, but he was a very self-willed man."

"Had you heard anything about this invention of Mr. Wayger's?"

"Yes. Only today I lunched with Mr. Suydam at Fernhurst. Miss Darnall waylaid me as I arrived, and carried me to her sitting room where she told me all about it, and implored me to use my influence to persuade her guardian to advance the money necessary to finance Mr. Wayger's invention. But, knowing Mr. Suydam as well as I did, I told her it was useless. The poor girl was much upset. 'Can nothing be done?' she cried."

"And what did you reply?" asked Judge Waynham.

Mr. Greenfield started to answer, then, as a sudden realization came to him, caught himself up and changed color painfully. "I would rather not answer that," he said in a muffled voice.

"I must insist," said Judge Waynham.

"I answered jestingly," said Mr. Greenfield anxiously. "It had no significance whatever. I said, 'Nothing short of giving Cornelius a whiff of poison gas.' It was only in jest."

"Oh, quite, quite!" said Judge Waynham, and both men laughed in a strained fashion. But the incident created a very unfortunate impression.

Judge Waynham seemed to give up hope. His kindly face sagged with weary discouragement. He hesitated, tapping the blotter with his glasses. It was obvious that he could not bear to condemn the daintily reared girl to a cell. "I am reluctantly forced to order that Miss Darnall be . . ."

Madame Storey interrupted him. Rising and throwing back her veil, she said in that arresting voice of hers, "Mr. Magistrate, before you close the case, if I might be permitted to put a few questions in the light of what I have learned . . ."

Judge Waynham's jaw dropped in pure astonishment. "But, madam, who are you?" he asked.

Alvan Wayger answered for her. "Madame Rosika Storey," he announced.

A general exclamation escaped from all. Every head in the room turned towards my employer as if moved by a common lever. For the moment even the unfortunate Laila Darnall was forgotten. At this time Madame Storey was the most talked-of woman in the country, I suppose. "The cleverest woman in New York" the newspapers were calling her. Everybody present had the feeling that her entrance into the case would make their insignificant village famous.

The good little magistrate flushed and stammered in his gratification. "But of course . . . of course. . . . I am honored, Frémont is honored by your presence amongst us, Madame. Won't you be good enough to join me on the bench . . . I mean at my desk . . ." He relieved his feelings by suddenly shouting for the maid: "Nettie! Place a chair for Madame Storey."

Serenely oblivious to the goggling eyes, my employer seated herself beside him. "A prima facie case appears to have been made out," she drawled; "still, there are one or two little matters that might be gone into further."

Instantly everybody realized that the case, instead of closing, was only just starting.

"Miss Darnall required a large sum of money," Madame Storey continued; "therefore the few pieces of jewelry that were taken could have been of no use to her. The theory is, of course, that she opened the safe and took the jewelry merely to make it appear that robbers had done the deed . . . A very, very clever plot! Well, if she was such a clever plotter why didn't she plot a little further, and leave a way open to return to the house? She must have realized that someone would likely be awakened by the shot? There is a discrepancy here."

I saw a hope dawn in the magistrate's harassed face.

"I have made a hasty examination of Mr. Suydam's study," Madame Storey went on, "and . . . er . . . some other rooms in the house. Unfortunately for my purposes, the body had already been removed to Mr. Suydam's bedroom. I should therefore like to ask the butler a question or two concerning it, if I may."

Judge Waynham made haste to give an assent.

"Lumley," said Madame Storey, "you told us you left your master reading when you went to bed. But when you found his body he was sitting at his desk. This was not a position for reading, was it?"

"No, Madam. When I found him his fountain pen was still grasped in his right hand, and his left hand was spread on the blotter in such a way as to suggest that it was holding a paper. He was undoubtedly writing at the moment he was shot."

"But the paper itself was gone?"

"Yes, Madam."

"This suggests that he was writing something which was of interest to the murderer," remarked Madame Storey, "who therefore carried it away. That's all for the moment, thanks. . . . On Mr. Suydam's desk," she went on to Judge Waynham, "I found an ordinary calendar and memorandum pad on the top leaf of which he had written: 'Write G. G.,' then a dash and the word 'will.' Underneath was another memorandum: 'Write Eva Dinehart.' Now I take it 'G. G.' is Mr. Greenfield."

That gentleman spoke up for himself.

"Yes, Madam. Such was Mr. Suydam's nickname for me."

"Had you had any discussion with him today about his will?"

"No, Madam, it was not mentioned."

"Have you his will?"

"Yes, Madam, I drew it up. It is kept in my safe."

"Had you had any talk with him that would make it necessary for him to write to you?"

"No, Madam. Whatever it was, it must have come up after I had gone."

"What time did you leave him?"

"Three o'clock."

"Thank you. . . . Now, Lumley, what did your master do after Mr. Greenfield had gone?"

"He had Miss Beckington into the library, 'm," the butler answered with a wondering air. None of us could see which way this questioning was tending. "It was their day for going over the household bills."

"Can you tell me anything about what took place between them?"

"N . . . no, Madam."

"Why do you hesitate?"

"Well, there was an incident which was a little unusual."

"What was that?"

"Mr. Suydam called on the phone, and asked me to connect him with Central. Ordinarily he would let me get him what number he wanted."

"You listened?" suggested Madame Storey with a bland air.

"Well . . . yes, ma'am," said the butler in some confusion. "Mr. Suydam asked for information. He read the names of three New York business firms over the wire, and asked to be given their telephone numbers. I remember the firms. They were: N. Hamill and Sons; Nicholas Enslin; and Dobler and Levine. And information reported to him that no such firms were listed."

"What did your master do after Miss Beckington left him?"

"Went to the country club to play golf, Madam."

"And Miss Beckington?"

"She went into the city by train."

"Rather a hasty trip, wasn't it?"

"So it might seem, Madam."

"When did she get back?"

"Just before dinner."

"Carrying several parcels?"

"Why, yes, ma'am," said the butler with a look of surprise, "now that you mention it."

"Wasn't that rather unusual?"

"Yes, ma'am. Ordinarily everything would be sent."

"That's all, thanks." Madame Storey turned to Judge Waynham. Her beautiful face was as grave as that of some antique head of Pallas. "I then asked to be shown Miss Beckington's room," she went on. "The door was locked, but the constable obligingly forced it for me. I am aware that this was a high-handed proceeding on my part, but I was sure that the owner of the room would forgive me if her conscience was clear . . . In the room was a desk which I likewise forced. In a drawer of the desk I found these papers." From a sort of reticule of black velvet that she carried, Madame Storey took a sheaf of papers and spread them before the magistrate.

He blinked at them owlishly.

"They are, you see, blank bill heads for the three firms whose names you have just heard mentioned; N. Hamill and Sons; Nicholas Enslin; Dobler and Levine . . ."

"But what does it mean?"

Madame Storey held up her hand to bespeak a moment's patience. "I returned to the library. I found in a cabinet all the household bills for many months past. Upon consulting them I found every month a considerable bill from each of these mythical concerns . . ."

"You don't say, Madam . . .

"It means," said Madame Storey with her grave air, "that Miss Beckington has been systematically swindling her employer out of hundreds of dollars monthly."

Every eye in the room turned on the housekeeper. Laila Darnall jerked herself free of her arms, looking at her in astonishment and dismay. Miss Beckington, who had been pale before, now looked livid. There was an awful terror in her eyes. Her attempt to smile in a scornful and superior way was something you could not bear to look at. I mean, it seemed indecent to see a human creature expose herself like that.

"I take it that Mr. Suydam discovered the thefts today," said Madame Storey. "That brings us back to the will. Mr. Greenfield, is Miss Beckington mentioned in her employer's will?"

"Yes, Madam. A comfortable legacy."

"I thought so. Naturally, his first act upon discovering her treachery would be to write to you to cut that out. Now as to the second name on the memorandum pad: this Mrs. Eva Dinehart happens to be an acquaintance of mine. She conducts a special sort of employment agency. You go to her for help of a superior and confidential sort such as a social secretary or a lady housekeeper—need I say more?"

"But the murder, ma'am, the murder?" asked Judge Waynham excitedly.

"I am establishing the motive," said Madame Storey gravely. "Dishonor and disgrace faced this lady. At the very moment he was shot, her employer was writing the letters that would have ruined her."

"But have you any evidence?"

"I found none in her room—or next to none," said Madame Storey dryly.

Miss Beckington preened herself, bridled, smiled in that ghastly, would-be contemptuous manner.

". . . but I recommend that you have her searched," added Madame Storey quietly.

At these words, the woman sprang up electrified. "I won't submit to it!" she cried in a shrill, hysterical voice, and made as if to bolt for the door.

Lavell the constable seized her. She struggled like a wildcat. Everybody looked on dazed. It was inexpressibly shocking to see the elegant Miss Beckington suddenly reduced to such a state.

"Take her into the dining room," said Judge Waynham. "Lumley, will you please help him?"

Madame Storey added to me: "Miss Brickley, you search her while the men hold her."

It was not a job I relished, but I had no recourse other than to obey. To make a long story short, I found, firstly, in her stocking a handkerchief bearing Miss Darnall's initials; secondly, fastened inside the lining of the raccoon coat a pair of sport shoes; and thirdly, the strangest of all, wound around and around her body under the top part of her dress a ladder made of thin strong cord. Fastened to one end of it were two steel hooks. I returned across the hall, and laid these things on Judge Waynham's desk.

"I thought so," said Madame Storey offhand. "You see she had had no opportunity to dispose of them." She lifted up the objects one by one. "The handkerchief she stole from Miss Darnall as she sat beside her, hoping thereby to make the poor girl's story sound more incriminating. The shoes you see are replicas of Miss Darnall's from the same manufacturers. Miss Beckington bought them today, I have no doubt. She knew that Miss Darnall always wore such shoes in the park. The rope ladder she used to leave her room and to return to it. If you look for them you will find the marks made by the hooks on her windowsill."

At this sudden upset of the case, every vestige of order disappeared. All the people came pressing into the back room, crying out and attempting to congratulate the one or to abuse the other. Miss Beckington shrank from them. Judge Waynham's mild face crimsoned with anger, and above all the racket I heard his trembling voice.

"You miserable woman! You deliberately set out to fasten a horrible murder on this helpless child. In all my experience I have never known the like!"

Miss Beckington had collapsed now. All the fight had gone out of her. "I didn't! I didn't!" she wailed. "I tried to make it appear that a robber had done it!"

"Your purchase of the shoes doesn't bear that out," said the judge sternly. "All through the proceedings you sat there with your arms around her whispering hypocritical comfort in her ear, while the evidence was produced against her. It is horrible!"

Miss Beckington's voice rose almost to a shriek. "I knew they wouldn't hurt her!" she cried. "Young and pretty as she is, and with all her money, no jury would convict her! She was safe!"

"Silence!" cried the magistrate. "Your excuses aren't helping you any! . . . Lock her up!" he said to the constable.

When Miss Beckington was removed, the crowd threatened completely to overwhelm Madame Storey and the young lovers in their well-meant efforts to congratulate them. Madame Storey regarded this demonstration with good-humored dismay. I opened the door into the hall to allow them to slip out, and held it until they had secured themselves in the dining room opposite. Over there, I presume, the lovers thanked Madame Storey in their own way for saving them. I was not present at the scene.

Presently the young couple escaped through a side door of the house, but were seen as they ran hand in hand for a car, and the crowd pursued them cheering.

IN THE ROUND ROOM

A TALL GENTLEMAN of thirty-eight having still something of the boy about him. Nice eyes, but otherwise a little soft in the face. A man of quick, warm emotions one would say, but perhaps not much staying power. Dressed like an Englishman, which is to say in comfortable clothes of good material, not ironed and fitted to extinction. But notwithstanding the clothes, unmistakably a good American by his glance of slightly derisive good humour. Not at all a remarkable person, yet he brought a certain high assurance into my office, that I was at a loss to account for until he gave me his name: Norbert Starr. I looked at him with a quickened interest; it was his vast wealth, of course, which had given him that air of being set a little apart from his fellows. Everybody knows more about the Starrs than about their own best friends; all the brothers and sisters have so thoroughly and repeatedly aired their domestic difficulties in the courts. Norbert's case was not the least conspicuous among them.

I carried his name into Mme. Storey, and presently ushered him into her presence. From the manner of their greeting I gathered that they had met before, but only casually. Mr. Starr cast an appreciative glance around at my mistress's room.

"I wish I could get an effect like this," he murmured, "but it takes genius."

Mme. Storey smiled in her slow way. She is not insensible to the right sort of flattery.

Mr. Starr's eyes twinkled at the sight of Giannino in cap and bells, making faces at him from a corner. The man was no fool. One liked him rather, in spite of his disgusting riches.

I understood by a private sign from my mistress that she wished me to remain in the room. When he saw me sit down, Mr. Starr looked a little blank. It became evident that under his air of careless good humour he was nervous. He was understood to murmur politely that he would like to speak to Mme. Storey alone, to which she made her usual reply:

"Miss Brickley is present at all interviews. She is my memory."

He took the seat she indicated, but seemed to be at a loss how to begin. Mme. Storey offered him a cigarette, and took one herself. That helped. He presently said with a careless laugh, which was not, however, without a note of bitterness:

"I assume that you know all about me from the newspapers. It will save time."

"I know what the newspapers report," said Mme. Storey dryly, "but I do not suppose that is the whole story."

"Oh, it's true in the main," he said. "We Starrs seem to have made a mess of things generally. We're not a bad lot, either. But I suppose we haven't got the moral natures to measure up to our incomes."

"Nobody has," said Mme. Storey. "Moral natures are only developed by poverty."

"You're right of course," he agreed. "Money's a curse, just as the copy-books say. But what is one to do?"

Mme. Storey shrugged.

"Life gets you into a net," he murmured, lowering his eyes. "Not being of heroic stuff, I have never been able to cut myself out."

This was rather painful to hear from the boyish man with his happy-go-lucky air.

"You are frank about yourself," said Mme. Storey kindly.

"Not much use my coming to see you if I were not," he murmured.

Mme. Storey merely waited for what was coming.

"I was married when I was twenty-three," he said, plunging all at once into the middle of his story. "I was seeing life, you understand. The usual young fool! My father gave me as much money as I wanted on condition that I used an assumed name in my pleasures, and did not run any bills. . . . Did you ever meet my wife?" he broke off to ask.

Mme. Storey shook her head.

"No, you wouldn't," he went on. "She was Bessie Jewett, the elder of the Jewett sisters, famous music hall stars of that day. They were the queens of the silly little world I moved in, *the* world, I thought it was. That is, Bessie was the queen, for Tessie, the quiet one, was no more than a foil for her. I thought in my youthful vanity that Bessie was taking me for myself alone. I meant to surprise her on our wedding day with my real name. But it was no surprise to her. In fact, she . . . Oh, well, I don't want to abuse her. I need only say that she was ten years older than I. I was married before I had time to take a long breath.

"I was speedily disillusioned, of course. From the first day she had me with her bad temper. I hate rows. I gave in to her, and of course every time I gave in, it made my position more abject. She retired from the stage and set up as an exemplar of respectability. She assaulted the citadels of society—there was a society in those days, and was humiliatingly repulsed. She found to her astonishment that money couldn't buy some things. It turned her temper worse than before. Like most violent people, I believe that she is a little unhinged. But that doesn't help me any. Her mother is quite mad.

"Her crowning folly was the building of Bolingbroke Castle— she claims to be descended from Henry Bolingbroke, you know. Not that it matters. A castle she had to have, reproduced stone by stone from one of the mediæval fortresses of England. I weakly assented—anything for peace, without realising what I was being let in for. It was from the castle that she designed to make her grand sortie upon society. It was five years building; five years it kept me poor. I never told anybody how much it cost me; I was ashamed. I will say, though, that during those years I enjoyed a kind of peace. She had an absorbing object in life that kept her busy; then, too, she had to be halfway decent to me in order to extract the vast sums of money that were called for.

"But when it was finished I discovered that she expected me to go there and live with her. I balked at that. It is really a magnificent pile, I believe; she had the wit to employ the best talent. In fact, it made the fortunes and the reputations of a small army of architects and decorators, though it never did its owners any good. Perched up there on Patching Mountain overlooking a sea of suburban villas with fertilizer factories in the distance! How unspeakably ridiculous! A donjon keep with battlements and machicolations. Stone-vaulted corridors and vast chambers. Fancy living in such a place. A common or garden American like me. It made me turn hot and cold to think of the way my honest neighbours would grin when they caught me driving in or out of the place.

"It was the castle which finished me. I visited Bessie there two or three times, but the spectacle of the ex-music hall favourite established amidst such grandeur was too much. My God! she was so *common!* It gave me the courage to chuck it altogether. She raged like a madwoman—she always claimed that it was my abandonment of her that prevented her from getting into society, but I kept out of her way. I felt as light as air.

"In the course of time she resigned herself to the situation and set her wits to work to devise ways of tormenting me. That has become her grand object in life. She sued for and obtained a judicial separation, and the court awarded her an enormous allowance which I do not begrudge her, God knows! I'd give up every cent I possess sooner than live with her again. She still lives with her mother and sister in that nightmare of a castle. With what guests she can bribe to come visit her. Second-rate hangers-on.

"One of her latest caprices was to drive tally-ho up and down the precipitous Patching roads. Oh, she has courage of a sort. The spectacle has been described to me; the gargantuan purple-faced Bessie, attired in pale pink perched up on the box screaming curses at the horses, while some trembling sycophant beside her held a pink parasol over her head. Ah! if she had only broken her neck that way! After one or two narrow escapes of doing so, she probably reflected that the risk of giving me my final release was too great, and she gave away the horses.

"I was not long exulting in my freedom before I learned that I was not free at all. Therein lay her cunning. Legally I am still her husband, and she takes care not to let me forget it. She is continually bringing ridiculous suits against me, which she invariably loses, but she gains her object, which is to drag my name into the newspapers again. And one way or another I always have to pay the costs. She is a woman who must continually be engaged in litigation.

"She has me constantly watched and followed. She has a trick of turning up to accost me when I am entertaining friends, or whenever she thinks it will most humiliate me. There have been times when I have been ready to die under the crude humiliations she has put upon me—this woman who spends a thousand dollars a day of my money. I needn't go into details. She is certainly insane. Her hatred of me has become a mania, and she will stop at nothing in order to gratify it. Nevertheless, until lately I was prepared to put up with all this. A man always has ways of escape. But now . . . but now . . ."

He hesitated. It was not hard to guess what was coming next.

"I came here to make a clean breast of the matter," he presently went on in a lower tone. ". . . I have fallen in love with another woman. The real thing. It is the first time I have experienced it. It changes the whole colour of my life. With the help of such a woman I might make something of myself. I feel as if she were my only hope of salvation. I may say that she loves me in return. . . . But with such a woman as she, there could not be any relation except an open and straightforward one. I am bound to this other! Is it any wonder I feel as if I were going out of my mind!"

"You have all my sympathy," said Mme. Storey gently. "But—if you will pardon the blunt question, why do you come to me? Should you not rather consult your lawyer?"

"Oh, I've been in the hands of lawyers for the past eight years!" he said hopelessly. "What Bessie has left me they have taken. I have sued her for divorce. My case was thrown out of court. She takes good care to give me no legal cause. Moreover, it appears that the judicial separation militates against it. Oh, she has me tied hand and foot."

"I must repeat my question," said Mme. Storey. "Why do you come to me?"

"You are a psychologist," he said with a wistful air; "not a mere professor of psychology, but a practising psychologist. On every hand I hear of the wonderful things you have accomplished through your extraordinary insight into the human heart—particularly the feminine heart . . ."

"Mostly in the direction of solving crime, was it not?" asked Mme. Storey with rather a wry smile—this is a sore point with her.

"Yes," he admitted, "but why stop with crime? The same gifts would enable you to . . ."

"Surely," said Mme. Storey. "When I began to practise, I scarcely considered crime. I hoped to do a little towards straightening out tangled human relations. . . . Unfortunately I soon discovered that wrong people do not want to be set right. So crime was about all that was left for me. . . . What is it exactly, that you wish me to do?"

"See my wife," he pleaded. "With your skill you can surely bring her to listen to reason. She has nothing to gain by her present course. She . . ."

Mme. Storey interrupted him with a grave shake of the head. "You overrate my skill," she said. "I am sorry, but I cannot undertake it. In the first place it would make matters worse—you have drawn only too convincing a picture of your wife. Any move that I might make would only gratify her hatred. . . . In the second place, after one or two unfortunate experiences I was obliged to make an absolute rule never to undertake anything in connexion with marital relations."

It was only too clear that she meant what she said, and Mr. Starr wasted no time in attempted persuasion. He got up heavily. There was now no look of youth about him. "I scarcely expected you to say anything else," he said dully. "I just took a chance. One snatches at anything. . . . It is only too true you cannot touch pitch without being defiled. . . . You think there is no hope for me then, short of my wife's death?"

"I must be honest with you," said Mme. Storey gravely. "I see none."

He went out without another word.

"A pitiful case," murmured my mistress, abstractedly extinguishing her cigarette. "The girl he is in love with is Mary Lansdowne. I had it from another source. She's a girl in a thousand . . ."

2

DURING THE AFTERNOON of the same day, the door of my office was rudely pushed open, and a monumental female strode in. I knew at a glance it could be no other than the famous Bessie Jewett Starr. Monumental! I ought rather to have written mountainous! A tall woman and fat beyond all credence. Her fat was accentuated by the harness she wore which thrust it out at you, so to speak. And all this was swathed in yards and yards of mauve chiffon which made her look even bigger. Her face was puffy and, I suspect, scarlet in its natural state. Coats of whitewash had reduced it to a strange violet hue. Perhaps that was why she wore mauve. She was dressed to represent thirty years old; a simple-minded person might have been deceived. You could see that she had once been a gloriously beautiful woman; that made the ruin more tragic. She demanded to see Mme. Storey. Her arrogant glance bade me to fall down and grovel at her feet.

I did not.

"If you will wait a moment . . ." I began.

"I am Mrs. Bessie Jewett Starr; I am not accustomed to be kept waiting," she said, and thrusting me out of her path (she was several times my size) she opened the door of Mme. Storey's room.

I was not much put about, for I knew she'd meet her match in there. I followed to see the fun.

Giannino fled to one of the picture frames where he sat squeaking with indignation.

Mme. Storey was writing at her table. She looked up calmly. "Ah, Mrs. Starr," she said at once.

"You know me!" exclaimed the fat woman, somewhat taken aback.

"How could I fail to do so?" said Mme. Storey sweetly. "Won't you sit down?"

HULBERT FOOTNER

Mrs. Starr sat on the edge of a Florentine chair, which creaked alarmingly. I saw a lightning glance of anxiety cross Mme. Storey's eyes—not for the woman, but for the chair.

"You'll find the upholstered chair more comfortable," she said politely.

Mrs. Starr merely glared at her and at me, and settled herself more firmly where she was.

"A cigarette?" asked Mme. Storey.

"I don't use them," snapped Mrs. Starr.

Mme. Storey helped herself from the silver box, and lighting up with a malicious deliberation, puffed a great cloud of smoke towards the ceiling. Mrs. Starr watched her, biting her lip. Her brusque entrance having fallen flat, the fat woman found herself for the moment at a loss. Her eyes glittered painfully and hatefully at my mistress. Mme. Storey, beautiful, slender and smiling, was a ghastly reproach to the other woman. Under any circumstances Mrs. Starr would have been obliged to hate her.

Suddenly Mrs. Starr said, like the villainess in a melodrama, through her teeth: "My husband's been here!"

"But yes!" said Mme. Storey, elevating her eyebrows. "Why not?"

"I can see that he has filled you up with his slanderous lies about me!"

"Oh, I wouldn't say that," said Mme. Storey deprecatingly. "He must have drawn me a fairly true portrait of you, mustn't he? because you see, I recognised you at once."

The fat woman snorted with rage. "What did he come for?" she demanded.

"I must plead privilege there," said Mme. Storey blandly. "A professional matter."

"Professional! Do you call this a profession? Snooping, *I* call it!"

Mme. Storey smiled delightedly at her cigarette.

"I know what he came for!" Mrs. Starr went on in a strident, hateful voice that made one ashamed for her; made one wish not to see her give herself away like that. "He came here to hire you to help him get rid of me! Well, I wish you joy of the job! He's tried everything already. And here I am still. I'm a healthy woman, too, thank God! I'll live for twenty-five years yet to plague him! I'll outlive him, the poor weed! He has no constitution."

"Ah," said Mme. Storey, "you are strongly attached to him!"

"Attached to him!" shouted Mrs. Starr. "I despise him! A worthless idler. Never did a day's work in his life. Always going around and whining against me to anybody who will listen to him! He's not a man! There isn't a bone in his body. A jellyfish!"

"I should think you would have cast him off long ago," remarked Mme. Storey with a dry affectation of sympathy.

"Oh, do you," said Mrs. Starr with a hateful smile. "Well, that's my affair. . . . I don't believe in divorce."

The last statement sounded unspeakably droll from those angry lips. Mme. Storey looked at me, her face broke up incontrollably, her silvery laugh was heard. The sound of it set me off, too.

It infuriated the fat woman. She sprang up and started cursing us like a drunken teamster. It was startling, but it was very funny. I'm afraid we only laughed the more.

Mrs. Starr shook a stubby forefinger at Mme. Storey. Until I saw her, I didn't think anybody did that except on the stage. "I came here to warn you to keep out of this," she shouted. "If you don't, you better look out, that's all. I can make myself damned unpleasant when I want . . ."

"So I see," murmured Mme. Storey—but I doubt if Mrs. Starr heard her. She was shouting too loud.

"If anybody makes an enemy of me, I don't care what I do! If you don't believe me, ask your friend Norbert! He can come snivelling around to you or anybody, but he dare not stand up to me!"

There was a lot more of this. Mme. Storey, making her eyes big, wickedly led the woman on. I'm afraid my mistress was enjoying the situation. Giannino got hysterical. I was obliged to capture him, and put him in his box in the middle room.

Mrs. Starr did not see my mistress press the button under her desk, but I did.

"I'll expose you in the newspapers," the former was shouting. "I can command as much space as I want! How will you like that? How will you like that?" More play with the forefinger.

The door from my office opened, and John, our stalwart young engineer, appeared. He had eyes for no one in the room but Mme. Storey. John would jump off the top of the Woolworth Building to serve her.

"John, this lady feels unwell," said Mme. Storey blandly. "Will you please assist her to her car downstairs?"

John got it. "This way, ma'am," he said briskly.

For the space of a moment Mrs. Starr was struck dumb with indignation. Then speech returned with a roar. "I'll go when I get damned good and ready!"

John merely smiled hardily, and made a significant move towards her.

"I am Mrs. Bessie Jewett Starr!" she shouted. "Don't you dare to lay hands on me!"

"I don't care if you're Mary Queen of Scots," said John unabashed. "Come on, if you don't want to be helped."

Mrs. Starr suddenly thought better of it, and bolted through the door. These people who deal in imperatives always run the risk of coming up against an imperative. For a fat woman she moved with an astonishing celerity. John touched his cap to Mme. Storey, and followed, grinning.

Presently we heard the resounding slam of a car door in the street. Mme. Storey disdained to look out of the window, but I could not be so strong-minded. I saw the superbly appointed car move away, with the wooden chauffeur in front—he kept his face though his mistress could not. I saw her, and she saw me. She leaned over and, looking up, shook her fist at me like a washerwoman. I burst out laughing afresh. It was so exactly in character!

"What a woman!" I said as I left the window.

"Suffers from an inferiority complex," said Mme. Storey, lighting a fresh cigarette. "That's always what's the matter with these shouters."

3

WE SUPPOSED that the incident was closed as far as we were concerned, and thought no more about it. Three days later, at noon, a man's voice on the telephone asked for Mme. Storey. I did not recognise the voice, but I did apprehend the tremor of a desperate agitation in it; and, as I switched the call into my mistress's room, I wondered what new excitement was in the wind.

Almost immediately she came out of her room, and I saw by her face that I was not mistaken as to the seriousness of the matter.

"Bella," she said, "Mr. Norbert Starr telephones that his wife has just committed suicide while he was in her house."

A quiet announcement like this does not alarm the nerves. I suppose I said: "Is that so?" or something like that. A moment later the sense of it reached me. "My God!" I weakly ejaculated, staring, no doubt, like a clown.

"He begs me to come to his aid," said Mme. Storey.

"But . . . but . . ." I stammered in confusion, "if she's killed herself he doesn't need any aid, does he?"

Mme. Storey looked at me queerly. "Think, Bella! Is it likely that that woman would kill herself? . . ."

Horror grew in me. "You think. . . ?" I began.

"I think nothing yet," she said crisply. ". . . Come let's go. I really feel as if I owed it to the poor wretch. Did I not as good as tell him there was no release for him except through her death?"

I could not pull myself together all at once. In our business we are used to dreadful happenings, dear knows! But this was too shocking. Had not the woman herself been in our office three days before? Ordinarily we first hear of our tragedies after the event. *We are not consulted in advance!*

"Come, Bella, your hat!" said Mme. Storey impatiently. "We'll taxi out to Upper Bellaire. It will save precious minutes."

The entrance to the park surrounding Bolingbroke Castle was guarded by a pair of immense and beautiful wrought-iron gates. Just inside was a picturesque stone lodge in the English style. The gates were closed. When our chauffeur sounded a summons on his horn, the lodge-keeper hastened out of his door, but after looking us over, undertook to wave us away. Our Broadway chauffeur remarked upon his inhospitality with more force than politeness. The lodge-keeper merely pointed to a little sign outside the gates which had hitherto escaped our attention.

"Hired vehicles will use the East drive."

Mme. Storey and I looked at each other. How exactly characteristic of the chatelaine of Bolingbroke! The woman was rather splendid in her way. Certainly she stopped at nothing. Perhaps mediæval chatelaines were like that. Sooner than waste time by arguing with the lodge-keeper, who obviously did not yet know that the author of these regulations was lying dead in her castle, we obediently turned around and sought the humbler entrance.

The castle was truly magnificent. The approach was from below, and the foreshortened view of the piled, grey masses of masonry struck powerfully upon the imagination. There was a squat, grey central keep, with encircling walls flanked by smaller towers of different sizes and designs, all of the very stuff of romance. One wondered if after all there had been a strain of romance in the coarse-grained woman who had it built to order. Probably not— still it was a disconcerting thought. From the top of the great central tower a flag fluttered insolently against the sky. It bore a white swan on a red ground, a device that the owner had chosen for her own. A swan! Its purpose in flying was to advertise that the owner was in residence. Nobody had thought to pull it down.

It made one rub one's eyes to come upon such an apparition in Upper Bellaire. Of course when one looked closely there were certain anachronisms; the plantations were rather immature, and the rear premises had somewhat of a Bellairish look. One remembered the thirty tiled bathrooms the place was said to contain. I think it was thirty. That would have amused the Normans.

I had only time to receive the swiftest impression of the place ere we were swallowed up in the tragedy which filled it. The inside servants knew what had happened. They stood or moved about in dazed attitudes as if a spell of horror had been laid on them—men in gorgeous liveries and maids peeping from around doors. It was touching, the eager expectant way they looked at my composed mistress, counting on her to lift the spell.

We were received in the gloomy lower entry by the butler, quite a personage on his own account in sober dress. But a shaken personage now. His face was ashy, and his hands trembled. Without a word being spoken, he led us up a shallow, sweeping stone stairway into the great hall of the castle. The entrance had purposely been made dark and restricted. Rising from those depths one's breath was taken away by the great hall. It soared thrillingly to a pointed roof like a cathedral; there were no windows low down, but the whole place seemed to sing with the warm colour that was admitted through the painted glass above. Fancy all that to house one fat woman! Why, the coal necessary to heat it in winter would have kept a whole village comfortable.

As received from the architects and decorators I expect the place was all in keeping, but it was inevitable that innovations should have been introduced. One perceived examples of the Jewett taste here and there; a large phonograph in a Jacobean case à la Camden, N. J.; a pair of those perfectly useless torch lamps that have lately become so popular. Among such objects my eye was attracted by a large photograph in an over-elaborate silver frame. It depicted two young women in incongruous costumes consisting of ragged short skirts, torn blouses, expensive slippers and enormous picture hats. Tasteless photograph, tasteless costumes, but the girls were of really remarkable beauty. Their faces haunted you. I did not need to be told who they were. They were very much alike, but it was not hard to pick out the bold Bessie from the meek Tessie.

All this I got in passing. Crossing the tessellated floor of the great hall, we struck into a corridor whence we entered a beautiful panelled chamber—filled with stuffed velure furniture. Such were the contrasts of Bolingbroke. In this room Norbert Starr was walking up and down with a tragic assumption of composure. For his lower lip was hanging down loosely, and his eyes were simply witless from shock.

Before Mme. Storey was well inside the room, he ran to her and picked up her hand. His face worked so, he could scarcely get any words out. "Ah, you've come! Thank God! How kind of you! I had no right to expect it! . . . But if I had not someone to turn to, I'd go out of my mind!"

Mme. Storey sought to stiffen him. "Ah, come!" she said resolutely. "We are grown-up people. We can look ugly facts in the face, I hope. Why should you. . . ?"

"Ah! you know what they'll say! you know what they'll say!" he stuttered with a distracted gesture. "Come!"

He led the way out of the room. We walked the whole length of the stone-paved, stone-vaulted corridor, which was lined with armour and antique weapons and conspicuously worm-eaten oaken furniture. No one had given the butler an order, but he followed at our heels with his head sunk between his shoulders as if he simply had to attach himself to somebody. Obviously a man accustomed to command, it was disconcerting to see him so unstrung. All the doors opening out of the corridor were shut. One wondered what was behind them.

The end of the corridor was closed by a little pointed door with great ornamental hinges stretching all the way across it, nicely blacked. Such are the things that one notices at such a moment. Opening this door, we passed through a sort of vault, and thence into a smaller corridor running transversely to the other. On our left it was closed by another pointed door. This door had a knob sticking through a hole; you lifted it to raise the antique latch within. As Mr. Starr put his forefinger under the knob he hesitated, and I heard his breath hiss between his teeth. The heavy door swung slowly in, and he quickly averted his head.

We looked into a perfectly round room which evidently formed a storey of one of the flanking towers of the castle. It was very bare. One's eyes marked only a great flat-topped desk in the centre. On the floor between the desk and us lay what had been Bessie Jewett Starr. A great, inert huddle of flesh, all her violence was stilled now. She was enveloped in pale blue chiffon fresh as flower petals, which, like the costume of an actress in a tragedy, seemed to have been put on especially to enact this scene. One thick arm was extended before her, and the puffy fingers clasped a blued revolver. There was still a suggestion of gunpowder on the air. Her head and face were covered with a napkin.

From behind us like scurrying dead leaves came Mr. Starr's whisper: "She has not been moved not been moved. . . . We waited for you."

And the butler like an echo: "Not moved . . . not moved. . . . I just covered her face."

"Have you notified the police?" asked Mme. Storey.

"Oh, no, no, no, no, no!" stuttered Mr. Starr.

"But they *must* be notified!"

"What am I to say to them?" he wailed.

"The truth, I suppose."

"Of course . . . of course! . . . But I looked to you to steady me a little first. I am so unnerved I could not even be sure that I was telling the truth. . . . And if they confused me, it would look . . . it would look . . . they would naturally believe . . . everybody will be prepared to believe . . ."

"Tell me what happened," said Mme. Storey quietly. "My mind is open."

He drew her a little away from the open door. He told his story in a whisper as if he feared the dead might overhear.

"When I left your office I didn't know what to do. . . . I sat down and wrote to my wife asking her to let me talk to her. I thought perhaps I might buy her off. A foolish hope—but I was prepared to go high. . . . After making me wait two days, she wrote, appointing eleven o'clock this morning. I had a premonition that my coming would be worse than useless . . . but one must do something!

"She had me brought to her in the round room here, which she uses as a sort of office. All her private rooms open off this corridor . . ."

"One moment," interrupted Mme. Storey, "where are the other members of the family?"

"Early this morning Miss Jewett took her mother in to New York to the doctor's. They have not returned."

"Go on."

"My wife received me with the sort of smile which always presages her most insane bursts of rage. I immediately regretted my coming; nevertheless I persevered. All the way here I kept saying to myself over and over: I will not lose my temper; I will not lose my temper; no matter what she says, I will not lose my temper. But that was the worst course I could have pursued. In her eyes the unforgivable sin was not to lose your temper. . . . Need I say what passed between us? The usual thing. In fact I can scarcely remember. She deafened me with her screaming . . ."

"Better tell me as far as you can remember," said Mme. Storey.

He lowered his head. "She insisted on dragging in the name of a certain lady," he whispered. "The one I told you about. I thought I had been able to keep that . . . even from her. But it seems not. She made gross accusations. I could afford to smile at that. But finally it turned out that she had seen this lady. That . . . that was very hard for me to bear . . . But I swear to you, I stuck to the line I had laid out for myself. That was to ask her how much she'd take to release me. She said if I was ten times as rich as I am it wouldn't be enough. . . . I permitted myself one retort. I did say that I would be happy in spite of her. Then she . . . she . . . then I got out . . ."

There was a fatal stammer at the end. One could not escape the suspicion that all had not been told.

"Go on," said Mme. Storey.

"I had no more than got out of the room when I heard the shot and the fall. I ran back. I saw her just as she is now. There was smoke floating in the air . . ."

"Where did she get the gun?" asked Mme. Storey.

"I . . . I don't know. I didn't see. Out of her desk I suppose."

"How long was it, precisely, after you had left the room when the shot was fired?"

"It was no time at all. I pulled the door to after me; my hand had no more than dropped from the knob; I had not taken a single step when I heard the shot."

"She must have moved with marvellous quickness," said Mme. Storey. "To get around the desk, I mean; to get the gun out; to get back in front of the desk where she now lies."

"I don't know . . ." he said, vaguely passing his hand over his face.

"Had she said anything to lead you to suppose that she might . . . ?"

"Oh, no! no! . . . That was what shocked me so. I never dreamed of such a possibility. Not Bessie! . . . When I saw her lying there I could not believe my eyes. Bessie kill herself! My thought was there must be some humanity in her after all. Years ago there seemed to be . . . Her hatred of me was just a sort of obsession. She had had a lucid moment, and aghast at herself had snatched up the gun to set me free . . . That was what shattered my nerve. To find her lying dead by her own hand. Dead to set me free . . . And I hating her so. . . . !"

Some moments passed before he was able to go on. "I ran down the corridor shouting for help," he whispered huskily. "Down the main corridor. I met no one until I got to the great hall. Pascoe was coming up the stairs. I brought him back with me. That's all . . . In my confusion my only coherent thought was of you. I telephoned you. I have simply been waiting . . ."

The butler kept up a sort of whispered chorus to this. "That's right . . . He met me coming up the stairs . . . I went back with him . . . It was terrible . . . terrible! . . . He telephoned. We've simply been waiting . . ."

"Did you hear the shot?" Mme. Storey asked the butler.

"No, madam. It was too far away. The doors are very thick."

Mme. Storey went into the round room, leaving us in the corridor. Mr. Starr still kept his head averted. My mistress went down on one knee beside the body. She did not raise the napkin as yet, but examined the revolver with close attention. Without removing it from the dead woman's clutch, she broke it, and looked in the magazine.

She presently arose, and her face was like a mask. I caught my breath, for I had learned to dread that look. "This pistol has not been discharged," she said. "The magazine is full."

There was a dreadful silence. Mr. Starr looked at her witlessly. "Wh—what did you say?" he stuttered.

"You said you found smoke in the room," Mme. Storey went on. "This pistol contains only modern smokeless shells.'

"She *must* have killed herself!" he said stupidly. "There was nobody else here . . . no other gun."

Mme. Storey shrugged her shoulders. She went down beside the body again. This time she lifted the napkin. I involuntarily turned my head. Thank God! it was not my business to make an examination.

"She was shot from behind," Mme. Storey said impassively. "This hole in her forehead was made by the issue of the bullet."

The man fell back against the wall. His voice scaled up shrilly. "Do you realise what you're saying?" he cried. "Do you think I have been lying to you . . . lying. . . ?"

"Not necessarily," said Mme. Storey mildly.

"Oh, my God! what has happened then?" he cried, clutching his head. "What devilish combination of circumstances has come about? Who was it? Who was it? . . . You *must* believe me! You must! Why, if I had done it, how easy it would have been for me to discharge her pistol while I was waiting. But it never occurred to me. I was sure she had done it herself. . . . Merciful Heaven! what will I do now?"

"Nobody has accused you," said Mme. Storey patiently. "With your help I will get to the bottom of the matter."

"Ah, no one will believe me now!" he cried despairingly.

"The police must be sent for," said Mme. Storey.

"Wait!" he cried sharply. "Give me a chance to collect my wits. First let us find out for ourselves what has happened."

"I can do nothing," said Mme. Storey firmly. "I must not disturb the body until the police have viewed it."

"Ah, wait! wait!" he cried. "You must listen to me. If it is true that you can read people's hearts you must know that I didn't kill her. But no one else will believe me. . . . Before they come let me let me fire a bullet out of her pistol. Where would be the harm? . . . If I don't do it, it will mean the ruin of two lives. I swear I am not thinking of myself alone. There is another. . . . I cannot bear the thought of wrecking her life . . ."

"This is useless," said Mme. Storey. "You know it is useless. . . . Pascoe must telephone at once. In this county, I understand, the county prosecutor takes direct charge of all criminal investigations. Pascoe, telephone to his office and ask him to come at once."

The butler disappeared. Mr. Starr turned from us, wrapping his arms around his head like a man who had given up all hope.

I thought Mme. Storey was extraordinarily patient with the abject creature. A hint of disapproval must have shown in my face, for she murmured while his back was turned to us:

"Do not be too quick to jump to conclusions, Bella."

"But this unmanly panic!" I said.

"It doesn't prove anything. A guilty man is prepared for an accusation. An innocent man might well be thrown into a panic by it."

To Mr. Starr she said hearteningly: "Pull yourself together. Answer me a question or two."

"What's the use?" he said apathetically. "I'm a goner. . . . I'd better blow my brains out at once and save the state money."

"And convict yourself without a hearing?" suggested Mme. Storey.

"It's nothing to me what they think. If I want to live it's for myself and one other. Popular opinion is nothing to me. I'm hardened to it."

"Then, for the sake of that other?"

"What is it you want to know?"

"What you held back when you first told your story. She could not possibly have got the gun out so quickly."

"No," he said dully. "She got it out of her desk while I was still in the room. She threatened me with it. That's why I got out."

"That alters the case somewhat," said Mme. Storey.

"It is useless for you to advise me to plead self-defence," he said. "If I had Bessie's blood on my hands, no matter how it came about, how could I . . . another woman . . . surely you must understand."

That simple cry of pain aroused my sympathies for the unfortunate man. I began to change my opinion.

Mme. Storey said quietly: "I was not going to advise you to plead self-defence. . . . But, tell me, why did you keep this fact back in the beginning?"

"For a simple enough reason," he said with a shrug. "When I thought she had turned the gun on herself it seemed as if there was some good in her after all. I didn't want to blacken her memory any further. I thought she was sorry. I was sorry for her."

"Have you anything else to add to your first story?"

"No, I told you the truth. . . . I don't suppose it matters."

4

THE HINT OF A CASE within the very walls of Bolingbroke Castle brought Mr. Ira Anders, the county prosecutor of Middlesex, on the run. He proved to be a slender little man with a big head and great round black-rimmed glasses. Dominant masculinity was his line. You know the type; the little dog making out to be a big one. His brow was furrowed like a mastiff's. Pascoe had given him no particulars over the phone, and when he learned that his "case" dealt with no less a matter than the apparent murder of Bessie Jewett Starr herself, his self-importance was shaken for a moment. But only for a moment. As the sweet assurance of undreamed-of publicity and fame stole into his soul, he began to swell bigger and bigger like the frog that sought to rival the ox. The magnitude of his opportunity rendered him a little breathless; the round glasses became moist with emotion, and he had frequently to wipe them. He looked around furtively for a telephone; clearly he burned to spread the marvellous news. But decency restrained him for a while. He brought with him a crude sort of county detective; an honest, red-faced yokel whose "bright" air was on a par with his master's heavy air. This creature's name, as I heard it, sounded like Kelliger.

Mme. Storey had refused to make any further move until the prosecutor arrived, and we were all waiting for him in the great hall. When he was introduced to my mistress it was clear that the name Storey suggested nothing to the suburban lawyer. He took it that she was merely a friend of the family's, and she let it go at that. Her beauty won a suitable tribute from his masculinity; he was very gallant. You know the sort of thing; so comical in a little man addressing a superb woman. He all but patted her hand and assured her that everything would be all right now that he had been called in. One foresaw a rude awakening for the little man. It was almost a shame.

On the other hand, the name of Starr had a magical effect on the attorney. His manner towards the unfortunate husband was as smooth as velvet. Mr. Starr merely looked at him in a bitter silence.

We all returned to the scene of the tragedy. There was a horrible formality about the procession; two and two down the long corridor. Mr. Anders, his eyes darting right and left to spy out the wonders of Bolingbroke, offered professional condolences to Mme. Storey the whole way, like an undertaker. Behind him walked Mr. Starr unseeing, unhearing, like a man in a trance. He had become so apathetic that he walked unmoved into the round room with the rest of us. But I noticed that he never looked directly at what lay on the floor.

"Ah, *suicide!*" said Mr. Anders with a world of melodious compassion in his voice.

"The pistol in her hand has not been discharged," said Mme. Storey.

"Eh, what?" exclaimed Mr. Anders, blinking behind the round glasses, and wrinkling up his forehead like our Giannino.

"She was shot from behind," said Mme. Storey in her quiet voice.

It was then that Mr. Anders really began to swell. A murder in Bolingbroke Castle, and he the prosecutor!

I went out of the room while he made his examination of the body. Afterwards somebody covered it with a green velure drapery brought from another room. It did not look any the less dreadful under that shroud.

Mr. Anders then set on foot a regular investigation. Such a man rejoices in formalities. He seated himself at the big desk, and had additional chairs brought in for the rest of us. There we sat. A curious inconsequence seemed to attach to the proceedings. The grim reality at our feet mocked at them.

Mr. Starr was the first and the principal witness. As he told his story the prosecutor's eyes glittered. His manner towards the witness underwent a notable change. He became the stern avenger of crime. In the end he even dared point an inquisitorial forefinger at the millionaire. Mr. Starr took his arrogance as he had taken his obsequiousness with the same dreary indifference. He answered all questions unhesitatingly, however they seemed to strengthen the case against him. Mr. Anders, satisfied that he had his man, only asked him such questions as would tend to incriminate him. Mr. Starr did not change his story in any important particular.

The butler, Pascoe, followed him. This Pascoe was a self-respecting middle-aged man with a manner considerably above that of a servant. I suppose his job at Bolingbroke called for a good deal of administrative ability. The prosecutor's aggressive manner had the effect of stiffening his backbone, and he gave his answers coolly enough. So far as it went his story corroborated that of Mr. Starr, and Anders naturally assumed that they were both lying. The prosecutor brought out one new point to which he made believe to attach great importance.

"When you were coming back to this room with Mr. Starr," he asked, "did you hear him say anything?"

"He was like a man half out of his senses," answered the butler. "He kept saying over and over: 'Oh my God! the poor soul! How I have wronged her!'"

"Ha!" exclaimed Anders, busily writing it down.

"I understood by that . . ." Pascoe went on.

"Never mind that."

But the butler persisted. "That as the result of a quarrel she had shot herself, and he regretted the quarrel."

"I am not interested in your deductions," said Anders loftily. "As you see, she did not shoot herself."

"But he thought she had."

"Please confine yourself to answering my questions."

Later Mr. Anders proceeded to delve a little into the past of the Starrs. "What were the relations between Mr. and Mrs. Starr?" he asked Pascoe.

The butler glanced at Mr. Starr and spread out his hands deprecatingly.

"That is no answer," said Anders.

"They have been separated for the past eight or nine years," said Pascoe.

"How long have you been working here?"

"Ever since the castle was completed, sir. That is ten years in the Spring."

"Then Mr. and Mrs. Starr were living together when you came here?"

"Mr. Starr occasionally visited the castle."

"What were the relations between them then?"

"Bad, sir," said Pascoe laconically.

"Very bad?"

"Very bad."

"Quarrels?"

"Continual quarrels. Mrs. Starr was a woman it was impossible to get along with."

"Yet you stayed with her ten years."

"I was not her husband, sir," said Pascoe dryly.

"You were her servant."

"Oh, she got to know a long time ago about how much I would stand. I was useful to her and she left me pretty much alone."

"In these quarrels that you refer to, did you ever hear any threats passed?"

"What sort of threats?" asked Pascoe guardedly.

"Threats of personal injury."

"From Mrs. Starr, often, sir. Not from Mr. Starr. He would simply leave the house."

This was not the answer Anders wanted, and he sneered. "You do not seem to have retained much loyalty towards your mistress—after taking her wages for ten years."

"I earned my wages, sir," said Pascoe quietly.

After Pascoe, Anders examined a number of lesser terrified servants. From none of them did he obtain anything of significance. None had been in that part of the castle. None had so much as heard the shot.

From the sample of Anders's cross-examination which I have given, it may be gathered that he asked only the obvious questions to which of course he received obvious replies. It was impossible for Mme. Storey to betray much interest in what was going on. She was not idle, though. I saw her fine, keen eyes travelling about the room, taking in every detail, from which, assuredly, she was drawing her own conclusions.

The round room was not the least incongruous in that incongruous castle. Wall and ceiling were hidden under a glorious oaken panelling, rich with antiquity, that must have been raped entire from some European stronghold. There were two Gothic windows filled with exquisite tracery containing leaded glass. Yet the floor was covered with battleship linoleum, and the dingy, flat-topped desk might have come out of a city editor's den. The other movables in the room were in keeping; some plain wood chairs, a filing cabinet, a typewriter on its stand and a cheap rattan sofa. Nevertheless, Pascoe had testified it was in this room that his mistress spent most of her time.

Mme. Storey, reading my thoughts, murmured: "Even Bessie Jewett Starr discovered at last that magnificence is fatiguing."

Pascoe, released from the witness chair, sent up trays of sandwiches and bottles of ginger ale, which we partook of very thankfully in an adjoining room.

Back in the round room again, it was Mme. Storey who discovered the bullet lodged in the panelling alongside the door. She called Mr. Anders's attention to it.

"Ah, yes, thank you," he said with rather a strained smile. "I have not come to that yet."

Mme. Storey made a whispered request of one of the footmen for a tape-measure which was presently fetched her. She measured the distance of the bullet from the floor. Mr. Anders affected to take no notice of what she was doing, but he looked rather annoyed.

It was about this time that the proceedings were interrupted by the sounds of an arriving automobile that reached us through the open windows. One of the windows of the round room commanded the main entrance to the castle, and Pascoe, glancing out, said with a dismayed look at the rest of us:

"It is Miss Jewett and the old lady coming home."

A horrified silence fell on the room. Who would tell them? was the general thought.

"It will have to be you, Pascoe," said Mme. Storey with concern. "I can't go to meet them in their own house. It would be an impertinence."

Pascoe bowed and went out of the room, leaving the door open.

During the succeeding moments the investigation faltered. Mr. Anders was nervous. I suppose we were all unconsciously listening for sounds from the house. I recalled that Mr. Starr had told us the mother of the two women was mad, and I shivered with apprehension.

But no distant shrieks, no sounds of any sort reached us until in a few moments there came soft hurrying footsteps along the corridor. Tessie Jewett came into the room, and stopped with a jerk just inside the door. Pascoe was behind her.

She presented a startling contrast to her sister. The strong facial resemblance was still there, but how different, how extraordinarily different! Tessie Jewett had grown gaunt and dull-looking with the years. It was well-nigh impossible to reconstruct the former music hall favourite from this dispirited and frankly middle-aged woman. Dull, worn and apathetic, the skin of her face was flabby and greyish; her hair dust-coloured. She was dressed in a ridiculous travesty of her sister's style, i.e. the ultra-fashionable woman. The rich garments hung anyhow on her angular frame; on her head was balanced some sort of tasteless hat that had no relation whatever to her dulled, simple face and sparse hair. To remind you of her former beauty only the large, dim blue eyes were left. They turned helplessly this way and that behind the old woman's spectacles that she wore. In a word, the very picture of an unmarried household martyr. Between a domineering sister and a mad mother what a life she must have led!

Her dazed and uncomprehending gaze fixed itself on the shapeless huddle under the green velure drapery, and her lips shaped some indistinguishable words. Raising her eyes at last, she looked at each one of us in a puzzled way, but the body, like a magnet, dragged them back to itself. She half lifted her hands in an ineffective way and let them fall again. Then I made out what it was she was trying to say.

"Oh, my God! What next? What next?"

It was unspeakably affecting.

Mme. Storey went to her in her large, grave way, and said simply: "I am Rosika Storey. I am here to help if I can."

Obviously the name meant nothing to Miss Jewett; nevertheless she retained Mme. Storey's hand, and pressed closer to her like a bewildered child. "I'm glad there's someone here," she whispered, "some woman. I wouldn't know what to do, myself."

All this time her fascinated gaze had never budged from what lay under the green velure. Everybody else in the room was silenced. According to their natures some looked out of the windows, and some gaped at the stricken sister.

At length she murmured huskily: "Who did it?"

"That's what we're trying to find out," said Mr. Anders, briskly moving his glasses up and down on his nose. His voice sounded thin and pert in that highly charged atmosphere. Puff himself up as he might, he was unable to measure to the situation.

"Don't you know who did it?" she asked in a curious, far-off whisper.

"It is not proven," said Mr. Anders significantly.

Miss Jewett slowly raised her dim, great beautiful eyes and let them rest accusingly on Norbert Starr. A shiver went through all of us. There was something so remote, so disembodied about her. That involuntary glance was more convincing than any of the evidence which had been brought out against the husband. I confess I was shaken by it. Yet Mr. Starr seemed not to be affected.

"Have you any reason to suspect anybody in this room?" asked Mr. Anders with a preternatural air of acuteness as if he alone had been capable of seeing what would have been patent to a child.

She quickly veiled her eyes. "Oh, I accuse nobody, I accuse nobody," she said nervously.

"Do you feel able to answer a few questions?" asked Mr. Anders.

She kept her eyes fixed on the body. "Ask me anything you want," she murmured dejectedly. ". . . What does it matter?"

"Did you know that Mr. Starr was coming to see your sister this morning?"

"No, sir."

"She did not tell you, then, that she had written to him, making the appointment?"

"No, sir."

"Do you not think she would have mentioned it to you if she had written such a letter?"

"I can't answer for what Bessie might have done."

"Has Mr. Starr been here at any other time recently?"

"No, sir."

"Your sister and he have not met at all, then, of late years."

"Bessie went to see him sometimes—when she wanted to plague him."

"I understood that you took your mother to the doctor today. Is that a regular duty of yours?"

"Yes, sir, every Thursday morning I take her in."

"It is well known then, that you and your mother are always away on Thursdays."

"I suppose so."

"Could not Mr. Starr have been aware of this fact?"

"Bessie told him, maybe. I don't know."

"Have you ever overheard Mr. Starr threaten harm to your sister, or do you know that he has ever done so?"

She shook her head heavily. "I accuse nobody."

"Have you ever heard your sister express a fear of him?"

Something about this question had the effect of unlocking the frozen woman's speech. But it still came out of her involuntarily, like the mutterings of one asleep. Her remote, bewildered eyes seemed to have no part in what she was saying. As is sometimes the case with elderly unmarried women her voice still had a suggestion of the immature girl in it, and she had reverted to the homely idiom of the village she had left so many years before.

"Oh, Bessie often said he'd like to do her in, but she wasn't really afraid of him. Bessie wasn't afraid of anybody. She had everybody afraid of her except Momma. Momma wasn't afraid of Bessie. They never could get along. Both too quick-tempered. And lately

Momma brooded. She's not herself, you know. She'd done Bessie a hurt if she could. I had to watch her and keep her away. Momma's not herself any more."

What a picture of life in that tragic household this drew!

The apathetic voice droned on: "Of course, we could have put Momma away somewheres. Bessie wanted to. But I said no. No hired nurse could manage Momma like I can. I keep her with me. I sleep with her nights. Of course I wisht that Momma and I could have gone away somewheres together. But Bessie wouldn't let us. It would have left her alone here. She wouldn't have had anybody to jaw at but the servants. And they leave."

"Yes, yes. Most distressing!" said Mr. Anders impatiently. "But it hasn't got anything to do with the tragedy before us. I do not suppose that you mean to suggest your mother might . . ."

"Momma was with me all the time."

"Kelliger," said Mr. Anders, "uncover the hand."

A corner of the cloth was lifted, and the fat ringed fingers clutching the revolver were revealed once more. Though we had been conscious of it every minute, there was nevertheless a horrid shock in finding that it *was still there*. The hand had changed colour a little in the interim; grown more clayey.

"Do you recognise that pistol?" asked the prosecutor.

"I suppose it is Bessie's," Miss Jewett answered. "She's had it a long time. She threatened people with it when she was mad, but I don't know as she ever fired it off. . . . The last time I seen it—if that is the same one, was one day when she run into the house in a passion to get it, saying that some common Irish from the village had brought their lunch into the Park . . ."

"Yes, yes," said Mr. Anders, "but that hasn't got anything to do with the matter before us . . ."

Once started, it appeared that the gentle, disembodied voice was not to be shut off. ". . . I never heard how it turned out. I expect it was Mitchell Crear, the tinsmith. Bessie's had trouble with him before. He was one of these red republicans that have it in for the rich. He'd go out of his way to spite Bessie, and made remarks as she passed by. . . ."

Mr. Anders shook his head. "I'm afraid this has been too much for the poor lady," he remarked *sotto voce* to us. "It is impossible to get anything out of her."

"I will take her away," said Mme. Storey.

We left him to his ridiculous "investigation."

5

As we walked through the corridor, Miss Jewett murmured: "You mustn't mind Momma. I let her dress up to please herself. She is always quiet if you put her before a mirror."

I wondered if I could believe my ears.

Out in the great hall under the watchful eyes of two maids, we came upon the third member of the strange household. It was a woman incredibly old, incredibly made up. Her hair was dyed a strange bright red hue; her seamed and sunken cheeks were carmined. This strong colour simply obliterated the faded eyes that she could not restore. She seemed to have no eyes. Her thin bent frame was dressed in—how shall I describe it?—gewgaws and ribbons and laces seemed to be pinned at random all over her. She had all the tricks of a stage *ingénue*. One of the maids was holding a large hand mirror up before her, into which she smirked, endlessly prinking. The sight was too tragic for tears.

She saw us coming from afar, and simpered, and put her head on one side, and waved her hand in an affected fashion. When we came close, she said to Mme. Storey in her cracked old voice:

"How are you! I suppose I know you, but I forget who you are. I think you're very pretty."

"And I think you're pretty, too," said Mme. Storey, taking her hand, and smiling down at her.

A quick look of gratitude shot out of Miss Jewett's dim eyes. When she came into the presence of her mother, she no longer looked so remote and wandering. Her spirit seemed to brood over the helpless old woman.

Mrs. Jewett bridled and simpered and raised her shoulders in a killing way. "Me!" she said. "Oh, no! I can no longer pretend to have any looks with two such great girls. There was a time, my dears, when the gentlemen did not pass me by. . . . Hold that glass up, girl. . . . This is my baby, Teresa. She is a little backward. . . . Have you lost your tongue, Teresa? Can't you speak to the lady? . . . My other girl Elizabeth has more of a spirit . . ."

Mme. Storey looked at Miss Jewett, and her lips shaped the words: "Have you told her?"

Miss Jewett nodded. "She can't take it in," she whispered.

"Can't take what in?" instantly demanded the old lady. "What are you keeping from me?"

"Bessie is dead, Momma," said Miss Jewett.

But the old lady's attention had already wandered. "Heigho!" she sighed. "It's a great responsibility bringing up girls! I was married at seventeen and left a widow before I was twenty. How'm I ever going to find husbands for them when the time comes. . . . I hope you've come to lunch. We have better food when there's strangers here. Too many fal-lals. Don't you like apple dumplings?"

"Momma, Bessie is dead!" cried Miss Jewett in a dreadful low voice of pain.

Mme. Storey quickly laid a hand on her arm. "What does it matter?" she whispered. "It is better so."

"Apple dumplings," repeated the old lady unctuously. "Baked. With hard sauce. Um yum . . ."

Presently a footman came to tell Mme. Storey that Mr. Starr would appreciate it, if she would return to the round room for a moment. I was thankful to get away.

As we entered the round room Mr. Starr said in a voice of cynical despair: "He's ready to lock me up now. I thought you'd better know about it."

Mr. Anders spread out his hands. "In view of what I have learned it has become my painful duty to order Mr. Starr detained in custody," he said. "You will appreciate, I am sure, that no other course is open to me."

Mme. Storey bowed without committing herself.

Mr. Starr sneered at the prosecutor's elaborate phraseology. He went direct to the heart of the matter. "You can't hang me until you find the gun with which I am supposed to have done it!" he cried in a voice reckless with pain. "That won't be easy. Why, it would have been suicidal to come to see that woman with a gun in my pocket."

"You have a perfectly good plea of self-defence," said Mr. Anders. "Why aren't you satisfied with that?"

"Ah, you're a fool!" said Mr. Starr.

Mr. Anders, with the expression of a man sorely-tried, looked towards Mme. Storey for sympathy. But my mistress kept her eyes down.

"You make a great point of the fact that I had a reason to kill her," Mr. Starr went on, "but you overlook the fact that I had a reason, every reason to live! I left my gun at home in my desk, where it may be found if you send for it."

"I suppose there is no reason why you may not have stopped on the way here and bought another gun," said Mr. Anders with that acute smile of his.

"Well, find it then," said Mr. Starr sullenly.

"That I shall," said the prosecutor. "You may remain here while we look."

A haphazard and unsystematic search followed. The bare room offered but a certain number of possible hiding places, and they looked in these over and over. The corridor down which Mr. Starr had run to summon help was searched, and finally Kelliger was sent outside the building to see if the pistol had been tossed out of one of the windows. Nothing came of it all.

While it was going on Mme. Storey sat in the round room pondering. That is how she generally looks for a thing. She was of course trying to reconstruct the assassin's course of reasoning. When Anders and Kelliger had come to a stand, and were looking around rather foolishly for new places, she said dryly:

"You have not moved the desk. There is room under the drawers on either side for a gun to be hidden."

"I was just coming to that," said Mr. Anders.

The desk was a heavy piece, and it was not upon casters. It required the combined efforts of Kelliger and Pascoe to move it. And there, on one of the dusty oblongs of linoleum that were uncovered, lay as if by magic another pistol. It was a bigger pistol than the one clutched in the dead woman's hand, an old-fashioned pistol.

It created an immense sensation in the room. Everybody (except Mme. Storey) looked at Mr. Starr as much as to say: That finishes you! I myself was badly shaken. Mr. Anders plumed himself ridiculously. He said with a sneer:

"I hope that satisfies you, Mr. Starr."

That unfortunate man was not thinking about *him*: He stared at the pistol as if it was pointed at his own heart, and a low, anguished cry escaped him. "God help me! How did *that* get there!"

Mme. Storey gave the pistol a close examination. She was rendered a little impatient by the general excitement. With her magnificent common sense she said:

"I cannot see that the finding of this gun alters the situation. It was conceded beforehand that *somebody* shot Mrs. Starr."

Her irony failed to reach Mr. Anders. He bustled in his triumph. "Kelliger," he said, "telephone to the Central station for the sergeant and a constable to come here and take Mr. Starr. Let them come in a taxicab."

Mr. Starr glanced imploringly at Mme. Storey, but she was still busy with the pistol. She scribbled the number of the weapon and the maker's name on a bit of paper and handed it to me.

"Telephone," she whispered, "and see if you can learn when that gun was first sold."

I left the room.

For some little time past I had been chafing at Mme. Storey's apparent supineness. Of course I knew she was simply biding her own time, but I wanted to see her *show* these people. When I returned, apparently the time had come for that. She arose.

"Mr. Anders," she said with the satirical-seductive smile that is her most effective weapon against men of his sort, "of course I'm only a woman, but I've been trying to put things together. I wish you'd let me tell you my theory."

That smile brought him up on tip-toe. He smiled back *so* gallantly, *so* indulgently. "My dear lady! I should be charmed to listen to anything you may have to say."

Said Mme. Storey: "I should say that Mrs. Starr was shot by a tall woman or a man of average height."

Mr. Anders blinked. This was hardly what he had expected. "What reason have you to think so?"

"The dead woman was five feet nine inches tall . . ."

"How do you know that?" he interrupted, round-eyed.

"She visited me three days ago, and my secretary happened to remark that she was the same height as myself."

"Very interesting. Very interesting. But, if I may ask, how does that apply here?"

"The bullet is lodged in the woodwork yonder exactly five feet seven inches above the floor. Mrs. Starr was shot, as near, as I can determine, two inches below the crown of her head. It must therefore be obvious to you that the bullet pursued an exactly horizontal course across the room. Need I go on?"

Mr. Anders's jaw had fallen lower and lower as she proceeded. Such words from the lips of a pretty woman! Trying to teach him *his* trade!

Mme. Storey continued, since he did not seem to be able to supply the rest. "A person must aim a gun on the level of his eye. It is true one reads in fiction of marvellous Westerners who shoot from the hip, but I think we may safely disregard that possibility. . . . If I am right, Mrs. Starr must have been shot by a man or woman of about her own height, while Mr. Starr is . . ." She looked at him.

"Six foot one," he stammered, a wild hope dawning in his eyes.

Mr. Anders was very much discomposed. The gallant smile had become strained. "Very interesting; very interesting," he said, looking at his fingernails. "But I am afraid your ingenious theory will hardly stand against the stubborn facts. If there was a third person in the room while Mr. and Mrs. Starr were talking, where was he hidden?"

"Under the middle part of the desk at which you are sitting," said Mme. Storey softly. "There is room there, you see, for a person to hide even from the sight of one who might be seated at the desk."

Like a wondering child, the little man ducked down and looked under the desk.

Mme. Storey went on: "Mr. Starr says he found her lying on the very spot where he had left her standing. And why not? The murderer had only to stand up to shoot. The shot came from the direction of the desk. And when the desk was moved you noticed, of course, when you examined the dust, that the revolver had been pushed under from the middle part."

"Of course I noticed it," said Mr. Anders.

"There was plenty of time for the murderer to escape while Mr. Starr was away fetching help," said Mme. Storey.

"How could he escape without being seen?" stammered Mr. Anders.

"Well, for one thing, there's another door in this room," she said coolly.

"Another door!" he echoed, gaping.

"Pascoe, is there not a door about there?" she asked, pointing to the panelling behind the desk.

"Yes, madam," he said unhesitatingly. "In the sixth panel counting from the other door."

"What is on the other side of it?"

"A circular stairway. There is a door at the foot of it leading to the rose garden. Mrs. Starr frequently went in and out that way. There was no secret about it."

"Can you open the door, Pascoe?"

"I think so, madame. I have seen Mrs. Starr open it when I have been in the room."

He went and felt about the woodwork. At length his fingers met the concealed spring, and the panel slid slowly back, and thudded against its stops. Within the dark aperture a circular stone stairway was revealed mysteriously rounding from above, only to be swallowed up below. What a glimpse!

We all peered fearfully into the place and listened.

"Why wasn't I told of this?" Mr. Anders demanded of Pascoe.

"You didn't ask me, sir," said Pascoe dryly.

"How did you know of its existence, madam?" the prosecutor asked my mistress with a glance of dark suspicion.

She smiled. "Oh, there's no magic in it. As we drove up to the castle I happened to notice that each of the flanking towers had its attendant turret built alongside, topped off with an extinguisher. It was customary in the period. The turret always contained a stairway with an opening to each floor of the tower."

"Hum!" said Mr. Anders.

He drew a revolver from his pocket, and started down the stairway.

Pascoe picked up a great key on the desk, saying: "I believe this is the key to the garden door, if you require it."

"That door is kept locked?" asked Mme. Storey.

"Oh, always, madam. Mrs. Starr would not have allowed anybody but herself to use that entrance."

"Well, if it's locked now, and the key's been lying here all the time, the murderer could not have got out that way."

Mr. Anders came back for the key, and resumed his way down. Mme. Storey followed, smiling. Pascoe and I brought up the rear. Mr. Starr was left under guard of Kelliger. The reawakened hope and anxiety in the unfortunate man's face was painful to see.

Well, we marched down the stairway, took a look at the rose garden, and marched back again. The garden, by the way, which was surrounded by an arbor vitæ screen, was a dream of secluded loveliness. But the door was locked, and it was evident no one could have got out that way.

Returning, Mr. Anders did not stop at the room we had set out from, but kept on up the stair. It was not absolutely dark, for there was a loophole or two in the thick stone wall. One made so many turns one lost all sense of direction. We came to a door which presumably gave on an upper chamber corresponding to the round room. It was locked, and having no key we kept on. Higher up, an arched opening led to another and a larger round chamber which was perfectly empty, floored, walled and vaulted with stone. It contained no windows, but in the edge of the floor all around there were curious holes, through which one could peer down to the ground far below.

"Machicolations, they are called," said Mme. Storey. "Through these holes the defenders could drop stones on anybody who might attack the base of the tower."

Fancy, in Upper Bellaire!

Continuing still higher, we issued out through the candle extinguisher she had spoken of, on to the flat roof of the tower. It was floored with thick sheets of lead—think of the expense nowadays! and surrounded by battlements. There was a widespread view of the salt meadows; a light haze lent even the distant fertilizer factories a charm; but at the moment we were looking for something else besides a view. The battlements were a good twenty-five feet above the main roof of the castle. No one could have escaped that way. There was nothing to do but go down again.

We paused by the locked door.

"What is this room used for?" Mr. Anders asked Pascoe.

"It has never been used, sir, so far as I know," the butler replied. "It is too remote from the rest of the house. Mrs. Starr may have stored some personal belongings there. I have never been in it."

"The key?"

"It has always been in her possession, sir."

"Well, if it's in her possession there's no use our looking in," he said, taking a leaf out of Mme. Storey's book.

But it is not safe to try to borrow her thunder. "May I have your flashlight?" she asked sweetly.

It was handed over to her. She turned it on the keyhole, and bent down to look.

"The key is on the inside," she said quietly.

6

HER QUIET WORDS had all the effect of a small explosion among us. My heart began to beat thickly. Somebody was in that room! What fresh horror was in store for us? I heartily wished myself back in my quiet office. I do not like these sensational scenes.

Mr. Anders in great excitement beat upon the solid wood with the soft side of his fists. "Open the door!" he cried. "I am an officer of the law!"

No sound came to us from the other side.

He used the handle of his flashlight upon the door. "Open!" he cried louder; "or I'll break it down!"

This was easier said than done, for the door, like all the others, was presumably of two-inch oak, and there was not room enough on the narrow landing to wield a battering ram or to swing an axe.

"What shall we do?" the little prosecutor said helplessly.

"We can lower a man through the machicolations above, and let him smash a window," said Mme. Storey.

Before there was time to make a move in this direction, we heard the great key creak in the lock, and the door swung slowly in. It was not a formidable figure which faced us, but a woman with hanging arms and lowered head. A beautiful, slender creature with hair wall-flower brown, and dark curled lashes that swept her cheeks like an infant's. Her soft cheeks were hollowed and bloodless and when, finally, she raised her blue eyes they looked most piteously as if they had wept themselves dry of tears. One side of her pretty mauve dress was all fouled with brown dust as if she had flung herself down on the floor in her despair.

"Who are you?" gasped Mr. Anders.

The girl's pale lips essayed to move, but she was incapable of making a sound.

"Who is she?" Anders demanded in turn of Pascoe and Mme. Storey. They shook their heads.

Mr. Anders took her by the arm, and started to lead her unresistingly down the stairway. Before following, Mme. Storey took a survey of the room she came out of. It corresponded to the room below, but the stone walls had never been finished off with panelling. It contained nothing but some miscellaneous litter such as bundles of old papers, books, etc., all thick with dust. One of the books was a big scrap-book stuffed with press clippings. Mme. Storey's eyes gleamed at the sight of it. She said:

"Bring it downstairs, Bella. It may prove valuable."

As we were rounding the stairs, we heard a strange cry from Norbert Starr below: "*Mary!* . . . Oh, my God, what are you doing here?"

"Ah, poor souls!" murmured Mme. Storey.

When we got into the room the two had run together. Seizing Mr. Starr by his two elbows, the girl gave him a little shake in her relief and joy. Her frozen face melted; speech returned to her.

"Oh, Norbert! . . . Oh, Norbert! Thank God you're all right. I could not be sure. . . . I could not be sure what had happened!"

The man's harassed face grew soft and youthful and he looked down at her. Clearly he forgot everything else when their eyes met. The girl, too.

"But, Mary, how did you get here?" he murmured.

"Oh, how can I tell you?" she said with a shudder. "It's been so dreadful and confused! . . . But it doesn't matter now. If you are safe."

Anders grew very impatient at being excluded from the scene. He assumed to be filled with moral indignation. "Come, Miss," he said sharply, "you must give some account of yourself."

The girl turned from Mr. Starr. A little colour had come back to her face, and she was getting her grip again. She had not yet perceived what was lying under the green shroud, because the big desk was in the way.

"What is your name?"

"Oh, don't drag her into this!" Mr. Starr exclaimed involuntarily.

"I don't mind telling him," she said. "My name is Mary Lansdowne."

This name suggested nothing to Anders. Mme. Storey and I knew it before it was spoken of course. I was filled with a great compassion for the pair—a great curiosity, too. What on earth was the girl doing there?

"Please explain your presence in this house," said Mr. Anders.

"I came to see Mrs. Starr at her request," was the rather surprising reply.

Norbert Starr was frankly amazed.

"You were on friendly terms with her?" asked Anders.

"I was not on any terms with her. I had never seen her before."

"Yet you are friends with her husband, I judge."

"Mr. Starr and I are friends."

"Very intimate friends, I take it."

The girl's chin went up. "That is not a question, but an insinuation," she said with spirit. "What right have you to question me, anyway? Who are you?"

"Anders, County Prosecutor of Middlesex," he said with an affectation of boredom.

The girl was shaken. "What has happened here?" she demanded.

"Do you not know?" sneered Anders.

"If I knew I would not ask you."

"Mrs. Starr has been shot dead."

The girl gazed at him in silent horror; glanced around at the rest of us for confirmation. Involuntarily, our eyes turned toward what lay on the floor. She ran around the desk and looked. She drew a gasping breath in her throat, and turning, flung an arm up over her eyes to shut out the sight. Strong shudders went through her slender frame. Mr. Starr's eyes dwelt on her, half sick with solicitude; but he made no move to go to her.

Presently the girl said nervously: "Has been shot . . . has been shot? You mean she shot herself?"

"I do not mean that," said Mr. Anders.

"But she *must* have shot herself. There was no one else in the room."

"Where were you?" he asked significantly.

The girl pointed. "Behind the sliding door."

"Mary! . . . In God's name . . . !" gasped Mr. Starr.

Anders shrugged. "Well, Mrs. Starr was shot from behind. That's proven. Moreover, we have the pistol from which the shot was fired."

The girl looked at Mr. Starr with a horrified question in her eyes. Clearly, she could not put it into words.

A new strength had come into him since she had entered the room. "Yes," he said quietly, "they accuse me."

"That's ridiculous," she said quickly. "You were outside the door before the shot was fired."

"How do you know if you were hidden behind the panelling?" Anders asked quickly.

"I could hear everything in the room. I heard the door slam before the shot was fired."

"How do you know he didn't push the door shut and then shoot her?"

The girl faltered. "She . . . she had threatened to shoot him."

Mme. Storey said softly: "The bullet is over here beside the door."

Anders smiled at her in an annoyed way. "Er—of course, of course. Supposing the girl to be telling the truth about the slamming of the door. But I am far from satisfied as to that. Her own position is a highly suspicious one." He turned to the butler. "Pascoe, did you know that this young woman was in the house?"

"No, sir."

"How could she have got in without your knowing of it?"

"I can't say, sir."

"It was by no honourable means, we may be sure," said Mr. Anders, answering his question to suit himself. ". . . What were you doing locked up in the room overhead?" he suddenly barked at the girl.

"I thought she had shot at Norbert through the door," the girl answered simply. "I was afraid she would try to shoot me next. I couldn't get out of the garden door, because she had locked it and taken the key. So I ran into the room overhead. The key was in the door, and I turned it to protect myself."

"Why did you not throw open one of the windows above and call for help?"

"I suppose that is what I should have done," she murmured. "I can see it now. But I was half distracted. I dreaded being mixed up in an ugly scandal. I thought it would only make it harder for Mr. Starr. I hoped that I would be able to find my own way out later."

"Ha! that sounds at least as if we were approaching the truth," sneered Mr. Anders.

Norbert Starr glared at him.

"Perhaps Miss Lansdowne will tell us how she came to be in the house in the first place," suggested Mme. Storey mildly.

"Certainly," said the girl. "I received a note from Mrs. Starr yesterday asking me to come to see her at ten o'clock this morning. I was astonished to hear from her at all, and still more astonished that it was a kindly seeming letter. She said in it that if we could talk together woman to woman perhaps I would find out that she was not so black as she had been painted. She . . . she . . . ." The poor girl faltered. "It is difficult to speak of these private matters," she whispered.

"You are not obliged to tell!" Mr. Starr burst out.

"Silence!" cried Mr. Anders.

"Silence, yourself!" retorted Mr. Starr. "This happens to be my house!"

When this little flurry blew over, the girl said firmly: "I will tell everything. Everything must come out now . . . Mrs. Starr intimated in her letter that she was prepared to set Mr. Starr free under certain conditions. She asked me to meet her alone in a certain spot in the castle grounds, giving as her reason that she was continually spied upon by servants and others. This seemed like a natural enough reason to me. She further asked me not to tell Mr. Starr that I was coming, or he would be sure to dissuade me . . ."

Norbert Starr's face was a study throughout this. "Oh, Mary!" he murmured.

"It was a very clever letter," the girl continued, "and I was completely taken in by it. I have every confidence in Mr. Starr, but even so, it seemed natural to me after the intolerable injuries he had received at her hands, that he might not be altogether fair to her. Nobody had ever acted hatefully or maliciously to me, consequently I believed that everybody must be good at heart.

"So I came. I followed the directions in the letter; entering the park by a little-used gate, and meeting Mrs. Starr in the spot she had described. In manner she was as kind and gentle as her letter had been, and I was glad I had come. She frankly acknowledged her former faults, but said she had experienced a change of heart.

Her whole object now, she said, was to make up as far as she could for all the unhappiness she had caused Mr. Starr. She said that the reason she had sent for me was to make sure that I was the sort of woman who could really make him happy. If I were, she would put no further obstacles in his way, she said.

"In a little while she suggested that I come to the castle with her, where we could talk more at our ease. She brought me here by a way known to herself through the woods and the rose garden. We met nobody. We entered this tower by a door from the garden which Mrs. Starr locked behind her. We had not been in this room but a few moments when there was a knock at the door. Mrs. Starr asked me to wait on the stairway while she found out who it was. I did not like that sort of thing, still under the circumstances it did not seem unnatural that she should ask it. So I waited on the stairway, and she closed the panel behind me.

"It was a servant who had knocked. To my dismay I heard him announce Mr. Starr. When Mrs. Starr told the servant to bring Mr. Starr to this room, I realised that I had been tricked.

"I rattled the panel—I did not know how to open it from that side; I begged Mrs. Starr to let me out before he came, or at least to give me the key that I might get out through the garden. She only laughed at me. What I heard would open my eyes, she said through the door.

"At first I would not listen to what took place between them. I ran down to the foot of the steps. But when the woman began to scream at him, I became afraid on his account. I came back . . . then I heard all that was said . . ."

"Oh, Mary!" Mr. Starr murmured in horror.

"It didn't hurt me," she said stoutly. "I am not made of glass. . . . I believe the poor woman was mad; mad with malice and hatred. Her object in getting me here was evidently to have me overhear her triumphing over Mr. Starr. But if that is so, it was not realised, for her foul abuse only reacted on herself. It never touched him.

"Her failure to move him aroused her in the end to a perfect frenzy. She screamed out that she'd kill him. I heard her fumble in the drawer of her desk for a gun. Then the door slammed and the shot rang out. I thought she had fired after him."

"Very interesting," said Mr. Anders with a disagreeable smile. "I am just going to ask you one little question." He paused for effect.

The girl looked at him as if puzzled to know what sort of disagreeable insect this could be. That glance of hers was a deadly affront to the little egoist.

"Are you prepared to produce the letter you say you received from Mrs. Starr?" he asked with an air.

"No, I burned it," she answered at once. "As she had in the letter asked me to do."

"How unfortunate!" said Mr. Anders sneering. "For I have established the fact that Mrs. Starr was shot by a woman or a short man."

This was pretty cool. I looked at Mme. Storey full of indignation, but she only smiled. When, oh, when, would she arise and crock this insect, I wondered.

"Miss Lansdowne is hardly five-foot-nine," Mme. Storey murmured.

"Oh, you cannot figure to a fraction of an inch," he retorted loftily. "A very pretty little plot is suggested here. It is too miraculous, the set of coincidences that brought them here at the same moment, the two people in the world most interested in putting this poor woman out of the way. Just what part each one played in the matter, I am not prepared to state without further investigation. In the meanwhile I shall of course order Miss Lansdowne's detention also."

"My detention?" gasped the girl, opening her eyes very wide.

"Detaining *her!* . . . Oh, you fool!" burst out Norbert Starr.

"Oh, doubtless, doubtless," said the little man, with a jocose smile at Kelliger, whose sympathy he could depend on; "but time will tell!"

7

MR. ANDERS had not yet published the sensational news broadcast, but he could not quite keep it to himself, either. He had telephoned to a certain Mr. Beckwith, who, it appeared, was chief of the selectmen or burgesses or whatever it was they called them, of Bellaire. In other words, the leading citizen of that suburb. He arrived at about the same time as the sergeant and constable.

Mr. Beckwith was a large, smooth, highly polished man. Besides running Bellaire in his off hours, he was a New York business man; vice-president of some Trust Company or another. In short, much more the experienced man of the world than little Anders, whose horizon was bounded by Patching Mountain and the Hohokus' meadows. When he was introduced to Mme. Storey, Beckwith's pale face shone with excited gratification.

"Mme. *Rosika* Storey?" he asked.

"The same," said my mistress.

"I am honoured . . . I am honoured," he said, bowing again and again. "Good Heavens, Anders!" turning to the other man, "how lucky we are to have the great Madame Storey to take an interest in this case."

Anders's jaw dropped as if its prop had been knocked from under. Behind the owlish glasses his eyelids made a thousand revolutions a minute. "Of course, of course!" he pattered. "Lucky indeed!" Meanwhile his bewildered face was mutely demanding: "But who the Hell is she?"

"Of course, in your business you know more about her work than I do," said Beckwith.

"Naturally."

"I shall never forget how she solved the Ashcomb Poor case. And the mysterious murder of that unfortunate girl up in Westchester County."

The prosecutor looked at my mistress as one might suppose the ugly step-sisters looked at Cinderella when the glass slipper went on. He gulped over the bitter pill. "Wonderful work," he said with a sickly smile. One could almost have felt sorry for him.

My mistress was too big a woman to rub it in. She smiled good-naturedly at little Anders. No one who did not know her as well as I did, could have perceived the humorous mockery in it.

"Mr. Anders," she said, drawing him a little apart, "before you have this man and woman taken away, indulge me just a little."

He was knocked quite flat. "Anything in my power," he murmured quite humbly.

"Let us suppose for the sake of argument that these two may be telling the truth. We have to admit that their stories dovetailed remarkably well."

"Oh, they fixed that all up beforehand," he said.

"Possibly. But just for the sake of argument. . . . If they were telling the truth, there must have been a third person present in the room all the time."

"Obviously. But . . ."

"Well, before taking any action, let you and I pursue that possibility as far as it will take us."

"Just as you say, ma'am."

"If there was such a person in the room," Mme. Storey went on, "after firing the fatal shot, he or she ducked under the desk again as Mr. Starr ran back to see what had happened. Then when Mr. Starr ran out again to summon help, the murderer must have followed him out of the door, since Miss Lansdowne was hidden behind the door in the panelling. And since the murderer had been in this room even before Mrs. Starr and Miss Lansdowne talked here, he or she knew that Miss Lansdowne blocked the way out by the circular stair."

"Most ingenious," murmured Mr. Anders.

"But merely theorising, you would say," she put in good-naturedly. "Quite right. . . . Well, give up ten minutes to accompany me on the trail of this supposed person, and if within that time we do not discover some facts to support the theory, I will retire."

"I am in your hands," he murmured submissively.

"Bella, you come with us," she said, "and you, please, Pascoe, to guide us through the house."

"May I come, too?" asked the fat Mr. Beckwith, eagerly.

"Ah, this is purely professional," said Mme. Storey with an apologetic smile. "We mustn't be too big a crowd."

He fell back disappointed. Anders, Pascoe and I followed Mme. Storey out of the room. Mr. Starr and Miss Lansdowne were left under guard of the various constables.

It was a queer sort of personally conducted tour that Mme. Storey took us. "The murderer would scarcely have followed Mr. Starr out into the main corridor," she said. "Let us see what alternatives there are. There are three other doors on this rear corridor. The first . . ."

"Mrs. Starr's bedroom," put in Pascoe.

"Ah, a noble room," said Mme. Storey as we entered, "with three tall windows facing the east such as a bedroom ought to have. The windows are open, but there are screens outside which have not been disturbed. The ground is about twenty feet below. There is but one other door in the room, and that leads to . . ."

"The bathroom," said Pascoe.

We all crossed this most luxurious cabinet which had nothing mediæval about it. It was lined throughout with green marble, and there was a vast bath let in flush with the floor, and quantities of brass-piping—or gold-plated, for aught I know.

"It has a door on the corridor we have just left," continued Mme. Storey, like one thinking aloud, "and a third door leading to . . ."

"Mrs. Starr's dressing-room," said Pascoe.

The dressing-room contained nothing but a great table standing in the window embrasure surmounted by an ingenious arrangement of mirrors which gave you a view of every angle at once without moving your head; also chests and chests of drawers. The walls all around were lined with wardrobes having glass doors.

"A businesslike place," remarked Mme. Storey dryly.

"Shall I search the wardrobes?" asked Mr. Anders.

"You may if you wish. But I think so cunning a criminal would scarcely . . ."

"The wardrobes are always locked," said Pascoe. "The keys are never out of the possession of Miss Woodley, Mrs. Starr's own maid."

So we went on.

There was no door from the dressing-room into the corridor, and we proceeded directly into the last room of the suite, which was known as the boudoir, according to Pascoe. In this, her own sitting-room, the mistress of the castle had given herself a free hand, and the resulting effect was one of the weirdest we had seen.

Imagine a magnificent lofty chamber with a massive beamed ceiling, a superb fourteenth-century fire-place with projecting canopy, and along the south wall a whole row of tall pointed windows which looked out upon the central court of Bolingbroke, brilliant with clipped grass and parterres of many-coloured flowers. To complete it there should have been arras hanging before the stone walls, old faded rugs and a few pieces of heavy oak. But instead of that the stone walls were concealed behind hangings of pink taffeta—one wouldn't have thought there was so much pink taffeta in the world! The windows were curtained with it, the great corpulent chairs were upholstered in it, and there were besides a myriad lamp shades, cushions, screens. The floor was covered with a vast pink Aubusson carpet. Come to think of it, Mrs. Starr's instinct was not so far wrong after all. The boudoir must have made a fit setting for her.

Mme. Storey looked around her in an eloquent silence. Mr. Anders goggled at the pink taffeta.

Besides the door through which we had entered, there was a door from the corridor, and, diagonally across the room, a third door. Mme. Storey immediately proceeded to it, and opening it revealed a narrow landing and a stair descending. She looked at Pascoe inquiringly.

"For the servants," he explained. "So that Mrs. Starr could be waited on directly from below."

"This is the natural way out," said Mme. Storey. "Let us go down."

At the bottom of the stairs there was an ordinary door and window—once you left the show rooms of Bolingbroke the construction was frankly modern. Mme. Storey opened the door, and we looked into a sort of central servants' hall, from which corridors radiated in several directions, to storerooms, pantries, kitchens, no doubt. Half a dozen servants were within view. It appeared that work was still going on after a fashion, though the end of it all no longer existed.

"The murderer would not go this way if there was any other," said Mme. Storey. "Let us look at the window."

A sharp exclamation escaped from Pascoe. "Why, it's open!"

"Should it not be?" asked Mme. Storey.

"No, madam, by Mrs. Starr's express orders this window was always to be kept locked. It afforded a direct entrance to her rooms, you see."

"Ah," said Mme. Storey. "Let's look at it. The sill is three feet from the floor. An active woman would have no particular difficulty. . . . Unfortunately there's no dust on the sill . . ."

"You think it was a woman, then?" said Mr. Anders.

"My opinion inclines that way."

"What further grounds have you. . . ?"

"Well, it's the result of a rather lengthy course of reasoning," said Mme. Storey with a smile. "I'll tell you as we go along. Let's look out of the window first."

She suited the action to the word, and little Mr. Anders stuck his head out alongside her.

"Someone has gone out this way with fear at his heels," she said quietly. "Observe how the chrysanthemum plants are clumsily broken and crushed."

"I see! I see!" said Mr. Anders, like a child.

Mme. Storey withdrew her head. "Are you willing to come a little further with me?" she asked with a smile.

He spread out his hands in token of surrender.

"Then let Pascoe show us how we can reach this spot from the outside. He can then carry back word that we may be gone some time."

We left the butler at the service entrance to the castle. A moment later we were standing outside the open window above the chrysanthemum bed. Bending down, Mme. Storey carefully separated the broken plants, revealing a fairly perfect footprint in the loose mould.

Seeing it, the depressed Mr. Anders brightened up maliciously. "But that is a very large foot," he pointed out. "A man's, surely, and a big man's."

"So it would appear," said Mme. Storey cheerfully. "However, we shall see. . . . The next question to decide is which way she—he went. Only two steps to the service driveway, you see. Only one way to turn in the drive, because it ends yonder at service door.

Walking along the driveway this person would not be especially conspicuous, but I feel sure that with fear at his heels he—she would take to cover as quickly as possible. To run across the lawn would have been fatal; but observe, two hundred yards ahead of us, how a sort of promontory of the shrubbery almost touches the road. That would be the most likely place."

"It begins with the revolver we found under the desk," said Mme. Storey. "You observed, of course, that this revolver had a fresh, new look, though it is of a style which has long been discontinued. A close examination of the hammer, the chambers and the barrel suggested to me that it had never been shot off until today. The working parts have been kept free of rust by grease, but the shells are slightly rusted to the chambers. Now it is scarcely possible that a gun could pass from owner to owner and never be shot off, never even tested, so I assume that this pistol has been continuously in the possession of the person who first purchased it.

"It has been kept closely wrapped in a rag, as you could see from the particles of cotton still adhering to it. Now a revolver kept on hand for ordinary emergencies is never kept wrapped up that way—takes too long to get it out. I assume therefore—kept all these years without ever having been discharged—that it was purchased for a particular purpose, in short, the purpose for which it was used today."

"But why by a woman?"

"I'm coming to that now. The next question I had to answer was: How many years? That was easy. I had my secretary telephone to the manufacturers to find out about when the weapon bearing such a number had originally been sold. The answer was 1908. Fifteen years ago. The year of the marriage of Bessie Jewett and Norbert Starr. Now if anybody had a grudge against Bessie Jewett Starr that dated from her wedding, it would naturally be another woman, wouldn't it? a jealous woman? And anyway who but a woman would nourish a grudge for fifteen long years? Who but a foolish woman would undertake to use a revolver that had not been cleaned nor tested in so many years? It's a wonder she didn't blow her own hand to pieces."

"You bewilder me," murmured Mr. Anders.

"Theorising! Theorising!" said Mme. Storey cheerfully. "I never insist on my deductions until they are bolstered up by solid facts."

"But that was certainly a man's footprint," insisted Mr. Anders.

Mme. Storey merely smiled. The twinkle in her eye caused me to suspect that she was keeping her most important evidence to herself.

When we reached the point in the drive that was nearest the shrubbery, Mme. Storey bade us wait there so as not to mess up the earth with our tracks. Meanwhile, like a graceful hound she beat back and forth among the bushes. She presently gave tongue. As we joined her she pointed out a series of scarcely discernible depressions in the mould.

I would never have been able to follow them unaided, and I'm very sure Anders wouldn't—he was like a lap dog lost in the woods; but Mme. Storey with her marvellous eyesight led us on unhesitatingly. In the woods she was a dryad just as naturally as in town she was the fine lady. Through woods-mould, grass and last year's dead leaves she followed the trail. The shrubbery was backed by a thickly springing young woods of deciduous trees; oak, beech and ash; a natural wilderness with little open glades where rabbits scuttled and quail whirred up.

Presently Mme. Storey confessed that she had lost the track. However, she kept on, averring that it didn't matter, since she now had the woman's general direction. The woman must know what she was about. She would be heading for the shortest way out of the woods.

Mr. Anders hazarded the information that we could not be far now from the Greenwall road which bounded the rear of the Bolingbroke place.

Sure enough, we soon heard the sound of passing motors. A thickly planted border in the English style screened us from the road. Bidding us stand still again, Mme. Storey searched up and down until she found the place where the woman had forced a way through. Even I could see the marks of her passage, but Mme. Storey was not content; she was still searching for something.

Presently she made a pounce under a laurel bush, and held up a pair of large, new men's rubbers.

"I was sure she'd cast these before venturing out on the high road," she said.

Mr. Anders gave up. He cringed before Mme. Storey now. He stuffed the rubbers, one in each pocket.

Forcing our way through the thicket, we were still cut off from the highway by a barbed-wire fence. Before attempting to pass it, Mme. Storey looked keenly along the wire.

"It is difficult for a woman to get through barbed wire without leaving a souvenir," she remarked.

From one of the barbs she picked a thread. "What do you make of it?" she asked Anders, handing it over.

"A black thread," he said, blinking owlishly.

"But what sort of thread?"

"A cotton thread."

She shook her head, and broke off a piece. "A strong fine woolen thread with a crinkle in it. Crêpe. Our friend hung a crêpe veil from her bonnet so that she could hide her face, if need be. It is of a piece with the rest of her actions."

We assisted each other through the fence by holding the wires apart. On the hard macadam road the tracks were swallowed up. We could not even tell which way they turned in the road.

"No matter," said Mme. Storey. "It ought not to be difficult to figure which direction she took." She pointed to the left. "This would take us back to Upper Bellaire, wouldn't it?"

"Yes, madam," said Anders. "It runs into the main road to Bolingbroke Castle about a quarter of a mile from here."

"Then she wouldn't have gone that way," said my mistress, turning in the other direction.

We proceeded along the country road three abreast. The passing motorists looked at us curiously. And in truth we were an oddly assorted trio: Anders in his little cutaway coat and patent leather oxfords; the tall, elegant Mme. Storey in a champagne-coloured frock and a little red hat, and red-haired me with my note-book.

"The three musketeers!" murmured Mme. Storey.

We passed a few sporadic commuters' bungalows, and Mme. Storey sent Mr. Anders in to each one to inquire if a woman wearing a crêpe veil had been seen passing about noon. It was rather a trial to the county prosecutor's dignity to apply at the doors. In each case the answer was in the negative, and he began to pluck up a little spirit again.

"The person we are following may have had a car waiting for her," he ventured. "If so, we are certainly wasting our time."

"It is possible," said Mme. Storey calmly. "Anything is possible. On the other hand, this crime bears all the ear-marks of the single-handed crime. A crime long brooded upon in solitude and secrecy. I am as sure as one may be, that she came alone and departed alone. . . . One begins to be able to reconstruct her character. A strange mixture of naïveté and cunning. She took chances, you observe, that would have appalled a prudent person. That was how she was able to get away with it."

After having gone say three quarters of a mile, we came to a single-track railway. There was a small solitary station where the line crossed the highway. The sign upon it read: "Greenwall."

"The Longwood Lake road," said Mr. Anders.

"That station, I take it, was our friend's objective," said Mme. Storey. "She had evidently familiarised herself with the neighbourhood, and with the timetables, too, no doubt. Let us inquire." She looked at her watch. "It has taken us twenty-eight minutes to make it. She would do it quicker. It was eleven twenty-six when Mr. Starr called us up today. Let us assume that the shot was fired five minutes before that."

The station-agent was one of those typical, lean jacks-of-all-trades that one associates with country stations; one who is prepared to perform any office for a traveller from sending a telegram to trundling a trunk.

"What is the first train that stops here after eleven-forty A.M.?" asked Mme. Storey.

The man hesitated, all agog with inquisitiveness. He greatly desired to obtain information before giving away any.

"Anders, County Prosecutor," spoke up our escort brusquely. "Answer the question, please."

The agent quickly changed his attitude. "Eleven fifty-one, madam," he said.

"Bound in which direction?"

"To New York."

"Did a woman wearing a black veil get on here?"

"No, ma'am. Nobody got on here."

Anders rubbed his upper lip, and tried not to look too pleased.

Mme. Storey was undisturbed. She looked around, fixing the lay of the land in her mind. "The conductor of that train?" she asked, "when will he pass through again?"

"He comes out on the four-eighteen," was the reply. "Twenty minutes from now."

"We'll wait," said Mme. Storey.

The three of us sat down on a baggage truck. Mme. Storey lit a cigarette. Mr. Anders was comically divided in his mind between masculine admiration, and professional jealousy. They discussed the novels of Emile Gaboriau. It appeared that Mr. Anders took him quite seriously.

"A better story-teller than a detective, I should say," remarked Mme. Storey.

When the antique local train with its leaking engine drew in, a single passenger alighted and scurried away. The conductor was somewhat astonished to be accosted as he was about to wave his arm to proceed. Anders got off his formula:

"Anders, County Prosecutor."

"When you stopped here at eleven fifty-one did you pick up a woman passenger?" asked Mme. Storey.

"Why, yes, ma'am," was the unhesitating reply. "Big woman, all wrapped up in black like she'd been to a funeral."

Mr. Anders's face was a study. To do him credit, he never after that offered to set himself up against my mistress's opinion.

The station-agent was standing close, of course, with his ears stretched. "I never seen her," he put in.

"She paid her fare on the train," said the conductor.

"She would have waited behind the section hand's shanty across the track until the train pulled in," said Mme. Storey. "And got on from that side."

"Yes, ma'am," said the conductor. "Now you speak of it, she got on on the wrong side."

"Where did she go?"

"New York City, ma'am."

"You did not see her face, I suppose."

"No, ma'am, she kep' it covered."

"Can you add anything to your description?"

"Not much, ma'am. Large, stout woman dressed in plain black. Not young, I should say. But real spry; energetic in her movements; determined-like."

"A very good description. That's all; thank you."

The train went on.

Mr. Anders was left in some little excitement. "Now we have a definite clue!" he cried. "We know where we are. We have something positive to go on. I will follow to New York by the next train."

Mme. Storey shrugged. "Just as you like," she said dryly. "Won't you find it rather difficult to trace a woman in a crêpe veil through the streets of New York? . . . Besides, she'll take it off at the first opportunity."

His face fell absurdly. "What are you going to do?" he asked.

"I'm going back to Bolingbroke Castle," said Mme. Storey. "I must discover who the woman *was* before I can *find* her. I want to ask Norbert Starr a question or two."

Mr. Anders suddenly struck his fist into his palm. "Of course!" he cried. "This woman was a creature of Starr's! He hired a woman, thinking that the trail would be less likely to lead back to him through her. I see it all now!"

"I don't," said Mme. Storey with an enigmatic smile.

8

FROM THE STATION we telephoned to Bolingbroke Castle to ask that a car be sent, and in ten minutes or so we were back there. Though we had been gone an hour, the persons in the round room seemed scarcely to have moved. The body had been taken away. No one else had been admitted to the room, but in the corridors of the castle I met many new faces. Goodness knows who they were or what right they had to be there. Not the least dreadful thing connected with having a tragedy in the house is that it robs you of your privacy.

In the round room everybody was furtively watching Mr. Starr and Miss Lansdowne, who supported the ordeal as best they could. They were sitting beside one of the windows with their backs partly turned towards the others. They occasionally exchanged a whispered word, and continually sought to keep up each other's courage with confident and smiling glances.

But oh! with what a poignant anxiety Norbert Starr's eyes flew to Mme. Storey's face when she entered.

"Be of good heart!" my mistress said instantly. "We have established the fact that there was a third person in this room."

A long breath of relief escaped Mr. Starr. His eyes turned to the girl. Her clear glance answered back: "I knew they would clear you!" But Mr. Anders frowned; on general principles he disapproved of having the spirits of the accused bolstered up.

With half a glance at Miss Lansdowne, Mme. Storey said to Anders, aside: "I think I may get more out of Mr. Starr, if I question him without anybody being present except yourself, of course, and my secretary."

Anders nodded. "Suppose I have him brought to you in the end room on the corridor, the boudoir. Kelliger can wait outside the door, in case we need him."

"Oh, I shouldn't say Mr. Starr was dangerous," Mme. Storey said with a smile. ". . . Let a few minutes elapse. I don't want him to attach too much importance to the matter." To me she murmured: "Bring the big scrap-book to the boudoir, Bella."

Mr. Anders followed us to the boudoir. He had become my mistress's little shadow. He looked to her for his impetus. In that giddy pink room, Mme. Storey sank into one of the corpulent armchairs, crossed her legs comfortably, lit a cigarette, and opened the big scrap-book on her knee. For a few moments she studied it in silence, holding her head on one side to keep the smoke out of her eyes. Mr. Anders, lost in another pink chair across the fireplace, tried to look as much at his ease as she did, and respectfully waited for the oracle to give some sign.

In due course Norbert Starr was escorted to the door of the room. He was allowed to enter alone. Mme. Storey closed the book, and glanced at me. I put it on a table.

"Sit down," said Mme. Storey with a friendly smile. "This is not going to be an inquisition. We want your help. I think I may say— may I not, Mr. Anders?—that you need no longer consider yourself under suspicion."

"Just as you say, Mme. Storey," Anders said very reluctantly.

Mr. Starr sat down rather gingerly in another of the pink chairs between Mme. Storey and Anders.

"Have a cigarette?" asked my mistress.

He took it thankfully, and, lighting up, puffed at the weed deeply. He needed it.

"I want to ask you a question or two in reference to your marriage," said Mme. Storey.

"Anything you like," he murmured.

"Where were you married?"

"In the Little Church Around the Corner."

"Can you name the principal persons present?"

"There was nobody present but our two witnesses and some newspaper reporters."

"Who were your witnesses?"

"Mrs. Jewett, and Miss Jewett's manager, a man called Fazenda."

"Rather a hasty marriage, eh?"

"Decidedly," he said bitterly. "We made up our minds one night after the theatre, and were married next morning."

"You suggested in my office the other day—if you will forgive me for reminding you of it, that you were rather a passive agent . . ."

"Well, my wife was many years older than I," he said with a shrug.

"Didn't *you* want to marry her?" Mme. Storey asked softly.

"I thought I did," he said with a painful smile. "I was dazzled by her prominence and notoriety. I thought, God help me! that it would make me famous!"

"Now for a delicate question," said Mme. Storey. "Were you interested in any other lady at the time?"

He started to answer thoughtlessly—then pulled himself up with a startled glance at Mme. Storey. "Why . . . why, no," he stammered.

Just a startled flicker of his eyes, but it meant everything. I realised that Mme. Storey had asked the significant question, and that we were on the brink of a disclosure. Ah! I knew her so well! That was the way she did it. Seemed at the point of falling asleep just when she touched off the powder magazine.

"Ah!" she said with a disappointed inflexion. ". . . Are you sure?" she persisted softly.

"For your own sake you'd better answer frankly!" barked Mr. Anders.

Mme. Storey affected to look at him in astonishment, and he subsided.

Mr. Starr's agitation greatly increased—but there was a difference now; he was not agitated on his own account. "Why . . . why, what do you mean? Why do you ask me such a question?"

Mme. Storey's candour is notorious. She always tells the truth when she is able. "We have reason to believe," said she, "that Mrs. Starr was shot by a woman who had borne her a grudge ever since her marriage to you. In other words, a jealous woman. I am asking you if you know of any woman who had reason to be jealous."

Mr. Starr's horrified glance seemed to be turned inward. Clearly he was pursuing some private train of reasoning that brought him to an impasse. "Impossible . . . impossible!" he whispered, and a fine sweat broke out on his forehead. Then in a louder voice, with an attempted laugh: "Of course there was no other woman!"

Seeing that Mme. Storey did not appear convinced, he added with a cunning assumption of bitterness: "No woman ever cared for me. My money outshone my personal qualities."

"No woman but one," said Mme. Storey softly.

Norbert Starr's glance seemed to be fixed in space as if she had conjured up some dreadful ghost out of the past. "No! . . . No! No!" he whispered.

There was a silence.

Anders, thinking that Mme. Storey was at a loss, rushed to her assistance. "You're not telling the truth!" he cried, stabbing the air with a prosecutor's forefinger.

This only angered Mr. Starr. "Keep a civil tongue in your head!" he retorted haughtily. "You've got nothing on me. You know damned well by this time that *I* didn't do it!"

"We don't know that you didn't hire somebody to do it!" cried Anders.

Mr. Starr laughed contemptuously. "You'll have a job to prove that, old man."

"Gentlemen! Gentlemen!" admonished Mme. Storey with a bored air. She rose languidly. To Starr she said: "Thank you very much; that is all I wanted to ask you."

Manifestly relieved, he left the room. As soon as the door closed after him, Anders cried, "He knows who killed Bessie Jewett Starr!"

Mme. Storey shook her head. "No. He only knows somebody who had a motive for doing it."

"Well, that doesn't advance us any."

"On the contrary," said Mme. Storey with a subtle smile, "his refusal to tell me, tells me."

"Who is it?" cried Anders.

Mme. Storey regarded the end of her cigarette. Whether she would have answered him or not, I don't know. Before she had time to do so, the door from the corridor was softly opened. Around the door sidled the gaunt, awkward figure of Tessie Jewett with her dim remote gaze and half smile. A premonition of the dreadful truth gripped my breast. It stopped my breathing.

"Excuse me," murmured Miss Jewett, without looking directly at any one of us, "it has just occurred to me you have been here since morning. You have missed your lunch. May I. . . ?"

"No, thank you," said Mme. Storey gravely, yet kindly, too. "Pascoe gave us an excellent lunch. We need nothing more."

"Oh, excuse me for disturbing you," murmured Miss Jewett, immediately turning to creep out again.

"Miss Jewett, why did you shoot your sister?" asked Mme. Storey quietly.

The suddenness of it made me feel a little sick. It seemed like the very refinement of cruelty. But Mme. Storey knew with whom, with *what* she was dealing, and as it proved, she adopted precisely the right means.

The woman at the door did not start at all. With her hand on the knob she merely turned her head, and a dreadful sly smile overspread her face that instantly made her madness manifest. "She was too fat," she said with a chuckle. "I was tired looking at her."

Mr. Anders jumped up. His eyes seemed to bulge against his glasses. "You're mad!" he gasped.

"Well, I ain't as crazy as Bessie was," retorted Miss Jewett. "She was *plumb* crazy!"

"Come in," said Mme. Storey soothingly. "Tell us about it."

Miss Jewett obeyed unhesitatingly. As soon as she left the door, Mr. Anders made a hasty detour to reach it from the other side. He peeped out, and beckoned to somebody to stand near.

Meanwhile Miss Jewett seated herself on the edge of the same chair that Norbert Starr had occupied. The woman seemed to be completely metamorphosed. She sat up stiff and straight; her eyes sparkled behind her thick glasses and hard, bitter lines appeared around her mouth. All her movements were definite and purposeful; we saw before us the "spry" woman that the conductor had described. She had exactly the look of an honest village wife sitting down with her company manners for a good gossip with a neighbour. It was very dreadful to see.

"I been thinking about it a long time back," she began. "I always kept a pistol by me for the purpose. . . . But mostly I'd forget. May didn't want to do it. May's a Christian soul. I have to bear with her."

This was incomprehensible to me, but Mme. Storey got it. "So there are two of you?" she murmured.

"Yes, that's it," said Miss Jewett, grateful to be understood. "There's May and there's me. And folks don't know the difference. May's a fool. Her spirit is broke. She's one of these bearers and forbearers . . . But me! I'm fed up! fed up! I never say nothing, I let May talk, but I think a lot! . . ."

A different delusion intervened here, and the sharp, firm voice faltered. "There's too much eaten and drunk around here," she muttered, "and not any honest work done. All sorts of goings-on. It's like Babylon. And a voice told me it was my job to clean it up . . ."

Her voice trailed off into an indistinguishable mumble, and her eyes bolted. Mme. Storey sought to recall her with a question.

"Why did you choose today?"

She instantly picked up the thread as if she had never dropped it. "I always meant to do it of a Thursday. That's the day I take Momma into town to the doctor's. I knew I could steal back. I had it all planned out. . . . But one Thursday was just like another . . . so many Thursdays! I couldn't fix on any particular Thursday. May was always interfering. May was scared . . ."

"Why did you fix on today?"

"Yesterday Bessie told me that Norbert was coming today. Eleven o'clock in the morning. So I knew this was the appointed day."

"You told us that you didn't know Mr. Starr was coming to-day," put in Mr. Anders.

"That was May talking," she instantly retorted, with her sly smile.

"What has Norbert got to do with it?" asked Mme. Storey softly.

"Norbert's the cause of all the trouble," she answered darkly. "He made bad blood between Bessie and me. He's false-hearted. I was the instrument appointed to chasten him. A voice commanded me, saying . . . *And he had in his right hand seven stars and out of his mouth went a sharp two-edged sword . . .*" She became quite incoherent again.

"You took your mother to town," prompted Mme. Storey.

"Yes. I had to start real early so's to get back in time for Norbert. We drove to our house on Fifty-Fourth Street, which is all locked up and nobody there. We stop there every Thursday to make sure it hasn't been entered. But today I took Momma in with me. I told the chauffeur I had to pack trunks and he needn't wait. I told him when I was ready we'd drive to the doctor's in a taxi, and he was to come back to the house for us at one-thirty. So I got rid of him."

"And your mother?"

"Oh, I locked Momma in a small room upstairs. She bit and scratched and cursed when I put her in, but she don't mean nothing by it. There wasn't anything there she could hurt herself with, and I laid down a matteress so's she could lie down and take a sleep when she got tired. . . . Then I dressed myself in a black dress I had ready, and stuffed it all out with things I picked up to change my shape. Because everybody out here knows me. And I had Momma's widow's bonnet with the crêpe veil to hide my face. I had everything ready to my hand. A long time ago I planned it. . . . When I was all dressed I got a taxi and drove out to the hotel in Upper Bellaire. It's only ten minutes walk from the Castle. I had time and to spare . . ."

"How did you get into the castle?"

The sly smile returned. "Oh, there's plenty of ways, if you know them. I had planned it often. They never could catch *me!* I hid in the bushes and watched, and I saw Bessie come out of the rose garden and go into the woods. So I sneaked through the rose garden and got into the tower through her door, and went up to the round room. When I heard her close the garden door, I hid under the desk . . ."

"How did you know she would see Mr. Starr in the round room?"

"Because she could say anything she wanted in there, and nobody could hear. . . . But I was there hidden under the desk so snug. I could hear everything. I squeezed against the back of the desk, and when she sat down I could have tickled her fat feet . . ."

"She was not alone."

"No. She brought another woman with her. They talked, and pretty soon I made out the other woman was Mary Lansdowne. It was like the Lord had delivered her into my hands. I was going to shoot her, too. I had six bullets in my pistol. But the voice commanded me to wait till Norbert came. I wanted him to see it . . ."

She came to a stop, and sat staring before her, rubbing the silken arms of the chair with a curious circular motion of her palms. Mme. Storey made no attempt to prompt her.

She resumed on a sharp staccato note with breathless pauses. "Bessie didn't want Norbert to see the girl . . . So she put her behind the panel before he came in . . . Norbert came in . . . His voice . . . his *nice* voice . . . Norbert says to me: 'Why don't you join in the fun?' And I says: 'Oh, I'm nobody when Bessie's around.' And he says: 'Well, I'm nobody, too. So we're a pair!' How I laughed! . . ."

It was evident that the poor soul had jumped far back in her mind to quite another scene. She presently recalled herself with a jerk.

"Norbert came into the round room. I could hear every word. . . . He offered Bessie her own figure to let him marry Mary Lansdowne. . . . Bessie began to scream at him. . . . And then . . . And then . . ."

The bony breast began to heave tumultuously; the big blue eyes were utterly distraught. Mme. Storey made haste to carry her over the dangerous spot.

"Yes, we know what happened after that," she said quickly. "And you got out by the window at the foot of the service stairs. You were clever!"

"Yes," she said, relapsing into her old dull self. "May was askeared Norbert hollered so. May was askeared of Mary Lansdowne, too. She couldn't get out by the garden door because Mary was behind the panelling. But she thought of the window at the foot of the little stairs . . ."

"Then she made her way to the Greenwall station, and took a train to town," prompted Mme. Storey.

"Yes, the eleven-fifty-one," said Miss Jewett dully. "Tessie knew what time the train left. She had planned it all out. . . . Tessie's a terrible woman. She's got a scorching fire burning inside her. But it never shows. . . . I'm afraid of what she'll do. . . . And when the chauffeur called at the house at one-thirty Momma and I were all ready to come back with him."

"Weren't you afraid your mother would tell?" asked Mme. Storey.

"She ain't got the sense," was the apathetic reply. "Momma's like a baby. Soon as a thing's over she forgets it. . . . We're all crazy. . . . It seems kinda hard. . . ."

It was heartbreaking. Mme. Storey and I could not bear to look at each other. The wretched woman had sunk down in her chair, her mouth had fallen, her eyes were staring glassily. I suppose, to do him justice, that Mr. Anders was moved, too; but unfortunately he had not imagination enough to change his role. He must still be the public prosecutor.

"Are you capable of realising the sense of what you have told us?" he harshly demanded.

Mme. Storey sought to stop him with a little cry of warning, but it came too late. The sound of the harsh voice seemed to electrify the insane woman. She sprang to her feet; her great eyes blazed; her voice rose to a shriek.

"Yes, I know what I did! I shot Bessie! I shot her dead! I always had it in mind to do it! And I'll shoot you, too, if you bark at me. . . . I'm glad I shot her! She stole Norbert from me. And every day for fifteen years she threw him in my face! I wish she had nine lives like a cat so's I could kill her nine times over! . . ."

It ended in mere insensate shrieking. Anders turned white as paper. Kelliger and a policeman ran in from the corridor.

"Take her! Take her!" gasped Anders. "She did it."

They seized the unfortunate woman by the elbows and led her struggling and shrieking from the room.

Mme. Storey whispered to me quickly: "There must be mental sanitariums out here. Find Pascoe. Have him telephone for experienced nurses. Let him send a car for them."

As I hurried along the corridor they were taking Miss Jewett into the round room. Every shriek of hers was echoed far off from the direction of the great hall. Ah! that doomed household! I ran into Pascoe, hurrying along the main corridor.

When I returned, Mme. Storey was alone in the pink boudoir. She sank into one of the great chairs, and pressed her knuckles to her temples.

"It was harrowing, wasn't it?" she murmured. "Ah! the poor, poor women! Happily they don't know their own situation; they still have their delusions."

Norbert Starr rushed into the room with Mary Lansdowne following more decorously behind him. The man was well-nigh hysterical in his joy. Snatching up Mme. Storey's hands, he poured out his gratitude. She turned it off in her own humorous, mocking style. Her manner towards Mr. Starr was a shade drier than in the beginning; still she was polite.

More polite than I could have been. In the light of the scene we had just witnessed, Norbert Starr appeared much less charming to me than he had. His "charm" had worked too much damage, it appeared. To give him his due, I don't believe there was a thought in his head at that moment save simple joy at being freed of a horrible accusation; nevertheless, the fact remained that by her insane act the unfortunate woman had ensured the happiness of the man who had wrecked her happiness. It gave a horrible irony to the situation.

There is no need of repeating all he said. Mme. Storey has heard it many times before. The girl was more restrained. She said a pretty thing, I remember.

"Whenever I have a happy day, my thoughts will fly to you!"

She was a lovely thing with her luminous, quiet eyes, and I was very thankful she had not overheard Miss Jewett's wild and pitiful confession. I prayed that she might never learn the purport of it.

Mr. Starr had a car waiting, and he besought Mme. Storey and I to accompany him back to the city. My mistress declined.

"I wish to make sure that the unhappy woman is well treated," she said. "You cannot always depend on the temper of a prosecutor who finds himself cheated of a culprit."

"That's good of you," said Mr. Starr, with perfectly genuine feeling. "I wish you'd act for me in the matter. Just as if Mrs. and Miss Jewett still had the closest claims on me, I mean. Whatever the expense may be . . ."

"You are generous," said Mme. Storey. There was no mistaking the dryness of her tone now.

But the two never noticed it. They went out with eyes only for each other.

I didn't say anything, but Mme. Storey could read my thought in my face, of course. She said:

"You are a little uncharitable, Bella."

"I am just thinking the same as you are," I retorted.

"Possibly," she said smiling. "Then I am uncharitable too. . . . One must not blame a man—or a woman either—for an injury of *that* sort. It is just the fortune of love. In love the wounds are dealt out, regardless. When you receive one, the only thing to do is to bind it up yourself and hide it. There are no surgeons on that front. . . . In this case it is not the man's fault that the sort of injury which is generally healed in a week festered for years. The barb was lodged in unwholesome flesh."

"You are right, of course," I said. "But it goes against the grain to see him *rewarded!*"

"Oh, destiny has no moral sense," said Mme. Storey.

"What a day!" I exclaimed, realising all at once that I was dog-weary. . . . "What was it that first put you on the right track?"

"Mrs. Starr's scrap-book," said Mme. Storey, putting her hand on it. "All the notices of her theatrical appearances are here—and her various appearances in court later on. An actress always keeps one. When I turned to the accounts of her wedding among the ordinary clippings, my eye picked out these verses. They are clipped from *Chatter*, that infamous but highly amusing weekly. Read them."

A Light Comedy
(With apologies to R. B.)

I

An unknown youth scarce-bearded, he
    Was the least-regarded swain
Among the many that bent a knee
    At the court of the sisters twain.

II

Marvellous sisters of beauty rare,
    And nothing to choose between;
But one had a meek and downcast air,
    The other the glance of a queen.

III

To arrogance, sure, the homage was paid,
    Men being what they are;
And the meek-browed sister served like a maid,
    Who attends, but may not share.

IV

The youth unnoticed and the woman unsought
    Drew together like magnet and steel;
And in that court of vanity wrought
    The only thing that was real.

V

Then he, 'twas brought to the queenly one,
    At whom her lip had curled,
Was in fact no other than Midas's son,
    And heir to half a world.

VI

Whereat the corners of her lips did rise—
    Poor fool! Need the rest be told?
He gave up the woman who smiled in his eyes,
    For her who smiled at his gold.

VII

Well, anyhow, here the story stays,
    So far at least as I understand;
And here Clyde Fitch, you writer of plays,
    Is a subject made to your hand!

THE ADVENTURES OF MADAME STOREY

Volume 1
ISBN-13 978-1-61646-236-9

Volume 2
ISBN-13 978-1-61646-237-6

Volume 3
ISBN-13 978-1-61646-238-3

Volume 4
ISBN-13 978-1-61646-239-0

Volume 5
ISBN-13 978-1-61646-240-6

Volume 6
ISBN-13 978-1-61646-241-3

Volume 7
ISBN-13 978-1-61646-242-0

Volume 8
ISBN-13 978-1-61646-243-7

COACHWHIP PUBLICATIONS

COACHWHIPBOOKS.COM

MURDER
IN STYLE

Emma Lou Fetta

ISBN 978-1-61646-232-1

COACHWHIP PUBLICATIONS

COACHWHIPBOOKS.COM

THERE IS
NO RETURN
THE ADELAIDE ADAMS MYSTERIES
ANITA BLACKMON

ISBN 978-1-61646-223-9

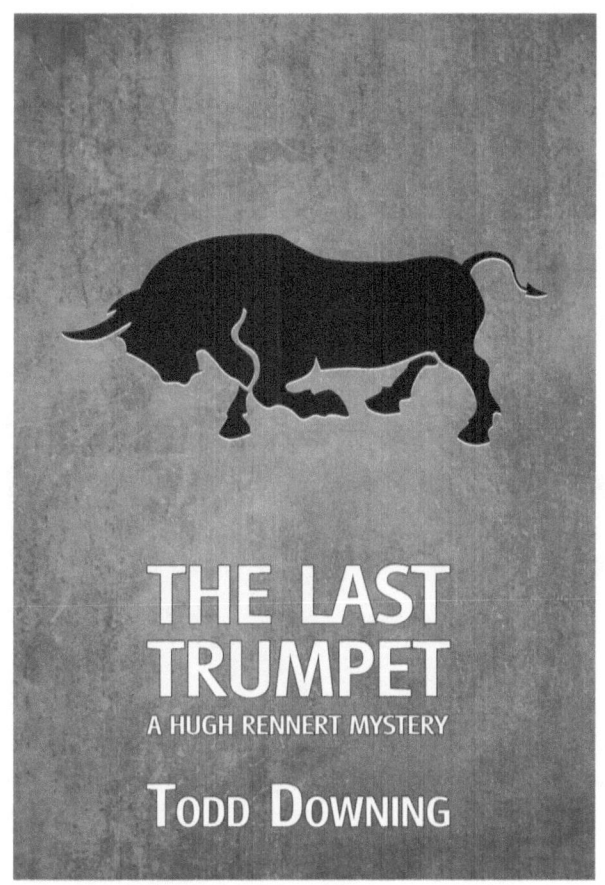

THE LAST
TRUMPET
A HUGH RENNERT MYSTERY

TODD DOWNING

ISBN 978-1-61646-152-2